Flames of Rapture

Book 1 in the Carnal Fever Trilogy

Riley Kade

Manifold Publishing LLC

Paperback: 978-1-957572-00-0

Ebook: 978-1-957572-01-7

Cover design by Ebook Launch

Internal design by J.W. Donley

Manifold Publishing LLC

315 Prospect St.

Unit 5206

Bellingham, WA 98227

Contents

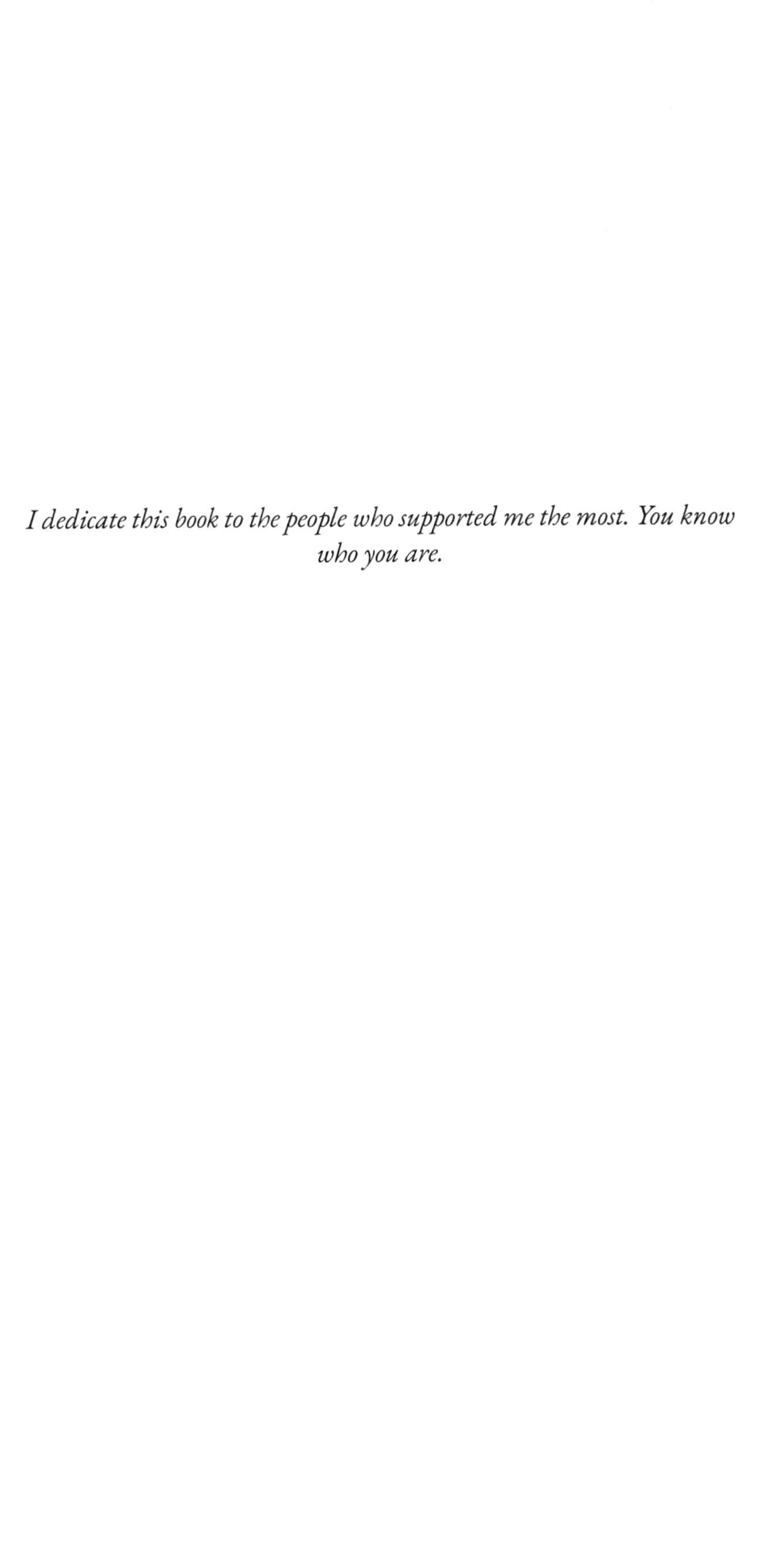

I dedicate this book to the people who supported me the most. You know who you are.

Prologue

The night held its breath as Gabriel approached the wrought-iron gates of the Siphon estate. It was the perfect night for a Becoming. The tension before the storm spoke volumes through its stillness. As for storms, this seemed to be the only little plot in the whole state of Massachusetts that wasn't currently riding one out. That could mean only one thing: the Siphons had a storm nymph in their employ. A powerful one, too.

The gates opened of their own accord. Gabriel stepped back in surprise. An earth nymph? Or did families this wealthy have electric power running through their whole property? Aware that he was likely being watched, he strolled casually through the entrance with his most confident swagger. This was just another Becoming, something he knew well. The fact that it happened to be for the most powerful succubus family in the country should matter little.

The heavy knocker resembled entwined lovers. Gabriel ran his thumb over a smooth metal thigh before pounding it heavily against the door. An old man, ungloved, greeted him. The man gave no response to Gabriel's introduction, saying only, "This way, sir."

The house was in line with expectation. Erotic paintings lined the walls, which were all painted a deep shade of red. Elaborate statues adorned ornate pedestals.

Gabriel's boots clanged on the hard stone floor as he was shown into a sitting room full of luscious sofas. Unlike the doorman, everyone in this room was gloved. Seven people, all clearly resembling each other and connected through strong pulses of blue light, chatted quietly from different corners.

"Thank you, Marty. You can go fetch the others now," the eldest male said.

"Congressman. It's... a pleasure," Gabriel said, extending a hand to the man.

"Derek. Please," the man responded in a pleasantly deep voice. "We're all family here."

Dressed in fine clothes like the rest of his kin, Congressman Derek Siphon stepped forward to take Gabriel's hand between both of his own.

"Welcome to my home. I've received several recommendations of your services."

Suddenly glad he'd put a shirt on under his leather vest, Gabriel stood up straighter.

"I'm sure I won't disappoint," he responded with a grin; an expression which turned out to be more forced than casual. The congressman smiled back knowingly. Gabriel, so used to being the center of any room, flushed slightly under the man's gaze. It was disconcerting being surrounded by so many of his own kind, he mused, as he took in the rest of the gathering.

"And your daughter?"

"Upstairs asleep. We'll wake her shortly. But first, let us get to know one another. My wife and I were just ruminating on what motivates someone so young to appoint himself with this noble responsibility."

"I had a bad time during my own change," Gabriel explained, accepting the congressman's offer to sit.

"I was alone. I didn't even know what was happening to me. Thought afterward that maybe someone should be looking out for those of us that had the bad luck of being born into human families."

The woman sitting across from him looked away at this comment, but the congressman moved forward in interest. "And how many of those have you found? How many Becomings have you presided over?"

"Eighteen. I try to stay on the move. Always looking. But I'm sure there's many I've missed."

"Certainly," the congressman said. "Since moving into the public limelight, we've had at least a dozen runaways show up at our doors. It's good work you're doing, son. It has been a generation since anyone came along with your particular talent."

"It's not talent, sir. Just practice, and passion."

"Yes. Like my late grandfather. You have taken up an honorable mantle, doing this work. It's important to look out for one another. Especially in these times. I encourage you to connect these lost souls with me and mine. If you have addresses...? I could write them myself."

"I don't know," Gabriel said. "Not sure I should share those without asking." He cringed at his potential rudeness, but the congressman waved, as if to say *no matter*.

The woman Gabriel presumed to be the man's wife rose to her feet. She retrieved something from above the fireplace and brought it to him.

"Well regardless, in appreciation for your role in our daughter's Becoming, we'd like to gift you this." Gabriel ran his fingers over the handprints on the surface of the box, surprised at such an offering.

"You know how to use it?"

Gabriel nodded.

"Then may it assist you in your work."

"Should I open it now?" he asked.

"Later. Now, we have other business," the man boomed as five new people were escorted into the room. He lowered his voice to add, "But I hope you know... you always have friends here. And so does anyone else you find. Additionally, I hope you know the contents of this box are for *our* eyes only."

"Of course, sir." Gabriel ran a thumb along his jaw as he turned to take in the newcomers. The two women were decorated with delicate stone jewelry, and the men had vines woven through their hair. Stone nymphs and wood nymphs. He could work with that.

"Shall we?" the congressman said once they'd completed their introduction.

Leaving the rest of the family behind, they entered a grand hallway.

"My daughter will of course be familiar with the process. You will merely be assisting her, not educating her," he explained, leading the party up a spiral staircase. "We have a dedicated room for the event, in fact. Though once a member of the household turns, we never re-enter it."

Stopping outside a bright red door, he added, "Which means this is where I leave you. After it's done, our butler will assist you with anything you may need for the next couple weeks. This floor is yours, along with the kitchen at the end of the hall. When she's ready, we'll greet our daughter with dinner in a grand celebration, which you will all be welcome to attend. See you in a few weeks." He shook Gabriel's hand, patted his human friend on the shoulder, and departed.

Gabriel cast one look over his party, contemplating how each person might best be useful, before pushing open the door. The room was beautiful, with a fireplace at each end and a four-poster bed in the center. Everyone hung back as Gabriel approached the object of attention. The woman rolled over in her sleep, a frown on her face. She looked about the right age. Maybe nineteen? Her long blond hair was soaked in the same sweat which covered the rest of her. She'd clearly tried to apply makeup, but it now dripped down her face.

Gabriel took out a handkerchief and began to wipe her clean. Leaving her eyes closed, she showed she was awake by saying prettily, "I thought you'd never get here. I've had to entertain myself all day."

When he was done drying her, she sat up and took in the rest of the new arrivals. Gabriel watched hot red light flash between her and several of the other members. He knew who she would choose before she said it.

"You." She pointed at one of the dryads. "Come here." The wood nymph smiled widely as he approached the woman, who was now kneeling at the edge of the bed. She kicked the blankets away, leaving her body visible through her wet nightgown. The man grew hard just looking at her, causing the woman to smile.

"I've already had a child and received copious instruction regarding sexuality. This isn't going to be new to me, understand?" she said as he reached the edge of the bed.

Gabriel could tell this was going to be a challenge. This woman was clearly hoping to remain in control of the situation, which was exactly the opposite state he needed her in if he was going to help her transition painlessly. Gabriel took a seat next to her on the bed. Removing his trusted leather gloves, he decided there was no time like the present to work his magic.

Leaning into the woman's ear, he said huskily, "That's not exactly true, is it? That this isn't going to be new to you? Before a Becoming, a person has no interest in sex. You may have read books, and even reproduced, after what I imagine was a boring one-night rutting. But you've never experienced this."

He stroked one finger against the bare flesh of her arm. She sucked in a breath. "I think you should experience it, before you give it," he whispered, biting at the lobe of her ear. "You'll enjoy it more if you know exactly what it is you're doing to someone." She turned to look at him, her face and neck growing flushed. He slid a finger under her shoulder strap and freed one breast. Reaching down to twist his fingers around her nipple, he felt his touch slowly penetrate her whole body.

It spread first to her lips and fingertips; a pleasurable sensation that made her breathing turn to a quickened pant. It traveled down her spine, managing to leave her chilled and warmed at the same time. As it reached her core, she couldn't hold in the sound that escaped her. She arched her back in a sudden jerking motion.

Sliding her knees apart on the bed, she clenched her thigh muscles, rocking her pelvis. Gabriel, able to feel every inch of her now that he'd made contact, observed the pressure building inside her. He felt the exact moment that the convulsions began. And with the little control he had over such things, tried to draw them out.

Normally he would stop at this point, leave her wanting more, but this woman needed to practice losing control. To increase the intensity, he climbed behind her and slid a hand down her body and under her nightgown. Pressing his bare hand directly against the warm, wet flesh between her legs, he held her firmly with his other arm below her breasts.

She cried out as she convulsed back against his chest. He didn't let up; taking her as high as he was able.

Only when she'd completely lost herself and he didn't think she could take any more, did he withdraw his attentions, allowing her to collapse back against the bed as the aftershocks subsided. Making small sounds of contentment, she kept her eyes closed for a full minute as her breathing returned to normal. When her lids came open and she fixed her gaze on the wood nymph still standing at attention in front of her, Gabriel saw the deep red of raw desire flash from her to him. The light this time was pure; the fire in her eyes full of promises.

Toying with the inside of her own thighs, she slowly ran her hands upward and slid the gown up over her head. Letting the nymph look for only an instant, she pulled his gaze to her face with the words, "My turn."

She sat back up in front of him and extended a hand to his lips. The man's face changed as he took the woman's finger in his mouth. She stared back at him intently, looking equally satisfied by the experience.

Removing himself from the scene, Gabriel leaned casually against a bedpost to watch. Observing the woman's subconsciously writhing body, and look of raw, carnal desire, he knew he'd done right. And so the night began.

Outside, far in the distance, he could hear the branches snapping and leaves whipping in the storm that someone very powerful was holding at bay.

Chapter 1

A farm girl

Sadie entered the open doors of her neighbor's barn, pausing to show her usual respect to Tina, the young cow. Having been there at Tina's birth, she always made sure to acknowledge her whenever she dropped by. Sadie reached to rub behind the cow's ears and the animal pushed her head into the touch, throwing her a contented, big-eyed smile.

The commotion on the far end of the barn, however, pulled at Sadie's attention.

Jimmy was shoveling fresh hay into the nearest stall, sweat glistening off his naked back. He turned as she approached, and she swore she saw him tighten the muscles of his abs. Only he really didn't need to flex to show off his form; they were well into adulthood now and he had more than grown into himself. He worked with his body every day, after all, caring for both his parents' farm and assisting hers. He was plenty to look at. What she didn't understand was why he cared what she thought. He'd never been vain. It was just one of his many new behaviors that had her on edge.

"Having fun?" she asked, looking at the load of work still left.

"Shoveling hay? Always. But if you've come to hang out, I could use a break," he said. He kept his gaze on her as he picked up his shirt to wipe his face and chest. Yep, this was another day of him being weird around her. She swore that every time she dropped by these days, he was trying to display himself like a rooster in spring. It must just be part of the weird mating habits she'd observed in her peers. Men in spring must display naked, sweaty body for passing females, even when said females are their entirely sexless best friends.

"Mom sent me to bring home Betty."

"Yeah, she's been up there an hour." They both turned to look at Betty's favorite wooden beam, from which the chicken was even now looking down on them.

"But she's so content there, I suppose we could let her stay a little longer." The chicken clucked along to Sadie's comment, as if to say she agreed with the plan.

"I brought you back your comics." Sadie swung the backpack off her shoulder and tugged it open while Jimmy went to kick open the cooler and pull out two beers. He twisted off both caps and handed her one as they squeezed together to share a seat on the cooler.

"And? What'd you think?" he asked as she laid out the comics on the flat surface created by their legs.

She wrinkled her nose. "I don't know. They seemed a little far-fetched. I mean, honestly. Why would Emilia have gone with Luis, when she had far more compelling reasons to trust Alejandro?"

Jimmy touched his favorite books affectionately.

"Perhaps because life is full of hard choices made on a bed of soft information," he said, in a direct quote from the comics. His familiar dark eyes looked so serious for a moment. Then he saw her watching and smiled.

"That's why I like them. In the moment, I can always understand each character, why they made the choices they did. Even if people can be foolish about other people sometimes." He looked intent again as he swept her curls over her shoulder and out of their lap.

She liked when he did that. It was as if her curls were his curls, like there was nothing in the world they didn't share.

"Well, I don't envy Emilia her choices, that's for sure."

Sadie was glad to see his expression return to normal as they argued all the minutiae of the plot and characters. And for once, it wasn't she who broke the moment.

"We should get Betty back to your mom before she starts wondering where you are," Jimmy said. She laughed and downed the last gulp before saying, "Don't worry, my mom will just hope we're making out. These past few years, she's gone from not wanting me alone with you to finding any excuse to send me over here. I think she's concerned by my lack of dating interest."

Jimmy, suddenly alert, gave her an unreadable look.

"I told her you were dating Kate though, and that—"

"Actually, we broke up," he cut in.

Damn. She had been happy he was finally dating someone. It removed the unspoken pressure from their friendship. Though Kate frequently took a lot of his time and didn't like for him and Sadie to be alone. That was a drag.

"Sorry to hear that. What happened?" Sadie wished her tone sounded a little more sorry.

Jimmy gave only a shrug in response, then broke the silence with, "Well I think your mom should be happy to have the daughter she has."

"Definitely. I was a good student. I'm a good farmer. And one day, when I take over the family farm, I'll already be best friends with the neighbor. Though I've gotta say now that it's over, you're going to need to pick a better wife than Kate. I can't say I'll approve of any woman who won't let us drink a couple of beers alone together."

"Noted. I'll make sure she gets your full approval," Jimmy said, reaching to clink his drink against hers.

"I think she's just stressed that her only child will never give her grandkids," Sadie said, still wanting to talk about her mom. "But since you're practically like her son, you can give her babies."

"Oh thanks, Sadie. No pressure. I think your mom is spending a little too much time breeding sows," he said, tossing their beers in the tub nearby.

"Clearly," Sadie said, before looking him up and down and laughing at the thought of her mom breeding him. "You'd probably make a terrible sow anyway, you'd get bored lying around all day."

He surprised her with an offended look before saying, "But you forget, if I was a sow…" He stepped into a nearby stall and emerged with a little piglet. "I could spend all day with little piglet-wiglet's with their noses so tiny…" His voice traveled slowly from its normal deep tone to a prepubescent squeak, as the words became mostly incoherent. Sadie could just barely make out, "-cute-little-kissable-feet…" before it was all just cooing noises.

While she watched her best friend hold the piglet in one hand and rub noses with it, she felt a sudden pain in her stomach, a deep longing for things to just stay the same between them. She hated this growing-up. Life became so stressful when everyone around her suddenly became interested in romantic relationships. And though she didn't want Jimmy like that, she also really didn't want to lose him.

"But things might still change for me." She broke in on his moment with the piglet. "I might give her grandchildren, I mean. I'm only twenty, for god sake. It's not like I'm an old hag."

"Hey, hags aren't always old. That's just a stereotype," he rebuked, hugging the piglet one last time before returning her to her mother.

"How would you know? When would you have ever met a hag?"

"I got it from the human species class I took last spring. Remember? The one you rejected in favor of another math elective?" he said.

"It was one class! Will you never forgive me for taking one class different from you?"

"I had to study with Matt Shmitt. All he wanted to do was tell me about chicks he'd nailed. I'll tell you what, I promise to ensure all future wives and girlfriends approve of our relationship if you never leave me alone again with Matt Schmitt."

"Deal. Now go find your ladder so I can get Betsy."

"Dad has it. He's fixing the roof. I say we do this old school." Jimmy squatted down. Sadie just assumed he was joking and so made no move to climb onto his shoulders as he was suggesting. When he didn't budge, she gave a loud guffaw.

"There's no way you can lift me."

"Are you saying I'm not strong enough?" he challenged up at her from the squat.

"I'm saying I'm too big for you. I'm not the scrawny kid I used to be."

His eyes flitted quickly over her curves before looking away. Sadie, not sure what to make of him these days, pretended not to notice. She opened her mouth to break the awkward moment, but he cut in. "Tell you what, if I can't stand up, then I will muck out your chicken coop this week. But if I can stand up, then you have to come with me to the party that's happening down by the river tonight."

Sadie threw her head back in exasperation at the thought.

"Those people don't like me any more than I like them. Those parties are always exhausting. Why do you even want to go?" Before he could speak she added, "People always like you less when I'm around anyway."

He shrugged. "I just thought it would be something fun for us to do together. Besides, those girls just picked on you because they were immature and you were an easy target. But that was high school. We're a year older now. And why are you always so sure people aren't going to like you? It's like you decide before they do." Then before she could launch her typical counterattack he added, "The bet is that you have to go with me, not that we have to stay long. If it blows, we'll leave."

Sadie shifted uncomfortably for a minute, thinking about just how smelly that chicken coop was at the moment, before giving a groan of reluctant agreement. She stepped forward and swung one leg over his shoulders, grabbing the top of his head for stability. He wobbled dramatically as he started to stand, but with an exaggerated roar of effort, lifted Sadie's head until she was staring at the surprised face of Betty.

Sadie grabbed the chicken harshly, as if Betty had intentionally conspired with Jimmy.

With Sadie and Betty aboard, Jimmy turned to face the barn doors.

"Well, let's get this chicken home," he said, taking a firm hold of Sadie's knees.

"Put me down!" Sadie squealed, squirming on his shoulders.

"But I could do this all day. I'll take you anywhere you want to go. Where to, Betty?"

Sadie thought he was really going to carry her out of the barn like that, but at the last minute he turned to face away from the pile of hay nearest the door and let them all fall straight backward onto the semi-padded bed. Betty gave a loud squawk; launching herself out of Sadie's arms, while Sadie's initial squeak of surprise turned quickly into laughter. Jimmy's head, now resting on her abdomen, looked up at her as he rotated onto his stomach.

"Betty's never going to forgive us for that," Sadie scolded.

"I think she will next time we feed her."

She agreed.

Neither of them made an effort to get up immediately, and as Jimmy continued to look up at her something strange happened. Sadie became acutely aware of his body between her legs. It was a peculiar feeling; something she couldn't explain. They had wrestled a hundred times over the years, and never had she felt something like this. It was a kind of heaviness in her thighs, a warmth in her stomach. She didn't want him to move. He seemed equally reluctant to dislodge himself, and when she relaxed into their position, he followed her lead. His weight settled over her as he reached up to pull a piece of hay out of her hair, casting her a serious look.

In the post-commotion silence however, they seemed to become aware at the same time of a third person breathing. They both cocked their heads to listen. It seemed to be coming from somewhere underneath them.

They jumped up. Jimmy tore away the top layer of hay just to the left of where they had been lying. Sadie gasped as a strange woman's head appeared, her blond hair mixing with the hay stuck to her sweaty face. She looked up at them in fear.

"Please," the woman croaked out. Her voice sounded dry and raspy, as if she had just emerged from a week-long trek through the desert with no water. "I just needed a place to rest."

Jimmy moved to finish uncovering her.

"No! Please. No one else can see me."

"Who are you? What is this?" Sadie asked.

"Nobody. I was supposed to meet someone here." She paused with her eyes half-shut. "They never showed."

"What's wrong with you?" Jimmy asked in genuine concern.

"Nothing. Hungry. I'm a water nymph. Bonded to the Atlantic Ocean... been away too long."

"The Atlantic? That's a far cry from Washington." *What could have brought her to the pacific northwest?* Sadie wondered. "I thought water nymphs could never leave their bonding site; like earth nymphs."

"We can. Just not for this long," the nature feeder said.

"How long since you've fed off your site?" Jimmy asked, suddenly in action mode.

"Ten days," the woman wheezed. "I was supposed to meet someone at your river nearby. Four days ago."

"What could be so important that you wouldn't have gone home by now?" Sadie inquired, a little harshly given the woman's fragile state.

"I have to deliver something." The woman appeared to weaken; lying back into the hay.

"We have to get you home," Jimmy said. "You're putting your life at risk."

"No. Can't leave yet."

"I'm getting help," Sadie said.

"No!" The woman sat up, grabbing hold of Sadie's waist. "You can't. You can't let any more people know I'm here. Please." Given her emaciated state, Sadie was shocked at the strength of the woman.

"Okay," Sadie assured her; afraid she might hurt herself. "But let us help you."

"Just let me stay here a few more days. I'll stay out of sight. No one will know."

Jimmy and Sadie exchanged skeptical looks. "Can I get you something?" Jimmy asked. "Is there medicine...?"

"Water." The woman spoke the word like it was the name of God, and relaxed back into the hay. Sadie sat down next to her and looked the nymph over with concern, while Jimmy disappeared. She closed her eyes completely then, apparently having decided to trust the humans.

Sadie looked from her gaunt face to her tattered clothes. What could possibly cause this woman to put herself through this?

Jimmy returned with a large bucket of water and a hose. The woman's face lit up as water poured from the hose to the bucket. Then at the look on her face, he turned the stream to flow directly onto her. For about a minute, her body just absorbed the liquid, leaving the hay around her dry. When she seemed content, and the hay began to soak, he finished filling the bucket and left to turn off the flow.

"We should move you to the old pig stall," Jimmy suggested. "That one over there. It'll be empty for a while. I can't ensure that none of my younger siblings won't come running through here, but I'll try to distract them for a few days."

"Thank you." The woman pulled herself awake just enough to give them both a small smile; a smile that didn't quite touch her eyes.

"A WATER NYMPH. From the ocean! Think of how powerful she must be to be bonded to such a large body of water. I didn't realize nature feeders of her kind could be so far from their bonding site," Sadie said. They were picking their way through the woods toward the river so she could make good on her agreement to go to the party, and it was a challenge to keep their animated chatter quiet enough that they wouldn't be overheard. "Should we tell someone? She could be dangerous," she added, looking over her shoulder.

"She didn't look dangerous. More of a danger to herself. But if she doesn't head home in the next few days, I'll bring Ma into it."

"I just wonder if we should even be helping her. I mean, we don't know anything about what she's doing here, or her reasons for staying hidden. What if she's smuggling something deadly?" Sadie said, stopping on the edge of exiting the trail. They could hear talking and laughing.

"Anyone that afraid must have her reasons. My instincts are to help her," Jimmy responded, pulling up next to her and placing a hand on her shoulder. "Can we give her a shot?"

Sadie bit down on her lip; looking in the direction of the commotion ahead, then back to Jimmy. Her feeling of concern slowly faded into an awareness of the person in front of her. Why did it feel strange to be standing so close?

Rejecting her desire to step in closer, she said, "First this party, then a half-crazed water nymph... what are you going to get me into next?"

Taking his hand like it was any other day, she led them toward the smell of food and fire. Neither of them had ever actually been to a bonding party before. Given the fact their small town had no human feeders and only a smattering of nature feeders, neither of them had ever been to any non-human ceremony whatsoever. But they both knew you were supposed to bring a gift for the guest of honor and deliver it with well wishes.

Unfortunately, the guest of honor was Ina, and Ina was a part of the grove posse. There were four earth nymph families in the area, and they'd all decided to have children at the same time. The gang of all girls happened to be the same age as Sadie and were as inseparable as they were exclusive. Their families often supported the crop growth in the many surrounding farms, and the girls, now women, had a way of letting Sadie know that they were infinitely more interesting and important than she.

The dynamic between them began to develop back in middle school. She had been friends with Ina at that time. Sadie had never quite been able to pinpoint what had happened to shift things between them, but she vaguely remembered that *someone* had said *something* about *someone*. And someone had definitely said something back. She also thought that she vaguely recalled the falling out wasn't particularly her fault.

Lost in her own memory, Sadie didn't notice her parents' appearance in front of them. They had just emerged from the trail and the party was in full swing. She quickly let go of Jimmy's hand as if they were still children getting caught engaged in *inappropriate affection*.

"Ahh, look at you two," said her mother, a curvy white woman with a mane of auburn curls, the spitting image of herself. "I'm so glad to see you out, sweetie." She wrapped one arm around Sadie's shoulders, pulling her in to kiss the top of her head. Sadie always liked this affectionate greeting of her mother's, but in this setting it slightly embarrassed her. She wiggled away and murmured something about Jimmy making her come. The comment successfully diverted her mother's attention onto him.

"Heading out so soon, Lillia?" Jimmy asked her mother mid-hug.

"Ahh well, Don's hip is acting up," she gestured at Sadie's father; a bearded man leaning heavily on a cane, "But you kids have fun tonight. This could be the only bonding ceremony any of us go to for a while, now that little Ina has reached maturity."

Jimmy pulled Sadie reluctantly forward. "We promise to make the most of it."

"And remember to offer your congratulations!" her mother added as they walked away.

"Can we get that part over with?" Sadie asked him, side-stepping a running child as they left her parents behind.

"I was going to suggest it. Figured you'd be antsy until it was over."

The party had a sizable turnout. It seemed half the families in town had some representation present. Ash River lay just out of town, and the site was a common gathering place for big events. Embedded in the woods, it was equipped with an abundance of barbecue pits, all currently lit, and makeshift seating. Ina's mother, the most powerful among the local nymph families, had grown several small trees into elaborate benches. For her daughter, the guest of honor, she had made an intricate chair of entwined living branches and woven flowers.

Ina stood out to the eye as they approached the crowd. Her seated form was surrounded both by gifts and by the elaborately dressed presence of her friends. All four women had flowing gowns and flowers in their hair, but Ina was dressed simply; looking radiant only in her happiness. Cassie Ash was draped over one side of Ina's chair, talking to her friend in a joyful tone.

"I always knew you would develop eventually. In a family like yours, there was no way you could be human," Cassie said, as if she was an authority on all things. "And you know what they say, late bloomers blossom brightest. And look. Bonded to a whole patch of woods." She recrossed her legs and smoothed out her elaborate dress. "Even your mother only has three trees. But we should've known you'd have a powerful bonding. I mean you have the strong mother and the late blooming. Both of those are good signs." Cassie spoke almost without taking breath. "We're going to miss you though, being so far out of town and all." She brushed a strand of Ina's hair behind her ear. "But we'll visit each other every day. Especially while we're building you a house out there."

"Actually, I was thinking—" Ina dropped her sentence as she noticed their arrival. Cassie's expression also changed into what Sadie always interpreted as aggressively bored annoyance. It was the same old look she was used to from her. Sadie directed her attention at the surrounding posse in an attempt to be friendly. She nodded first to Cassie Ash, her biggest critic.

"Cassie. Ilda," Sadie said. Her forced half-smile turned to the Canopy twins. "Marisa. Sarah." She bobbed her head to each of them.

"Ina." Sadie's voice turned small in her throat as she said this last name. "Congratulations."

Stepping forward, she held out a basket of freshly laid eggs. She felt someone take it out of her hand and heard Jimmy offering his own blessings as she and Ina looked over each other's faces. The two women looked similar in some superficial ways: of medium height, with dark brown eyes, sun-dyed skin, and auburn hair falling in curls around their shoulders. People used to think they were twins when they were together, but Sadie had never seen it. All of Ina's features were small, and somehow matched her quiet personality. Sadie had always liked Ina's face, and seeing it again brought back good memories.

Remembering they didn't like each other, Sadie straightened her back and withdrew a few steps.

"Thanks Sadie," Ina responded in an equally small voice, while Sadie put a hand on Jimmy's back to depart. Steering him away from the group, she directed them toward a barbecue pit. The smell of a chicken being roasted drew her onward.

The owners of the local pharmacy were tending this pit. Sadie also recognized her fourth-grade teacher, who was standing next to the pharmacist's daughter. Their friends and neighbors. If only she knew how to talk to them. As she and Jimmy nestled themselves into the circle, the crowd made room for them to join without pausing conversation.

"I tell you. Every year we hear about more and more attacks," the south end baker was saying.

"It's just the news! They're always fear-mongering," her teacher responded in exasperation.

"It's the human feeder population growth," someone else chimed in. "I heard they've gone and doubled their population over the 20th century. Of course there would be more conflict."

"It's true there are a lot more of them these days. When I was growing up, I met not more than two of 'em in my whole youth. Now when you turn on the television, it's like they're everywhere. And these attacks..."

"Did you hear about the one back east? It was somewhere along the Atlantic Coast. A group of feeders moved into a small town and slowly drove everyone crazy. They can do that you know? Some of them can. And then one of the humans they were feeding on went and shot up his whole family. Terrible tragedy."

"Yeah. Terrible," people agreed.

"It's a new world coming," one of them said.

Sadie leaned into Jimmy's body as he put an arm around her.

"Yeah. A new world," someone else agreed.

"Times are certainly changing," the baker concluded.

The conversation went quiet while the chicken crackled and dripped into the coals. Sadie felt she should care more about the happenings of the larger world, but it all seemed so far removed from daily life. After all, they didn't even have human feeders in their town. And apart from the handful of wood nymph families, they had no other nature feeders.

Not that anyone here was afraid of nymphs. It was human feeders, after all, who were the scary ones. Bonding to nature was one thing, but feeding off human emotion... well, Sadie at least agreed with her neighbors on this one, powers like that sounded scary.

But it was easy to feel overwhelmed when thinking about such things, and it was equally as easy to forget about them entirely. Which is precisely what she did as the comfort of fire and distant chatter mingled with the crisp night air. Relaxing for the first time since they'd arrived, she softened against Jimmy.

When the conversation picked back up, it was to focus on who was having babies. Wanting to avoid being a part of such a topic, Sadie drew Jimmy to the next pit, despite the fact no one had yet spoken to them directly and she had no reason to believe they would.

Hours passed with them floating on the edges of different circles. Occasionally Jimmy chimed into the discussions, but Sadie never spoke to anyone and found only one-word responses to the few direct questions sent her way. After getting some food in their bellies and taking a brief walk down by the river, Jimmy agreed to leave.

"You should've gone without me. You would've had more fun," Sadie said as they walked through the dark trail back home. Solar bulbs, charged up from the long day, glowed softly on either side of them.

"No, don't say that. It would've been no fun without you," Jimmy said.

"I just never know what to say to any of them. They must think I have no opinions of my own," she said.

"Then they'd be wrong. And it's not always so hard, is it? You're fine around my family. And me of course."

"With you, I'm always fine." Sadie stopped them so she could face him. All evening she had been staying especially close to Jimmy. She told herself it was for comfort, but there was no denying that there was something else going on.

There was a buzzing under her skin and a knot in her stomach she normally associated with public speaking. Wanting again to be as close as they had been in the hay earlier that day, Sadie stepped forward hesitantly. Jimmy's brow furrowed in a look Sadie interpreted as concern, but he didn't withdraw. He stood strong against her when she pressed both her hands against his chest. Sliding them up around his neck, she stepped into his solid form.

With a mix of confusion and impulse, she drew him into a hug. His cheek felt warm against hers and the same wave of pleasure she had felt earlier swept through her. As it travelled to her stomach, however, it became a wave of nausea. She swayed on her feet and held on for balance.

"You okay?" Jimmy's voice came out in a tender whisper.

"Yeah. Sorry. I think I might be coming down with something. I've felt strange all day."

"Let's get you home then," he said, reaching to take her hand. This time, however, Sadie avoided his touch.

She focused on the path ahead as a shiver of unease crawled over her flesh and pulsated uncomfortably in her gut. Sadie felt like the host of a war of impulses, only she didn't recognize either side. There was one thing she was sure of, though. She was definitely coming down with something.

Chapter 2

A fever

Sadie couldn't remember what had been happening in the dream that had just woken her, but it must have been a nightmare because her heart was pounding and she was covered in cold sweat. Rolling over into a ball, she cupped both her breasts in her hands. This seemed to quell some of the ache.

What was happening to her? Was it just that time of the month? She decided it must be when she noticed the wetness between her legs, but discovered in the bathroom that she wasn't bleeding at all. She stumbled back to bed, where the night passed in something resembling a drunken haze.

Sadie began to feel mildly more coherent when the morning broke and her mom came to find out why she hadn't come downstairs. She explained it was cramps and suggested she stay in bed for a while. Her mom agreed and asked her if she was up for any breakfast. At the churning in her stomach, Sadie squirmed away from the idea. Declaring she wasn't hungry, she managed to be left alone for most of the morning, during which time the situation only seemed to worsen.

It must have been mid-afternoon, according to the light wafting through her curtains, when another knock came at her door. Sadie mumbled some response.

"I hear you're not contagious," Jimmy said as he pushed open the door with a tray in one hand and a book in the other. Sadie sat up and wiped some of the sweat from her brow.

"Your mom said you need to eat something or you'll just end up worse off in the end."

He sat on the bed and smiled down at her.

"How are you feeling?" he asked.

Sadie tried to pull her thoughts and emotions into some coherent form.

"Oh, you know, just normal menstrual stuff," she said. With some men, this response might have been enough to turn off further inquiry, but this was Jimmy she was talking to.

"Have you been throwing up? Do you want a heating pad?"

She propped herself up against the wall and smoothed out the blanket in front so he could place the tray in her lap. She saw his gaze fall on her sweat-soaked white T-shirt but made no move to cover herself up.

"No. I'm plenty warm. As you can see." Her voice came out in an uncharacteristically husky tone as she toyed with the small hollow at the nape of her neck. Sadie watched him intently as she leaned down to suck a bite of eggs off her fork, suddenly ravenous.

In an equally uncharacteristic move, Jimmy dropped his gaze, flushing slightly.

"Well, I can read to you... I brought the next issue," he suggested, sitting down on the edge of the bed. Sadie didn't respond verbally. She was looking over his body and trying to remember her most recent dream. She was sure it had something to do with Jimmy's hands, and that smooth patch of skin right above his hip bones. That had definitely played a role somehow. She remembered he had a little scar above his right hip from that time they'd jumped into the river and he'd hit a sharp rock. She wished she could run a finger along that scar now.

When she continued to respond only through eating and looking at him, he slowly opened the comic and cleared his throat.

He began to read.

She cut him off.

"Do you remember that time, years ago, when you were down by the river alone?" Her words sounded slow and far away as if she'd drifted back to dreaming and the scene was just about to shift. "You were leaning back against a rock with your eyes closed, touching yourself. I ran into you there."

"What?" He looked alarmed at her question, but she was sure he remembered because he swallowed hard and she saw his breathing increase drastically.

"You opened your eyes when you heard my foot snap a twig, and you pretended like you'd just been about to go pee, but I'd been there for a few minutes, watching. At the time, I just thought it was fascinating and couldn't seem to take my eyes off you. I think I would feel differently if that happened again now."

"Sadie, I..."

"I never do that," she said. "Touch myself, I mean. What does it feel like?"

The book fell out of Jimmy's hand and landed in a flop on the floor. Her mom pushed open the door.

"How are you kids doing? Ah, you got your appetite back I see. Good for you, dear." Her mom lifted the tray off her lap, as Jimmy bent down to pick up the fallen comic.

"Is it too warm in here?" her mom asked, touching Jimmy's forehead.

Sadie awoke from the moment and felt a sudden embarrassment at her comments.

"It's too warm for Jimmy, but not for me," she said. "He should probably go anyway though. I think I need some more sleep."

ANOTHER DAY and night passed like this. Sadie told her parents she didn't want any more visitors, not even Jimmy.

Especially not Jimmy, she thought. Though she did go back and forth in her emotions between dreading seeing him again after what she had said, and hoping he was going to come crawling into her bed any minute.

At the end of the second day, her mom began to become concerned.

"Maybe we should have Doctor Harris take a look at you."

"No. I'm fine really. It'll probably be all gone by tomorrow," she told her mom frantically, trying to look like she was on the edge of getting better. She wasn't even sure exactly from what she was trying to recover. Clearly this wasn't her period. She just couldn't seem to focus her thoughts, and her body wavered between a kind of panting, sweaty excitement and an exhausted nausea. Maybe it was a strange kind of flu; some new strand. In which case, a doctor should probably take a look at her.

Though something stopped her from saying so. She was embarrassed at the thought of talking about *all* her symptoms with the elderly doctor, and she was sure that no permanent harm could come from a little nausea.

By the time the third night fell, she was desperately grateful for the solitude that night brought. With no one there to constantly ask her how she was feeling, Sadie could let herself get lost in her feelings; her increasingly feverish dreams.

She rolled over in bed to discover it was now made of hay. For a minute she was afraid she was alone, until she saw Jimmy wiggle out of the nearby stack. He moved to rest on top of her and she spread her legs to wrap around his waist. She arched her back in order to press against him, a feeling of intense pleasure rippling through her body. Sadie moaned his name as the dream shifted into a dark bedroom.

"Yes. It's me," she heard him whisper, before she slowly became aware that she was awake again.

"You're here," she said, trying to pull herself free of the tangle of blankets.

"Yeah. I need your help," he said. "The water nymph. I think she's dying."

"What?" Sadie sat up. She had completely forgotten about the nymph.

"I had planned to tell my parents about her yesterday, but she threatened to take her own life, and even half-threatened to harm my family if I told anyone."

Sadie kicked out of bed and began to search for clothes in the dark as Jimmy continued to fill her in.

"I don't know what she might be capable of and I'm scared. I don't really think she wants to hurt anyone, but she seems incredibly desperate. I've been taking her food and helping her down to the river every morning. She says she needs to be there at dawn to meet... *someone*, but *someone* never comes. Then she stands in the river to replenish her energy, but it's been working less and less. It isn't her river. We need to force her back to the ocean, but I can't seem to talk any sense into her."

Sadie had never heard this kind of fear in Jimmy's voice before. It brought her sharply back to reality. Putting on a sweater and some gloves to protect against what was sure to be chilly predawn air, they crept out her window and did the usual hop from tree branch to ground.

"Well, clearly, whatever plan she has brewing isn't working. If we can just figure out what she wants, maybe we can help her make a better plan," Sadie said, almost back to her usual tone.

"Better plan than dying in my family's barn anyway."

As they approached the broad red doors, Jimmy shook to life a flashlight.

"Psst. Ocean," Jimmy called. "That's what I've been calling her since she refuses to give her name," he whispered over his shoulder at Sadie. "I've brought my friend with me. Don't be alarmed."

They approached the stall cautiously. Sadie half-expected to see a crazed animal by the way Jimmy had been speaking about her, but the tiny woman curled up in the hay looked almost like a child. She barely acknowledged them when he opened the door and squatted down next to her.

"Do you remember Sadie?"

"I failed," the woman choked out in a high-pitched whine. "We failed. Should have been here earlier."

Sadie sat next to her, bumping into the nymph's backpack. The woman pulled it tight to her body, away from Sadie.

"What is all this, making you take this risk?" Sadie asked softly.

"Secrecy is key. Never know who to trust."

"How much longer can you stay here? Waiting for this contact?" Sadie asked.

The woman didn't answer.

"We've kept your secret so far," Sadie added.

"Take me to the river," she said, half-opening her eyes to look at Jimmy. He sighed and exchanged a look with Sadie, as if to say, *this again*. He hoisted her up as she clutched her bag. Sadie continued to try to reach her.

"What will you do if they never show?" she asked as they walked. The nymph never answered any of her questions and when they began to descend the trail to the riverside, she collapsed entirely into Jimmy's arms. He hoisted her up, and looked a question at Sadie.

"First the water, quick. Then we can take her back to the barn and get her some help." Jimmy hurried down the trail as Sadie pointed the flashlight ahead of them. When they reached the waterside, he didn't hesitate to splash into the dark depths and lower the woman in. Sadie watched frightfully as the woman continued to remain still. After a minute though, her leg twitched. Her head shot up out of the water as she gasped, throwing two arms around Jimmy's neck.

"Where is it? Where's my backpack?"

Sadie, in an attempt to do anything to calm her, ran back up the trail to fetch it from where it had fallen.

"Take it," the woman cried.

"What is it?" Sadie asked.

"Don't know. The key."

"The key?" Jimmy asked.

"To stopping the war." The nymph could barely speak now, her words were nearly inaudible.

"Andre Amadi," she said so lightly that even Jimmy could barely hear it. "Give it to no one, but Andre Amadi."

Sadie screamed as the form melted in Jimmy's arms. The woman's flesh turned slowly to water and he was left holding only her clothes.

"Holy shit!" he said, scrambling backward.

"Oh my god, oh my god," Sadie said as she launched herself forward to grab Jimmy's shoulders. When he was safely out of the water, he relaxed backward into her arms.

"Is she dead?" Sadie asked.

"I think so," Jimmy panted.

"Did you know that's how it happens?" she asked.

"No."

"We just saw a woman die. Possibly aided in it," she said, voice choking on the word *die*.

They continued to stare at the river in shock for several long minutes, until Jimmy asked, "What should we do?"

"We can't tell anyone," Sadie said. "We don't know what this woman was involved in, but it sounds dangerous. We don't want anyone to come asking questions. She chose this. She chose this to protect whatever is in that bag."

They crawled to the backpack and pulled it open together. The only thing of interest seemed to be a marble box, which explained why the bag had been so heavy. Sadie lifted it out and placed it in her lap. The box was just big enough to have two handprints covering its lid. The thumbs and forefingers made a triangle shape in the center, with all the other fingers splayed outward.

After confirming it was impossible to simply open the box, Sadie shoved it back in the bag and donned the backpack. They sat on the edge of the river for what felt like ages, neither speaking. Sadie wasn't sure what they were waiting for. Maybe it was them who were now waiting for this magical person to show up and remove this burden from their care. Maybe they were both afraid of returning to regular life after what they had just witnessed, but the sky lightened as they sat.

"I'll hide it under my bed until we can figure out what to do with it." Jimmy broke the silence.

"Okay," Sadie agreed, hearing the weak sound of her voice and feeling like she might cry.

"Hey," Jimmy said, moving closer to put an arm around her. "You alright?" The past few days had been an emotional rollercoaster and Jimmy's increased nearness did nothing to calm her.

Sadie stood and put some distance between them. "I'm fine. We should probably get back home before anyone wakes up."

They gathered up the water nymph's worn outfit and agreed to have a private funeral for her at some point, but for now they would hide her clothes as well. They walked back toward the farms, switching off the now-unnecessary flashlight. The presence of a few birdsongs lightened the somber mood, or perhaps contrasted with it.

As the fear of the moment wore off, Sadie found her previous condition returning. Memories of all her dreams over the past several days were coming back to her, finishing with an echo of her words to Jimmy in her bedroom.

"Wait." She grabbed his arm just as they were about to emerge from the trees. "Can we talk?"

"Maybe we should finish this conversation later, after we get more information, and after we get some sleep," he said.

"No. I mean about me? And us? And what's been happening."

He looked suddenly wary.

"I know I've been a little... different... the past few days, and I need some time to figure out what it means, but I'm sorry for the way I talked to you earlier. In my room..."

She hoped he understood so she didn't have to repeat any of it. He nodded. "S'okay." Stepping closer, she searched his face.

"You were definitely in a mood," he added.

"Yeah," she said.

It wasn't obvious to Sadie how to interpret the look Jimmy wore, nor was it clear if it was her moving into him or the other way around, all she knew was that in that moment, on the edge of the woods in which they had grown up, she desperately wanted to kiss her best friend.

A branch snapped as if someone had stepped on it. They both jumped and looked to their left. The forest felt suddenly very uninviting, and a twinge of fear crept up Sadie's back.

"Let's get out of here," Jimmy said, grabbing her arm and breaking into a fast walk. They both increased their speed until they found themselves running. Sadie passed him the backpack and hauled herself up the tree outside her window. Jimmy waited until she was inside before turning away. She watched him until he was out of sight, heading back to his own bedroom to pretend that nothing more had happened that night than the restful sleep of a young man with a long day of farming ahead. Now all Sadie had to do was put on an equal show of pretending as if her body wasn't going totally insane.

She decided to replace her bed with a hot shower. Stripping off her outer layers and her now-extremely-dirty pajamas, Sadie stood in front of the bathroom mirror. She examined herself, wondering how it was possible that she could look the same as she always did.

Something had changed. Something was happening to her. She admitted that now. Her real reason for not wanting to see a doctor was out of fear of finding out exactly what it was. Was it connected to the nymph? Had the woman somehow cursed her? Made her ill? Or was this all just a big coincidence? Maybe these were just natural hormones; hitting her system late in puberty; heightened by new and strange circumstances.

All she knew for sure was, if she didn't want Dr. Harris involved, she had to go downstairs for breakfast. Moving like some kind of zombie, she forced herself to bathe, brush her hair and teeth, don her best summer dress, and put on a smile. She thought she looked quite nice when she did a quick check in the mirror. A perfectly normal, happy daughter.

Her parents were both relieved to see her, and her mom immediately assured her that she shouldn't worry about helping out at the fair. She should take a day to recover fully. Sadie brushed that off. The midsummer festival was always a big event. Normally, she would help her parents set up their produce booth, then go off with Jimmy to help sell caramelized apples from his family's farm. If everything was normal now, she saw no reason she shouldn't do the same this year.

Which is how an hour later, Sadie and her parents were awaiting the bus in front of their house, stacked crates full of produce in front of them. Growing up, they'd always gone to market by horse and carriage, but when the federal government lifted some of the restrictions on resource extraction a few years back, the town had bought exactly five trucks and three buses.

No one had wanted to buy more after the nymphs had brought pictures of the extraction site to the town hall, but Sadie had to admit that getting around on festival days was a lot easier now. She coughed as the bus fumes hit her face.

The large vehicle was trailing a wagon to pick up the goods of all the nearby farms and they were clearly the first stop since the wagon was empty. The driver hopped down to help them load up. The driver's son, Clay, was also helping out today.

Clay was a few years older than Sadie, and built like he spent all day helping his dad load and unload cargo. He frequently paid her extra attention whenever they ran into each other. Usually, his gaze on her made her uncomfortable, but today she couldn't have been happier to see him.

Her dad, leaning back on his cane, directed the loading. When Sadie picked up a crate of lettuce, however, her mom stopped her.

"We got it, dear."

She waved her mom away and headed toward the wagon.

"Is everything all right?" Clay asked her. She passed the crate up to where he was standing in the back of the wagon and looked him over with the same interest he was directing at her.

"Everything's great," she said. And she meant it. She had never felt so good. It was as if her body had just woken up after a lifetime of sleep. Swaying her hips as she walked away from him, she looked back over her shoulder. He smiled at her. She smiled back, then had to put a hand on a crate to steady herself against another wave of nausea.

No. Not now.

She climbed up into the bus and took a seat directly across from Clay. Sadie watched his face as he made small talk with her parents during the two-minute drive to the Baker household next door. Her meditation on his jaw was broken only when the bus came to a halt.

Glancing at her parents, Sadie realized then that she had been avoiding looking directly into their faces all morning. What she saw there surprised her. They were both watching her intently, with matching looks of concern. They relaxed their faces under her gaze; her father looking away and her mother putting on a smile, but it was too late. Sadie knew they were worried about her. Why exactly, she wasn't sure. Was she behaving that strangely?

The Baker family consisted of Jimmy, his parents, and a hive of younger sisters. The youngest two girls had managed to get their fine dresses as dirty as possible before even departing for the festival. Sadie expected nothing less and smiled at the sight of them. When her eyes fell on Jimmy, however, her body jolted unexpectedly. They exchanged serious looks as she climbed out of the bus to help them load up.

The world felt increasingly far away, as if someone else had taken the wheel and put her on autopilot while she was hidden deep inside herself, feeling increasingly like a rabid animal about to break free. She sat far from other people each time they reboarded the bus, until it was too full to avoid it. For the final leg of the trip, she sat directly in between her parents and stared only at her hands resting in her lap. She told everyone she was feeling motion sick, which she thought might be true.

Sadie watched her hands moving as they helped her parents set-up their booth and unload all the crates. She heard her voice exchange words with a variety of people. She put herself at the cash register ready to help make a few sales. She knew she should avoid Jimmy, and told her parents she'd prefer to stick with them.

She sold people lettuce and cucumbers and cherry tomatoes for some amount of time. It was deep into the morning when a man approached the register. He didn't look local. He wore a leather vest, frayed at the edges around his bare shoulders, and leather gloves. His dark hair made a nice contrast against piercing blue eyes. He flashed her a devilish grin that seemed entirely out of place in the context. Everything about him captivated her attention, and for a moment she felt present in her body.

"Um, is that all?" she asked, nodding to the vine of cherry tomatoes he'd placed in front of her.

"How are you feeling?" he asked, leaning casually against the table.

"What? Fine. How are you?"

"A little hungry," he said with a wink.

"Well, these tomatoes might hold you over for a bit," she rambled, sounding a little breathless.

"For a bit," he agreed. "And what'll hold you over, I wonder?"

She swallowed.

"Umm. That'll be four dollars," she said.

He dropped a five-dollar bill and backed away in an alluring swagger, sucking a tomato off the vine. It wasn't until he turned away from her that she noticed there was another person trying to make a purchase. The woman followed her gaze and whistled.

"He's something isn't he? I'd be distracted too." Sadie's eyes snapped from the man to the woman. She had on a low-cut baby blue shirt and red lipstick. Sadie looked her up and down, eyes darting from the woman's waist to neck to hair. She felt almost nauseous when she looked at the woman's lips. Strangely, she found she wanted to reach out and run her finger along them.

"Sorry. I..." Sadie backed away from the register and called out to her dad to take over. She moved to sit down on the edge of the booth where no one would bother her. When she'd caught her breath, she decided she should take a walk. Sadie wasn't up for talking to anyone else just then.

She stood up to find her mom looking at her. When she said she'd be back later, her mother stepped forward and put a hand on her shoulder. Grabbing her attention with her gaze, she told her daughter softly, "I'll be right here, if you need me."

Turning away from her mom's serious expression, Sadie walked out into the crowd. The colorful dresses of people on a festival day swarmed in front of her eyes. Her feet carried her through the throng while her gaze danced from person to person.

She needed something. She wasn't sure what it was exactly, but it seemed to be in the swaying hips of the woman in the cut-off shorts walking ahead of her, or in the eyes of the young man checking her out as he passed. It was in the smiles and smells and mere presence of many of the people around her.

She spotted the man in the leather vest leaning against a tree. There was a young woman attempting to get his attention, but he was staring intently at Sadie. She looked away. After a minute, she glanced behind her to find the man was following. She attempted to increase the speed of her walk, but felt a little unsteady on her feet. Averting her eyes from anyone she recognized, she started to focus only on the ground in front of her as she trudged onward in search of something undefinable.

A pair of feet appeared in front of her. She tried to walk around them, but they stepped to remain in her path. She looked up. It was Ina Birch.

"Are you okay?" she asked. "Sadie? Can you hear me?"

"She's drunk," said a voice to her right. Sadie turned to see the grove posse girls sitting around in lawn chairs, watching her. The sweet smell of the corn on the cob they were consuming filled her nostrils. They appeared to be laughing at her.

"Little early in life to be drunk and alone, don't you think?" Cassie choked out through a guffaw. Sadie felt herself swaying and widened her stance to keep herself upright. Looking back at Ina, she stared blankly at her old friend's button nose and tiny lips. Her hair hung long down over her chest. It was so pretty. Unbearably pretty. Sadie ran her fingers through it. She heard the laughter increase.

"She's wasted."

"Or high as hell."

"What's going on here?" a familiar voice said. Sadie turned toward the sound of Jimmy, before noticing a small crowd had gathered around them.

"Hi," Sadie choked out breathlessly. "It's you," she breathed, placing a hand on his chest.

"What's wrong? Are you sick?" he asked, handing off his tray of caramelized apples to Ina and placing his hands on either side of her waist to steady her. He asked her another question, but Sadie couldn't make out the words. The sounds around her seemed to blur as she leaned toward him. Her skin tingled as the whole world melted. She brought her lips close to his and breathed in the smell of his skin.

"I wouldn't recommend that," a voice said sharply in her ear, as two large, gloved hands pulled on her shoulders. She regained some awareness as she turned to face the man in the leather vest. She stared into his handsome face and found herself suddenly closer. Had she leaned in? Her gaze was still fixated on his mouth when he cupped a hand around the back of her neck and pulled her lips to his.

Her body exploded with sensation. She melted against him as pleasure traveled from her lips to her thighs, pounding hot between her legs. An excitement built rapidly in her and she wanted to be even closer. When he began to withdraw, she rocked forward into him. He let her kiss him a moment longer, before pushing her back forcefully.

Holding her at arm's length with a firm grip on her shoulders, he looked over her face.

"It's time," he said.

The world snapped back into focus. She felt more steady on her feet and suddenly keenly aware of the watching crowd.

"The hell?" Cassie said, no longer laughing.

"I'm sorry. I don't know what came over me," Sadie said, directing the words first at no one in particular, but then back at Jimmy, who was looking at her with such a frightened expression she wanted to reach out and hug him.

"Now that you're feeling better, let's get moving. We can talk on the way," said the man in leather.

"What? Who the hell do you think you are?" she asked, pushing him away from her, suddenly angry.

"A friend," he said calmly.

"A friend would never kiss someone without their permission," Sadie barked, still shaking from the experience of her first kiss. Was it always that intense?

"Which I didn't. I only did exactly what you wanted me to, but you're further along than I thought and we have a ways to travel. We should get moving. If you'll trust me for now, I'll explain on the way."

"I'm not going anywhere with you." Sadie backed up to where Jimmy was standing and put a hand on his arm.

The instant their skin touched, a keen awareness of him spread outward from where her hand met his bicep to every part of his body. She could feel his heart pounding in his chest; his abs clenching. She could sense every cell in him as she traced in her mind the flow of blood through his veins. She observed it harden the soft flesh between his legs. Jimmy gasped audibly, then collapsed at her feet.

Chapter 3

A transformation

The man in leather grabbed both her hands.

"Here, put these on," he said. Sadie didn't see what he held out to her because she had dropped to Jimmy's side.

"Are you okay?" she asked softly in his ear, trying to make sense of what had just happened.

"A feeder," Cassie exclaimed in the midst of the whispering crowd.

"He's fine. He'll want a minute before standing up," the man said, thrusting two pairs of soft black gloves into Sadie's face. She looked up at him above her, framed by the mid-afternoon sun, and felt a wave of shock and fear. He was implying she had done this. She had done something to Jimmy. He was suggesting she put on gloves. She stood up.

"I don't know what's happening to me," she cried. The man stepped forward and placed a hand on her shoulder.

"I do. I know what's happening to you," he said, emphasizing every word. "And if you'll trust me, I can help you through it."

She took the gloves then, hands shaking, and slid them on. Jimmy stood up and looked at her with an unreadable expression. He seemed to be unharmed. The man took her by the arm and began to steer her out of the crowd.

"No," she said, swiveling back to face Jimmy as the man tugged on her.

"Stay with me," she called out to her friend. Jimmy closed the distance between them as the crowd parted to let them pass.

"He shouldn't come," the man said. "This is a private ceremony."

"I'm not going without him." Sadie balked against the man's grip. He let go immediately.

"Okay. If it's what you want." He pointed to direct their path rather than retaking her arm. They cut through an alley which led them quickly away from the crowd.

"I really am a friend, you know? Name's Gabriel."

Sadie and Jimmy introduced themselves, but her suspicions of the man didn't waver. She continued to follow him, however, as he directed them to the edge of downtown. When they reached the train station, the man paid for all three tickets and climbed aboard.

He didn't look back. Sadie thought he was too confident in his belief that they would follow, but follow they did. The train that ran between towns in this area was never particularly crowded. They only had to pass through six cars before finding one entirely to themselves. Gabriel sat down next to her while Jimmy took the seat directly across, but facing her; keeping some distance, she noticed.

"How far are we going?" Jimmy asked the man.

"Just one town over. I'm renting a cabin there. It's secluded; a little out in the woods to offer us some privacy." The conversation went quiet for a minute. Perhaps Jimmy was also contemplating the wisdom of following a stranger into a secluded area. The man broke their reverie by asking, "Do you remember the last adult whose skin you touched before today?" Sadie raised her eyebrows. "Touched in a friendly way. A parent patting your back? A hug from a friend?" Sadie thought back over the past several days. Had her mom touched her? She couldn't recall. She didn't think she had touched anyone's skin over the past few days. Then she remembered when she had hugged Jimmy as they were walking back from Ina's celebration, how their cheeks had touched. Sadie nodded in the direction of Jimmy, and Gabriel looked the two of them over.

"Remember that moment," he said. "It was the last time."

Sadie looked back at Gabriel. He seemed to be looking inward, but when he refocused on her, she was unable to keep the words down any longer.

"I'm a feeder?" she asked.

"Yes."

"A human feeder?"

"Yes."

"What kind?"

"What do you think?" Gabriel prodded.

It was obvious.

"I feed off of..." She looked at Jimmy and felt her face flush.

"You feed off of sexual desire. And pleasure. You're a succubus. Like me. Or... at least you will be soon."

She looked at their gloved hands as his words sunk in.

"And succubi can't touch anyone?" Jimmy asked, while Sadie felt panic welling up inside her.

"They can. They just probably shouldn't in public." Gabriel grinned.

Everything was different now, Sadie thought. Could she even return to her life? What did this mean? She wanted to cry or hit something, or scream. Why her? She already felt like enough of an outsider.

Jimmy stood up and moved to take the seat next to her. He was careful to avoid touching her skin, but he laced his fingers through her gloved hand.

"It's going to be okay," he told her. At first, she felt only comfort from the gesture, but as she turned to see him so close, her unquenched desire kicked back into gear. She imagined reaching out to touch him again and shivered. Dropping her eyes from his to look him up and down, she chewed her lip as her heart began to pound. He watched her taking him in, and when she remade eye contact, he returned the look unflinchingly. She made no attempt to hide what she wanted and he made no move to withdraw from her. What he wanted, she couldn't tell, but at least he seemed unafraid.

Sadie had more questions she had wanted to ask, but Jimmy's

proximity was making it hard to focus. She let go of his hand, immediately missing the contact, and moved to sit directly across from the two of them.

"Sorry. I need some space," she said. If Jimmy was hurt by her withdrawal, it didn't show on his face. Taking a few breaths to recollect herself, she directed her focus back to Gabriel.

"How did you know that this would happen? You've been following me?"

"It's a special talent I have. I was passing through your town a while back and spotted you."

"When? How long back?" She suddenly wondered if this man's appearance had anything to do with their water nymph.

"About a year ago. I knew you'd go through the transition soon and I've been keeping an eye on you."

"And why do you care?" she asked, in some attempt to determine his motives. She supposed a part of her blamed this man for what was happening. That was irrational, she knew, but she needed some outlet for the anger building up inside her.

"Because we should look after each other. A Becoming can be terrifying if you're alone. And occasionally dangerous to those around you."

"A Becoming?" Jimmy asked.

"It's what we call it when you manifest the succubus part of yourself. Most human feeders develop slowly, throughout their childhood, but for succubi it happens in early adulthood. And it happens suddenly. Not everyone with the gene transitions, but I can usually tell when someone will."

"You've done this before? Helped someone... change?" Sadie asked.

"Many times."

"Must be a lot of you. If you happen to run into so many others," Jimmy said. Sadie didn't like being a part of the *you* in Jimmy's words; something different from him; something other.

"No. I chose this role. It's what I do. I wander around a lot, scouting out those who might need me one day."

This last piece of information relaxed her a bit. That story at least made sense.

They sat lost in silence until the train ground to a slow crawl, then looked up at the map as Gabriel announced the name of their stop. She could see the little road attached to stop fifty-seven. It was the last stop before the train left town and there was clearly nothing else out here.

They hopped off the train into the bright afternoon sun and followed Gabriel down the dirt path. Sadie struggled to form more questions in light of the fear now building up in her. She desperately wanted to ask what was going to happen, but the words kept catching. She looked over at Jimmy several times. Once, he reached up as if he was going to stroke her arm before catching himself.

Gabriel looked back at her, then broke the silence with, "Sorry, I'm... not very good at the emotional support leading up to this. Why I don't usually reach out until it's time." He turned to walk backwards in front of her, his suddenly heightened swagger grabbing her attention. "But I promise you, I'm very good at what happens next."

He pulled open the buttons on his vest. "Just remember, this is all a matter of course. Your body is taking its natural path and nothing you're feeling is wrong." His movement and casual undressing, as well as the sudden purr in his voice, caused a reaction in her. As she was sure was his intention.

Behind him, the cabin emerged through the trees, and she was surprised to see they had company. Lots of company. A man and woman were swinging back and forth on a tire swing. An older woman sat on the porch, smoking a pipe. Three young men were tossing balls of fire between them like a baseball. Neither Sadie nor Jimmy had seen fire nymphs before. They gawked at their game.

Noticing their arrival, they all turned to face them.

"Everyone, this is Sadie Hall." Clearly Gabriel knew more about her than he'd let on, since she was sure she hadn't given her last name. Sadie waved awkwardly. Gabriel didn't introduce Jimmy. The two people on the tire swing jumped down, but their movement failed to make sense for a moment. It was as if a gust of wind carried them several feet forward. *Are they all nature feeders?*

The fire nymphs came and shook her hand. One of them, who introduced himself as Leon, also shook Jimmy's hand. He had a nice smile, and Sadie's gaze lingered on him a moment.

"Dinner's ready," a woman said. She'd just emerged from the cabin door with a bounce in her step. She had short purple hair and several piercings, and was carrying a tray. "Ahh perfect timing. The guest of honor. Can you help...?" she directed at the air nymphs before walking out into the yard and placing the tray on a long table.

They moved toward her while the air nymphs disappeared, returning a minute later with more trays. The table was already set. The napkins wafted in a cool breeze, and the surrounding trees provided a nice canopy for their meal. Everyone except the newcomers walked through the grass barefoot.

Sadie exchanged a look with Jimmy as they moved to take seats. Gabriel gestured for Jimmy to sit on the other side of the table, as the woman with purple hair pulled out a chair for Sadie.

"I didn't catch your name," Sadie said, taking in the woman's captivating face.

"Annabella," she whispered, almost touching their noses together. "You hungry, Sadie?"

Sadie leaned forward, but the woman pulled back. She moved to take the seat directly across from her and next to Jimmy.

The three fire nymphs stood staring at her succubus guide. Gabriel looked from Sadie to Leon and directed the man to take the seat to her left before sitting himself down on her right. The other two men slumped off to find other seats. When they were all in place, Annabella declared, "Dig in!"

Sadie didn't feel particularly hungry, and when she didn't reach for any food, Leon put some salad on her plate. Normally, she might have been embarrassed about all this attention, but the humming under her skin caused her to want even more of it. She watched the muscles in Leon's forearms working to scoop up the salad. He smiled at her attention on him.

"Fire nymphs, you know, are naturally good mates for succubi. We can always withstand the heat, if you know what I mean? We're particularly handy during Becomings." He rested his hand an inch from her forearm on the table. She looked at it expectantly, but he didn't move it further. "I'm not gonna touch you, but you can touch me if you like," he said.

Sadie blinked at his bold behavior. Then her surprise turned inward. Why did this not feel that strange?

She considered reaching for Leon's hand, and her blood seemed to boil at the thought. Aware that Jimmy was watching, she glanced at him. He didn't look away, but his expression still told her nothing. She had never seen Jimmy so subdued, and if she'd had the energy to, she'd have been worried.

Sadie's gaze fell on Annabella as she said, "We're all here to help out, just let us know what you want."

"Eat first," Gabriel ordered. "We've got a long night ahead of us."

Sadie did her best to follow his command, but couldn't stop staring at the people around her. She was grateful to see them passing around a bottle of wine – perhaps that would calm her nerves – but when it reached her, Gabriel stopped her from taking a sip.

"Not tonight. We need you level-headed. For everyone's safety." He too, drank nothing.

The noise level at the table grew from the casual conversation of the many guests. All Sadie could hear, however, were Leon's words echoing in her mind as she imagined reaching out to touch him. She felt the intensity of her desire increase back to the level it had been before Gabriel had kissed her, and she was finding it particularly difficult to focus on chewing and swallowing. And though she didn't feel much like small talk, she did feel like looking at Jimmy. She spent most of the meal watching him converse with those around him. How had she never noticed how appealing his jaw was? How handsome his dark brown eyes?

He turned from Annabella on one side of him to the old woman sitting on the other side and asked, "How do you all know each other?" The old woman tossed her cigar bud in an empty glass and immediately lit up a new one.

"Gabriel's only one I know," the elder woman said in a low, husky voice which broke into a cough mid-sentence. "Keeps me in the loop."

"On...Becomings?" Jimmy pried.

"On succubi," she said this last word like it was the brand name of her favorite cigar. "My kind; always looking for a little unmet desire. Unrequited lust. That's my favorite. The kinda thing follows succubi around, you see."

"Requited lust follows succubi around too," Annabella said in Jimmy's ear, "but siren don't give a shit about that." She winked at the old lady, who raised her wine glass in acknowledgement.

"Oh. And you? You here for the same reason?" Jimmy asked Annabella.

She laughed. "Oh no. I'm definitely no siren. More like the opposite, if you know what I mean?" It was unlikely Jimmy had even the vaguest notion of what she meant, but he nodded anyway. "Just a fan of the succubus. Gabriel keeps me in the loop too. I was in Spain when I got the call. Caught the first ride back."

"You flew? Across the ocean?" Jimmy asked.

"Ha! My parents don't have that much money. Na. I got the call back in January. It was enough time."

This woman had traveled from Spain for this? Sadie's thoughts refocused enough to register surprise. The knowledge made her nervous, as if she was about to go on stage in a famous opera house, only no one had told her any of her lines. And back in January? Gabriel said he'd known for a year that this might be coming, while Sadie had just been going about her life. The thought scared her. As if the ground she'd walked on for years had turned out to be quicksand.

If Jimmy was surprised at any of the things he heard, it didn't show. He continued to make polite conversation, as if he had spent his whole life around human feeders and nymphs alike. While in reality, neither she nor Jimmy had ever met a single feeder who fed off humans until Gabriel. And it seemed this old woman was also a human feeder, a siren. Was everyone else nature feeders? After all, you couldn't always tell nymphs from humans or human feeders. Not unless you witnessed some visible interaction like throwing fire, or they wore some signifying adornment. Human feeders were even harder to spot, since they often fed in silent and subtle ways. Sadie didn't know any details about that, however, and felt she could possibly be wrong about anything she did know. After all, who remembered all the details of sixth grade biology?

Regardless, it seemed Jimmy and she were the only humans. Or… Jimmy was, at least.

Sadie turned to look at her guide. Gabriel had a special kind of allure to him, and she wasn't sure if she should trust it or not.

"How are you feeling?" he asked.

She looked down at his lips as he spoke and suddenly found him even closer. Had she leaned in?

"Uhh. I'm not sure. Is…? Is it always going to be like this for me?" she asked, wishing he would just kiss her again. Instead, he brushed her hair back from her neck and placed a hand there. Then he rested his exposed forearm against her skin.

"No. It won't always be like this," he said softly, as a pleasurable sensation spread outward from his touch. "Life will be a little crazy for a while, but it will settle down." The sensation reached the base of her spine and she felt heat build between her legs.

"Succubi have almost no sex drive before the Becoming, making the experience kind of like jumping into the deep end of a very warm pool. But when it's over, your life will be more or less the same." She squirmed slightly, arching her back. "You will get hungry, like you do now for food, and then you will feed." He slid his right hand under the table and placed it on her knee. He had removed his glove somehow and the intensity of the feeling more than doubled.

"And… what does that… entail, exactly?" she asked. He slid his hand along her thigh and up her dress, stopping with one finger hooked under her panty line. She leaned closer into him.

"Exactly what I'm doing right now. I'm causing the pleasure, and then I'm feeding off it. This feels equally as satisfying from my end, though in a different kind of way. The satisfaction of my experience as feeder is bound up in the intensity of the sensation for you. And, if you want to get into some subtlety, it is also bound up in the emotional impact on you. This, right now, is very satisfying for me because pleasure is so new to you." He leaned in to whisper in her ear. "And I love causing it."

She felt the pressure inside her build and a small sound escaped her throat. He abruptly withdrew his touch and Sadie saw the old woman's head snap in their direction. Coming back to her senses, she expected everyone to be staring at them, but she saw that they were all still engaged in conversation as the sound of their chatter hit her ears again.

Looking back into Gabriel's eyes, she was on the verge of begging him to keep touching her. Why had he stopped if they both wanted it? She took a sip of water and tried to collect herself.

Then the question struck her, "Is that what I did earlier? When I touched my friend?" She was afraid to say Jimmy's name in case it grabbed his attention.

"Approximately. Though you weren't feeding. You won't be able to feed until after the transition."

She tried to scoot closer to him, but he sat up straighter. "And when you touch me... I feel a little better afterward. Like there's a buzzing in my head and I can't focus, and then you take it away."

"It's a momentary release. It will work less and less as the night goes on. But it's one of the ways I can help," Gabriel said.

"What are some of the other ways?" she heard herself ask. The words sounded as if they didn't belong to her. Was she flirting with this strange man that had pulled her out of her life? The concept felt so foreign and yet natural at the same time. Gabriel just smiled and went back to eating. As she withdrew back into her space, she noticed Leon watching her.

"How's the food?" he asked.

"Not really sure," Sadie said, only half-listening.

She took a sip of her water. Leon's words from earlier echoed again in her head. *You can touch me if you like.* With the bit of knowledge Gabriel had just thrown her, Sadie's curiosity and impulse to take Leon up on that offer intensified. She pushed a potato around her plate, contemplating the rudeness of not finishing her food. *You can touch me if you like.* She looked up to watch Jimmy again, his face both familiar and new. His smooth copper skin caught in the late-day sun. His kind eyes both attentive and hesitant. *You can touch me if you like.*

Sadie caved. Without looking at him, she gently pressed her left thigh against Leon's bare skin. She was impressed that he showed no reaction above the table. She saw him take a bite of food out of the corner of her eye as she observed excitement build slowly in his body. She was fascinated, and for a moment lost track of everything else around her. She wanted to look at his face, but was too shy. She kept watching Jimmy. He was turned toward the woman with the purple hair whose name Sadie couldn't recall just then. Sadie's thoughts again became muddled. She watched Jimmy speaking without being able to make sense of his words and suddenly she wished it was him she could touch. The instant she had that thought, she found she desperately wanted more.

"Time to go inside," Gabriel declared. She jerked herself away from Leon. Conversation halted as everyone looked toward them. She felt flushed and dropped her gaze to her plate; suddenly guilty about what she'd just been doing. Then the crowd stood up. A few people made to clear some plates.

"We've got it," one of the air nymphs said, waving them away. "Go on."

Sadie's eyes dropped to the bulge in Leon's pants, now visible to everyone. She looked at the faces around her in confusion and embarrassment, but no one else seemed to think much of it. Except for Jimmy, who registered some emotion in the coloring of his cheeks. Leon took her hand and began walking toward the house, while she looked back at Gabriel.

"I'm right here," he said, placing a hand on her back. Still looking over her shoulder, her gaze locked on Jimmy's, imploring him to stay with her. Jimmy moved to follow. Annabella opened the door for them and Leon led her into a dim entrance way, kicking off his shoes. Sadie did the same.

The cabin was mostly empty. No furniture to be seen. The floor was covered with a rug and a flood of pillows. The setting sun cast a warm glow through the skylight, but there appeared to be no other light sources available.

"Whose place is this?" Sadie asked.

"Ours," one of the air nymphs said, coming in behind her with a stack of plates. "Gabriel's an old friend. When he called, we said we'd be happy to host."

Leon dropped her hand and went to the fireplace. She watched as flames flickered down his arms, and a moment later, the room brightened with a roaring fire. Several of the others, including Jimmy, seemed to appreciate the heat and sat nearby, but Sadie felt too warm already. The old woman stacked a bunch of pillows and made herself at home next to Jimmy, pulling out another cigar.

"Oh not in the house June," the other host begged the old siren, entering with another stack of plates.

Sadie remained on her feet, still not sure exactly what she was supposed to do. One of the other fire nymphs stood with her. She turned to him and asked, "How did you find out about this?"

The man brightened. "The three of us perform with a traveling circus. We met Gabriel a few years back. He asked if he could call us sometime. We were in the area."

"Wanna see our act?" Leon asked. He stepped within a foot of her, his gaze studying her face.

She did want to see it. She wanted a lot of things. Sadie nodded and went to take a seat next to Jimmy. Gabriel intercepted her path, placing himself on a cushion in between her and her friend. Sadie initially balked at that, wanting to be closer to Jimmy, but perhaps she was better off with a barrier between them.

The three men pushed the pillows out of the center of the room and removed their T-shirts. The bustling in the kitchen ceased as the hosts rejoined them, making themselves comfortable on a couple of cushions to enjoy the show.

The fire nymphs started by creating a rhythm with hands and feet, urging everyone to join in. Once the onlookers were holding a steady beat, they began to dance. Strings of fire jumped to life, creating a light show on their bodies. Occasionally, the flames would exist independent of them. Two of the performers would create a ring and the third would flip through the hoop.

It was mesmerizing, and for a moment Sadie forgot all her fears. She felt her mind dancing right along with them, lost in the beauty of it. The sun set as they danced, and everyone seemed to be in a trance, stomping and clapping in time. Sadie watched until she could no longer ignore how overheated she felt. Moving away from the fireplace and everyone else, she placed herself near the window. The act seemed to be building to some kind of finale and she didn't want to miss it by going outside, but she felt as if it were her skin from which the flames were sprouting.

The onlookers responded appropriately to their increased tempo by speeding up the beat, and the energy of the crowd seemed to fuel the performers. They ended with a bang and everyone clapped, except Sadie. She pulled at her dress, which she suddenly noticed was soaked through. She needed air. Without saying a word, she moved to the door and pulled it open. She could feel a breeze hit her, but it felt no cooler than it did inside. In desperation, she stepped out into the night without her shoes and waited for the usual cool dusk air to have an effect. She felt nothing. Scared, she went back inside, where she found everyone watching her.

"I'm too hot," she said to Gabriel. "I think something's wrong."

One of the hosts came out of the kitchen and handed something to her guide. Gabriel brought it to her. "No, you're right on course," he said, before placing an ice cube on the back of her neck where it immediately began to melt.

It helped. Slightly. His assurance helped more; calming her panic considerably. Though she was still uncomfortable in her skin, Gabriel's hand on the back of her neck reminded her of when he had placed it there earlier, and her attention shifted from fear to lust in the course of a heartbeat.

She leaned into him, half-expecting to be pushed away. Instead, he pulled off his gloves and reached to pull off hers. Sadie moaned the instant their bare hands came in contact, and balked when he dropped them. He pulled open his leather vest, which had been hanging loose on his shoulders all night and dropped it to the floor. She panted as she looked him up and down. Gabriel let her look before pulling her to him and kissing her, gently prodding her mouth with his tongue. She pressed herself hard to him, forgetting all the world.

This was what she needed. She grabbed at his chest and arms, struck by the intimate sensation of his skin on hers.

When he did push her back to arm's length, she looked around, shocked to find herself in this strange place, doing these strange things. She looked at Jimmy. His expression was made of stone, entirely unreadable. Did he want her to be kissing him? Would Gabriel allow it? Perhaps he wanted to leave and have nothing to do with this. What if he was only staying because she'd begged him to?

Their air nymph hosts stood up and announced, "Well, we should give you all some privacy. We're going to bed, wake us if you need anything." They disappeared through a door next to the kitchen.

The instant the door closed, the energy in the room changed. It was as if everyone was suddenly holding their breath. Leon, whose torso had been covered in soot and sweat, dropped the wet towel he had been using to clean himself and came toward her.

"What else can I do for you, Sadie Hall?" He looked stunning in the firelight and she hesitated a moment over what she was about to do, but couldn't seem to access the emotions of shame, embarrassment, and shyness she had felt earlier.

Despite everyone watching, she walked toward the man, put a hand on his chest and kissed him. Sadie slowly pushed him to the floor with the kiss until she rested on top of him. Sitting up into a straddle position, she ran her fingertips down his torso.

"Ice," she said, picking open the button on his jeans, "More ice."

"You're not gonna to find it in there." He smiled through the pleasure on his face, looking down at her fingers unzipping his pants.

"Is this what I'm supposed to do?" she asked, her breathing hectic as she pulled down his boxers. His erection sprang free and she stared at it in fascination.

"There is no supposed to," Gabriel said, appearing behind her with more ice on her neck.

"But to me, you can do whatever you want," Leon said, putting his hands behind his head, "and I'll do anything you ask me to."

Sadie stared for a long time at his body, before tentatively taking hold of the thick shaft in front of her. It was warm and hard in her hand, and felt both familiar and strange. She swallowed as her desire mingled with uncertainty.

Gabriel appeared at her back, straddling the man's thighs with her. Handing the ice cube to Leon, he scooped his cold hand over hers. "Like this," he whispered in her ear, as he guided her fist in a slow stroke. "See how the precum pools here? You should take it and spread it."

Sadie watched their hands moving in fascination as the man they were stroking groaned. She'd never heard such an intoxicating sound, and as the sweet scent of him hit her, she felt she would go crazy with needing more. How had she been living without this?

Pleasure began to build between her own legs as Gabriel continued to make skin contact. Though it wasn't until Leon ran the ice over her nipples, that her whole body trembled. She slowly stroked him faster, taking more control.

"How does he feel?" Gabriel asked.

Sadie wasn't sure what to say, so she spoke simply, sticking to the truth. "He feels good. So good. Smooth and warm, and... just right." More precum appeared and their hands make a slick sound as they continued to stroke him together.

"I like when it pulses," she breathed, as Leon sucked in air.

"That's because he's close to coming," Gabriel whispered, before running his teeth along the back of her neck. "I'm holding him back, though. He'll wait until you've finished your exploration." Then he added, "And *it* has a name. His cock. Dick. Shaft. Pick one, and say it out loud."

Sadie chewed her lip as she stared at it. Then she whispered, "His cock. I like when his cock pulses."

Gabriel slowed her stroking, taking control again of her hand. "And this is the cockhead. It's very sensitive, especially to the bare skin of a succubus." He slid her hand in a slow stroke downward to scoop up the sack. "And here are the balls. Cup them. Yeah, like that." He let her explore awhile, until she had the feel of him, and then added, "Now. Do you want to make him come?"

Sadie's heart was beating out of her chest, her own body taut with pleasurable tension. She nodded her head.

"Then let me show you something." Gabriel directed their grip to wrap around the base of the shaft, but then he held them still. "Where you touch someone and how has an effect on the experience, but it's not necessary to move. If you're in contact with their skin, they will eventually climax."

Sadie could feel the moment Gabriel released his control over Leon's building pleasure. Though their hands didn't move, she felt the rush of sensation take him. Acutely aware of every inch of his body, she observed with rapt attention as Leon's heart pounded faster; every muscle grew taut, and his balls drew up tight and firm. Then the tension released in wave after wave as he cried out. A moment later hot fluid shot from him.

She looked up to watch his face at the last minute and the sight was utterly captivating. "God," Sadie said.

When the man had finally stopped shaking, Gabriel released his grip and slowly slid his hand up her thigh. "That was part one of your lesson." She knew what was coming and even so, she gasped as his hand slid into her panties. The pleasurable sensation that had been slowly building increased rapidly as he languidly stroked her.

"And *this* right here," he stroked over the place between her legs which was throbbing the hardest. "This is your clit. It's my favorite body part." He added in a purr that somehow made her thighs feel weak even though she wasn't using them.

For some reason, she suddenly remembered Jimmy was in the room. When her gaze locked on his, he looked rapidly away. But Sadie continued to watch his face as she rocked into Gabriel's touch. *Yes*, something was happening. The tension that had been building in her was finally reaching a peak. She found her mind going soft as she chased the sensation.

Suddenly, Gabriel withdrew his touch, and a moment later he'd gotten to his feet. The feeling stopped abruptly, leaving her with a throbbing ache. She gasped, and Jimmy, who was directly in front of her by the fire, looked her way. Everyone was watching her now. Everyone except the siren, who was fixated on Jimmy.

Jimmy, whose masked expression was now colored by flushed cheeks, clutched his knees to his chest as they locked eyes. *God, how she wanted him.* Could she do it? Touch him the way she'd just touched Leon? Suddenly, it was all too much, the desire building up in her too intense. She couldn't take it. Her skin was on fire and she wanted more.

"Ice," she cried, picking at her dress as Gabriel disappeared again into the kitchen. She wanted it off, but the bralette was built into the dress. Removing it would leave her topless. She felt that information was important somehow, but couldn't remember why in her haste to get it off.

Once she was mostly naked, she looked back up at Jimmy, but he was again looking away. She wanted desperately to be near him, but as she moved across the room Gabriel returned just in time to put a hand out in front of her.

"No, Sadie. He's off-limits tonight," Gabriel said.

"Why?" she whined.

Jimmy's eyes flashed briefly toward her, before dropping to the ground.

"You need to learn more control before you're ready to touch him."

Perhaps that was good advice, Sadie thought, as control was something she seemed to have in short supply just then. She felt an unstoppable force coming over her, and in search of something to satisfy the craving, approached the naked man she'd left lying on the ground.

Pulling off her underwear, she dropped back into a straddle over his thighs. He immediately hardened when their skin touched. "More," she said, reaching again for the now very slick shaft.

"Take as much as you want," Gabriel told her, as he ran the ice over her neck and back. This time, however, he avoided touching her skin. Sadie whimpered, and Jimmy glanced at her and then quickly away.

No. That's not what she wanted. She needed him to watch her.

"Look at me," Sadie said. "James. Look at me."

He did. At the same time, Gabriel slid a hand around her waist and cupped between her legs. Her mouth dropped open as her head fell back. She looked down at Leon, then up at the man she wanted most. The one that was finally watching. Holding Jimmy's gaze, she rocked her pelvis back and forth as searing pleasure coursed through her.

She was on the edge of something incredible; something new, but just as it arrived, Gabriel again withdrew his hands, whispering in her ear, "Not yet." She turned around to grab at him, but he had slipped back on his gloves and he stopped her with a firm grip on her wrists.

She was too hot. Her skin burned her. And she needed him to keep touching her. Why had he stopped? "It's too hot. It's too much. Can't you do something?" She tried to stand up, but felt dizzy and instead found herself on all fours. Sadie sat up with her legs beneath her and writhed back and forth in place. Gabriel kneeled in front of her.

"You want me to touch you?" he asked in a husky voice.

"Yes," she said.

He ran his gloved hands up her hips.

She reached for his chest, but again he stopped her, holding both her hands at rest on her legs.

"If you know it's what I want, and you're here to help, why don't you give it to me?" she asked. Sadie barely recognized her own voice. She watched sweat dripping from the ends of her hair and fall to the ground between them. Their faces were inches apart.

"Because I'm trying to help you turn, not give you satisfaction. Your body is changing and I'm here to help it. It's uncomfortable, believe me, I remember, but the speed of your transition is related to your level of desire. My goal isn't to give you what you want, it's to give you what you need." He kissed her lightly on the lips before pulling back.

"When I turned, I was alone. It lasted days and became unbearably painful." He kissed her again, then held her back. "It's your longing that needs to reach a climax."

She squeezed her thighs together, wishing he would push himself between them.

"You're saying..." Sadie began, before losing her thought. She took a steadying breath. "You're saying you're trying to turn me on?" she asked.

"Not trying. Succeeding." He kissed her again. She undulated under his grip, still firm on her hands, and felt her blood would boil.

Glancing at one of the other fire nymphs, she called him forward with her gaze. Gabriel retreated so the man could kneel in front of her. Sadie devoured him, holding the back of his neck as she firmly kissed him through multiple releases. She didn't know his name, but she knew exactly what his tongue felt like against hers as he thrust into her hand.

She exhausted him and moved on to the woman with purple hair – again, Sadie had lost her name. Sadie could barely recall her own name, in fact. She cycled through the fire nymphs and young woman twice before coming to lie on the floor. She wanted more. Sadie tossed and turned as she lost track of time. Occasionally, her thoughts would focus enough to remember to beg for ice, but she had no words for the things she wanted most.

"Is this normal?" she heard Jimmy whisper somewhere in the distance. He sounded afraid. Called upright by his voice, she turned again to stare at him. Out of the corner of her eye, she saw Gabriel jerk his head. An instant later, the third fire nymph appeared in front of her.

This time, things got a little out of control. Gabriel had to step forward and pull Sadie off the man, releasing him to rest in the corner. The spent nymph collapsed into sleep.

Leon stepped back into the picture. Everything seemed to consume her, his smell and texture and desire; her own earthly body, heated and alive; Jimmy's gaze on her; the moments of relief when cool ice caressed her neck.

An hour later, Leon was resting in the corner and she was back to writhing uncomfortably, propped upright on her knees.

Gabriel scooped her face up in his hands. "Come on," he whispered. "Let it happen. Let it go." He ran his lips along her neck. "You're almost there."

Her abdomen tightened suddenly and a shiver ran down her back. Every time he touched her, the place between her legs would throb out of control. He continued to caress her neck and face with his mouth as the sensation built to a peak. Then, just as he'd been doing all night, he pulled back, holding her down with his gloved hands.

She cried out. "Please. Gabriel, I need—" but she wasn't sure what she was seeking. "Please keep touching me. Just touch me. Please."

He nibbled at her cheek and his gaze flared as she panted with frantic desire for more. She found his lips, and he let her kiss him for one long precious moment. Then he pulled back once again.

Her body throbbed even more unbearably than before. This time however, a sudden surge of heat rose in her and she balked backward out of his grip.

"There," he said in satisfaction. Sadie convulsed forward, feeling the rug under her stomach. She gripped at it with both hands, before rolling to her back. A mix of sensations, both pleasurable and uncomfortable, swelled up inside her. She thought she heard someone screaming, then a man's voice yelling in anger.

Then she let go. Everything went still. The chaos in her thoughts paused even as the physical sensations intensified.

It came to her then. Clear as day. She knew the truth. She could reject it. She wasn't sure how she knew, but the knowledge coursed through her. She was about to change, forever, and right here and now, she could let the change take her or push it away. It must have shown on her face, because when she locked eyes with Gabriel, sitting a few feet away with an arm in front of Jimmy, he nodded.

Was he answering her question? Was he saying, *yes, you are choosing this. Yes, it's a choice.* She was sure he was.

The knowledge that it was up to her was the most terrifying thing that had happened all night. She could reject this, if she wanted. She could tell it no, and return to her life as usual. If she in fact, didn't want this new life. But what if she did? She had always felt like an outsider, without being able to identify why. Maybe it was herself she was outside of? The emotion coursing through her, the sensation, it felt right. How could she reject it? Beyond the fear of the unknown and the self-doubt, she knew it was what she wanted.

Gathering up all her reservations, she put them in a little corner of herself. Then she relaxed. She relaxed into it completely and let it consume. Flames kicked to life and licked down her skin, though the heat caused her no pain. On the contrary, she felt a kind of pleasure spread through her, a sensation that was wholly new. Sadie convulsed repeatedly as she lost track of all time and space. Her first orgasm hit every cell in her body at once. And the instant it was over, she had time for only one thought, *I am born*, before she collapsed.

Chapter 4

A choice

"Look at me. James. Look at me," Sadie called to him. He lifted his gaze to her. The scene in front of him was unreal. How had they ended up here? Just a week ago, they had been fishing and telling each other ghost stories. And now, they had witnessed the death of a half-crazed water nymph; met a siren, a succubus and a host of nature feeders, and they'd been dragged from their life so that one of them could become non-human. No, not become. She had always had it in her, he reminded himself.

Over the years together, he thought he'd been through it all with Sadie. He'd seen her break into tears and burst into laughter, but never in a million years would he have expected to see this. She was stunning. Her skin seemed to glow and her auburn curls clung wet all around her. The firelight cast shadows along her flesh. It was almost painful to look into her beautiful hazel eyes as she writhed in front of him, but he did look, and she looked back. Ignoring the men around her, he drank in the scene.

Images flashed in his mind from their shared lives. Sadie tackling him for the last cookie. Sadie's nipples in front of him, dripping wet. Sadie reading a poem in front of their eighth-grade class. Sadie's naked thigh muscles contracting and releasing. Sadie cuddled up next to him on a blanket under a starry sky. Sadie's head thrown back in ecstasy.

Jimmy had woken up that morning with his mind churning from her almost-kiss the previous night. He had been trying to make sense of the sudden shift in her behavior. And now he knew. It was her need to feed. It had all been about this, not about them.

She moaned.

But none of that changed the fact that her pleasure was intoxicating. A part of him wished desperately to be the person she was straddling, and another part was terrified at the thought. His mind snapped back to her touch from earlier. They had always been so physically close – now he wondered if that had happened because she'd had no sexual interest in him.

What did this new life mean for them now? It had been a shock to have her touch bring out such a reaction, and he was both excited and saddened by the thought. Everything would change.

She moaned again, louder this time. His erection strained against his jeans and he hugged his knees tighter. He found his body rocking slightly in time with hers.

When Gabriel again withdrew his touch from her and she began to plead with him, Jimmy's emotions hit a tipping point. He wanted to go to her; to kiss her; to hold her; to give her anything she asked for, but there was nothing he could give.

Why wasn't the succubus man doing more? Sadie looked like she was in pain.

Though it was hours later, when the man leaned forward and whispered something in her ear, that the scene became truly frightening. He had to do something. She panted and rolled and cried out.

Then she screamed.

Jimmy jumped up and yelled at Gabriel. He tried to reach his friend, but hands from behind stopped him from getting too close.

All of a sudden, she paused. The room stilled. Lying on her back, she looked at Gabriel. And a moment later her body arched dramatically. Her head fell back as her hips and chest rose. She stretched until only her fingertips and heels were touching the rug.

Sadie began to convulse as flames bloomed all over her naked form. Jimmy shouted as her body strained and muscles tightened, all while the expression on her face turned serene.

The room was momentarily lit up by her fiery form, and then she collapsed.

Jimmy had been focused all night on keeping his own emotions at bay in order to support his friend, but when he looked at her still form sprawled across the rug, he screamed. Again attempting to reach her, he felt people holding him back.

Her knees and chest were turned toward him, but her head was turned away. He stared at the line of her strained neck, trying to detect if she was breathing.

"Change seats," Gabriel ordered the room. Everyone else seemed to understand him fine, since they all got up and moved to a different pillow. Even June, the old siren, pulled herself up slowly and crossed the room. Jimmy, however, couldn't understand how such a strange order could be remotely relevant to helping Sadie.

"What?" he asked.

"It can take a long time to reorient after a Becoming. I've developed some techniques to help speed up the process. Trust me," Gabriel told him before moving himself to a new location. Jimmy grudgingly complied, not taking his eyes off the naked woman in the center of the circle.

The first sign of life in her was the smallest twitch of a finger, then a contracting of her abs. After what felt like a lifetime, she drew in a staggering breath.

Sadie sat up, slowly, and looked around the room then down at her own body. She paused for a long time, just blinking down at herself. She got to her feet. Her stance was strong and steady.

Gabriel spoke. "Do you remember where you are?" She stared at him for a minute as if she didn't understand the words, then nodded.

"In the woods. There were men of fire. I... collapsed." Her voice sounded uncertain, but clear. "The man in leather," she continued. "A succubus, he brought me here."

"Is that man still in the room?" Gabriel asked. Jimmy's head snapped to look at him, then back to Sadie when she answered, "Not sure".

"He is. Find him," Gabriel said.

Sadie turned slowly, looking at each person. She went around the circle twice, before pointing at Jimmy.

"That's wrong, but a good choice from your perspective," Gabriel said. "You were close. Try again."

What the hell was going on? Why couldn't she see them?

After a minute, Sadie pointed to Gabriel. He smiled.

"Good. Now, there was a fire nymph named Leon who you had sex with. Find him."

Again, strangely, after some thought, Sadie pointed to Jimmy. When Gabriel shook his head no, she immediately chose Leon. Jimmy felt his eyes tear up. She didn't know him.

"Now find your human friend," Gabriel said.

Sadie pointed without hesitation to the old woman.

"That was an unfair question, given your circumstances," Gabriel said. "We can work on this later." As if on cue, everyone except Jimmy rose to their feet. "You'll get hungry in the night. Pick someone to share your bed." Gabriel gestured at the three fire nymphs and Annabella. Sadie pointed at Leon.

"Good, the three of us will stay in here," Gabriel said.

And just like that, the night was over.

"Got tents outside," June said to Jimmy. "You can share mine."

"Or mine," Annabella said, following it up with a smile.

Jimmy mumbled that he wanted to head home. He shook off their protests that there were no trains, and went to the door. He looked back at Sadie, wanting to say some kind of goodbye, but she was turned away from him. Lacing on his boots, he nodded to June, and walked out into the dark night. Everything had changed.

THE NEXT WEEK passed almost in a blur for Sadie. It seemed she was hungry all the time. During the days leading up to her change, she had been hungry for something she had never experienced. Now that she knew exactly what her body wanted, she satisfied the craving the moment it appeared. And it appeared often. She understood now what all these people were doing here, for what Annabella had crossed an ocean, and she was grateful for their presence.

After the first few days, she no longer needed to constantly feed and sleep, and began to take long walks in the woods and help out in the kitchen. The cabin had no phone for her to call home, but Jimmy had dropped by while she was sleeping. He had delivered her a bag from home. It contained clothes, her favorite book, and a note from her parents wishing her well. The note was short, stating simply that they loved her and looked forward to welcoming her back home. There was no note from Jimmy.

Ten days passed before she dropped down to feeding only once a day. Her turbulent emotions had calmed considerably and she felt mostly like her old self again. It was during this time, while sitting in the garden next to Gabriel watching the other guests go about their business, that she finally asked, "What does it all mean?"

Gabriel rolled to face her.

She continued. "Everyone looks so different. I know you told me to give it time, but it's been over a week and I have no idea what I'm looking at."

Their hosts, Meesk and Deena, were sitting on a blanket in the grass, knitting opposite ends of a sweater. Gabriel nodded toward them.

"Tell me what you see," he said. She looked at the couple. There were strands of different colored light passing between Sadie and those around her. The light had been there since she'd woken up from her Becoming. It wasn't quite with her eyes that she saw the light, but rather with another new sense that felt like a filter over the visual world. Between Meesk and Deena, the exchange was especially strong. There was a streak of black entwined with red, and a solid pulse of green and blue. It flowed between them like an ethereal dance, ebbing and pulsing in tiny waves.

And when she looked at the people themselves, they seemed covered in... stories, only written in a language she couldn't read, and told through a slideshow of images. All of the images were sexual in some way, mostly involving the two of them. Though Meesk had images involving a young woman, which seemed almost faded in quality. As with the light, Sadie perceived these flashes of their sexual selves with something other than vision, as if the images were planted directly in her brain, like memories, whenever she focused on a specific person.

The information was overwhelming, however, and it was hard for Sadie to notice anything else about them. Their hair color, facial expressions, all faded in importance. It had taken her a full day to begin to recognize who was whom, and once she had, her picture of who they were was entirely different. But she couldn't summarize it.

"I don't know," she responded in the end. "Honestly, I don't know what to make of it."

"You see some colors?" he asked.

"Yeah."

"Are any of them unique to that couple?"

She looked at the fire dancers practicing in the distance and at Annabella reading a book in the tire swing. Everyone present seemed to be exchanging some light with each other, including herself. The dancers were mostly green light with a touch of blue. Annabella also shared green light with Gabriel and red with Sadie. Or at least those were the colors traveling from Annabella to them – Gabriel sent out very little light in general, a small amount of green toward Annabella and toward June before she had left. From both Sadie and Gabriel, red light flowed in varying degrees toward everyone present.

"The couple shares black light in both directions. None of the rest of us have black," she concluded.

"What does it mean?" Gabriel asked her. When he put it that way, it seemed a little more obvious.

"Love? Companionship?" She guessed, and it felt right.

Gabriel reached into his bag and pulled out a box. Sadie gasped, recognizing it as the box they had been left by the dead water nymph. Then she realized that made no sense. This was a different box, but it looked nearly identical.

"You've seen a thing like this before?" Gabriel asked.

Sadie shook her head, trying to recover. "No, no it's just beautiful."

"They're specially made for succubi. I'll be right back," he said and left the box next to her. Gabriel walked toward Annabella and she lit up at his approach. Spreading her legs with his hands, he pulled her to him. Red light pulsed even stronger between them while he kissed her. The tire swing swayed back and forth as she rocked into him. It took a good ten minutes before he returned.

Upon rejoining Sadie, he sat down with the box in his lap, and pressed his two hands into the space in the lid. It popped open and her eyes widened.

Sadie peered into the mysterious object. All it contained was a rather thick scroll.

"People would be uncomfortable if they knew we could see the nature of their relationships. What you have just begun to discover is an ancient secret, kept hidden among our people. It is impossible to force any individual succubus to keep quiet, and they sometimes tell those closest to them, but our people have managed to keep the information out of the biology textbooks. I believe the secret has kept over the years because we all recognize the danger in it getting out. We know who's in love and who has a friendly political alliance, who lusts after who and who's secretly fucking. No one wants such information to be so public. Or, they want to know it so badly that they would stop at nothing to get at the information. You see?"

Sadie nodded in understanding.

He took her hand. "Will you help, Sadie Hall, to keep our powers secret, as the long line of succubi before you have?"

Sadie was surprised at how moved she was at the question. It made her feel a part of something special. She would gladly keep this ancient secret. She nodded and he handed her the scroll. "Then here is everything we've collected about ourselves over the years. It should help you make better sense of what you see. When you're done, put it back in the box and replace the lid. It'll seal on its own. I can reopen it anytime you're ready."

Sadie ran her finger over the handprints. "Who makes them?"

"Made them. It was a couple, the wife a succubus and husband a stone nymph. No one has since been able to replicate it. I don't even know how many there are, but we use them to store all the secrets we collect."

She looked at it a moment longer in fascination, then went to open the scroll. Gabriel stopped her.

"First, make your own guesses," he said. "What does green mean?"

Sadie looked again at the fire dancers, the green light seemed to spark when they smiled at each other and glow strong when they were more in sync. "Friendship?"

Gabriel nodded.

"And the blue?" On this one, Sadie was less sure. She shook her head.

"Blue is family," he told her. "And red?"

This one was too obvious. "Desire," she said confidently.

He smiled, and kissed her cheek. She and Gabriel were no longer able to feed off each other now that they were both succubi, though they still triggered pleasure through their touch. Sadie had learned she couldn't feed off any other human feeders, though she could feed off nature feeders just like she could feed from humans, and in fact, fire nymphs tended to be a very fulfilling source.

She had noticed the difference in her strength after feeding off one of the fire dancers versus when she fed off Annabella, who had hinted she was some other kind of nature feeder.

"Why didn't you let me feed from Jimmy? How does it work with a human?" Sadie asked.

"It works the same. And since there are so many more humans than nymphs in the world, most of the time you'll feed off humans."

"Then why did you stop me? And why did he collapse when I touched him at the festival?"

Gabriel did up the buttons on his vest that Annabella had undone.

"I stopped you because I can also see the nature of people's relationships." He cracked his jaw. "And he collapsed because you were about to turn, meaning your powers would be extra sensitive to your emotions."

She nodded, though she didn't understand.

"Will I ever be able to see people as I used to see them?"

"Eventually, but it will take work. You'll have to relearn who the people in your life are through this new lens. You're getting so much more information now. It's not that you can't see people's physical selves, it will just take time to learn how to focus on that part of them, but it can be done if you want. Here, I'll show you." He pulled a deck of cards out of his back pocket. "I want you to tell me how many hearts there are."

He spread out ten cards in his hand and flashed them briefly at her before putting them away.

"Three," she said.

Gabriel nodded before asking, "And how many fives were there?"

She tried to remember. He had just shown it to her. "None?" she guessed. He showed her the hand. Two fives.

"It will be like re-meeting everyone in your life. But once you identify them, there will be no need to go back to seeing only their physical selves. You might just think of someone as the hand with three hearts for a while. Eventually you'll see the hearts and the fives. And you might even decide you don't care about fives at all, and only ever see hearts."

Sadie nodded. She was willing to believe that. It was already becoming more natural, day by day. Though she was anxious for a time when she felt like herself again.

Now that they were finally starting to talk about the details, she found she was hungry for more.

"The colors... They shift moment-to-moment and day-to-day. And even within a color, there are differences. Leon and I seem to share a rather deep blood red. But from me toward Annabella the red is so light it's almost pink, though from her to me it's the same deep blood red." Sadie thought she understood what all this meant, but wanted confirmation.

"Yes. There is a mismatch in attraction between you and Annabella, but not between you and Leon."

Sadie replied with, "And there's a mismatch in friendship between you and Annabella. I thought you'd known each other a long time. Do you share green or black with anyone out there, Gabriel?"

He didn't respond, merely smiled and directed her to the scroll, but Sadie had a particular burning question about her future that she'd been waiting to ask. This was clearly the right moment, but she felt her heart pound obnoxiously as she began to speak. "Jimmy and I... that is, say our relationship develops – I mean I don't know how he feels, but I've been having all these feelings recently... about him. And I just don't know how it works. Can succubi... can we date someone?"

Gabriel smiled sympathetically.

"The coexistence of the three species, humans, human feeders, and nature feeders, are held in a shaky balance. The relationship between nature feeders and the piece of the world they bond with is natural and mutually helpful. Between human feeders and humans it can be a bit more... complicated. Especially for our kind."

He put a gloved hand on her shoulder. "Succubi need many people to feed from, Sadie, and having serious attachments with one or even a few particular people is not a good idea. It happens. I've seen it, but it's best to keep ongoing booty calls, let's say, over taking on love relationships. It can also be dangerous for the people if it becomes an addiction. If you care about that human, I would suggest just leaving him alone."

Sadie felt a cold sweat break out on the back of her neck. She swallowed down her emotions at the news.

"And what do you see?" She forced out the words. "When you look at us?" She knew he would understand she meant Jimmy and her.

"I see two people that would be better off going their separate ways," he said. Sadie was glad Gabriel didn't look back as he walked away, because in that moment, she had no willpower to hide the emotion in her expression. Though it wasn't until hours later, when she began to read the part of the scroll about human-succubi relationships gone bad, that tears finally rolled down her face.

THE ONLY OTHER significant moment during her recovery time at the cabin happened a few days later. Jimmy hadn't returned since the day he had dropped by while she was napping. She missed her friend. They probably hadn't been apart this long since they were babies.

On this particular day, Sadie was out for a walk alone. She was bent over gathering some flowers when she heard a voice behind her.

"Will wildflowers never be safe around you?" She was hoping it was Jimmy's voice, but the sound too was filled with stories about the person producing it. She turned and looked at the shape in front of her and her eyes widened.

It was someone she knew, it must be. A thick stream of red and green light flowed between them. The red flowing from them was rich and deep and seemed to pulse, the red from her was light and smooth. The green was steady and laced with streaks of black. This person was clearly a friend, and a friend with an attraction to her that far surpassed that of Leon or Annabella. And furthermore, she largely felt the same way.

She had only one guess of who it could be, but was shocked by the knowledge. This was how Jimmy felt about her? How had she never known?

She said his name, and her thoughts registered the fact that he smiled. The smile was accompanied by a pulse of the green light of friendship and the black of love, and it gave the expression new depth. For a moment she felt she could see her old Jimmy in there. She tried to focus on only his physical features, but her senses were bombarded by a thousand lustful images, *about her*.

Sadie approached him cautiously. For a second, the impulse to push him against a tree and kiss him surged up in her. She imagined holding his face in hers and causing in him the same reaction she had spent days causing in all these strangers.

She stopped dead in her tracks. The words from the scroll pulsed in her vision.

...never the same... obsessed till the end...

She didn't want Jimmy to want her because of her power. In fact, the last thing in the world she wanted was for him to crave being around her because of what she was.

"Sadie?" he asked, right in front of her now. "Are you okay?"

"Yeah." She couldn't even hug him since she was wearing short sleeves and had left her gloves at home. In the end she just stood there, awkwardly, and said, "Thank you."

"For what?"

"Everything," she said before pulling her two wildflowers apart. She stuck one behind her ear and carefully handed him the other one. "And no, wildflowers might never be safe around me." She smiled sadly as he took the flower without moving any closer. He stuck it behind his own ear. She tried to focus on his expression, but there was too much to look at. She had no idea what she was getting from him, and in the end, decided just to resume walking. He fell in beside her.

"What now?" he asked.

"Well, I've gotta go home sometime." She kicked at the ground in front of her. "Might as well be today."

"Good, because I've been doing your chores on top of my own and I don't think I can take any more of your mom's gratitude cookies."

And just like that, things were almost back to normal. They stayed for dinner, packed up the clothes she'd managed to sprawl in every corner, and got ready to catch the last train home.

In the final few minutes before their departure, Sadie stood nervously near Gabriel, afraid to be leaving his side. "How do I do this? What if I get hungry and there's no one around?" she whispered, before biting her nails.

"There are lots of people out there who want to sleep with a succubus. Find one or two or five steady partners, fuck the milkman now and again, and you'll be fine. And if you're struggling, you can always head into the city. But don't worry, we'll stick around a bit longer. In fact, we'll come visit you tomorrow."

Before her Becoming, Gabriel had seemed so alluring and attractive, but now he seemed slightly sad to her. He had a strange aura about him that made him appear disconnected from the world around. Sadie kissed him on the cheek, causing the usual spark of excitement to pass between them, then turned her back on her perplexing guide and went out to face the world.

❧

SADIE WALKED UP to the porch of her parents' house, of *her* house, and had to fight back the instinct to knock before entering. She felt like an intruder as she pushed open the door. The house was quiet. She went to the kitchen and set her bag down on the table. It was covered with books. Brows raised, she picked one up.

Human Feeders, A Complete Guide. She looked up succubi. They were tagged on only one page. Flipping to it she found one brief paragraph.

The succubus requires a steady diet of sexual interactions. The creature must make skin contact in order to feed, and such contact always causes the recipient to pass through the four stages of orgasm. If the succubus remains in contact through the refractory phrase, the process simply starts over. This makes them highly sought-after and also highly dangerous. Interacting with a succubus often leaves the human prey depleted of energy. If the creature chose to continue feeding, they could leave the human for dead. It is not known as to whether succubi can feed from each other or from other feeders.

Below each description was a scale in which they rated to what degree the feeder was deadly. They gave succubi four out of five, explaining that: *Because the succubus has total control over their feeding, able to create the emotional reaction they need with a simple touch, they are one of the few human feeders that can easily kill. The only reason we choose not to give them five out of five stars is due to their often intimate emotional connection to their prey, which keeps them from overfeeding off any one person.*

Sadie snapped the book shut. She didn't think it was particularly well-informed, but then again, succubi had worked hard to ensure that would be the case. Another title caught her eye. *Mixed Families, How to Parent.* She flipped through it to find several bookmarked pages.

Just as she was reaching for *Help! My teenager is a harpy!* she heard the front door open and a minute later her parents were in the room. They froze at the sight of her. Sadie was in no doubt as to who these people were, given the black light of love and the blue light of family pouring from them to her and to each other. She also learned her parents had a healthy sex life, and was grateful the images were too muddled for her to pick out anything specific.

Her mom dropped her bag and covered her cheeks with her hands. "Oh sweetie, you're home!" she cried, moving to go in for a hug.

"No Lillia, remember," her father whispered, sticking his cane in her mother's path. "Welcome home, sugarbug," he said to her.

"How are you feeling?" her mom asked.

"Good, Ma. I'm… mostly back to my old self. How's the farm? Jimmy been helping out?" Her voice sounded unsteady.

"Oh yes. Yes, all the time, I feel I've barely lifted a finger the past few weeks," her mom said. "Such a sweet boy. And he told us all about the gentleman who's been assisting you. Such a good man. We should have him over for dinner to thank him properly." Sadie laughed inside at the thought of Gabriel at her parents table, but said only, "That's a good idea." Her parents seemed to be making an effort, and she wanted to make this as easy for them as possible.

"Will him and his friends stay nearby?" her mom asked.

"For a while," Sadie said. "I need some more time to get situated."

"Oh yes, come dear. See what your father's working on," her mom said and led her into the back garden, where a large muddy square had been dug into the yard. She looked at her dad, her face a question.

"For you. A bedroom and a bathroom. The Bakers are helping," he said, referring to Jimmy's family.

Her mom said, "You'll have some privacy when guests stay over." She paused to chew her lip before adding, "That is… if you want to stay."

Sadie looked into her mother's face just in time to see her eyes tear slightly. Sadie hadn't even contemplated leaving. She thought life would go back to normal eventually. How exactly the details would work had been too much to consider. Now, looking at the start of the house her family had begun to build for her, and all the effort they had been putting in to ensure her safety and comfort, she began to cry. Sadie was surprised at the strength of her own emotion as mother and daughter looked at each other, unable to hug, and mourned the loss of her old life together.

"Thank you," Sadie eventually said.

~

SHE CAME DOWN to breakfast the next morning having slept nearly twelve hours. In that time, a new question had come to her, and she was surprised she hadn't wondered at it before. Gabriel's scroll had spoken in length about succubi families, but her family was human.

Pushing away her empty plate she asked, "How? If I was born to humans. How did this happen?"

Her parents exchanged a look and a nod.

"Well now," her mom said. "When we got pregnant with you, your grandma, rest her soul, came over one night. She let me know that we had feeder blood in us, and that there was always a chance. But we never saw a reason to scare you over nothing. When you showed no signs of it, we thought there was no need to mention it. She wouldn't tell us what kind of feeder, only that it was human feeder and not nature."

Her mom began to stack their plates.

"I did a little research back then and learned that nymphs usually have nymph parents, while human feeders are regularly born into human families." She began to bustle around the kitchen as she spoke. "But I also learned that they often show feeder signs in childhood, so most parents know by then. I didn't look up succubi specifically though, so I didn't know that they don't develop until after puberty. Still, I kept watching for signs, all these years. When you began behaving differently, I did a little more research, and then I knew there was a chance."

The dishes splashed as her mom dropped them into the soapy sink.

"I should have told you then. I'm not really sure why I didn't. I'm sorry, sugarbug," her mom said without turning around.

Sadie didn't know why she wasn't angry at this news – perhaps because it had all worked out okay, perhaps because she didn't have the strength to be mad at the people whose support she needed most just then. Suddenly Sadie remembered her mother's final words to her before she'd wandered away at the festival. *I'll be right here, if you need me,* she'd told her.

"It's alright, Ma. It all worked out," Sadie said.

Her mother sniffed, pausing for a minute, before resuming scrubbing the dishes. Her dad turned on the radio. As she got up to wipe down the table and her father went to tie up the trash, Sadie felt the rhythm of her old life fill the air. The familiar voice of a newscaster broke the silence.

Another incident occurred early this morning in the aftermath of the feeders' announcement that they will be forming their own government, refusing to work alongside their human counterparts any longer. The animosity between humans and feeders has been increasing in leaps and bounds since two weeks ago, when the Human Council brought forward a proposal to reduce the size of the protected lands to ten percent of its current size, making way for a new industrial age. The HC insists this will not impact nature feeders, as there is plenty of land for all, but the nymphs, seeing this as a sign of human aggression, have just today joined with the human feeders to form their own government for the first time separate from humans. This split has been marked by an increase in—

Her father clicked it off. Sadie was shocked. How could no one have told her? She knew a little of the recent tensions, but something like this should be big news. Pushing her parents for more, they grudgingly filled her in, but they were so vague she felt as if they were trying to soften the information.

Sadie was distracted from further inquiry when the sound of Jimmy clearing his throat pulled her gaze to the kitchen entrance.

"Lillia. Don." He nodded to them before turning to her. "I thought you might want to go shopping, get some new clothes."

Her pulse increased at Jimmy's sudden appearance. The new sight of him was still overwhelming. He was leaning casually against the doorway with his hands in his pockets, a familiar stance, but the surrounding tumult of emotions and images struck her like a hurricane.

"Oh," Sadie said. "Yeah. Good idea, Jimmy."

"Maybe we should all go together today?" her mom chimed in.

She didn't really want her mom tagging along and shook off the idea, but when she continued to push, Sadie began to suspect something. She crossed her arms and narrowed her eyes.

"What's going on?" Sadie asked.

Her mother simply mumbled something about safety before letting it go.

"We'll be fine, Ma," Jimmy said. He always called her mother Ma when he wanted to show extra respect, which Sadie knew was whenever they were looking to spend a day just the two of them, perhaps goofing off by the river. It seemed Jimmy was anxious to get away too.

Sadie followed close behind her friend as he led the way to the side of the house. They smiled shyly at each other as they grabbed their bikes. Why did this feel so strange? They had done fine the day before.

Jump starting the conversation, Sadie continued her previous inquiry, now directed at a better target. "Tell me the truth, Jimmy. What's been going on?" They were straddling their bikes, still next to the house. Jimmy glanced at one of the open windows and nodded for them to head out.

On the freedom of the open road, he spoke in a straightforward tone. "Things have been tense, Sadie. On the news, in town. Rumors spread, of course, about what happened at the festival that day. Everyone needs to gossip. And then the very next day this terrible announcement came out. I thought it would pass. You know how politicians like to fight. But it seems like things have just gotten worse and worse since then. I was at the market the other day and I overheard the Wilson brothers arguing. They completely had it out, right there in front of everyone. Marty had to kick them out."

"What was it about?" Sadie asked in astonishment. The brothers shared a farm nearby and had always been so polite. When Jimmy hesitated, she found herself wondering if she really wanted to hear the answer.

"It was about whether or not feeders should be allowed to live here," he said.

Sadie almost lost her balance. "What? That's crazy. And the dryad families?" she asked.

"No one seems bothered by them. They aren't really afraid of wood nymphs. They're afraid of human feeders."

"But the nymphs are siding with the human feeders right? It was a split between humans and feeders?"

"Yeah, but since when are people rational?" he said. She must have looked worried when he glanced at her because he added, "I think it's mostly just a few loud voices in town stirring up trouble. Once the mania quiets down, I bet more people will come to their senses."

Sadie was only mildly convinced.

They pulled up outside a small clothing store, the only one in town for people their age, and ditched their bikes. Sadie caught sight of a person approaching them and whispered a request to Jimmy for their name.

"Meghan uh... Delany," he whispered. Sadie recognized it as someone she vaguely knew from large functions. She was on edge from their conversation though and frowned at the woman, half-expecting her to say something nasty. Instead, Meghan nodded at the two of them. Sadie relaxed a bit. The store owner also bobbed her head politely and inquired about the health of their parents, and by the time they had begun to browse the wares, it felt almost like a normal day.

They found gloves in a tiny bin in the back since it wasn't really the season for them. It was going to be a challenge to find things which covered a good deal of skin when winter was long since over, but she would need gloves at a minimum.

As they bent over the small selection, they were careful to not let their bare arms touch. It was such an odd thing, avoiding contact with Jimmy. She'd never been so aware of their bodies. They'd always been casual in their touching, but now she could feel the empty space between them as if it was an extension of herself, measured in desire and stretching across an infinite chasm. When they were especially close, she watched lines of deep red lust flare up between them. She could especially feel the emotion pulsing from him to her. On the outside, however, their interactions seemed benign. He gave no outward sign of the exchange. Though of course, he couldn't see it himself.

Jimmy held up some white-laced gloves. They reminded her of something her grandmother used to wear. "Too many holes," she said, running the ends of them through her fingers an inch from Jimmy's hand. Their eyes met. His outward demeanor contrasted sharply with the flow of information she was getting. He shrugged casually and dropped them back into the bin.

"How about these?" he asked, his voice and hands completely steady.

"Um, yeah, those could work," she said, sounding out of breath.

"I was joking. These are, like, for snow. Are you feeling okay? You look flushed?"

"Yeah, it's warm. And... I just haven't fed yet today," she said.

Now Jimmy seemed to register some nervousness. He avoided her gaze as he said, "Oh. I had been wondering about that."

It was going to take some time for her to figure out how to navigate conversations again with Jimmy. His flip from cool and collected to timid and flustered at the mention of sexual matters was confusing from her perspective. They were always half-talking about sex now as far as she could see.

She tried to see it from his perspective. A minute ago, everything was under the surface. They were just talking about gloves. Was this how people always interacted? With secret worlds writhing around inside them?

"You have a plan?" he asked, gaze roaming over the bin.

It took Sadie a minute to remember what they'd been discussing. Oh, she hadn't fed yet.

"Not really," she said. "Gabriel said they'd come visit. He seems to act like I'll be fine without him though. That it's easy to find people to feed from."

Jimmy cleared his throat. "You think that's what you'll do? Find people around town?"

"Could be. I haven't decided," she said. He looked up, then, and studied her face. They stared at each other in silence for several breaths. Perhaps Jimmy, like herself, was hoping the other one would speak next. They had to talk about it sometime.

"I heard she's back," someone said from the next aisle over. Jimmy's eyes widened at the sound of the voice, but Sadie didn't recognize it.

"Scary thought. I mean, I just can't imagine how she could go thinking she'd be welcome, after what happened." The voices appeared to be coming closer. Jimmy put a hand on Sadie's lower back and nodded to the dressing rooms. They took the closest one, pulling the curtain tight so they wouldn't be seen.

"You talking about the Halls' daughter?" chimed in a third voice. "You two were there, right?"

"Oh, we were there." The voice sounded suddenly animated.

"Is it true?" someone asked.

"Depends. What did you hear?" continued the first voice.

"I heard she just started staggering around, swearing and drooling, and then she saw that Baker kid and attacked him out of the blue." Sadie's eyes darted to Jimmy. They were leaning against the same mirror, less than a foot apart. Is that what it looked like? Her face must have seemed distraught because Jimmy began to reach to touch her shoulder before he caught himself.

"Then you heard about right," said the voice.

"Wow. Never thought I'd see something like that here."

"You don't think she plans on staying?"

"Might do. She's real close to that Baker boy. And she's the only child her parents got." This was the first voice again. As Sadie listened more closely, she felt she understood a piece of the information she was now receiving. So far, she had only been overwhelmed by what she heard when people spoke and what she saw when she looked at them. But in this voice, she thought she heard something about Jimmy. This person had something to do with her friend, something very specific. Was it... desire?

The voices slowly moved away, but not before they had to listen to the second person respond, "Yeah but... should she? I mean, it would be one thing if she were a hag or a muse, but a succubus? I mean, Congressman Matthews made some good points last week. They're not all the same, these feeders. Should creatures like succubi be allowed to just roam around unattended?"

The voices moved away.

Sadie put a hand on her hip.

"It wasn't like that. Was it like that?" she asked Jimmy.

"No." Again, Jimmy almost reached to touch her arm. Again catching himself, he put his hand on her waist instead, just below where her fist was perched.

"You were a little unsteady on your feet, but there was no drool," he said. "I promise." He pulled himself a few inches closer.

"And when I touched you, I... didn't know what was going to happen," Sadie said. "I didn't mean to..."

"I know," he said.

"I wasn't attacking."

"It didn't feel like you were." He gaze flickered from her lips to her eyes. They were very close now.

She put her hand on his chest and was unsurprised to feel his heart pounding as fast as her own. She looked at their reflections in the mirror, while he kept watching her directly. Sadie was slowly beginning to sort out the images surrounding him. She saw herself everywhere; all over him, and she'd be willing to bet that when Gabriel looked at her, he saw Jimmy.

It made sense, after all. He meant the world to her. Sadie touched her thumb to the glass and traced it along the image of Jimmy's jaw. But she didn't want to feed from him. She didn't want him to become addicted to her like those people in the scroll. She didn't want him to only want her in one way. She wished desperately that she could go back in time and kiss him just once, without her succubus powers.

It was clear from his taut, still form, that was exactly what he expected her to do. He seemed to be waiting for her to make a move, and when she tried to focus on what she saw coming from him, it was evident he was ready for her. She needed to tell him. Now.

"Jimmy," she said, turning back to face him directly. "I don't think you should be one of the people I feed from. That's, uh, not what I want." It was almost physically painful to say it, and she wanted to explain. She wanted to tell him that she wanted him and that she was making this choice to keep him safe, but saying that out loud would break her resolve and make it so much harder for both of them to resist. In fact, she was certain that if she did tell him that she desired him too, she wouldn't be able to stop herself from taking what she wanted from him. She needed to be firm now if she wanted to hurt them both as little as possible.

He pulled his hand off her waist and stepped back. His retreat caused her hand to drop from his chest and trail down his torso. She missed his nearness immediately and it was all she could do not to move in again.

"Oh. I had thought—" he said. "That's fine. I thought maybe you wanted that. Since it would be convenient for you." He spoke faster than usual.

It was strange watching him lie to her. Though then again, she was doing the same thing.

She chewed her lip. "I don't think it'd be right for us," she said. "Besides, it might hurt our friendship, and—" Sadie paused to keep her voice from breaking, "and I love you too much for that."

"Yeah, you're right," he said. "Good call."

As he moved the curtain aside, Sadie saw for the first time an image flash out of him that was clear as day. She knew exactly what it was she was seeing. It was her, naked on top of Leon. Only she didn't look quite like herself. She seemed to glow. It was the sound of her speaking, though it sounded erotic in an otherworldly kind of way. Her voice seemed to echo around the image. It was saying, *James*.

Chapter 5

A freak

The ride home was awkward. Not because of silence between them, but because Jimmy talked rapidly the entire time about any topic he could find that had nothing to do with sex or politics. Sadie had never heard him ramble like this, and it made her nervous. She was glad when they parted ways.

As she was making the short ride along the road from Jimmy's place to her own, she found Gabriel and Annabella waiting for her. They seemed to be having a heated argument and didn't notice her until she was almost on them.

"Hi," Sadie said, before she jumped down off her bike and reached for Annabella. She walked the woman backwards until they were hidden by some trees and kissed her firmly. A minute later Gabriel pulled up next to Sadie and said, "Easy there, it's been an exciting couple of weeks, and she has only so much to give."

Sadie didn't want to take it easy. She surged through the woman and Annabella gasped. Sadie wanted more. Gabriel pushed his knee between the two of them, forcing Sadie to break the kiss. She slid her bare hands up under Annabella's shirt as Gabriel swept Sadie's hair behind her ear. Leaning in to whisper so only she could hear, he told her, "He's not in there." When she didn't relent, he grabbed her by the waist and hauled her backward. Annabella collapsed back against the tree, panting as she rested her elbows on her knees.

"Whew! That was something." She smiled at Sadie. "I like you like this, farm girl."

Suddenly Sadie was angry. "I'm not a farm girl! The whole town wants me to leave. I'm a freak. I'll never have a normal relationship. And I hate it! I hate this. I should have stayed human."

She tried to pick up her bike, but tripped and fell forward onto one of her pedals.

"Ow. Shit!" She pushed herself up. A little blood oozed from her shin. Limping to a nearby tree, she plopped down in its roots.

Gabriel pulled a handkerchief out of his pocket and crouched in front of her.

"It's not easy, feeling like you don't belong," he said as he mopped up the blood. "But you'll have plenty of so-called normal relationships. Normal is relative. You're exactly how you're supposed to be."

She burst into tears. He waited for her to cry it out before sitting down next to her and adding, "And you don't have to stay here." As he said this, a thin line of blue passed from him to her. The second she noticed it, she watched herself send the same color back.

"There are places for us out there, Sadie. When I leave here, you could come with me."

"Where would we go?" she asked.

"To Massachusetts. I have a place there. And I could introduce you to some people. If you wanted, it could be your home."

Sadie felt empty at the thought of going so far from her family.

"I'll think about it," she said, collecting herself to stand up. "Thanks, Gabriel."

She returned home with a bruised and bloodied leg, a newly purchased black turtleneck, a rather fluffy pair of gloves, and a mess of confused thoughts. She must have looked wretched because her mother inhaled sharply at the sight of her.

"Oh dear, what happened. Who did this?"

"No one Ma, I just fell off my bike." She tried to put on a smile, but it felt forced. Her mother clearly wasn't buying it. Sadie tried to distract her by asking, "Chickens been fed? It's time I started helping out again." Then before her mother could reply, she dropped her bag and went out the back door.

Sadie worked hard the rest of the day, slept a few hours, and got up early to keep working hard. She threw herself into helping her father build the adjoining house. Jimmy didn't come by.

In the afternoon, she took the train out to the cabin to feed off Leon, and got home just in time for dinner. The next couple days looked more or less the same. It was the fourth morning since they'd gone into town, while Sadie and her parents were sitting around the breakfast table, that Jimmy finally made an appearance.

"Morning Lillia. Don."

Sadie looked at him in surprise, the lines of desire he had shown so strongly a few days before had lessened a bit. The change was slight, but enough to fill her with regret. He was moving on. Would he get over her completely one day? Sadie blinked away the beginnings of tears, annoyed at her confusing emotions.

"Sorry I haven't come by," he directed at her. "It's been a busy few days." He handed a handful of mail to her mother. "Dave asked me to bring this over."

Dave, their mailman? Why wouldn't he deliver it himself?

Everyone was quiet for a moment as they exchanged looks. She understood. Dave didn't want to approach the house.

"No matter. Thank you, dear," her mother said.

Sadie felt miserable.

And then, for no reason at all, she remembered the box. How could she have forgotten? She knew how to open it.

"Jimmy," Sadie stood up, "Didn't you need my help with that thing?" she asked. Jimmy blinked, but recovered quickly.

"Yeah, that's what I came here for," he said, playing along in a familiar way.

As they left, Sadie was acutely aware of the expression of her mother. She was certain to think Jimmy and she were together now that she was a succubus. The added pressure made Sadie even more uncomfortable with their situation.

The topic of the box was a welcome distraction.

"I know how to open it," she whispered the second they were out of earshot.

"What?" he asked.

He listened in fascination as they made the walk to his place. Then, for the first time in what felt like ages, Sadie entered Jimmy's bedroom. They dropped into silence as Sadie climbed onto the bed. He retrieved the backpack and placed the box between them, looking up at her expectantly.

"I—well, I don't know for sure if I can open it right now, but here goes nothing," she said.

Spreading her fingers as wide as possible, she placed both hands in the groove. Nothing happened. The reason seemed fairly obvious.

"Gabriel, he fed right beforehand. It's probably just been too long," she said.

The mood in the room changed.

"I'll have to take it with me." She kept her gaze on the box as she spoke. "The next time I go to visit Gabriel, I can open it there."

Jimmy was still.

"I'll do it tomorrow," she said to fill the silence.

"But not in front of him, right?" he asked. "You're not going to tell him about the box, are you?"

"No. Of course I won't tell anyone," Sadie said, as she put the heavy marble thing back in the bag. "I'll bring it back and share it with you tomorrow."

"Careful," he said, finally looking up at her. "We don't know those people that well. I wouldn't leave the bag unattended." Sadie didn't like the tone in his voice.

"Those people have shown me nothing but kindness, Jimmy."

He put his hands up, "I wasn't trying to—I only mean that we don't know what we might have here. It could be really dangerous, and maybe shouldn't end up in the wrong hands."

"Gabriel's not the wrong hands."

"Okay," he said, "but will you just promise to keep it secret? Please?"

"Yeah, I already said I would."

Sadie hated when they argued. It hadn't happened in years. And though both their feathers were already ruffled, she somehow couldn't stop herself from saying, "He's asked me to go with him."

Jimmy looked up, an expression of horror slowly covering his face.

"He thinks I could be more comfortable somewhere else," she said.

"More comfortable? Away from everyone you know? Everyone who's been with you your whole life? Gabriel thinks he can just walk in here and sweep you off to some new life as if nothing here matters? Who suddenly put him in charge?" His voice rose until he was almost yelling, and he spat out Gabriel's name like it was a curse.

Sadie knew he was just scared. He never yelled. And yet, she was too caught up in her own frustration to control her words.

"Things aren't exactly perfect here," she said. "And I might just need a new life. Gabriel's been a lifesaver. I don't know what I would have done without him." She pushed herself off the bed. "And I don't know what I'm going to do when he leaves. And honestly, Jimmy, I don't know what kind of life I can have here." She crossed the room. "So maybe you could be a bit more understanding of how hard this all is on me." She stormed out of the room before he could see the tears in her eyes.

Sadie immediately regretted her last words. Jimmy had been very understanding, completely supportive, and this was all at least as hard on him as it was on her. She had clearly been trying to push them apart. She just couldn't imagine staying here like this, unable to touch him, unable to talk about it, finding people from a town that hated her so she could feed.

But how could she leave?

She didn't feel like going back to her place, and her heart couldn't handle going down to the river when that had always been a place she shared with Jimmy. She wanted someplace new, somewhere she could think. Heading south, she followed a footpath through the woods to the edge of town.

As her feet carried her, the words of Gabriel's scroll ran on repeat through her mind.

Our people have never found it a struggle to feed. Succubi are often sought after as lovers. The challenge is getting rid of someone once they've latched on. For this reason, it is wise to set expectations early. Choose five to six steady partners and make sure they each know that they are not particularly special. If you desire a romantic partner, choose another human feeder, preferably a succubus. Deep, romantic attachments with humans are complicated by the often addictive tendencies of the weaker species.

Sadie didn't like the way the scroll referred to humans as weaker. There were, in fact, many things she'd read that she didn't like, but it was also her only source of knowledge about who she was. That, and the at-times closed book that was Gabriel.

Some of the information she'd read she'd yet to fully process in all the distraction, and the saddest piece struck at her now, as if she was hearing it for the first time.

After the Becoming, a succubus becomes barren, so we advise having children prior. To maintain the succubus bloodline, some families have chosen to pair succubi mates for the purpose of having children prior to their transition into succubus. For a complete list of families engaging in this practice and how to contact them, see Appendix A.

And there it was. How could she offer Jimmy anything but pain? A childless life of unrequited lust, built on lies about her own desires. And yet the idea of him with someone else made every cell in her body tighten. It was so unfair.

Sadie was pulled out of her lamenting by an awareness of a shift in her surroundings. She looked up in search of its source. Had the bird sounds become louder? Or perhaps the trees were denser. The air certainly smelled richer, heavy with the scent of earth and moss. She couldn't put her finger on it exactly, but the forest was suddenly present in a way that she couldn't hold separate from her mood. It calmed her.

Wanting suddenly to feel the earth beneath her feet, she bent down to remove her shoes. But before she could get them off a twig snapped to her right. Sadie jumped at the appearance of a person.

It was someone she knew.

They pulsed with the red light of desire mixed with a few pale strands of green. A friend then. A friend who was interested in her. What luck was this? But who could it possibly be? She didn't have any real friends apart from Jimmy.

"Hello?" Sadie directed uncertainly at the complicated figure in front of her.

"What are you doing out here?" the person said. Or at least those were the words. There were other things in the voice too. Most of them were lost on her, but she thought she detected it asking *Are you here looking for me?* There was longing in the question.

"I just needed to get out of town, you know," Sadie said, stepping closer. "It's nice out here."

Something caught her eye and she turned to see a half-built home. It was embedded around two large trees and the material was indistinguishable from the bark. Sadie stepped toward it to admire the beauty. From close up, she could see that the walls were grown directly out of the surrounding trees and were very much alive. There was little symmetry in the design, but it had a kind of organic beauty. She ran her hand along the arc of the half-finished doorway as the person stepped up to watch her caress the house.

It was clearly the home of a wood nymph, and as she caught the scent of banana chapstick, Sadie realized precisely who it was.

"Ina?" she asked.

"Sadie," Ina said. Ina, her childhood friend who had recently bonded to a patch of woods outside of town, had begun to grow herself a home. Ina also didn't dislike her as much as she'd thought. In fact, she was quite pleased at Sadie's presence as she invited her in.

Ina brushed off the clothes strewn over a bench at the base of one of the trees.

"Here, make yourself at home. I know it doesn't have a roof yet, but at least you can have some back support. Ina climbed onto the bench next to her, tucked her knees to her chest, and leaned back against the great oak tree, which happened to be big enough to make up an entire wall.

"What do you think?" she asked Sadie.

"It's beautiful, Ina. It almost pulled me in, I felt the shift as I got close," Sadie said.

"That's the nymph magic," Ina said in a quiet but animated voice. "It's why I wanted to live out of town, like my grandmother did. I haven't felt anything like this since she passed. All nymphs imbue the space around them with the emotion of their particular affinity, but when we live fully traditional lives, our homes themselves can become infused with almost an awareness of themselves. I've never been so content and I'm just getting started. Think of how it will be when it's all finished."

Sadie felt a sadness wash over her again. She envied Ina. If only her own transition had gone so smoothly.

"I heard about what happened," Ina said in a different, but hard to read tone. "How has it been for you?"

Sadie looked over at the streaks of sunlight penetrating the center of the structure, made visible by their interaction with the dense air, and began to cry. She didn't mean to. It was just so beautiful there, and she hadn't been asked that question yet.

Ina scooted forward to put a hand on Sadie's knee. Neither of them spoke while Sadie got the emotion out. Ina handed her a tissue and rubbed her back.

"I'm just scared," Sadie said. "Most people here don't like me, how am I supposed to feed?" Sadie looked up to see Ina gazing intently at her.

Ina shifted her weight so they were sitting up against each other. "Yeah," she said. "I know everyone's a bit afraid of you right now. But give them time. And... it's not the whole town that doesn't like you." Ina's lashes flickered in the sunlight as she looked over Sadie's face. This particular feature drew Sadie's attention to her physical form for an instant before the pulse of desire overwhelmed the sight of the woman. Ina leaned in first, and Sadie held her face as if she were a delicate thing as she kissed her.

She felt the tension and fear over finding people seep slowly out of her. Her thoughts turned to fascination at this experience. There was something different about it and she thought it had a lot to do with the fact this person had been a friend. Sadie hadn't touched anyone she cared about since turning. It was intoxicating. She wondered why there was no mention of this in the scroll. It seemed worth a footnote. And she barely knew Ina these days. It wasn't like she was a real friend. Her thoughts turned again to Jimmy and her whole body clenched with desire.

"What the hell?" someone said from the other side of the doorway.

Ina jumped up like she'd been bitten.

"Is this what you do now? Come find innocent girls alone out in the woods?"

"Cassie, uh, Sadie just went for a walk, and—" Ina began.

"It's okay, Ina, I've got it from here," Cassie said, turning on Sadie. "I know you think you can just chew people up and spit them out, take whatever you want, but I think you should find someplace else to do it." Sadie recognized this voice from the clothing store. She now knew it was Cassie and from the few images she could clearly decipher she knew Cassie had a long-held crush on Jimmy. Well, that explained some things.

Sadie got to her feet calmly, trying to communicate that she hadn't been doing anything wrong.

"Cassie, you can't tell me what to do. This is Ina's place. If she wants me here, I have every right to be here," Sadie said.

"Ina's judgement was compromised the second you touched her. I'm her best friend. It is my job to make sure she's safe. Now, I swear by my mother that if you come near here again, you are going to have much bigger problems than you can handle."

Cassie stepped between Ina and Sadie. Ina's gaze was on the ground and Sadie didn't know what else to do. "Fine," she said. Then, without even trying to catch Ina's eye, Sadie left slowly and with as much dignity as she could muster.

Her confidence in her future was even bleaker on the walk back than it had been on the way out. She couldn't even muster the rage to be mad at Ina. Probably because her hormones were still stuck on the taste of banana chapstick and sweet desire. Suddenly, Sadie understood all her classmates who'd gone through puberty years ago. She remembered thinking they had all gone crazy at the time. Now she was making up for lost time all at once and under extreme circumstances.

She'd resolved nothing by the time she walked into her own home. But when she saw her parents, she pulled out a big smile. "Sorry I'm late for lunch. Lost track of time."

Their plates were empty, though they hadn't yet left the table.

Sadie avoided her mom's worried gaze as she slunk passed her to grab a plate. Before she could take a seat at the table, however, she noticed a sound coming from the open back door.

"Is someone here?" she asked.

"Jimmy," her father said. "He's in the back, working on the foundation."

"He's working on my house? During lunch time?" Sadie asked, wrinkling her forehead.

"Couldn't persuade him away from it," her mother said. "He's done nothing else all day."

Sadie put her empty plate on the table and made her way out back.

Jimmy didn't turn around at the sound of her approaching. He was shirtless, putting all his muscle into mixing cement. Too focused on his task to notice her, she took the moment to really look at him. The black love lines seemed to ebb and flow less than red, and none of it had diminished in the past few days.

Sadie focused on the mess of scenes surrounding him, and practiced picking them out one at a time as the scroll had suggested. There was one that was particularly clear, though it was of something that had never happened. It was of him holding her face between his hands and kissing her. It was set among a million different backdrops, with the two of them wearing many different outfits. She imagined it was a history of every time he had imagined doing just that.

"Looks like a good foundation," she said.

Jimmy looked up. He was covered in grime and sweat, and as his physical form registered stronger in her attention, she thought he looked quite good like that.

He wiped some sweat from his brow. Clearly, he'd thrown himself full force into this distracting task and she felt guilty for not coming home sooner after their fight.

Dropping his gaze back to his work, he said, "Yeah. I think it is. A strong foundation."

She looked him over while he stared at her future house, and her heart felt ready to burst from her chest. She stepped up next to him and placed a gloved hand on his back while they looked down at the hardening cement.

"I know anything you would build for me would be exceptional," Sadie said.

She was unable to coax Jimmy to come eat with her, but she left a plate for him on the deck.

As Sadie was cleaning up her own dish, alone in the kitchen, Gabriel walked in. She turned at the sound and found him leaning in the doorway in the same posture Jimmy had taken just that morning. Gabriel must have caught the image in her mind since he correctly interpreted her annoyance at the comparison. He stood up straight and came into the room.

"Sorry. Just let myself in," he said.

"It's okay. My kitchen is your kitchen. Can I fix you a plate?"

He shook his head. "I just came here to tell you I've been called home, we'll be leaving a bit early."

"What?" Sadie felt the walls closing in around her.

"I'm needed somewhere else," he said.

A tear slid down her cheek. "I'm not ready. I need more time. One more week," she said.

He sighed. Then took her hands in his and held her firmly. "You'll be fine. And if not, you can always come stay with me. I'll help you get settled in the city. You can find a real home. You have until morning if you want to leave together. Either way, here's my address."

He slid a piece of paper into her pocket.

"Just don't let yourself get too hungry," he added.

Then, before she could protest further, he kissed her on the lips and departed.

She stood there trembling around the words *a real home* for so long it took her a while to notice the sounds of Jimmy working had stopped. When Sadie went to check on him, he was gone. Unpoured cement sat wet in the bucket.

Chapter 6

A parting

Sadie couldn't bring herself to tell her parents that Gabriel was leaving. The whole topic of her feeding stress was too uncomfortable to discuss with them. Instead, she took over Jimmy's abandoned project and finished the foundation. It was a good distraction from having to talk to anyone.

When it was done, she told her parents she wasn't hungry and wanted to head to bed. It was a lie. Once she had finally stepped away from the physical labor, Sadie became acutely aware of exactly how hungry she was, but it wasn't food she wanted.

It was too late to go out to the cabin, so she opted for a cold shower instead. She returned to her room just after dark. When she flipped on her light, she found Jimmy sitting in her windowsill looking out at the full moon. Sadie flipped the switch back off and let the night sky be their light as she disappeared into her closet to get dressed.

Then silently, she hopped up to join him. With their toes together, she leaned against the opposite edge of the window and looked up at the stars.

When she turned to watch him a minute later, he kept his gaze averted. Maybe it was her hunger, or maybe it was the emotional day they'd had, but he'd never looked so beautiful or so sad.

"Please don't go," he said, still not looking at her.

"It feels like I have no choice," she said.

He turned to face her. Sadie pushed away all the excess information for a minute and tried to focus on just his eyes. Even in the dim light, she could tell he'd been crying.

Jimmy leaned forward, took her gloved hands and pressed his forehead to her knuckles. He followed this with briefly holding her fingertips to his lips, before releasing her and dropping onto the roof.

"There's always a choice," he said over his shoulder.

Within a blink, he was gone into the night.

Sadie couldn't sleep. If she was going with Gabriel, either the next day or shortly after that, she needed to pack and tell her parents. Instead, she just lay there, fully clothed on her comforter with the moonlight washing over her, waiting for answers to come.

Sometime just before dawn, she lost consciousness.

It was a painful minute of remembering her dilemma upon waking, but she had bigger problems when she noticed how late it was. It was almost noon! She jumped out of bed. She didn't have time to prepare anything—she just needed to get to the cabin as quickly as possible. Sadie bolted out of the house in the same clothes she'd worn yesterday. She could always pack later. Right now, she needed to talk to Gabriel. There were so many more questions to ask. Why hadn't she found out more yesterday?

When she arrived an hour later, she could tell immediately that they'd gone. Meesk and Deena were sitting on the porch having a quiet lunch. Gabriel had left a phone number for her, but he wouldn't be back home for several days so she shouldn't try to call just yet. Sadie thanked them for everything and declined to stay.

That was it. She was officially on her own. The bigger question of what to do with her entire future was shoved in the background of the very real question of whom precisely she was going to feed from. Not tomorrow or the day after, but today. She thought of the bus driver's son, Clay. That was a safe bet. She was pretty sure she remembered which bus stop he used to get off at on the way home from school. One train and bus ride later, and she found herself wandering along the sidewalks of a little cul de sac.

A face peered out from behind thick curtains to watch her progress. Sadie didn't know precisely where to find Clay, and she suddenly felt terrified at the thought of knocking on any of the doors. With thoughts of Jimmy increasingly pulsing through her mind, Sadie reluctantly set off for home.

Gabriel didn't seem to understand her place in this town. She couldn't imagine finding someone, especially not after what had happened with Ina. And the wood nymphs were the only other feeders in town. If they didn't trust her, it seemed unlikely anyone else would.

If she stayed, she would just end up giving in and feeding from Jimmy. If she truly wanted to avoid that, it was time to go.

Having made the decision, Sadie was surprised to find herself feeling calm for the first time in days. No tears disturbed her as she planned everything she would need to bring with her and where she would go. Arlington was the closest town with a lot of people, so she would head there today. She tried not to calculate exactly how long that would take or when, after arriving, she would be able to feed.

Sadie entered her house to find her parents finishing up with lunch. Her mother seemed weary when Sadie said, "We need to talk." She did her best to convince them that it was right for her to go without making it seem like a forced decision. Sadie underplayed her problems, opting instead for making it seem like she wanted to get out and discover the world a bit. Spread her wings. That kind of thing.

Her mother protested, trying to offer other ideas. Even her father made an appeal: "But, sweetie, what about the house?"

"I'll come back." Sadie said, not exactly sure when or how that would be.

"And Jimmy? He'll go with you?" her mom asked.

"No, I don't think so. Jimmy and I need some time apart. We've been together so long, you know, and with all these changes... We just need some space to grow," Sadie said, trying to convince herself as much as them.

Her father nodded like that sounded reasonable. Then the next big hurdle hit.

"And I need to go today," she said.

"What? No, there's no rush. Take a week… at least," her mother said.

Sadie wasn't about to explain the truth.

"Look, this decision is really hard for me. I feel that if I don't go right now I never will." Her voice choked and she paused to breathe. "Please, Ma. Don't make this harder on me."

The pain in her voice must have won them over, because they went silent. Her mother followed her up to her room to pack. She needed to travel light if she was going to be on foot. Sadie gathered up her favorite summer dress, as well as several long layers. When her mom wasn't looking, she tossed in the stone box.

"How are you going to say goodbye to little Jimmy?" her mom asked as they wrapped up.

"Not so little anymore, Ma." Sadie heaved a sigh. "And I'm going to write him a letter."

"A letter? Don't you think he deserves more than that?" her mother asked.

"He deserves a lot more than that, but it's all I got. I can't face him. He'll never let me go. And I'll never want to." Sadie brushed away some tears. "You'll give it to him for me? A few hours after I leave?"

Her mother responded to the heaviness of her daughter's mood and moved away from interfering and toward giving practical advice.

"We have some money saved up we can send with you. It should last you a while if you're careful. You don't know this, but your father and I used to travel around quite a bit before we had you. People are friendly to travelers in general. So long as you keep an eye out for trouble you should have places to stay on the road. Cities are pricey, but they often have plenty of hotels and restaurants."

As her mom spoke, Sadie became even more nervous about this task of being on her own. She realized there was a lot she didn't know.

She'd never been afraid of learning though, and she always enjoyed a fresh challenge.

"Just be smart out there, baby," her mom concluded. "And it's the twenty-first century. Every town has a pay phone now. I'll expect you to call home once a week."

"I promise," she said.

~

SHE CAUGHT A TRAIN SOUTH, still shaking from the tearful goodbye with her parents.

In search of a distraction, she quickly pulled out the mystery box. Tracing her finger over the outline of the handprints, she wondered at the importance of the object she was carrying around so casually. Maybe she should have been taking it more seriously? Thought of it earlier and opened it by now?

She felt guilty for not paying it more attention and vowed to open the thing at the next opportunity. Meaning she would open it immediately following her next sexual encounter, which was a horizon she couldn't seem to see beyond.

Her body had slowly begun to ache with a subdued longing. It was nothing overwhelming, but it was constant. She clenched her thighs together on the seat and rubbed her breasts. Touching her own body, though, seemed only to make it worse. It drew her attention to thoughts of sex, even more than they already were. She stopped and closed her eyes, trying to focus all her attention on the image of a clear lake.

The lake, still and calm, morphed into a river, fast and loud. Jimmy was on the edge, about to jump in. His back glistened in the sunlight. Sadie wanted him to turn around, but when she called his name, no sound escaped her lips. Gabriel laced an arm around her waist from behind and kissed the back of her neck. A surge of pleasure ran through her and she tried to call out to Jimmy again. He still didn't turn. All she could do was stare at his back as she writhed in Gabriel's arms. This wasn't how she wanted it. Why was this happening? Why was—

Sadie woke as the train slowed. She couldn't remember falling asleep, but she pushed herself upright and looked up at the map, keenly aware of the dampness in her panties. Arlington was the next stop.

Some strange colors caught her eye and she turned to look out the window. Her jaw dropped. There were buildings in every direction. Tall ones. This was definitely a *city,* and it was the first one she'd ever seen in person. It was a lot more overwhelming when it was towering over her than they made it look on television.

Many of the buildings appeared to be a mix of stone and nymph-grown wood. The architecture was elaborately beautiful. Complex patterns of interwoven branches had been grown up pillars, serving as both decor and structural support. Wooden sky bridges had been grown between buildings, creating a network of paths up above. Sadie imagined someone could travel all over the place without ever setting foot on the ground.

As she hopped down and caught a full shot of the majestic Arlington, she wondered why her family had never visited together. In between the two buildings in front of her was an open-air market swarming with people. Sadie checked to make sure her gloves and turtleneck were firmly in place, secured her backpack, and headed into the crowd.

The presence of so many humans made Sadie's hunger a very real force. Colors flowed between the people like a spiderweb made out of a rainbow. She occasionally caught quick flares of desire directed at her, but they were all too small to catch her interest. She thought she was in luck when a man cat-called her from an alleyway, but when she turned she saw he had no red streaks at all for her. *Lies,* she thought, and stormed on.

She needed to find someone soon, but who and how? An image came to her of her grandmother grabbing her hand right before she dropped a too large handful of salt into a pot: less is more, she'd always say. *Yes,* she needed someplace more intimate with a smaller crowd.

She turned down another street, this one made for buses, and was shocked to see such a steady stream of traffic. One bus after another passed by. She didn't know how she was supposed to cross it. Changing her mind, she turned back toward the market.

She wanted somewhere she could interact with a few people over some amount of time. She looked at the names of the places she passed by. It all seemed to be shops. She needed to find a little diner and hit on the waiter or some lodgings and try to pick up someone from the lobby. She had no experience doing either of those things and the thought sounded terrifying, but she was sure her hunger would provide her the confidence when the time was right. She wanted to ask for directions, but everyone seemed caught up in their own world.

Stopping to purchase some roasted nuts from one of the vendors, she asked the man if he knew where she could find housing for the night.

"Fifth floor," he said.

"Scuse me?" Sadie responded.

"Temporary housing is fifth floor." He gestured for the next customer and Sadie found herself pushed out of the way. She glared at the rude stranger before looking up at the building next to her. Time to explore indoors. As she approached the elaborate entranceway, she noticed someone watching her intently.

The person wasn't sending out light of attraction, but rather a tiny line of green. Did she know them? She pushed back the images surrounding them and focused on their physical features. As usual, she was only mildly successful. She could tell it was a man. He had on black leather pants and nothing else. He threw her a flirtatious smile. "Not here, love. This is my corner."

When she only stared, he laughed.

"Just a little joke. You're a tourist or I'm celibate! Danny at your service. Or... probably not *your* service, but it's nice to meetcha anyways." He held out a hand, it was gloved. As she shook it, understanding hit her. She let the totality of what she saw from the man flow back in and tried to sort through it. He was covered in sexual scenes, too much of a blur for her to pick out any details, but clearly involving many different people. He also appeared to have five different romantic partners.

"You're a succubus," she mumbled.

He clapped a hand to his thigh and guffawed. "I'll be goddamned. Am I the first one you met, girl? Sides yourself?"

"Almost," she said.

"Well, what can I do you for? You're clearly hungry. Over a day since you fed. My gracious," he said, putting a hand to his chest.

It didn't completely shock Sadie that he knew this, since she'd read in Gabriel's scroll that such things were possible, in that some succubi saw very particular things beyond the standard stuff, but she was still surprised.

"You can really see that?" she asked.

"Sure can. And where's that brown-haired fella? Cutie. If he's your only main squeeze, should be with you, right?"

Sadie didn't particularly want to talk about Jimmy with this stranger, but she wondered if he could help her figure out how to feed in the big city. It was at this thought that Sadie became aware of the other people mulling around. She forced herself to notice their clothes and saw they were dressed scantily. She watched one of them be propositioned. They disappeared into the building together.

Sadie turned back to the man and opened her mouth to speak.

He cut in, "Not your best option. Feeding from complete strangers, well, it'll hold you over a minute. You can even live off it if you're in the life, doing it all day. But if you're looking for a real feeding... you gotta make a *connection*. The people come to us, they're just bored, a little lonely. Not what you need."

Sadie was beginning to understand that it wasn't all the same, but the thought just made trying to find someone even more terrifying.

"Then how?" she asked, feeling a little woozy.

"Stop moving 'round so much. Find a spot. Try to really see people. Give them a chance to see you. Most importantly, talk to 'em." He pointed to a building a little ways down. "Can find a room there. Not too pricey and the lounge might be just what you need. Good place. You'll see."

She vigorously thanked the stranger before fighting her way back through the bustling crowd. She was fascinated by the chaos of it all, but equally grateful to step out of it.

The entrance to the building was a broad stone archway with no door, though inside had a very different vibe from the street. It smelled of cigar smoke and alcohol with an ample amount of red light passing between people, frequently flowing in only one direction. Dark red tapestries covered the walls and a small fountain sat in the center, giving it an elegant atmosphere. The tables surrounding the fountain were populated by people playing cards.

Sadie wandered in slowly, examining the inhabitants. The network of interests was too complex to pull apart. She tried to focus in on the folk with several lines to others, figuring those people didn't have their hearts focused on someone in particular. There was one man with particularly strong chords of lust. Concentrating on him, she attempted a more intimate reading. He had no romantic attachments, but was pulsating desire toward several of the people around him. None of these people were returning the emotion. He seemed a little desperate for some contact, exactly like she was at the moment, but curiously, he wasn't making any attempt to talk to anyone.

He was perfect.

"Is this seat taken?" she asked, and a small burst of desire shot from him as he shook his head, but after she'd settled in, he made no attempt to talk to her either. In an effort to engage his attention, she asked him to show her how to play. He seemed to light up and gestured for her to be dealt in.

He leaned in to show her his hand as he explained the rules, along with some strategy. She found herself drawn into him as he talked. She liked his mannerisms and the images wafting off his voice; they were beautiful somehow, despite her inability to clearly interpret them. At one point, she smiled at him and caught a distinct picture from him of the two of them kissing. She watched actively as the attraction between them grew.

After an hour of play, when she began to feel anxious with hunger, she decided she needed to take drastic action. As someone redealt another hand, she turned to the man and whispered, "I was about to go get a room upstairs. Um... do you want to, like, come with me?"

He looked at her, radiating astonished silence. "Uh, what do you mean?" the man asked, then added, "I... don't have a lot of money. And, I don't really like to—"

"Oh, no! That's not what I meant. I'm not..." She knocked over his wine glass as she gestured dramatically. It poured red over the table and into his lap.

"Oh shit. I'm so sorry," she said.

"It's okay. It was an accident," he told her, before making for a hallway at the back of the room, clearly heading for the bathrooms. She was getting increasingly desperate and thought she had to try again. She followed the man. Catching up just as he was about to enter the restroom, she rapidly shouted after him, "I meant, do you want to sleep with me. But not for money, but because we both want to."

She was grateful Gabriel wasn't here witnessing this. In fact, she was glad that no one was observing this profoundly embarrassing attempt. The man just stared at her with a mess of images flashing around him.

"I don't understand," he said finally.

She moved slowly forward as she said more boldly, "I want to have sex with you. Right now." Her body throbbed with the truth of her words. "If that's not what you want, tell me so and I'll leave." But she already knew it was exactly what he wanted. He didn't speak, but began pulsating a desire so strong it made her knees feel weak.

She stepped until she was nearly touching him. He still didn't reply, only sent out such a flurry of sexual images that it made her dizzy to look at him. The physical arousal of his body pressed against her.

"Want to go in there with me?" She was breathing in quick, frantic bursts and could feel herself shaking. He pushed the door open as if in a trance. She entered the men's room first, her gaze fixed on him. There was no way to lock the door so she pulled him into a stall before bending down to check the other stall was empty.

"What is this?" he asked. He didn't seem to trust her and he made no move to come closer, but the desire wafting from him was clear.

"I'm a succubus." She had to tell him, since he was about to find out anyway. He inhaled sharply. She watched as the news crashed through his emotions. His posture softened ever so slightly and he moved an inch closer. Sadie didn't hesitate, she tore off her gloves and moved in.

Something about the desire of the man was intoxicating, and she struggled to pace herself. It was impossible to keep totally silent when someone came in, but neither of them seemed to care. It was in moments like this that everything suddenly felt right. Having to leave home, having to face the ridicule of neighbors and supposed friends. It all seemed trivial up against the power she felt when in her element.

She stuck to using her hands for most of it, but took him in her mouth when he got close so things wouldn't get too messy. They were at least alone when he cried out, loud enough to echo around the small chamber. Sadie gasped and moaned along with him as if it were her own climax, her mind going blank with the raw pleasure of it.

Immediately following the last spasm, someone again entered the restroom. Sadie stood up as the man grabbed for some tissue. Then they both went still, their repressed breathing intimate between them. She reached up to caress his face. The texture was strange enough to cause her to notice something different about it. She briefly saw that it looked melted, as if he'd been badly burned. Then more compelling images distracted her. He had a kind of tenderness overlaying a very active libido that defined the feel of him to her. He looked like something beautiful that she could eat right up.

When they were alone again, he pointed to her shoulder.

"I hurt you." His voice came out in a breathy croak as he pointed to a small bruise developing on her upper arm.

"Yeah," she said. "It's okay. Not your fault. I… haven't actually done this kind of thing before. Picking up a stranger, I mean. I need to work on my self-control." She scooped her hair behind her ear, a little embarrassed. She knew that what had just happened had been a little inappropriately intense. After all, she didn't want a complete stranger to get addicted to her.

"Could've fooled me," he said, caressing the wound. He looked back into her face and added, "Thank you."

Sadie's skin buzzed with satisfaction. "You too," she said, a small smile playing at the corner of her lips.

His gaze dropped to the floor.

"Can I ask though... why me?"

She shrugged. "Why not? You attracted me." Sadie had found she felt comfortable with vulnerable honesty right after feeding. "You're beautiful." She leaned in and kissed him, grabbing his face with both hands.

Just before she broke away, she felt a single tear escape him and fall into one of her palms. And that was the start of round two.

The second she had satisfied one hunger, another one roared to life. Having eaten very little that day, Sadie found herself suddenly ravenous. Though before she could go in search of food, there was something rather important she needed to do. Wandering back out into the lobby, she spotted an elevator. The fifth floor was in fact labeled, lodgings. Exiting the lift, she found a check-in desk immediately in front of her.

She asked the person behind the counter for the cheapest single-person room available. When they told her the price, however, she paled. The succubus had told her this place was cheap! Her mom had been right. Money didn't go far in the big city. She handed over a large chunk of change.

The hallway to her room was also made out of nymph-grown wood. Whoever had done the design was incredibly talented. They had grown knots into the wood at regular intervals and swirled them into a large pattern in the shape of a galaxy. She traced the design with her fingers, fascinated by its beauty.

Sadie had never stayed in a hotel before, and as she entered the small single room, she gazed around in curiosity at the little dresser and bed. The single lamp cast a soft yellow glow and she beamed at the pleasant atmosphere. For the first time since leaving that morning, Sadie felt a small thrill of adventure.

Pushing away thoughts of missing Jimmy, she sat down on the bed, extracted the box, and looked at it in nervous anticipation. Setting it firmly in her lap, she pressed both hands, fingers splayed, into the small depression.

Nothing happened.

Sadie focused on her connection to the object, attempting to calm her racing thoughts. She could feel a bond with the stone, a small humming in her flesh. Her instincts told her to treat it like a lover. She imagined the surface as the skin of a person's chest and tried to travel inside the material. This seemed to be the right path since it was made for succubi and Sadie was pleased at the cleverness of her idea, but still this failed.

She tried this tactic with different moods and intentions. She tried to hold the memory of her last sexual encounter in the front of her mind. She tried thinking of Jimmy. She conjured up the sensation of her own pleasure. She attempted to feel excited, anticipatory, gratified, and elated. She sat there for almost an hour before giving up.

Eventually the gurgling in her stomach won her attentions, and she went out in search of a real meal. And by the time she'd sat down to eat, the thrill of adventure had worn off. She realized then that this was the first time in her life she had ever eaten alone, and suddenly the loss of Jimmy at her side hit her with an unbearable pain. That was when it struck her, she might have just made a horrible mistake.

Chapter 7

A city

Jimmy bolted off the train. Sadie had to be here! Arlington was the closest town with a lot of people. As he entered the alleyway between the two buildings directly in front of him, however, he despaired. The place was colossal. A part of him knew that he stood no chance of finding her, but his legs continued to carry him forward regardless. He barely noticed the handful of vendors packing up for the night as his gaze darted from person to person, frantic in his search.

A rather attractive man called out to him, "Hey cutie."

Jimmy briefly looked at the man before guessing his intentions. He mumbled, "Oh, no, I'm not interested," and began to move on.

"In finding your girl?" the man asked.

Jimmy almost tripped in his haste to come to a stop.

"What?"

"The amiable newbie with the appealing eyes? Don't know her name. Likely find her in there though." Jimmy looked toward the building at which the man pointed. There was only one explanation: this man was some kind of human feeder that could tell when a human was searching for something. Brightening at his luck, he thanked him profusely and took off running.

The sun was setting. Jimmy feared if he didn't find Sadie on the first day, there was no hope for it afterward. If she kept on the move, who knew in which direction she would head. He darted through the archway and found a fairly crowded social space. Every table was packed with people, and he had to scan the room carefully before deciding she wasn't among them. He waited outside the women's bathroom for five minutes before moving on.

Jimmy couldn't think of what he would do if he couldn't find her. He tried to push the thought away as he ran through the lobby to an elevator. He calmed when he saw this place had lodgings. Perhaps the angel on the street had meant Sadie was upstairs.

He got off on the fifth floor and emerged facing an elderly woman behind a counter, smiling kindly at him. When he inquired about a Sadie Hall, however, the woman crossed her arms high on her chest and refused to confirm if anyone by that name was staying there.

"Did a young woman alone check-in at all today? Auburn hair with curls? About this tall?" he pushed in desperation.

The woman shrugged. "Maybe so, maybe not. If she'd wanted your attentions, I'd think she'd a told you where she's at, no?"

Jimmy took her comment as some confirmation that Sadie might actually be back there in one of those rooms and looked longingly at the hallway behind the old guard dog. She stared him down, eyes narrowing. He briefly contemplated running past her, shouting Sadie's name. If he could have been sure Sadie would answer him, he would've done just that.

Instead, he took the elevator back to the ground floor. Looking around at the busy tables, he dreaded the notion of sitting down and interacting with anyone. Also, such a thing might distract his attention. Jimmy plopped down next to the elevator door and glared out at the room.

He would stay there all night if he needed to. He could think of no better plan at this point. As he sat watching the dedicated players, he went again through the events of the past month. How could it have come to this? And how could she have made this decision without talking to him, and so abruptly, without giving him the option to go with her? Though he'd been bracing for this, he had never expected her to just up and leave him. Perhaps, and the thought terrified him, their relationship didn't mean as much to Sadie with all the changes she'd gone through recently. Maybe she'd moved past him.

As the weight of that thought hung over him, he began to be aware of his body again. All at once he realized how hungry and thirsty he was. He wished he'd brought more with him when he'd been frantically packing. An hour passed. Then another. The yearning for something to drink increased to a peak, but he refused to leave. Then his body gave him something he couldn't ignore. It was time to find a bathroom.

He approached the table nearest him, thinking he could ask them to keep an eye out for him. The group broke out into laughter at something just as he reached them and he had to say "Excuse me" rather loudly before anyone looked around. The man nearest him shot him an expectant look, but by that point Jimmy's attention had been entirely refocused elsewhere.

Sadie had just entered the far end of the room. She was holding the hand of a man with a strange face. As they neared, Jimmy saw the man's skin was half-melted. He looked like dried wax. Jimmy heard the man at the table ask him something.

"Oh, no, I'm good thank you," he mumbled to him without looking down.

Jimmy watched as Sadie and the wax man made their way toward the elevator. Then his feet kicked back into gear and he crossed to them in a rush. As he approached, he heard the blessed sound of Sadie's voice.

"Are you sure you feel up for this? I'm really not supposed to feed off the same person this much," she said.

Jimmy didn't hear the man's response because Sadie had just spotted him. A half-eaten burger fell from her hand and hit the floor with a thud. Her eyes widened and, if he wasn't mistaken, glistened slightly with tears. Was she upset or happy he'd come after her?

Unfortunately, his friend had on blue jeans, gloves, and a tank top, leaving her arms exposed. So with Jimmy also in short sleeves, it was impossible to hug her. He limited himself to raising a hand awkwardly in greeting. The wax man looked at him, then back at Sadie as she returned the gesture. The elevator door opened. She reached down to retrieve the smashed burger and emerged looking flustered. Tucking her hair behind her ear and adjusting her shirt, she made her way into the elevator, not taking her eyes off Jimmy. He followed right behind her, but the wax man hesitated.

"Should I... still come up?" he asked.

"Of course!" Sadie gestured for him to follow as the doors tried to close them in. The man squeezed through and the three of them faced forward as the lift rose. Jimmy opened his mouth to ask the many questions he'd been debating all day, but in the end wasn't sure how to phrase them. The presence of the other person created an additional barrier. No one else spoke either. Though more than once Sadie made like she was about to speak, she contented herself to twisting her hips side-to-side and pawing at the ground with a foot.

The old woman narrowed her eyes when she spotted Jimmy re-emerge, but softened when she saw his company.

"Hi there, Delilah." Sadie smiled as they approached the desk. "You have another key for my room? I had a friend join me."

She nodded to Jimmy, who smiled at her. His smile might have turned a little smug when it fell on the old woman. Delilah slid a key at Jimmy with one finger and cast a look which let him know she'd be watching him.

"Wow. What did you do to her?" Sadie asked Jimmy once they had entered the hallway.

"She didn't like me trying to find you. She said I'd already know where you were if you wanted to be found." Jimmy said it as a question, and Sadie dropped her gaze. She looked guilty, but that didn't tell him much. Was it wrong that he'd followed her? Should he have just let her go? He felt awkward walking toward her room with this strange man, but he needed to talk to her privately. Though she was obviously busy at the moment, or at least she was about to be. But he just couldn't let her out of his sight now that he'd found her.

The hallway was continuously curved. New doors popped out of the unknown as they walked in silence. Sadie pulled up next to one and looked him over. "You don't have more stuff with you?" she asked, eyeing his half-filled backpack.

"I left in kind of a hurry," he said.

Again she looked guilty. The wax man retreated into the background as they stared at each other.

"Well, if you wait here..." Sadie began to speak before Jimmy's bladder interjected.

"Can I use your bathroom?" he asked.

"Oh... yeah." She pushed the door open and let the three of them in.

"I'll just be a minute," Jimmy said over his shoulder.

As he entered the tiny restroom he couldn't help but think the words, *her* bathroom in *her* hotel room in *her* life. He felt in the way already.

Though he was only behind closed doors for a minute, when he emerged it was to the sight of them pressed together next to the bed. Sadie broke the kiss away like it was an effort to do so and looked at him as if she'd already forgotten he was there. What place could he have in her new world?

Her eyes were dilated as she licked her reddened lips, but then her gaze refocused on the man and Jimmy was out-of-mind. He spotted the damaged burger on the nightstand and grabbed it to take outside.

Jimmy took a seat just outside, leaning uncomfortably against the curved wall, and casually dusted off some dirt before scarfing down the burger.

It seemed to take an eternity. What could they possibly be doing in there? He tried not to picture it, but sounds of pleasure occasionally reached his ears. He could have moved further away if only he hadn't been glued in place by his desire to hear Sadie's voice.

He ached with longing for the woman he had loved most of his life, and though he could no longer picture what the future looked like with her, he couldn't imagine a path without her in it.

He was there to stay, he decided, as long as she wanted him around. He would take whatever part of her he could have. Even if it meant sitting on the other side of closed doors while—Good god, what was going on in there? He did move then, glad no one was walking past, as his arousal was visible when he stood. He covered his ears and tried to name the state capitals.

The door opened.

The wax man gave a cordial nod to him as he left. Jimmy took a deep breath to calm his heart rate before entering. The room was empty and the shower running. The bed, surprisingly, was unruffled. He found an empty glass and downed three cups of cool water as the shower turned off.

Jimmy heart raced as Sadie emerged from the steam of the bathroom, wrapped in a towel.

They stared at each other in awkward silence. She opened her mouth twice to speak, but didn't get anywhere. Eventually, he decided it was going to be his lead.

Shifting uncomfortably, he tried to sound casual as he asked, "That was twice today with him?"

"Yeah, he was a lucky find."

Jimmy was curious what exactly that meant, but asked a different follow-up question. "Is that how many times you should feed a day?" He was babbling, but couldn't seem to bring himself to start with the question *why did you leave me?*

Sadie saddled toward the other side of the bed and, securing the towel, bent down to retrieve something.

"No, usually just once, but I wanted another shot at this." She tossed her backpack between them and climbed on the bed before extracting the ornate container.

The box! He had completely forgotten about it. Apparently so had she. How could she not have opened it yet?

"I can't figure it out. Gabriel made it look so easy," she said to his unasked question. She placed her hands into the lid and closed her eyes. He watched her, lips slightly parted, forehead creased in concentration.

"Ugh! What is my problem?" She withdrew her hands. "I've tried everything I can think of."

"What does that mean? What have you tried?" Jimmy asked.

"Well, let's see..." Sadie pulled her clothes from the bag as she explained her various strategies. She slid off the bed and paced once back and forth. Then she dropped her towel unexpectedly, causing Jimmy to jerk his head away.

"Sorry…" she said in a small voice, "I forgot." She seemed to lose her train of thought because she finished dressing in silence. A minute later, he felt her weight back on the bed. "I'm dressed," she told him.

He looked at her. She'd put on the turtleneck they had bought together, as well as long pants and gloves, despite the fact it wasn't remotely cold.

She looked down at her attire and said, "So we can share the bed."

It took Jimmy a moment to register. "So, you want me to stay?"

He felt so vulnerable asking this. Jimmy knew he would melt if she said no, but he supposed that he'd tracked her down solely to ask that question. The *why* she had left was obvious. The *why* she had left without talking to him was not obvious, but he wasn't ready to hear the answer anyway. So it all came down to one thing: did she want him with her or not?

She reached out and rested her hand over his. "Yes," she said simply as she squeezed his hand. An expression of guilt flashed briefly over her face, but then it was gone and she said, "I'm really glad you found me."

She placed the box on the ground next to the bed and pulled back the covers to climb in. Jimmy hesitated only a moment before kicking off his shoes and joining her.

"So what's your plan?" he asked, feeling every tense muscle in him relax.

She laughed. "Oh, I forgot to get one of those. Do I need one?"

Sadie lay propped on one elbow to talk and he copied her.

"Suppose not. What money do we have?" he asked.

"My parents gave me what they could. Don't think it'll go too far in the big city though. I just came here first since it seemed easier to feed with more people around."

Jimmy nodded. "Right. I got a couple bucks too. Plus a bit of Grandma's jewelry to sell in an emergency. It should hold us for a while." It was good to say the word *us*. Sadie must have thought so too, since she smiled and sunk more comfortably into the bed. As the mood relaxed, he could almost imagine things were back to normal between them. Apart from the fact they were about to sleep in the same bed.

Sadie filled him in on what had happened over the past several days. Jimmy told her about what his dad had overheard the Johnsons' saying about what one of the O'Connors thought about the news the town now had a succubus. For some reason, sharing this gossip so far from home made them both laugh.

"Doesn't matter now," Jimmy said, feeling a little homesick already.

"I guess not. Now all that matters is finding food and shelter and exploring new places," she smiled.

"And finding people for you," he added, and her smile faltered slightly.

"Yeah, which should hopefully be easier here," she said.

"Was it easy? I mean how do you...? I can't imagine...."

"Um... yeah. It wasn't too bad." She shrugged. Her face said lie and he narrowed his eyes. She buried her head in her pillow. "Okay, it was awful. So embarrassing, Jimmy."

Then she told him a ridiculous story of hitting on the wax man. He laughed so much he had to sit up to hold his side. When he finally lay back down he said, "Wow, I'd never thought how awkward it would be... being a succubus."

"It is definitely awkward. Sometimes." Then her smile turned to contemplation. "And sometimes it feels exactly right. Like it's all the most natural thing in the world. Isn't that strange?"

It was strange. He couldn't picture himself in her place, not in any of a thousand parallel universes. Though he didn't really have any idea of what she was going through. They hadn't talked much about any of the details and it was odd to not be up on her life.

Jimmy looked back at the bathroom. "What's it like?" he asked. He was genuinely curious and meant it to be conversational, but couldn't keep his heart from racing.

She raised her eyebrows and asked with a grin, "Taking a shower?"

He dropped his gaze at the look on her face. It was a strange thing, feeling nervous around her. He'd been around that grin his whole life, but now everything was different. He didn't want it to be though. He couldn't lose what they had over something as small as a complete and sudden identity change. Jimmy laughed at that thought.

Determined to maintain some normalcy, he looked back at her with what he intended to be a casual expression. Sadie reached out and slid her gloved fingers through his. Dropping her own eye contact, she stared at their adjoined hands as she explained, "It's like my mind goes blank, and my instincts kick in. My whole world becomes simple. As if nothing has ever made so much sense. Like reaching into someone with every part of yourself." She played with his fingers. "And when it's with someone you really connect with, it's a whole other thing." Her eyes seemed on fire when she looked back at him. He wondered if she was thinking about the wax man, or Leon, or that succubus with the stupid leather vest and penetrating stare.

"Was that what it was like with Gabriel?" he asked, trying not to choke on the name this time.

"Oh. No... um. Succubi can't feed from other human feeders. Nature feeders, yes. In fact, fire nymphs are particularly resistant to fatigue from succubi. This makes it easier to push them further; to feed longer and more frequently. That's why Gabriel brought them for me. I didn't really get to explore that idea much though. I was sort of all over the place during the first few days of feeding. But I think that was the point. They could take it. I feel like I'm gaining more control now though. I wish I could've had more time with them."

Jimmy wondered if Sadie was aware of the way she was slowly leaning into him as she spoke. He remained perfectly still, trying to interpret her behavior.

"No," she went on, "it was like that with Ina. I ran into her in the woods. I think it was because we had known each other so long. And because she really liked me." Her voice sounded a little drunk.

Jimmy had the urge to also lean in, but worried he'd be taking advantage of her in her clearly aroused state. She wasn't thinking of him, but her body language was confusing. She ran her hand up his forearm as she inched a bit closer. "I think it also made a difference that I liked her." She ran one finger up and down his bicep. "It seems the intensity of what I can do goes up when I like them and the response goes up when they like me. And the more they enjoy it, the more I have to feed off of. And that feedback loop pours into me, filling me up. And that's the feeding." She delivered this speech in a dreamlike tone.

She was very close now. For a moment, Jimmy thought she was actually going to kiss him. Excitement pulsed through him as Sadie's eyes lit up on his. What was happening? Had she changed her mind about him? He didn't know what to do. The casual conversation had disappeared, and his body throbbed with arousal.

Then Sadie took in a deep breath and seemed to shudder as she let it out. She blinked several times, retreated, and lay down on her back. "We should get some sleep. It's been a crazy day," she said.

Adjusting himself so he could lay on his stomach, he agreed, "Yeah. Crazy."

SADIE AWOKE to the sound of the shower. It took one long, foggy minute for her to realize where she was. Her sleepy gaze rested on the indent in the pillow next to her. Jimmy was here. In the shower. And she'd slept in this bed with him. All night.

Granted, she had nearly kissed him before gaining control. Her stomach clenched in guilt at her mixed signaling, but this just showed the importance of not telling him the truth about her feelings. If not for his belief that she didn't want him, she knew she wouldn't be able to hold herself back.

She was waiting just outside the bathroom when the door opened.

"Morning," he said, leaving slightly more room than was necessary as they switched places in the doorway. "How'd you sleep?"

"Uh... good I think. You?" she asked.

She missed what he said in words as a rush of images from the last eight hours hit her. He had slept fitfully, waking after every sexual dream until finally sneaking into the bathroom to take care of business.

"Right, well, let me just..." she said, gesturing to the toilet.

Sadie wasn't sure if she was pleased or not that her ability to pick out specific scenes from the images was improving. Gabriel's scroll had said eventually she'd be able to tell memory from fantasy from dream, and as Sadie took in the rather vivid mental images in Jimmy's head, she decided that was definitely the flavor of dreams. Whereas, the scene of him touching himself while thinking of her had actually happened, right where she was now standing.

She splashed several handfuls of cold water on her face and practiced smiling at herself in the mirror in a casual, non-seductive way. Just two friends exploring the world and sharing a room. That's what they were. She could do this.

They made their way down to the street below. The market was as alive at this time as it had been the day before. Did nothing ever stop here?

"I say we just walk, see where it takes us," Sadie said.

"I'm in," Jimmy replied, handing her half a cinnamon roll. Not wanting to get her gloves dirty, she removed them to take it. This made the careful passing of food rather awkward. She juggled not touching his skin with not losing any of the delicious-smelling frosting.

"Which way?" he asked.

Sadie chose at random and they set off.

The bustle of vendors and large crowds didn't persist down every street. In fact, as they moved away from the train station, the city felt a lot more like a cramped version of home.

Though strangely, there weren't any houses. In fact, there weren't individual buildings of any kind. The entire city was one interconnected web as tall as a forest. Where did people live? Were they all above ground level?

"How do we get up there?" Sadie asked, gesturing to one of the many sky bridges above them.

"That looks promising," Jimmy said, pointing with a bob of his head.

There was an elevator mounted between two buildings, and they took it to the highest floor.

Sadie licked the frosting from her fingers, acutely aware of Jimmy watching her do it, and replaced the gloves. When she looked over at him, he redirected his gaze to the buildings passing by. A slight blush colored his cheeks.

That was new.

Had she messed up last night more than she thought? Had she given him a glimmer of hope that things weren't totally closed between them? She again felt guilty for her moment of weakness. If she really loved him, she would make it easier on him.

"Damn, look at that," he said, and Sadie turned back in time to catch the view as the door opened. An explosion of color greeted them as they stepped into a garden as dense and varied as it seemed possible to be. The path before them ran directly between two buildings and was open to the sky above. Sunlight rained down through the gap, and they stepped into it with matching smiles.

Sticking to the path, they walked between the gardens on either side. Regular pillars supported the ceiling while keeping the place open to the elements. Sadie looked up just as two birds swooped down through the crack to land on a bush to their right. Flowers, as vibrant as the ones all around them, ran up the sides of the buildings, clinging to the structures with their fingers made of vines.

Sadie heard a giggle to her right. There were a group of children playing hide and seek. They all wore flowers in their hair and around their necks. A little girl squatting behind a rose bush held up a finger to her lips to tell them not to give her away. As she sat there, the rose near her face opened a little wider, stretching its petals to caress her cheek.

Sadie smiled at the little nymph. She felt suddenly lighter and had to fight the urge to giggle herself. Then she felt something touch her fingers and looked over expecting to see that a child had appeared between them, but it was Jimmy. He laced his fingers through hers, a little tentatively. She couldn't help it – she clasped down.

They were both smiling as they stepped out from between the buildings onto a skybridge. Tentacles of green hung down from an arched lattice. The surrounding railing was thick with growth, which obscured the view, so they didn't try to look over the edge. The bridge branched into three separate bridges, each with unique architecture.

"Which way?" Jimmy asked, smiling at her.

Sadie took them right. "We can try the middle one tomorrow," she said, looking forward already to days of exploring this place together.

As they made their winding way deeper into the city, there was a distinct change in the tone of their surroundings. It was gradual, but the corners, sharp edges, and walls turned rounded, gnarled, and free-flowing. By the time Sadie had decided that they were no longer standing in a building, but rather a nymph-altered tree which was very much alive, she began to notice the same feeling she'd had when approaching Ina's place. The nymph magic that infused the wild-flowers behind them morphed into the magic of the deep forest.

Bird songs punctuated the silence, which otherwise felt heavy with stillness, and Sadie was entranced by the warm feeling of the surrounding life. The next bridge was made up of the tightly woven branches of the adjacent trees reaching for each other like long hands, and when they crossed it, they found themselves in a little neighbor-hood. The homes were nest-like in their construction, and the people had mixed reactions to the appearance of outsiders. Some smiled, or raised a hand, but many narrowed their eyes suspiciously.

Jimmy continued to follow Sadie's direction while she followed the feeling of serenity, which only increased the deeper they went. The journey ended when they reached a giant spiral staircase wrapped around the largest tree Sadie had ever seen. Her parents' house could've fit in the interior.

Squeezing Jimmy's hand, she led them down, wanting to save the view from above for last. The railing, like many of the houses, was wrapped in strings of lights, which glowed a gentle yellow. Sadie was curious how they were powered. They looked like the solar lights from home, but there wasn't much sun in here.

As they neared the bottom, engraved images appeared on the trunk. The outer bark had been peeled in places and carved to show elaborate scenes. Paragraphs of text added detail to the tails, but Sadie thought the pictures spoke for themselves. They first showed nymphs working together to construct and grow the city, which had happened hundreds of years prior. Then came the growing commu-nity of nymphs, feeders, and humans living together. Next was a series of experiments to interweave different nymph and feeder abilities.

"Hey, that box is mentioned here," Jimmy said, pulling them to a stop. The little blurb didn't say more than Gabriel had already told her. A succubus and stone nymph pair had constructed the boxes. Still, Sadie traced the text longingly before moving on. The text next to it explained how the bulbs lighting the heart of the city were especially crafted right here, made by fire and earth nymphs and powered by the trees themselves.

Their feet reached the dark soil of the earth and they continued around the base of the tree, continuing to read through the history. They paused simultaneously when they spotted a very different scene. Sadie's eyes darted over it with alarm.

"Why haven't I heard about this?" she asked. "Was it mentioned in school somewhere?"

Jimmy shrugged uncertainly.

"Can I help you?" someone asked from behind them. It was a woman with several fresh scenes involving a man who loved to go down on her. She was formally dressed.

"Yes, um, we're new here. Are we intruding?" Sadie asked.

"The museum is free and open to all. Did you want to hear about the fire?" she asked.

They nodded.

"It was fifteen years ago. There were three of them, humans, who took public credit. They spouted an ideology that nymphs were becoming too powerful. They said they wanted to burn down this whole area. Did you know that Arlington has more nymphs than any other city in the United States? Proportional to its population, that is. And most of them live here in the center. Well, the trio lit a blaze that went up so fast that even the fire nymphs were slow to contain it. All of the houses just above here burned down, including mine. But this tree stayed standing. It was all charred of course, but we were able to heal it over time. For ten years, humans were not allowed in the inner city, but things have opened back up."

She walked them around to the scene immediately following the fire.

"Here we list the names of everyone who helped us rebuild. It was remarkable – the next day, several powerful human feeder families came in to help clean up while we were in mourning. People had died. Many families lost someone. It took a while to heal. But we made new friends during that time."

Sadie traced the name Siphon with her finger.

"Siphon... like that congressman?" she asked.

"That's right," the woman said.

Sadie read over the other names as the woman looked them over.

"Are you moving to the city permanently?" she asked.

"No, just visiting," Jimmy said.

"Well, let me give you some advice anyway. Humans are still a little unwelcome around here." She looked only at Jimmy as she said this. "Not that everyone has the same opinion, but things remain tense. You should be aware. If you're looking for a good wedding spot, I would go elsewhere."

"Oh, we're not together," Sadie said, finally releasing Jimmy's hand, while he asked, "How did you know?"

"That you're human? Well there are human feeders at all four entrances to the inner city, older ones who have learned to pick out humans on sight. An alert went out about your presence. You're welcome to look around, but I wouldn't linger."

Jimmy thanked the woman for the advice before pulling Sadie away from glaring her down. They followed the stairs back up, not talking about what they'd just learned. Sadie's mind was on the violent scene of the fire. Though she forgot about it the instant they stepped onto the large platform toward the top of the tree.

Sadie had never been so high nor seen anything so spectacular in her life. They had a view of the entire city. The midday sun lit up the tops of the buildings and trees, which were too close together to see the streets below, but they had a glimpse of tiny people milling about the train station on the edge of town.

As they gaped out at it, Jimmy put an arm around her waist. It felt familiar, and yet not. Should she discourage them from touching as they used to? She patted her side to make sure her clothing was securely in place. She didn't want to lead him on, but she also didn't want to lose what they had. She resolved to not have any more moments of weakness like she'd had before bed, but to otherwise allow their closeness to stay intact. Afterall, it was the only intimacy they had; she couldn't force it away.

So she rested her head against his shoulder, her curls serving as a barrier between their skin, and enjoyed the moment. He held her tight. And for a few glorious minutes, everything felt right as rain.

A WEEK PASSED LIKE THAT. Their room wasn't exactly cheap, but they couldn't drag themselves away from exploring such a captivating new place. They wandered through the many connecting skybridges, getting lost in the maze of it all, and through the various markets, watching the street dancers and listening to the musicians.

Looking down at the city from a bridge one sunny afternoon, Sadie took Jimmy's hand.

"Thank you," she said. "For coming after me." He looked at her and she met his eyes. "And I'm sorry for leaving you."

Then, true to her promise to herself, she resisted leaning closer. Instead, she dropped her gaze back to the people below, squeezed his hand once and let go of it. Though she'd successfully navigated the line between them, she did wish she could say more. The trouble was finding the words. The truth was that as hard as the situation was, she had been radiant in her contentment since Jimmy had arrived. It felt almost as if they were two people on their honeymoon. Almost. Apart from her sleeping with strangers and him taking a lot of showers. But in that moment on the bridge, she felt completely in love.

At times she thought she had the worst end of the stick, getting to know exactly how they both felt about each other. It was a kind of pleasurable agony watching the love and lust lines grow stronger between them. And it was nothing but a nightly challenge falling asleep next to Jimmy. She was completely sure now that his belief she didn't want him was the only thing keeping things at bay.

Though despite their challenges, their overall happiness during those days seemed mutual. They were so lost in it, in fact, that it was jarring when life brought them back down. They had just stepped into the elevator in their building, ready to collapse into bed, when a couple of men pushed in after them. Instead of looking away like people usually did in such situations, they glared down at her from a few feet away. Sadie was immediately alert – she didn't like this at all. She also didn't care for the images from the men's sex lives. Though it was when one of them spoke to her that the full force of her instincts kicked in.

"Hey succubus, when do I become worthy of your attention?" one of them asked.

And she was right on. Apparently the word had gotten out about her, and to the wrong people. Attempting to avoid conflict, she stepped closer to Jimmy and didn't respond. She felt her friend tense next to her.

Then everything happened at once. One of the men threw a punch at Jimmy while the other one grabbed for her. She saw Jimmy cleanly dodge the punch, while she kicked the second guy full force in the gut. The man stood up and threw himself toward her. She lost track of what was happening with Jimmy, because her guy grabbed her by the hair and placed a bare hand against her face.

The words of Gabriel's scroll came back again. She could defend herself, she knew. There was a very clear reason her kind had never been turned into sex slaves or anything like that. She didn't think too hard about it, trusting her instincts as something deep inside her roared to life. She grabbed the man by the hair and aggressively pulled his lips to hers. Then she reached inside him in all directions. Sadie let her mind flow into every cell in his body and then, all at once, she pulled. It took a heartbeat. He cried out and a second later he was on the floor. She turned to see the second man down with a bloody nose and looked up to see Jimmy with a matching one. The elevator door opened.

Delilah took in the scene as Sadie bent down to feel the man's pulse.

"He's alive," Sadie said, before exiting the elevator.

"Oh my." Delilah said. "What happened here?"

"Sorry ma'am," she replied. "They attacked us. We weren't trying to cause trouble." Her whole body was shaking and she felt like she might throw up.

Delilah came around and stepped into the elevator, crossing her arms. "Don't you say you're sorry, now. This wasn't you. Go on and take care of yourselves." She gestured them to go.

Sadie helped guide Jimmy down the hall, while he kept his head back. Her head was pounding too, however, and she couldn't account for it. Was she having sympathy pains? They went straight to the bathroom and Sadie frantically handed Jimmy tissue before she collapsed against the wall to put her head between her knees.

Jimmy mumbled something that she interpreted as "Shit Sadie, what the hell was that?"

"Don't know," she said, her stomach turning over.

"Neat trick," he said.

A few minutes later, he must have recovered and caught sight of her because his voice came from close by. "You okay?"

"Don't know. Maybe," she said.

"What exactly happened?" he asked.

Sadie looked up at him, testing how she handled moving her head. The nausea seemed to be decreasing.

"He touched my skin. I sucked the life out of him."

"Oh," Jimmy said. "Just the standard life-suck. Well, I went for a punch myself. Thought I'd stick to the classics for today."

Then he dropped his tone and asked again, "Seriously. Are you okay? And I don't just mean physically?"

"Yeah. Or I will be. I'm angry and my head hurts, but at least I know I can do that now."

She looked at his nose, it didn't look broken.

"You held your own," she said.

"Yeah. Impressed?" he asked.

"Only a little," she said. "I've seen you plow a field."

He grinned at her compliment.

"Well. I have half a mind to plow the rest of that man's face, but I think they learned their lesson," he said.

She moved to sit next to him.

"We should probably keep moving," she said. "First thing?"

He agreed.

They sat a while with her head resting on his shoulder, staring at the bathroom floor. Having been forced from their mutual bliss, Sadie felt the weight of the future looming on the horizon. Tomorrow they faced the open road.

Chapter 8

A revelation

They departed the city on foot first thing. The dirt road leading south was large enough for a tractor, but the only traffic they saw all morning was a couple of people on horseback who veered off into the woods shortly after passing them.

"So," Jimmy said after they'd woken up a bit, "we can't afford to just travel forever on our parents' money. What do you think?"

"We need a mid-sized town with enough people for me to feed from," she said.

"And it needs to be friendly for humans and feeders," he said.

"With affordable places to live," she added.

"And we'll probably both need jobs."

She sighed. "I guess we'll have to ask around. But Jimmy, I don't want to end up too far from home. I don't know when or if I'll ever be ready to go back there, and I want to be able to visit easily. If we're going to settle down somewhere, it just needs to be good enough and nearby."

He rubbed her back. "We'll do our best," he said.

Sadie appeased herself with the knowledge that whatever happened, she wouldn't have to do it alone. Then, having finally talked about what they were headed for, she was able to relax.

It was a beautiful sunny day, and they were a bit giddy with freedom as they talked and laughed their way through the woods. They had agreed to enjoy the open road over paying for another train ride. A decision that had made sense that morning, but by mid-afternoon their stomachs were protesting. Sadie was also more than ready to feed.

Shouldn't there have been more along the road? A small town at least? She'd expected they'd run into something after a half day's walk. Just when Sadie began to get nervous about having left the abundance of city life, the sound of music hit them. A few minutes later, they found its source.

Just off the trail, clearly visible through the trees, was a small gathering of people. It appeared to be made up of two families by the way they were connected. There were children running and adults cooking over a fire. Surrounding them was a smattering of tiny houses.

Sadie's stomach churned at the smell of meat slow-roasting over open flame.

One of the people spotted them standing on the edge of the road and gestured for them to join. "Come on in here now! We don't bite!" they called.

Perfect. This was more like it. People stopped what they were doing to greet the strangers. Jimmy shook hands with a few and began explaining their situation. Sadie noted he left out some details and agreed that was wise given the fact they couldn't know how these particular nymphs felt about succubi.

Sadie looked around at each adult, taking in the lay of the land. There were three couples, heavily romantically and sexually involved in pairs, a few older folk, and the rest were children. Two of the adults were likely siblings, given their familial attachment, and there was a small sexual line between two people in separate pairings.

Sadie saw the children as she saw all children since her transition. They had no scenes surrounding them and came only with blue lines connecting them to various adults. She could see their physical selves easily, and noticed they were all dressed in the free-flowing clothing she associated with water nymphs depicted in books. Sure enough, there was the trickling sound of a brook coming from behind the houses. Some of the older children were in their early teens and had started to develop a sexual identity. One of the preteens had exactly one image surrounding him and it was that of a teenage girl, not present from what Sadie could tell.

It was clear that none of the people were potential partners for *her*. Feeling anxious again, she tried to smile as they introduced themselves.

"You must stay for dinner," one of the mothers said.

"And the night, since it'll be too late to keep traveling," added another.

Sadie wasn't sure how to accept the first and decline the second.

"That's very kind," she said. "We'd love to."

A man beckoned them to take a seat by the fire. It was clear the meal was nowhere near ready, and they both looked longingly at the meat.

"Here. Help yourself. Guests are family," someone said, passing them a basket full of bread.

Thanking them, Jimmy asked if the river water was clean to drink.

One of the adults said, "Yes, Cory just went to get some. Here he is now."

Sadie looked up at the person approaching from between the trees and her hope rose. Cory was fully grown, but clearly in the height of late puberty. He was surrounded by sexual imagery without being tied to anyone. When he was introduced to them, his thoughts locked down on Sadie immediately. Relief washed through her.

She was so focused on him, that she'd missed the question he'd just asked her.

"Sorry?" she asked.

"Do you have water bottles?" he repeated.

"Oh! Yes," Sadie said and they both held out their bottles. Cory put his hand above Jimmy's bottle and water poured from his palm. "It's clean. I just collected it and cleansed it on the way back," he explained. When the young man reached over Sadie's bottle his sexual images became hectic, and when he held out his hand to fill it nothing happened. Sadie saw the older person behind him smile.

"Sometimes you just need to collect more. It happens to all of us," the person said.

"Yeah, I'll... be back," he mumbled.

When Cory was out of sight the person over the fire turned to her. "My uncle married a succubus. He always wore gloves, and there was a similar thing in his eyes when meeting new people."

Sadie swallowed.

"We're friendly here. Don't you worry about that. But go easy on my grandson. It'll be his first time, I suspect."

Several of the adults chuckled. Sadie blushed. "No, I..."

"It's okay, girl. You should stay the night. We have a tent for when family visits. We'll set you up by the river. What happens beyond that is none of my business."

"Thank you. We're very grateful," Sadie told them.

A couple hours later and they were all happily eating what Sadie discovered was deer meat and passing around a bottle of red wine. One of the adults had insisted on opening the bottle in light of the presence of guests, and it had the effect of increasing the general merriment.

Cory finished eating and picked up the fiddle. After a few false starts he stopped and apologized for making them listen to him when he was still learning. Once he got going, however, the music was incredible.

Sadie licked her fingers clean and squeezed Jimmy's knee in parting before moving to sit next to Cory. The fiddle screeched a bit as he missed a few notes. After a few more mistakes, he decided to stop and pass the fiddle to his aunt. As the woman began to play, Sadie understood what Cory had meant when he'd said he was a beginner. This woman was something else.

Mesmerized by the music, Sadie lost track of her intentions. When she came back to herself, however, she found Cory's eyes on her. She could feel Jimmy watching her as well. As she struck up a conversation with the former, she was half-distracted by the conversation from the other side of the fire.

Sadie asked Cory how old he was while someone directed at Jimmy, "So boy, tell us what it's like to be courted by a succubus."

"Uh, I just turned eighteen last week," Cory said, while Sadie listened to Jimmy trip over his response, trying to explain they were just friends.

"Ahh, but that's not what you want now is it?" the man chuckled, clearly having drunk enough for the night.

"Leave him alone, Len," his sister said.

Sadie's gaze darted from the woman back to Cory.

"Oh, well, happy birthday," she said.

As the separate conversations continued, Sadie caught glimpses of the way in which Jimmy looked at Cory. She had begun to notice that he seemed to get jealous of certain people. She wished that jealousy was one of the things she could read directly, but she was pretty sure from his body language that she was interpreting him correctly. Sadie hadn't been able to detect any pattern in who Jimmy liked or disliked, but she was sure he did not like her attention on Cory. She wished there was another person to pick from. If there had been, she would have switched just to make it easier on him.

Though on the other hand, she was glad she didn't have the option, since she could tell she would quite like being with Cory. His untried lust was intoxicating. The pictures surrounding him were pretty nondescript, made more of a general feeling, but she did keep catching a glimpse of the same nude and wrinkled photo.

The sun was an hour away from setting when one of the adults said, "We should probably set up the tent. Cory?" He nodded and disappeared into one of the nearby houses. Emerging with a compact tent bag, he went off toward the water.

Sadie looked across the fire at Jimmy. Yep, he didn't like this. Sadie, however, was excited and quite ready to feed by this point. Trying to brush away a creeping feeling of guilt, she smiled at Jimmy as if everything was normal between them. Then she rose from the fire and followed Cory without further explanation to those around her.

She found him spreading out the tent near the edge of the water.

"Is this, uh, good here?" he asked breathily, when he noticed her.

"Do you know I'm a succubus?" she asked.

His eyes went wide. "No. Um... no I didn't know that."

She took off her gloves slowly, not looking away from him.

Sadie experienced again one of those rare moments in which she was perfectly glad to be who she was. *This* was going to be fun. Putting away all the complications with Jimmy, she allowed herself to enjoy the moment.

A half-hour later, Cory was getting dressed to head back to the fire. Sadie decided she could use some clean-up, and told him not to wait up. Heading down to the river, she lay her dirty clothes on a rock and tiptoed across the rocks.

The water was warmer than she had been expecting, but it still sent goosebumps all down her. Her nipples hardened into rocks themselves as she trudged carefully forward. It wasn't particularly deep, but she bent her knees a bit and submerged herself up to her shoulders.

This was a beautiful place. She looked around at the orange glow of sunset bouncing off the trees and water. The soft trickle sound danced through her ears, casting a calm feeling all around her. It smelled both earthy and tangy, and she filled her lungs with the cool, moist air.

She caught a motion out of the corner of her eye and turned back toward the tent. Jimmy was standing on the edge of the shore. She felt so at peace she could only look up at him lovingly, temporarily letting go of any attempts to hide her feelings.

He kicked off his shoes and removed his shirt. The orange glow struck his skin. He pulled open his belt and dropped his pants, kicking them aside. The next thing was a surprise. He pushed off his boxers and stood up. Sadie's heart pounded.

She tried to push away all the images and light and just see his physical self. She'd never seen him like this, and she wanted to drink it in. Thank goodness she'd just fed, or they'd be in trouble. What was going through his head? He stepped into the water and she watched his muscles move and flex as he entered its depths. She found her feet moving almost of their own accord as she walked in his direction. His gaze dropped briefly to her breasts as she rose out of the water.

They met about halfway, the water up to their waists. He stopped walking when they were just outside of arm's reach. Jimmy stretched his arms to either side, splaying his fingers and asked, "What do you think of me, Sadie Hall?"

She could tell he'd had a bit to drink by the slight slur in his speech. She'd never seen him drunk though, and it took her by surprise. As to his question, she had a million answers, none of which would likely make their situation any easier. She thought of saying, *you know exactly what I think of you,* and stepping forward to kiss him. Or perhaps babbling like the brook as she explained what was really going on.

Instead, she looked him up and down slowly and he returned the gesture. She watched his semi-erection stiffen under the water. Then they locked eyes and she decided to at least tell him something truthful. A little honesty was all she felt she could offer in return for this surprise moment of vulnerability.

"I think you're beautiful," she said. As these words passed her lips, she let his full sexual self rush back into her senses. She took in the way he felt and the rush of things he thought and was struck by the full weight and presence of him. A single tear fell from the corner of her eye. She stepped closer. Sadie trusted he would not try to touch her, even in his intoxicated state.

"I think you're perfect," she whispered.

Then she gathered up all her self-control and stepped around him. He didn't turn to watch her walk away, but she did. She watched him wade out a bit further and dive under.

Sadie felt a rising fear for tomorrow. Would they be able to go back to half-pretending he wasn't interested, after that? They'd been tiptoeing around acknowledging that fact, and she felt it was for the best. After the rhythm they'd gotten into last week, Sadie wondered what exactly had brought this on now. Whatever it was, it seemed their situation had just gotten even harder.

JIMMY'S FACE was the first thing Sadie saw the following morning. The tent was hot and humid enough to wake her early, but Jimmy remained deep asleep in his own sleeping bag. Looking at him, she was filled with sadness about the previous night. She hadn't exactly been clear in her signals. This was why she hadn't wanted him to come. She'd almost given in last night. And she was sure that if she allowed herself to touch him, even a little, that she would lose all control. She didn't think she could hold back with him, and then they'd both be in trouble.

One thing was for sure: she couldn't keep holding him so close while turning him away. It was too much for both of them. She vowed to be different with him, starting immediately. This meant she definitely couldn't get caught watching him sleep. Creeping quietly from the tent, she went in search of Cory. Now that she was out of the city, she didn't want to take any more risks on the open road. If she had someone to feed from, she was going to take advantage of it while she could.

Jimmy joined them at breakfast an hour later. Saying hello was uncomfortable, but at least there were people around to add a barrier. The real awkwardness began when they set back out on their own. They both made some effort at small talk, clinging to any topic they could until silently agreeing to finish the trek lost in their own thoughts.

It was late morning when they finally came upon a little town. Farms began to appear around them, sheep and cows casting them wide-eyed glances. When they reached the small, cobbled streets of downtown, Sadie felt as if they'd returned home.

They stopped at a diner to get out of the summer sun for a minute, which was quite sweltering, even for the Pacific Northwest. The place was colorfully lit. Paintings of teddy bears adorned bright yellow walls.

"Cheery place," Jimmy said, after they'd sat down to await their coffees.

"I know, right? Can you imagine being trapped here all day?" Sadie said with a grimace.

"What do you mean? I was thinking of doing my bedroom just like this," he said.

"Ha. I'd like to see you try to bring a girl home to that," she said.

Dangerous topic. Why had she said that?

"Well, I was going to do mine pink with paintings of baby dolls," she added quickly, glancing away. There were two other people in the diner, both sitting at the counter. One of them was buried deep in a newspaper, and the other was completely in love with the waitress, who did not even remotely return the affection. When she looked back at Jimmy, his brow was heavily furrowed.

"Not really," she said, looking at his expression with concern, afraid she hadn't properly changed the subject. "I would do paintings of baby cows."

He continued to frown.

"You know? With their big eyes—"

"Andre Amadi," Jimmy interjected.

"Sorry?"

"That's what she said. Ocean, the water nymph. She told me, right before she died. She said, give it to no one, but Andre Amadi."

"That name mean anything to you?" Sadie asked.

"I went to the library and looked it up," he said. "I did a full search of anyone by that name, but nothing came up. He's not in the system. I forgot to tell you about it. Maybe if we can't open the box, we should be trying to find this man."

"Maybe. But geez Jimmy, where would we even start? It might be a dangerous thing to just go asking around about."

He nodded, but continued to look thoughtful.

They kept traveling around in silence as they made their way further into town, eventually ending up at a duck park. There was a little archway over the ducks with an ornate bench in the center. They waited impatiently for the two teenagers making out on the bench to depart before claiming it as their own.

"Hey," Sadie said, nodding to a man with a newspaper. "That's the same guy from the diner."

"Is it?" Jimmy asked, but the sound was muffled as she pulled off her turtleneck. She suddenly couldn't take the heat anymore. She stripped down to her tank top and removed the gloves. Jimmy looked at her.

"I'll just be careful," she told him, scooting a few inches away. Sadie watched the diner man find a spot on the grass to their right and resume reading.

Glancing back at Jimmy a few minutes later, he was again wearing a look of concerned concentration. She didn't want to ask what he was thinking, but she couldn't ignore the furrowed brow. She cleared her throat to get his attention and looked a wordless question at him.

"I was just thinking about something you said the other day, when you were explaining how you feed." Sadie was nervous to hear where this was going. "And when you talked about how you brought down that guy that attacked you. You said you pulled on something. You pulled something out of him. With the box... you tried to do a similar thing to when you feed." She turned toward him now, curiosity getting the better of her.

"Yeah..." she said, raising her eyebrows.

"Maybe you should try it the other way around," he finished.

"What?" She frowned.

"Don't pull. Push. Right after you feed, try to push it into the box."

Sadie sat bolt upright. *Oh my goodness!* Why hadn't she thought of that sooner? She should do the opposite of what she did when she fed, like Cory probably did with the water. She looked around the park. No one appropriate.

"Let's go!" she said, jumping up and shoving her clothes into the backpack. They wandered through the town looking for someone she could feed from. There weren't many people in general.

The first sign of hope came from someone they found in a bookstore. Sadie and Jimmy were perusing the aisles, pretending to look at books, when Sadie saw the person at the end of their row.

Her jaw dropped at the sight of them. They were more experienced than all the other people she'd been with so far. They radiated confidence and sexual power. Images flashed around them, filled with scenes of passion. Sadie was immediately attracted to them. She hadn't replaced her gloves, so she coughed to get Jimmy's attention and pointed with her eyes.

Jimmy looked at her like she was crazy and leaned in to whisper, "The old woman?"

Sadie looked again at the person, this time trying with great effort to push away everything nonphysical. *Oh, look at that.* She was an old woman. It was hard to hold the rest of it at bay, however, and her full self came rushing back in to fill Sadie's attention. Sadie found she was still attracted to her. Handing Jimmy the backpack, she approached the end of the row.

Sadie attempted small talk, asking the woman if she were the store owner and if she knew of any good places to stay the night. The woman told her she was not the store owner, then directed her toward the only inn in town and went back to reading her book.

Sadie tried again, feeling increasingly nervous in the woman's presence. "What are you reading?"

The woman looked up with just her eyes, then flashed her the cover of a book with a muscular and shirtless man holding the waist of a petite woman with fire coming out of her hands.

"Oh. Is it any good?" Sadie asked, trying to make her voice sound soft and seductive.

"No," the woman said, turning back to her book. At no point during the exchange did the woman give off even the slightest flare of interest in her. Sadie gave up.

The instant they left the bookstore, Jimmy began to laugh out loud.

"I will never buy another comic. From now on, any time I'm looking for entertainment, I'll just go with you to pick up old ladies!" he said.

Sadie pushed him playfully away from her.

She pushed him with her bare hand on his bare arm.

Everything stopped.

Time seemed to slow as she felt every cell in his body respond to her. His heartbeat pulsed in her like it was her own. It felt like fire consuming her, stronger and more intense than she had experienced with anyone else.

She jumped back. Jimmy's eyes were wide, the laughter gone like a distant memory. He tried to cover his erection with a hand, looking around. No one seemed to be watching, but they darted to the side of the building anyway.

"Sorry," she said, looking at the ground to give him some privacy.

"Wow. Is it always like that?" he asked through heavy breathing.

"Um, yeah. More or less," she lied, not wanting him to know how different it actually was with him. But she felt a powerful ache in the core of her, and suddenly, she wanted to feed for more than just opening the box. Jimmy sat down and leaned back against the building, closing his eyes. "I'm gonna need a minute."

A minute turned out to be half an hour. Sadie had melted in the heat bouncing off the bricks by the time Jimmy finally got to his feet. They didn't talk about it.

Sadie took them in the direction of the inn. The old woman had said it could be found in the middle of town, and since the town only had one main road, they followed this easily to a stone building bearing the name The Rabbit's Den.

It was cool and dim inside, and the ground floor was a bar. Walking up to the bartender, she asked who to talk to about the inn.

"That'd be me. Just the two of you?" The bartender looked at her with a slow gaze that took in her whole body. She focused on trying to see the person and found a man not much older than she, fashionably dressed with an attractive face. A line of red began to pass from him to her. He was interested. She wasn't. The images surrounding him were not pleasant. As she looked more closely at them, she ruled him out completely. Moreover, the red coming from him was an off color; it looked burnt and crusty. Just looking at him left a sour taste in her mouth.

She stumbled over her response, but Jimmy came to the rescue. "Yeah, the two of us."

"How many nights?" the man asked.

"Don't know yet, how about—" Jimmy started to say.

"Just the one," Sadie cut him off.

She glared at the bartender's back as he opened a cabinet next to the liquor and extracted a key.

"Room 11, but you can't go in there yet. Still needs cleaning," the man said.

Jimmy picked up the key and pocketed it. "What time is check-in?" he asked.

"Don't know. Give it a couple hours."

They ordered some drinks and Sadie directed them to the booth furthest from the bar. Jimmy sat down across from her. "Wow, he really got your tongue. It looks like we found someone to help open that box." He sounded a little disappointed and turned to look again at the bartender with a frown.

"No," Sadie said quietly.

Jimmy snapped his attention back to her. "Really? I don't understand. Earlier you were settling for an old woman and now you don't want *that guy*. Not that you should. He's all funny-looking with his perfectly symmetrical face and well-styled hair." He smiled, suddenly in a better mood.

"*You* can have him," Sadie said. "Actually, I take that back. You should stay away from that one. He's trouble."

"How do you know? I don't understand how you've been choosing people." He frowned. They were back in dangerous territory, and Sadie wanted to change the subject, but she couldn't think of a quick way out of it.

"When I look at people, I just know some things. I can tell if we're compatible or not. That's how I decide."

"Oh." Jimmy looked suddenly somber. His eyes travelled back and forth over the tabletop as he took in this news. "Oh, I see."

She understood. He was coming to the conclusion that she'd rejected him because they weren't compatible. It hurt her to have him think this, but as she watched the emotion pass through him, she realized it might have been the best thing she could've done to ease their current tension. He looked back into her face with an expression of acceptance.

"Okay," he said with a nod of finality. She felt she'd finally given him a satisfactory answer to explain what was going on between them. Even though this particular consequence to her words had been an accident. She also felt she'd just unintentionally told the biggest lie of her life. Sadie put back on her gloves, reached across the table, and squeezed his hand. She trusted herself to do this. She didn't trust herself to speak, knowing she wouldn't be able to resist telling him the truth. He squeezed back.

And from there, things gradually seemed to relax between them.

Sadie took a sip of her drink and glanced around the room before nearly choking mid-swallow. "Jimmy. Don't look, but there he is again."

"Who?"

"The man from the diner and the park. He's following us," she hissed.

"This is a small town, Sadie. And if he's staying at the inn, he's an out-of-towner too. It's not strange we'd run into each other at the one diner and one park."

"But he keeps appearing right after we do. I tell you, he's on our trail."

"On our trail? What are we, spies?" His grin looked more like his old self than she'd seen in days.

She leaned forward conspiratorially. "Don't reveal our identity so loudly. You'll make it easy on him."

Looking back at the stalker, she noticed someone new had also just walked in.

"Gotcha," Sadie said. Throwing a last look at Jimmy, she handed him the backpack and got to her feet. An hour later, Sadie was ready to once again try her hands at opening the mystery box.

Chapter 9

A stranger

Jimmy kept on a good face all the way to the shower. Well, at least now he knew. He climbed under the warm water. He had just been misinterpreting her behavior. And it wasn't anything he had done or anything else about him. She wasn't on the fence about how she felt. They just weren't right for each other. He scrubbed soap vigorously over his skin, trying to wash it all away.

This wasn't a big deal. It didn't mean that much. They were still best friends. They were intimate and caring and would always be there for each other. All they were really talking about was sex. Just one little thing. He rubbed at his face, washing away the emotion.

He pictured that man Cory, who looked so like himself, lying naked with Sadie by that beautiful brook. They just weren't compatible. That was the end of it. Who knew why she wanted that stranger more than him? In fact, who knew why he'd always wanted her more than anyone else. There were other women in the world. He'd get over it.

A half-hour later, and he'd succeeded in lecturing himself into calm.

Jimmy stepped out of the shower feeling slightly less clean than when he'd stepped in. Clearing a spot in the mirror, he looked himself up and down. She had told him he was perfect. Looking back, it seemed she had been doing her best all along to tell him she cared, despite not wanting more. He'd just misread her, caught up as he was in his own desire. What he needed to do now was make sure not to ruin their friendship. He would step out of that bathroom and begin anew. Jimmy smiled into the mirror, testing out the feel of it.

He heard the door click open. Emerging from the bathroom, he caught sight of Sadie with her hair all askew.

"Hey!" he said with a little too much gusto. "Went well? You know I really can't keep wearing the same dirty clothes. Getting a few more shirts is becoming high-priority."

"I didn't want to say anything," she said, pretending to wave away the air in front of her face. He laughed, also a tad unnaturally, and extracted the box. They stared down at the thing.

"Here goes nothing." Sadie put her hands in the lid. It took the length of one slow breath for it to pop open. Her eyes shot wide.

"Ha! Jimmy. You're a genius!"

She lifted the top carefully and they leaned in to look at the contents.

"Huh," Sadie said, reaching in to extract the leatherbound book, while Jimmy pulled out the only other object. It was some kind of button. Cased in protective glass, it looked like you could turn the little ring inside, currently set at *off*.

"Huh," Jimmy said, mimicking Sadie.

The glass had a metal latch outside that could be turned and then pushed inward, and all that just to remove the lid and get to the switch inside. The motion had to be very intentional. Clearly, the button wasn't meant to be accidentally pressed.

They turned their attention to the book as Sadie flipped open the first page.

"Maybe this explains," she said.

He watched her read a few lines. Looking even more confused, she flipped forward and read a few more lines from the middle. She snapped it shut and stared at him with her mouth hanging open.

"It's a diary," she said.

"Can't be. A woman died for this," he said.

"Maybe she died for the button. Or maybe the book contains a code," she said.

"Can I?" he asked.

She passed him the book. It was a beautiful dark red leather. The binding was worn, but in better shape than the pages. Opening it carefully, he flipped through and read a few snippets.

"It's the diary of a succubus, Sadie."

"Well... it *is* in the box of a succubus. What a coincidence though. That this would all fall into my hands."

"Yeah. Maybe," he said. "I mean, she was told to deliver it right next to your house."

"True. And then Gabriel showed up a few days later. Was it supposed to go to him you think? Maybe he wasn't there for me at all. It was just sheer luck he was there when I needed him. Wait no, that doesn't sit. He told me that he had a knack for spotting unturned succubi, and I believe him. He assembled all those people for me. He knew for months that my transition was coming."

Jimmy started to feel a cold creep up his spine.

"I have a number for him," Sadie added.

He didn't like where this was going. "But we can't know for sure. What if we tell him and he turns out to be the bad guy?" Jimmy said.

"Bad guy? What's a bad guy? That's a little simplistic, don't you think?" she said.

"Fine, you're right. But we still don't know for sure. Ocean died to get this into the right hands."

"And how do we know *she* wasn't the *bad guy*?" Sadie asked. Her shackles were raised. Gabriel seemed to bring out the worst in their communication.

"You're right." He raised his hands in surrender and got off the bed, feeling restless.

"Do you want to go get dinner?" he asked.

"No." Sadie flipped open the diary. "I think I want to read for a bit."

"Want me to bring you something?"

"No. Not hungry," she said, her eyes already traveling over the words. "Thanks," she added, just before he disappeared, looking up in time to catch his eye. He nodded, then went out to eat alone.

August 3rd 1920

WELCOME, my dearest diary. And don't go acting for a moment like you believe yourself to be something else. Though I had planned to use you toward my education, I ran rather abruptly out of space and was forced to commandeer your pages for this purpose. After all, is it not the purpose of a thing which defines it? And since you will be serving me in this capacity, you must tie yourself to those of your kind which came before, despite your rather superior leather binding and thick, creamy pages.

Now if you'll recall, I was just telling you about the affable Dr. Bronze. A man of such fortune, both in wealth and looks, could surely pick from among any of the succubi families, though only four of them have available young daughters at this time, but two nights past, as I was reading to Nan, he came by to speak to my father! I'm sure he favors me! He looked rather flustered when I greeted him in the hallway, the way young men who have turned do in front of feminine beauty. So I made sure to smile most appealingly, and then he ducked his head, and disappeared into my father's study.

And this brings me to the most lamentable truth. The confession of my deepest hope and fear. No self-respecting succubus would select his wife before she has turned. After all, isn't there the chance that, mercy save me, I never do so? And I fear most fervently that if I do not turn soon, his affections will move on to that girl of whom we do not speak. And I couldn't bear such a thing! I could never hold up my poor, rejected head long enough to pass her by on the street. Nor would I be able to avoid going out in public if with no husband and no estate I

had to do all my own shopping, or be forced to marry a less noble suitor.

Lust spare me from this gloomy future, as I would surely not be cut out for a life in the shadows. After all, am I not radiant in all my physical splendor? Do I not please my family and all those who ask after me? Though I do apologize here for my vanity. It is only that I want no one else! Please let me turn in time to be swept up by the kindly, the venerable, the sophisticated Dr. Bronze. For now that my heart is set on it, I can imagine no other future, and would surely wither if such a one were forced upon me.

SADIE SNAPPED SHUT the leatherbound book. A woman had died for this? It must be a code book. Would this Andre Amadi know what it all meant, or were the contents of the box a misunderstanding? Sadie replaced the diary and button back in the box and resealed the lid. Out of all the things she had been expecting to emerge from this unwanted gift, this certainly had not been on the list.

JIMMY SAT AT THE BAR. He was there only a minute when the man from the diner moved to sit next to him. The man was several years older than he, with fair hair and pale skin, which left the impression he spent most of his time indoors.

The man smiled at him and Jimmy laughed inside, wishing Sadie was here to see their stalker initiating contact. He was sure it would just add fuel to the fire that was her theory.

"Alec," the man introduced himself, leaning in for a firm handshake. They made small talk. It was a welcome distraction. Alec told him that his people owned a casino in Seattle and that he was just taking a break to get some country air.

"Though," Alec told him, "I'm not tied to the casino world. Not really my thing, feeding off humans hoping to get richer while actually getting poorer. It seems an empty kinda longing."

This man sounded like a siren if he fed off unrequited desires. It was strange that he would share this information with a stranger in a small town. Jimmy felt a suspicion creep up his spine as the man asked, "Your friend you're with, you sharing a room?"

"My friend? Um yes. We're together. In a room." Not liking where this might be headed, Jimmy looked at the man straight on, crossing his arms high on his chest. "You know... she thought earlier that you might be following us."

"Clever then. I was following you." The man returned the posture, but added a smile. "And let's face it, you two aren't *really* together. But you're traveling together, sharing a room, in each other's space all the time. It's wonderful really. Don't think I've seen anything I've wanted more."

"I'm not following." Jimmy turned away, but continued to stare at the man through the mirror behind the liquor. His response was a lie. Jimmy knew exactly what was happening.

"All's I want is to stay near you. Physical closeness, s'all I need. Your friend seemed wary of me, but I mean no harm. What d'you think, can you convince her to let me travel with you?" the stranger asked.

"No. We'd rather be alone," Jimmy said.

"I'll pay you. And you don't have to tell her the reason. Just say we hit it off at the bar. And I'll be joining you on the road."

"You'll – pay me? I don't understand. I thought sirens could feed easily. Aren't there loads of people who want something they can't have?"

"Hmm, yes. But I got high tastes, and I'm not likely to find anything as good as what you two have going on." The man winked. This irritated Jimmy.

"I'm glad my pain is so enjoyable for you," he mumbled.

Alec put a hand on Jimmy's shoulder to draw his attention. His eyes were alight with excitement.

"It is. And I think you should be more grateful for it. Better to feel something than nothing, no? Longing is a powerful thing. You're a lucky man." Jimmy shook his hand away. The man had some nerve.

Jimmy got to his feet, but Alec's hands caught his attention in the corner of his eye. He was counting out hundred-dollar bills; three of them. Alec held them out between two fingers. Jimmy wouldn't play the fool. They needed money, and this stranger was asking for nothing.

"How close?" Jimmy asked.

"Within spitting distance. I'd be happy with the room next to yours for now."

Jimmy half-nodded, not quite ready to commit yet. He looked the cash over one more time before deciding.

"On one condition." He stepped closer to lower his voice slightly. "You never tell Sadie you're traveling with us just to feed off me and my... feelings."

"Deal," Alec said with a grin.

The following morning found the three of them together at a table in the bar.

"Jimmy says you're looking for a good place to settle a while. Thought about Seattle? I'd show you around. S'long as you're willing to take your time getting there. I'm still on vacation. Don't really wanna return before Monday."

Sadie studied the stranger from across the breakfast spread.

"If you're not in any hurry, we could make our way on foot," Alec added.

Sadie wasn't sure where this guy had come from, but she didn't trust him.

"He wasn't following us. It was just a coincidence. He seemed like an alright guy just looking for traveling companions," Jimmy had told her before he'd gestured Alec over.

In response to Alec's suggestion to head to Seattle on foot together, Jimmy looked a question at Sadie. She directed her response at Jimmy, turning slightly away from the stranger. "The train is faster, but more expensive. I guess it'd be okay if we took a few days."

"Excellent," Alec said. "I have a tent should hold all of us. I left home planning for a little adventure. Don't intend to return before getting one. It was lucky for me to find such a friend to travel with."

He gestured to Jimmy. Sadie looked at her friend with narrowed eyes.

Though he was smiling, he clearly didn't feel about this man the way Alec seemed to imply he should. And strangely, the man wasn't sending any of the green light of friendship toward Jimmy that she would expect to see if they had hit it off. Sadie would play along for now, but something was going on.

They left the tavern an hour later, the three of them, walking in silence. The town had several dirt roads heading away from it. They took the one that put the sun on their backs. As the buildings disappeared behind them, they again found themselves on a small trail surrounded by woods. Alec pulled up next to Sadie and struck up a conversation while Jimmy wandered on ahead.

Sadie, wanting to avoid giving the man too much information about her home, directed questions back at him. "So what do you do when you're not wandering the countryside?" she asked.

"Family runs a popular casino. Had it for generations," he said.

"And you work there?"

"Yep. It suits us well enough. Sirens do well in the gambling biz. But... it bores me. Pays the bills though. But for me... seeking out star-crossed lovers is my preferred pastime." He winked.

Sadie stumbled.

"Never actually met a succubus though. Feels like I won the lottery."

"How did you know?" she choked.

"My people are sirens. We grow up hearing about you. We appreciate the way your kind seems to always have a following of unrequited lust. You are clearly brand new since—"

"Oh shit. You *were* following us!" She cut him off.

"True story."

"Does Jimmy know?" she asked.

"Not exactly. Just convinced him I wanted some traveling companions. He was nice enough to do a guy a favor."

Sadie relaxed. Of course. It all made sense now.

"Can you do me a favor?" she asked the stranger.

"Anything," he said.

"Don't tell Jimmy why you're with us," she said.

He grinned.

"Deal."

~

AFTER THAT CONVERSATION, Sadie lightened considerably, her arms swung wide at her sides, and she smiled as they talked in earnest. She felt the bounce of excitement at this shared adventure with another human feeder.

"You know, Jimmy's not following me because I'm a succubus. We grew up together. We've always been close. And he's been there for me through all of this. My Becoming—"

"Really? He was in the room for that? Gods. Wouldn't I give my grandma's left tit for the chance to have been a fly on that wall."

Sadie pushed him lightly away from her, but her smile only grew. "Don't be insensitive. It was the most intense moment of my life, and I'm sure it wasn't an easy position for Jimmy to be in. I didn't know at the time how he felt or what would happen. If I had – I don't know. Maybe I wouldn't have asked him to stay."

"You really think you did wrong? S'nothing bad about wanting something. This is how it's supposed to work. I think you should be happy."

"Well I don't know about *supposed to*, but you're right. Maybe being a feeder isn't so bad." She paused to think for a minute before continuing, "Except for the fact I can't touch Jimmy, and the fact my hometown hated me enough that I had to leave."

Alec patted her shoulder. "The humans are too caught in their own fear to show us proper respect. We've all had a run-in. You're not alone."

Sadie was glad to hear it. "You have a lot of sirens in your family?" she asked.

"Most of my family is siren. Haven't mixed too much with humans, so it's rare when one of us turns out to be one. Which we shed no tears over. We haven't exactly had the best of luck with humans. 'Cept as customers of course."

"Oh?" Sadie encouraged.

"Humans attack the casino, time-to-time. And the human-run casino in town has never been hit. It's like they're trying to drive us out of town, just like as happened to you."

"I'm sorry." Her voice came out in genuine compassion.

"That's why we've got to stick together, huh?" Their walk slowed as they turned to look at each other and she watched herself send out a tiny thread of green light.

"Are there a lot of human feeders in Seattle?" she asked.

"Oh sure. Tons," he said.

"And humans?"

"There are a lot of humans everywhere," he said.

"Do you think Jimmy and I would fit in there? I need a place I can feed and we want to stay together. Somewhere we both feel comfortable."

"S'only one way to know. But yeah, I think you'd do just fine. Specially if you hung around with me," he said. She smiled, relaxing at this new plan.

Around midday they passed a sunny glade that caught all their attention at once. It looked inviting in its beauty and they wordlessly agreed to pull over for lunch. The grass looked velvety and wild, while rays of light filtered through a haze of pollen and dust. The effect was ethereal. Strangely, despite the direct sunlight, the clearing was a perfect lukewarm temperature. Sadie could find no reason for this to be the case on such a hot day. There wasn't even a breeze to account for it, but the world there seemed held in stillness.

They passed around the bread and cheese in silence, each seeming lost in their own thoughts. When Alec told them he was going to take a short nap, Jimmy agreed that sounded like a nice idea. Hours later, no one had yet moved from their initial chosen locations, and Sadie decided to go from staring at the sky in contemplation to reading a bit more of the diary.

She knew they should get back on the road, but it was just so comfortable to lie in this particular field. It seemed made for long hours of drowsy reverie.

Riley Kade

Pulling out the diary, she stared at the beautiful cover for a long time before opening it.

August 11th 1920

Dearest secret holder,

It has come to my attention that most people in general, but young men in particular, are rather foolish when it comes to the matters of love and lust. My brother has confessed to my parents his intentions to steal the priest's daughter, despite the unfortunate fact she is to be married in two days. When asked what earthly reason he could have for being so ridiculous as to stir up unnecessary trouble where a tenuous peace has been struck, he simply declared that he wanted her and walked out. Such incidents make me dread the day when I feel such emotions. Though my future will only be secured by the Becoming, I can't see it as beneficial in general to experience such irrational compulsions.

If my adolescent sanity is to be fleeting, I must seize it for all it is worth and cement my future now. For after I turn who knows what horrid choices I might make against my better judgement. Oh how I fear my own mind! Is there anything more dangerous than desire? I only hope I can recall these words here. Remember who you are! For no temporary lust can compete with long term happiness.

August 14th 1920

Oh dear. The most dreadful thing has happened. Dr. Bronze was scheduled to join us for supper, proving he has not yet given up on me. I was going to wear my finest red dress, and I had Charles drive me into town to get my hair done up finely.

As Dr. Bronze has long since turned, he obviously can be affected by such things, and I plan to use all that is available to me. I'd spent the previous three days reading newspapers from all over the country as I know the doctor is always impressed by my mother's knowledge of current events.

Anyway, the supper had to be cancelled! Those humans tore down the fence and released all the hens. Then they nearly broke into the cellar. There are still giant axe marks where they tried to chop their way in. Father only just repaired that door! It couldn't have been worse timing. Who is to say if the doctor will persist through all these ill-omens.

AUGUST 20th 1920

IT HAPPENED. I am finally a woman in full. I need not recall the details here as I will never, in all the rest of my days, forget a single piece of it. Mother is ecstatic. She recognized the symptoms immediately and began making preparations for the ball. To think, just ten days past I was miserable in my uncertainty, and now tomorrow I will get to enter society in the most glorious way imaginable, since you know Mother always outdoes herself.

Oh, but everything is so remarkably strange now.

Dr. Bronze is entirely in love with my mother. Which, I now realize as I write this, everyone must have known all along. But since she does not return the sentiment, this development seems unlikely to affect my own prospects. It has been a most peculiar experience, discovering the secret lives of everyone around me.

We had the Maddoxes over for tea a few days ago. Thomas is perfectly infatuated with me and has been for years. The things I've seen in his head! The scenes would have made me blush a month ago. Though I see no reason to entertain the notion of lavishing my affections on someone who cannot feed me, unless they are my husband of course. Only, and this I tell only to you... I apparently return the sentiment! And I wish with all my soul that I did not. Thomas is such an inappropriate choice.

Also, Mother evidently disapproves. Thomas walked in the door, I took one look at him, and she promptly rearranged the seating to place us as far from each other as possible. Mrs. Maddox was astounded at the strange request to vary our usual places, but at the scolding look Mother gave me, there was no doubt in my mind as to the reason. Though I do not see how I can help my emotions. Father says that one can sometimes change such connections through persistent rejection of them. I must trust his judgement on the matter, however, as I cannot possibly imagine it myself.

Though he did seem to disapprove mostly on my mother's behalf, because when he called me to his study to ask how my education was progressing, he casually mentioned that Thomas had taken a room in town for a few days. Then he winked at me. Thank the heavens I have two parents! Though I know my mother is right, she usually is, and I promise to abide her wishes after I have one night with Thomas. I will not fall into the trap of behaving as my ridiculous brother has done.

SADIE FOUND it a pleasure to get to read the diary of a succubus. At least here was a woman she could relate to. Maybe it would even help her through her situation with Jimmy. Though her stomach clenched as she read the next words.

AUGUST 27th 1920

NOT IN ALL THE finest prose from all the languages of the world can words be found to describe my night and a day with Thomas. I was loath to return home too quickly and made brother cover for me, which he did in exchange for a portion of my future wealth as we both know I am more likely to find myself a secure future. I shall have to ensure the need for a reciprocal favor, since I have no desire to share a penny with that man.

Regrettably, Mother will still be able to see it on me when she returns home and it will not be so easy to construct a similar rendezvous in the future. If only we could pause time and spend one lifetime in each other's arms before this next one begins.

SADIE PUT the book down with a sigh. She, too, wished for such a thing. Rolling closer to Jimmy's sleeping form, she watched him with longing. For once, he wasn't thinking about her and his quiet dreams only added to her tranquility. She put a hand absently on his chest to feel the pleasant drum of his heart, and a minute later, sleep claimed her.

Chapter 10

A temptation

Sadie blinked her eyes open in the meek sunlight, finding Jimmy on his back in front of her. As she watched his chest rise and fall, Alec shifted position, pushing Jimmy on his side and much too close to her. She shifted back but still the movement brought Jimmy out of his slumber.

Blinking the sleep away, they locked eyes, their faces a foot apart. Jimmy's gaze sharpened as he took in her expression. She wasn't sure what he saw as she was too busy looking from his eyes to his lips and back again. She needed to be closer to him. Her body called for it like an unstoppable force. There was a hum of resistance in her thoughts, a whisper of "shoulds" and "shouldn'ts" but she managed to suppress it easily.

Against her better judgement, she relaxed her weight forward; reaching her safely gloved hand to caress the side of his thumb. Jimmy raised his eyebrows at the gesture. Trying to wordlessly communicate what she wanted, she made a show of securing her clothing. She pulled her hair around to cover the side of her face and looked at the curve of his shoulder.

Understanding what she was after, he opened his posture to allow her to move in. Sadie rested her head against his chest and her hand against his heart. She pulled one leg up over his thighs and pressed herself tightly against him.

Had they really cuddled like this in the past? She couldn't remember her heart ever beating so fast or his body feeling so warm back when they used to do this while stargazing.

She knew she shouldn't, but she arched her back slightly, reveling in the feeling of the friction between her legs. She was obviously hungry and having him so close to her was predictable trouble, and yet she couldn't seem to care.

Sadie was playing with fire, and yet she seemed to have no control over her thoughts. Not even the presence of a stranger lying so near to them was a deterrent. She found his hand and put it on her thigh as she arched into him a second time. He was still as a rock. She couldn't even detect him breathing, though the pace of his heartbeat matched her own. She could feel his desire, but it too seemed frozen, like it had been tightly bound and stored someplace deep and safe inside him.

She should leave it there she knew, but instead she took his hand and slid it up to grip the side of her ass. A dam broke. His heartbeat skyrocketed along with her own as the red light that always connected them grew strong and thick. He gripped her against him and a second later, she began to move in a steady rhythm against his hip. The sensation of pleasure exploded through her, mingling with her emotions in a way which was wholly new. Her desire was immediately intensified by the sight of the growing bulge in Jimmy's pants and the pulsating red light flowing from him. She desperately wanted to lift her chin and kiss him; to surrender completely to the moment before she could question it.

Clenching her fist against his chest to keep herself from something she might regret, she inhaled the sweet smell of his sweat mixed with the scent of the precum glistening through his pants. Her thighs felt weak against the force of her desire. She gasped audibly when he gripped her tighter, exaggerating her movement. Gradually, she let him take the lead, letting herself be moved by his firm hold on her backside.

They had both begun to pant. Though the motion was small, it felt like the whole world was rocking with them. She felt her mind was dissolving in the ecstasy of the moment. The only clear thought was that she wanted more. More of him wanting her. More of him holding her. More of her own rapidly building pleasure.

Sadie got all of those things as she built quickly to climax. It took no more than a few breaths before it crashed into her without warning. She spasmed against him as they both stopped breathing.

Wet heat spread between her legs. Jimmy gripped her tightly for a minute before taking in a staggering breath and relaxing his muscles the tiniest fraction. Her heart continued to race at the same pace, while he loosened his grip on her to run the tips of his fingers gently from her hip bone down through the groove of her ass.

He had never touched her like that before. The soft exploration somehow felt even more erotic than what had just happened. She clenched her thigh around him once before forcing her muscles to relax, but the tension in her body only barely quieted. She reveled in her own stickiness as she stared at the damp spot in Jimmy's pants, now stretched to the limit over his own arousal.

She decided she was going to wrap her mouth around that hard mound and taste that most intimate part of him. She could both feel and see his readiness; it rolled off him in waves, consuming all her senses. She took that moment to look up into his face; suddenly wanting desperately to see his eyes. His warm brown eyes were full of love and painful desire. She imagined the look on her face was the same. Her face screwed up; her lips parted; so ready to feel his tongue against hers.

Then something shifted. She couldn't know what he saw in that moment, but there was a sudden and disappointing change in his mood. He slowly withdrew some of his intense emotion; all the while continuing to search her face. He looked... concerned? She thought she saw concern, then sadness, but when a look of fear appeared, there was no mistaking it.

Confused, she looked down at his erection. It hadn't changed. She looked to his face as she moved to touch him. He stopped her quickly with a hand over hers. They swallowed simultaneously, sorting through each other's reactions. She pushed off his chest to prop herself up and look at him, searching for something to say. Alec took that moment to stop pretending to sleep through all of this and loped off through the tall grass.

Jimmy still had a hand over hers when he said, "You haven't fed." His tone was a mix of surprise and resignation.

"No," she agreed guiltily. His sudden rise to a sitting position pushed her away.

"We shouldn't have done that," he said.

Though she knew she would've agreed with that sentiment yesterday, all of her reasons for keeping them apart seemed suddenly silly.

"No, it's fine," she panted, inching closer. "It's what I want." She tried to reach for his hand, but he moved further away. "It's what you want too," she said, looking pointedly at him.

He wrapped his fist over the erection and closed his eyes. Taking a deep breath, he shook his head. "No. Not like this. This... isn't what you want. It's not what you wanted yesterday. You're just hungry, Sadie." He sounded on the edge of anger and took another steadying breath before adding, "We shouldn't have stayed here. We need to get moving. Now." He stood up, adjusted himself and disappeared in the tall grass nearby.

Sadie's head cleared a bit the second he was out of sight. He was absolutely right. They needed to hit the road. This had been a disaster. She jumped up, searching for the sun. It was in the wrong place. It was – *oh my god.* They'd stayed here all night! It was the next morning.

She hadn't fed at all yesterday and had slept next to the person she wanted most in the world. No wonder she was out of her mind. And now she'd really made a mess with Jimmy. She needed to pull herself together; think rationally.

She stumbled off through the tall grass to relieve her bladder. As she was making her way back, though, a feeling hit her. It was one she had felt a few times while traveling with Jimmy, only this time it was filled with the very real memory of what had just happened between them. Somewhere to her left, Jimmy was thinking of her. And touching himself. She could always feel it a little when he did that, even though she couldn't see him.

Often, he would be in the shower, and she would be struck by erotic images of herself or of them together, accompanied by the feeling of his pleasure. The experience wasn't like feeding, it didn't make her feel fulfilled. It was exactly the opposite. It opened an unquenchable well of longing. And in that particular moment, it brought her to her knees.

She didn't see the ground in front of her face, or notice her hands gripping the grass below her, all she could see was her own naked body, her hazel eyes. All she could feel was the sensation of running a hand over her hip and ass. All she could smell was the scent of her hair as Jimmy experienced it.

The sensations built to a climax. Sadie begged for it to end; she didn't think she could take much more when she was already so hungry. And at the same time, she wanted it to go on forever. Jimmy's pleasure and thoughts of her seemed to live in the intersection of heaven and hell. Her mind went blank with his, as somewhere nearby, hidden by tall grass, Jimmy spasmed into his own hand.

Sadie opened her eyes. Her breathing was ragged and her whole body ached. She pushed herself back to her feet, but had to bend over and wait for the pounding in her head to let up before she could stand upright. Slowly, she began to walk.

Alec emerged behind her as she caught Jimmy's eyes from across the field. They both flushed and looked away. What had she been thinking? Getting trapped with no one to feed from! Making things ten times more complicated for them just when she'd finally found a way to put the tension to rest behind her accidental lie that they weren't compatible.

They gathered their bags quickly and fought their way back to the road. The tall grass that had been so cooperative on the way in, seemed to fight them as they waded back through it. Off to their left, Sadie heard the lightest trace of voices wafting in on the wind. She squinted at the grass domes on the other end of the field.

"Nymphs?" Jimmy asked.

"Well, that explains some things," Alec said.

"What do you mean?" Sadie asked.

"Nymphs can imbue places with their affinity," Jimmy said, as if just now working something out.

"Yeah, and if their affinity is a sunny glade, I guess the instinct to lie around in it is going to be strong." He laughed. "Damn. What a night. I for one feel great." He grinned at Sadie, who blushed and dropped her gaze. Afraid to look directly at Jimmy, she pushed onward through the grass.

Emerging on the wide trail felt like waking from a dream she hadn't been aware she was having. The temperature went up ten degrees at the same time the sound of bird chatter hit her ears. Reality sunk in harder than it had all morning.

They fell into silence, while Sadie and Jimmy picked up yesterday's path with determined steps. Alec bounced along next to them, occasionally attempting small talk, until he grew bored and sped up to walk on ahead.

After hours of awkward trudging, Jimmy asked, "So... how long, uh, can you go without feeding exactly?"

Afraid to talk about this, Sadie stalled by meticulously adjusting her backpack straps. The truth was, she didn't have any idea. She'd read something about it in the scroll, but the range seemed to vary drastically from person to person. There had been one account of a man teaching himself to feed only once a week. Allegedly his body had adjusted, but it was also reported that all his hair fell out and his fingernails stopped growing.

"Maybe up to a week," she said, trying to sound confident. Though her nauseous stomach and shaking hands called liar. Sadie could tell from Jimmy's body language at the edge of her vision that there was more he wanted to ask. Several minutes passed, however, before he followed up.

"And... are there ways to stall for time? Are there *things* that help I mean?" He tightened the pack's strap around his waist.

"This morning...?" he went on.

"Made it worse," she said. "Skin contact is the only way. Anything else just makes me... hungrier." They were both determinedly looking forward. Silence.

"Well, if we keep moving we'll find you someone soon," he said, as if confident statements were the source of reality.

JIMMY EVENTUALLY DROPPED BACK, letting Sadie and Alec walk together ahead. He stayed intentionally out of mind some fifty feet behind them. Walking next to Sadie, he had been craving a minute alone with his thoughts, but now he found himself regretting that desire. The memory of that morning rushed back to the surface like liquid heat to all his senses. That had been... unexpected. He should have understood right away what was happening. He'd let himself get swept up in the excitement of the moment. Clearly, he hadn't been thinking straight.

Now his emotions were a mess of guilt and elation. None of his previous fantasizing about being with Sadie could have prepared him for the reality; her attention and desire focused solely on him. And she had wanted to keep going. Things could have gone so much further if he'd let them. If he hadn't realized what was happening. But a hollowness followed this thought. It wasn't what she really wanted. The memory was soured by the flavor of guilt at having enjoyed it at all when clearly she had been in a vulnerable position. He resolved to never let such a thing happen again. He was going to make sure she was safe from doing anything she didn't want to do, even if it meant keeping her away from himself.

Several hours passed with them alone on the trail, and after a brief pause for lunch, they regrouped to discuss their plan.

"Maybe we should head straight to Seattle? I don't think there's too many people on this road," Jimmy said.

"Nah. There's plenty of little pockets this way. Don't worry. They'll show soon. This is farming country coming up," Alec said.

Sadie was looking at him intently, but he couldn't tell who she agreed with.

"What do think? Should we keep going this way?" he said to her unreadable expression.

"What? Oh yeah. Yeah. Let's keep going," she said and turned to face the path.

Night came. They couldn't prevent it. Eventually, the sun was setting and they had no other choice but to set up camp. The clouds overhead, which had sprinkled on them a few times during the day, threatened to drench them in the night. Unfortunately, Jimmy's idea to sleep outside the tent shrunk under the weight of the sky cover. He knew how quickly the weather could change.

Alec took the middle. He was also the only one who seemed to sleep. Sadie appeared to be awake most of the night. Her breathing never took on that deep, natural sound of slumber, and she tossed every five minutes. Jimmy was too concerned about her to rest much, even if he trusted it was safe to do so. For some reason, he was worried she'd just get up in the night and wander off. Perhaps it was the out-of-focus expression she had worn most of the afternoon. Occasionally her gaze would sharpen suddenly on him, but then it would go soft again. Her behavior was unpredictable and it had him on edge. He just hoped they found someone first thing.

Jimmy woke from his half-sleep to the sight of Alec unzipping the tent. It was really a two-person tent, and they were all too close for him and Sadie to be left alone. The light of day was bright, in spite of the steady rain coming down. And despite his restless slumber, Jimmy was suddenly wide awake. Sitting up in a panic, he darted a look at Sadie. She was finally fast asleep. He hurriedly pulled on some more layers and shoes and followed Alec out.

After relieving themselves, the men regrouped under the tree serving as shelter for the tent.

"You shouldn't leave us alone like that," Jimmy said brusquely.

Alec shrugged. "You were both hard asleep."

Jimmy sipped some water and forced himself to calm.

"I'm just worried about what's going to happen. Things seem to be getting worse quickly. I don't think you should leave us alone at all."

"It's not like she's in any real danger. She can always feed." Alec nodded at him.

"No! That's not – that's not what we want. Do you understand that?"

"Not really, but human society is a mystery. You're there for her to feed from. I see no problem."

Jimmy scrunched his forehead. What a thing to say. He was beginning to suspect that traveling with Alec was only going to be trouble.

Though right now, they clearly needed him. He was the only buffer between the two of them, after all.

They ate in silence. Moody silence on Jimmy's part, nonchalance on Alec's. The moment broke when Jimmy suggested in a decisive tone, "We should split up. You can stay with her while I scout out alternate paths, look for a larger gathering of people."

Licking his fingers clean, Alec responded without looking at him, "That's not our agreement. I'm looking to travel with the both of you. If that's changing, I'll start on home."

Jimmy sighed in frustration. "Well, we should at least turn south. Hit the train station and hop the rest of the way to Seattle. How did we let ourselves end up so alone?"

"You agreed to travel through nymph protected land; a smattering of farms and nature feeders to keep it interesting. S'almost like you wanted to be alone." Alec looked at him briefly, merely to smirk, then turned to walk toward the road. "I'll check out the surroundings. See if I can find anybody," Alec added, and before Jimmy could protest further, he was swallowed by trees and rain.

An hour passed. Or what felt like an hour. It was difficult to properly measure such things when you were cold and damp. Jimmy became increasingly anxious when neither Sadie nor Alec appeared. Eventually, he decided to approach the tent. Crouching down at the flap, he said Sadie's name twice. No response. Unzipping the opening he saw a lump in a sleeping bag, unmoving. It must be nearly midday. How could she still be so deep in sleep?

Reaching hesitantly for what felt like an ankle, he shook her gently. She gave out a soft moan before rolling over. That was disconcerting. Taking off his dripping rain jacket and shoes, he climbed into the edge of the tent. It wasn't large. Really it should hold two, but had accommodated three out of necessity. Though somehow it felt infinitely smaller now that they were alone in there. He knew this wasn't a good idea, but they needed to get on the road. He had to wake her.

Leaving the flap open in case he decided to leave suddenly, he tugged on a shoulder and rolled her toward him. Two, sleepy eyes flickered open, searched for something to focus on, and locked on his. Her gaze became sharp and intent. She began to sit up.

"Jimmy?" she said breathlessly, almost as if she was surprised he was there. Getting only halfway up, she quickly collapsed back onto her back.

"Sadie? Are you okay?" He almost reached out to stroke her hair before catching himself. Switching gears, he went on, "It's late. We should get on the road. We need to find you – someone." Her focus softened as she rolled her head away from him. Kicking the sleeping bag off, she lamented, "I don't feel good. Can't we just curl up and stay here? Forever." Her tone would sound childish if not for the seductive undertone.

He swallowed, not sure how to respond to an obviously rhetorical question as she traced the hemline of her tank with her finger. Instead, he watched the path she drew, slowly, lovingly, across her chest. Reaching to scoop up her breast in one hand she massaged gently. Before he could look away, she caught his eye and explained, "They ache."

This, he definitely didn't know how to respond to. He shifted his weight to hug his knees in front of his growing erection and tried to focus on the pitter-patter of tiny droplets striking the leaves around them. But when her next words came, his mind couldn't keep her out.

"I ache all over, Jimmy. My stomach and head; full of nausea. My nipples heavy. And between my legs, there's a craving. A pulsing. Insatiable. All I want is to hold someone deep inside me." She rolled her head back to look at his flushed face, then traced down his body, lingering on his clutched knees as if she knew exactly what they hid.

"I want to climb inside them too. Under their flesh, spreading pleasure, warmth. I want to feel them vibrating; aching right along with me." She was panting and flushed.

Through the humming feel in his brain, Jimmy tried to think of a reply to rescue them both, but he couldn't shake the picture of climbing on top of her and giving her exactly what she appeared to want. He'd known it would be dangerous entering the tent, but this was too much. Frantically looking for anything to say, he stuttered,

"Maybe you're pregnant. Aren't uh – sore glands a sign of pregnancy?"

The comment served its purpose. She grinned and relaxed. "I'm not pregnant, Jimmy. You know that's not it." She turned to stare down the roof of the tent. Afraid of what else she might say and how he might respond, he considered plugging his ears and running away, but then he remembered he was, in fact, a grown-up. Relaxing onto one elbow, he reminded himself he was here to support a friend, and all he had to do was listen. When Sadie went on, however, there was more sadness and less breathiness in her tone.

"Actually..." She paused, swallowed, and then continued speaking as if the words had a mind to come out on their own. "Succubi can't have children." He blinked in surprise at the change in topic, then felt the same sorrow she had on her face spread through him. "At least, not after the Becoming."

She looked back at him and added, "Sorry. I've been meaning to tell you."

Why was she apologizing? Her guilty expression didn't make any sense. He looked at her silently for a while until he realized his reaction was only increasing her suddenly nervous mood.

She continued, "Succubi are born into families carrying the gene, but once it is expressed during the Becoming, that person can no longer reproduce. Or so Gabriel taught me." She was obviously upset about this, and he wanted to say the right thing. He searched for comforting words, but before he could locate any she continued with more revelations, "Or catch STDs. It must be an evolutionary development, given how often we need to feed."

"Oh. I'd been wondering about that," was all he could think to say. Then he pulled himself together and added, "Well, there're lots of people who can't have kids who still make families. It'll be okay. Your body is smart. We're lucky you can feed without repercussions."

She rolled onto her side to face him. "Without repercussions? Repercussions like having to leave home? Like—" she extended a hand to rest in front of him, a few inches from his ankle, "never being able to touch you again. Never being able to curl up in your arms? Like having to sleep with strangers constantly just to survive?"

Wanting to take her hand, he erred on the side of caution and leaned back. A long, hard look passed between them. The silence eventually broke when she let out a third confession.

"I could've rejected it."

His brow furrowed. "Rejected what?"

"I could feel it, Jimmy, during my Becoming. I could have stayed human... if I had wanted."

He sat up. "Sadie – are you sure?"

"I'm sure."

Surprised at his own sudden anger, he tried to understand. She could've rejected it? Everything that had happened had been a *choice*. All these new problems between them... Another voice in his head added, then again, would she have been happy, rejecting such an important part of herself? He tried to hide the various thoughts from showing on his face as he asked, "Do you regret it?"

She lay back and looked at the ceiling, silent as she searched the fabric with her eyes. In the end, she responded by quoting a line from the comics he had lent her.

"Life seems nothing but hard choices made on a bed of soft information."

When Jimmy left the tent, he found Alec sitting under a nearby tree, smoking a pipe. Sadie had fallen back asleep, entirely unresponsive to the urgency in Jimmy's voice imploring that she needed to get up. He flopped on the soggy ground next to Alec, as exhausted as if he had just run a marathon, not spent an hour talking quietly in a tent.

"Okay. We need to go find someone. It shouldn't be hard if we can just get back around people. I say we look through the nearby woods, and if we discover nothing, I'll go on ahead. I won't be gone long!" He cut off Alec as he opened his mouth, presumably to protest. "I'll run if I have to. We're finding her someone before the end of the day."

Alec interjected to say he'd already searched the surrounding woods. Damn. He'd have to leave Sadie here then. Jumping up, he declared, "No reason to delay then. I'll be back. And I swear Alec, you better not leave her here. Just look after her for half a day, okay?"

Alec gave one of his typical shrugs, causing Jimmy to narrow his eyes in annoyance. "I won't be gone long. If you're still here when I return, I'll repay half the money you gave me." Waking up at this comment, Alec reached out to shake his hand.

"Deal," the man said.

Only mildly convinced he was doing the right thing, Jimmy pulled up his hood and took off toward the road.

He returned several hours later, with a feeling of growing panic.

Finding Alec preparing cold sandwiches, he shoved one in his mouth without asking. Savoring the sweet and spicy flavor of salami, he tried to imagine going days without eating.

"Went well then?" Alec smirked obnoxiously.

"We need a new plan. Has she eaten? Food, I mean?" he asked without glancing at his unwanted companion.

"Not yet. She mostly slept."

"Well, it's time to end that." Walking determinedly toward the tent, Jimmy pulled the zipper aggressively. There was a lull in the constant drizzle, and a small ray of sunshine swept past him to land on her sleeping form.

"Sadie! You need to eat and get up. Now!" he tried to say firmly, but kindly. Grabbing a gloved hand and pulling, he tried to get her to sit up. She groaned in annoyance, resisting half-heartedly before slumping upward.

"I can't. Don't feel good." She went to collapse back down, but he leaned forward and scooped one of her arms over his neck as he reached behind her back. Pulling the sleeping bag down he darted a hand under her knees and hoisted her in his arms. Her eyes opened slowly, found his face, and she was suddenly sharply awake. He stepped out of the tent as her lips swelled red and her gloved hand touched his lips. "Jimmy." She leaned forward to kiss him and he all but dropped her on the log.

"Sadie, no. I'm here to help you get moving. That's all. Here." He handed her a sandwich. She slumped in front of the log, but remained upright against it.

"Not hungry," she protested.

"Not what it looks like," Alec said.

"Sadie." Jimmy crouched in front of her and switched to his most gentle tone. "You have to eat this. And then we have to get moving. Nothing good will come from us staying here another night." He held the sandwich in front of her face until she grudgingly took a bite. "Clearly your estimate of a week was wrong. You can't stay like this."

"Jimmy, I—" She looked attentive again. "I know. I'm just so weak. I don't think my legs will support me. I'm supposed to need to feed more often in my first few years. It was irresponsible ending up here." She disappeared one sandwich and then grabbed at the second one he offered, her voice gaining strength. "I'm sorry, but I think—" she began, but paused to take another bite, swallowing almost immediately, "that I might need you to help in another way."

He withdrew his third offering. Slumping back to sit on the wet ground without a care; he searched her face.

"It would only be this once," she went on. "We could wake up tomorrow and never mention it again." Her face looked fully alert then.

She made it sound simple. And oh, it would be so simple to agree. He wanted to, of course. And furthermore, he suspected she knew he wanted to, though perhaps she didn't know how badly. But how did he know they wouldn't wake up tomorrow with her resenting him for taking advantage of her? And how would he move forward after that? He didn't want just once.

"Jimmy. This, it's what I want. It's what I need. I won't think you've taken advantage of me," she said as if she'd read his thoughts. "It's the best solution."

His mind filled with a background humming that quieted the completion of any attempted thoughts. His blood began to heat right as he realized he was going to agree. He was going to give in.

Fuck, they were really going to do this. It had come to that. He didn't want to glance in Alec's direction, though he could feel the man's gaze intent on them. Wishing he would just disappear and leave them alone, Jimmy shifted his weight to put their third party directly behind him. Then, letting his gaze flicker from Sadie's eyes, to her lips and back, he nodded ever so slightly.

Her eyes flared like fire. She looked fully awake then as she reached out unhurriedly and took the third sandwich in both hands. Moving slowly enough to wrap his hand in hers before withdrawing, she laced her fingers briefly through his. She consumed the last sandwich in two bites and licked her fingertips clean around the glove, gaze locked on his. Done consuming food, she asked with a calm, serious expression that stood in contrast to her previous demeanor, "Ready to take me back to that tent, James Baker?"

Chapter 11

A rainy day

Having come to the decision, the urgency of their situation morphed into unhurried deliberation. Jimmy knew one thing for sure: he wasn't going to let this be a memory they'd regret. He wanted to dry off, get them both into clean clothes and give Alec something to do; something far away. He searched around for a dry patch of ground to make a fire. Centered in a cluster of three large Douglas firs was the perfect little patch for a fire pit. It had remained dry from their cover, and if it continued to trickle rain, he was in little danger of setting any of the ancient trees alight.

Returning to the fallen log still supporting Sadie, he found her alone and quite soaked. She had leaned her head back, mouth open to the sky as if the rain was some kind of gift. She threw him a big smile, like they were kids again playing some kind of game, before resuming her consumption of rainwater.

"Don't you want to know what it tastes like?" she asked mischievously. He couldn't help the grin that came out of him at her pointed question.

Kneeling at her feet, he took both her hands in his. "I'm going to build us a fire. Just over there. I want to get dried off. Then we'll go inside." He kissed both her knuckles and stood, pausing to ask, "Where's Alec?"

"I asked him to take a hike." She twirled a strand of hair around one finger. "He was gracious enough to oblige. At least after I threatened a curse upon all his ancestors living and dead, to be personally delivered. The fact I was serious seemed to register anyway."

Jimmy felt some personal satisfaction that it had been Sadie who'd gotten rid of the man. Tightening down his raincoat as the weather threatened to worsen, he went off in search of rescuable wood with a smile on his face that resisted suppression despite all his half-hearted attempts. Jimmy crossed the road to where the trees had been thicker and scoured the ground in search of semi-dry branches. He knew how to make a good fire, in a variety of conditions. He just needed a half-decent haul.

Clawing his way through increasingly dense woodland, he fought with the underbrush bent on living up to its name. The tension under his skin felt good for once as he let himself picture what was about to happen. He was surprised to find his lust was far outweighed by the simple desire to finally kiss the person he loved so deeply. He realized now that it was the closeness of contact, of intimacy with Sadie that he longed for more than anything else; the same intimacy they had shared in other ways for years, not the simple fulfillment of desire. He was excited to be able to hold her again.

He gathered a long, thick branch from the underbrush and broke it in half with a heavy boot before stacking it under one arm. The cracking sound, however, was followed by a different, but distinct noise. One he recognized well. Looking in its direction, he detected a possible end to the trees. He stepped over a fallen fir and pushed through the tall ferns, to emerge suddenly into a wide expanse of deforested land. Surprised at the abrupt change in scenery, he took in his new surroundings.

They contained a little house, a barn, a field of various vegetables, and most notably, a man chopping wood. The man, likely in his thirties by Jimmy's estimate, stood in the shelter of an open barn. He had no shirt, but seemed perfectly warmed by his efforts. Jimmy could see no lights on in the house. No one else was in sight.

Did the man live alone? Shifting his weight slightly, another farm came into view just over the hill. There were people here. He'd found the farmland Alec had mentioned. Jimmy didn't understand this. Alec had investigated this direction. Had he really not stumbled upon the farm? He hadn't had to travel far to find it.

But... with all these farms, it was very likely they could find someone for Sadie. A glimmer of both hope and despair hit Jimmy in a stampede of emotion. A sinking feeling settled in the pit of his stomach as confusion beat against his skull.

If they had an out, how could he pretend not to see it? Wouldn't he be taking advantage of her if he acted like he was her only option now? He dropped the kindling and clenched his fists, standing there a long time with his ragged breaths punctuated by the steady sounds of the man chopping wood. Images of Sadie's red lips and hazel eyes kept flashing in his mind.

Then the memory of sweat dripping from her nipples hit him and Jimmy groaned as if in pain. He supposed it was news, not firewood, with which he'd be returning.

Feeling uneasy at assessing someone for their potential as a sexual partner for Sadie, he tried to look the man over. Young enough. Alone. His skin slightly sunbaked, like Jimmy's own. The build of a man who spent most of his hours working with his body. What did Sadie look for? He had never understood the choices she made, but this man seemed like a good fit.

Though he didn't have to do this, a voice whispered in his mind. Guilt at even having the thought crawled on top of his other emotions. Perhaps Alec had withheld the information for his own selfish reasons, causing this whole mess. Jimmy would not do the same. And this wasn't really what he wanted. Not like this. Not because she had to; because she needed him to. He wanted her to want him, freely, like he wanted her.

Jimmy squared his shoulders, took a steadying breath, and made ready to bring Sadie the good news.

Dominic didn't have to chop in such conditions when there had been plenty of sunny days that week, but the cool, fresh smell of summer rain had always been his preferred working weather. The day his wife had passed had been a hot summer day, and he always felt sorrow during the season. But when that rain hit, it was all good memories of times spent running around the barn, back when they were kids. Or of much more adult times, when they were married and had inherited the property.

He could still picture her perfectly, standing in the door frame watching him chop. She'd wear that thin white dress and no panties. They'd talk for hours. He'd take off his shirt, trying to impress her while he worked. They'd both know what was coming. Eventually she would lean against the doorframe and give him a particular look. And that's always when he knew the work was finished for the day.

Such memories couldn't help but be tinged with sadness now, but the excitement of them nevertheless worked its way through his body. Enough time had passed that the sharpness of specific memories had become more of a blur of that general time; an overall feeling. And that feeling was overtaking him in that particular moment. Maybe the work was done for *today*, in fact.

Just as he was contemplating going inside, a twig snapped loudly in front of him. He looked up to see a man carrying a woman out of the nearby woods. Was she injured? Leaning the axe against a bench, he called out to them. Neither responded until they had finished crossing the short distance to him. They stepped under the cover of the barn and out of the rain. The man was breathing heavily and the woman did in fact look ill. Stopping a good ten feet away with her still in his arms, the man greeted him and gave their names.

But when Dominic asked what he could do for them, he was met with a long moment of silence. The woman looked at Dominic from the man's arms as the man studied her face. Then turning to gaze into the eyes of her companion, she nodded once. The exchange happened quickly and Dominic could tell there was a lot in it he didn't understand, but never in a hundred seasons would he have predicted the man's next words.

"My friend is a succubus who hasn't fed in several days. We were traveling and went too long without running into the right person. She thinks you're the right person."

Dominic stumbled. He had moved to clear the bench for them to sit, but instead found himself plopping down in surprise. He searched his brain for what he knew about succubi. Their kiss caused pleasure. They could be dangerous, sucking the life out of you in an instant. One of their congressman was one and there was some trouble going on there, but he couldn't remember about what.

"Uh... what does that mean exactly?" Dominic inquired directly. The woman, *Sadie,* squirmed out of his arms and came to her feet, seeming to get a second wind. Though when she tried to walk, she stumbled, leaning on her companion. He guided her to the bench.

"May I?" she asked.

Dominic gestured for her to sit.

"I feed off sexual pleasure. And I create it easily through skin contact." Her voice had an allure to it that captivated him. Her wet curls clung to her face and shoulders. "It's usually safe, but I'm pretty new at this and, like Jimmy said, I'm pretty hungry. I'm not exactly sure what it'll be like. I don't want to lie to you."

Dominic thought he understood, but what exactly was the *it* she was referring to. Was she asking to kiss him? Touch him? Sleep with him? He looked her up and down. Though she was drenched from head to foot, he did think she was beautiful.

Was this really happening? A succubus had just wandered out of the woods and asked to feed from him? Would he be a fool to refuse?

Dominic looked out over his field as he thought about the risk. His life here had been pretty quiet for a long time. He wasn't sure he had anything to lose. Even not knowing exactly what he was agreeing to, his heartbeat pulsed at the thought of jumping into the unknown.

"Sadie?" he asked, wanting to confirm he'd remembered the introduction correctly.

She nodded. He tested the name again on his lips before giving her his.

"Dominic," she whispered, scooting forward a few more inches.

"What do I do?" he asked. Her face registered no change at his agreement, as if she had already known his answer. She pulled off her gloves and swung a leg over to straddle the bench a few inches from him. Her gaze was fire as she said, "Just this."

Reaching one hand to his face, she lightly grazed his cheek with her fingertips. A sensation shot through him, traveling to his lips, fingers, nipples. A pulse of heat and his pants were suddenly much too tight. Out of the corner of his eye, he vaguely registered her companion walking back out into the rain as Sadie pushed off her jacket. *Perhaps*, he managed to think, this was an elaborate robbery. Though if so, he would still cooperate, he realized, as she leaned to kiss him and the feeling in his body exploded.

The woman ran her hand down his naked chest. She did so very slowly, from collarbone to his lower abdomen, and as her touch traveled he went from heavy arousal to orgasm, gasping in surprise as he soaked his pants. She pulled away abruptly. They gazed at each other, her expression as surprised as his. The rain increased around them, creating a steady background roar.

"Sorry," he gasped, not quite sure if he had done anything wrong. Was that enough for her? Had that been what she wanted even if it was over quickly? He stood up to find his shirt to try to clean himself up, but she grabbed his hand. She rose too, but swayed slightly and had to grab onto him for support. Leaning into his chest, she kissed him again.

Before he could worry that he had nothing left to give her, his body began to respond as it had before. In less than a minute he was panting into her mouth. She broke away to tear her shirt over her head and the growing pleasure stopped long enough for him to catch a breath and clear his thoughts. It turned out he had just one thought, and it was how much he wanted to rip her bra off. Unhooking it with one hand, he scooped her up in his other.

As he ran a thumb over her nipple, they both moaned as he climaxed again. He needed to get these pants off. He reached for his belt, but she stopped him.

"Not yet," she breathed. Breaking contact, she backed up toward the barn, dropping down to her panties as she went.

He followed her and they stepped in sync until her back was against the entrance frame. Scooping one hand under her ass and the other under one thigh, he lifted her around him. She clamped her legs tight around his hips as he began to thrust against her. He hoped the feeling of his slickened jeans sliding up and down her wet panties felt good to her. He was sure it did when she began to moan every time he passed over her.

Or was she moaning because he was? Every time he pressed against her, she shuddered, and then immediately a wave of pleasure ran through him. The feedback loop escalated rapidly, but he at least saw his own climax coming this time. Just as he was worried he might collapse to his knees if he came again standing, she said, "No. Not yet." And wiggled back to her feet.

"Here," he said. He pulled her further into the barn, grabbed a towel hanging from one wall, and tossed it over the hay. There he lay her down and slid off her panties. He put his head between her legs and tried to lick her, but the second his tongue made contact, his delayed climax from before arrived. He gripped her hips and pressed his forehead into her stomach.

The second it was over, he found he wanted more. He hadn't felt this free in a long time. He ripped off his pants, staring at her sprawled, naked form, before trying again to lick her. This time he was able to get all the way through; not stopping until she shuddered against him, gripping his hair in both fists as her heels dug into his back.

As he crawled up to her face, he regretted no longer keeping condoms in his pants' pocket. He held himself above her as she ran her hand for the second time slowly down his body, this time coming to wrap around him. He was more than well-lubed by now, and she slid her hand smoothly over him once. It was an explosion. He had never experienced anything remotely like it. He bucked uncontrollably as she pumped him again.

Putting her hand against his backside she pulled him into her. Dominic slid through her warm entrance and could feel another climax around the corner. Only this time, something different happened. He kept climbing. Heat soared through his whole body; pleasure filling all his senses. He smelled cherry pie and tasted sweet liqueur. He was vaguely aware of himself swearing, of gripping fistfuls of straw.

And this time, when climax struck, it didn't subside. He convulsed into her repeatedly, expecting it to pass any second. But it didn't. She pushed hard against his chest and bucked her own hips, until she was the one on top. Still, it didn't stop. He opened his eyes and looked at her with some struggle. He was aware his face was all screwed up and that he appeared to be crying out in a voice he barely recognized.

But he couldn't feel subconscious. All he felt was absolute euphoria as he watched her beautiful form begin to ride him. His vision blurred, and he realized he hadn't taken in air in the same moment that she leaned down and whispered "Breathe" into his ear. A cool breeze struck his nipples as he filled his lungs, and they burned with sensitivity.

He wasn't sure how much time passed as he continued to orgasm. He thought of counting her undulations, but his thoughts couldn't focus. His gaze flashed from her hungry eyes, to her full breasts, to a leak in one corner of the barn, to a million different things.

At some point, with a final "Fuck" drawn from his lips, he collapsed into darkness.

Sadie stood and looked down at the man's spent form. She thought she should probably check his pulse, but as she crouched next to him, she realized she could still sense his heartbeat, even though they were no longer touching. In fact, she could feel his whole body as if it were her own.

Her thoughts darted to Jimmy. It could've been him. It almost had been. What that would've been like; to do with him what she had just done with that stranger. She hadn't known, all this time, that she could do anything like what had just happened. It was both thrilling and terrifying.

Thinking about Jimmy out there in the rain somewhere, she felt almost sick with regret. She could've nodded no; told him the man wasn't right. Asked him to take her back to the tent and forget about the fire. Though at the same time, she was incredibly grateful someone else had come along. She had been out of control back there. Insatiable. Greedy. She didn't want to turn her oldest friendship into a drug that she needed, that he needed. A drug they were both addicted to.

She felt immune to the cool air as she walked naked to the edge of the barn. Her skin vibrated with lingering pleasure as she breathed in the scent of the rain. Thunder boomed in the distance. A storm then. How appropriate. Jimmy shifted weight, catching Sadie's attention. He stood with his back to her at the very edge of the covering, his face an inch from where the rain fell in sheets. His stance was wide, hands behind his back. He looked like a pillar of strength.

Her pillar. That's what he was. The red light that always pulsed from him to her had grown when she'd asked him to take her back to that tent. Though now that it was all over, the pulsing hadn't shrunk back down. Jimmy wanted her more than ever, just like she did him. And she was sure he was filled with the same regret and longing. Only he didn't know, as she did, that it was reciprocated. That was her burden to bear. And if she didn't bear that secret, she was sure the dam between them would break in a heartbeat.

"Did you leave him alive in there?" he asked without turning around.

She stepped barefoot through the grass to stand behind him. "I hope so," she whispered. "He was a good find. We were lucky and I was reckless to put us in this situation. It won't happen again. I swear it."

"Now we know," he said. "What we can and can't handle."

Sadie thought there were several layers hidden in his words.

She didn't reply to this. There was nothing to say.

"Suppose we should get back to a city," he added.

"Yeah," she said, scooting an inch closer. She clenched her hands into fists to keep herself from hugging him, from reaching out and sliding her fingers between his clasped hands. Instead, she placed one hand on his back.

"Thank you, Jimmy. And… I'm sorry. For everything." She turned away to dress herself as her eyes filled with tears. She had no reason to hide them though, as he wouldn't turn around while she was naked. Eventually, without another word, he walked out into the rain.

JIMMY'S GAZE locked on Alec's black raincoat, bobbing through the trees ahead. Thunder roared again above them, closer this time. The sound of the storm masked his approach, though Jimmy was doing nothing to keep quiet as he tramped determinedly toward the blond rat. Alec turned at the last minute, "Hey, there ya are. I was looking to—"

Jimmy shoved him by both shoulders. Alec stumbled onto his backside at the foot of their tent. "You knew! You had to have known. You said you searched this whole area? Including all those farms just a minute's walk from here? You searched those?"

Alec threw out his typical grin. "Don't be so dramatic, farm boy. You wanted her to take you. More than anything. You just feel guilty that you said yes. Now looks like you're all butt hurt cuz she found some other little farm boy." He got to his feet. "Why are you raging at me, anyway? I was helping you out, don't you reckon?"

Jimmy clenched his fists to keep from punching him. "You don't help anyone but yourself. You did this for a reason. What is it? What game are you playing here?" Jimmy didn't touch Alec again, but he stepped right up to his face; his body tensing for a fight. Jimmy had only ever been in that one fight in the elevator. Usually, he had been the one breaking them up, but he was sure instinct and blind rage would help him out now if he needed it.

"Tell me! I thought you were into people not getting what they want. Isn't that the whole reason you're with us? What are you about now?"

"Who says it was you I was feeding from? I hadn't known my own self what a hungry succubus held till yesterday, but they should sell it by the ounce. Wasn't gonna end that too quickly."

Jimmy was livid at this. And confused.

"What? I thought human feeders couldn't feed from other human feeders?"

"Oh, some can. It's type-dependent. Sirens can feed from succubi. There's an evolutionary relationship there, so I'm told," Alec said.

Rage continued to pulse through him. "You'd have her do something she'd regret just for your own gain. You lied to us. You're done. We're done." Jimmy pulled the cash out and threw it at his feet.

"Ha. Don't matter now," Alec said. "I'm in. She likes me well enough. Think she's going to tell me to bugger off, just cuz you say I'm no good? What makes you so sure she'd trust your opinion on the matter? Seems like you could have a lot of motives if you ask me."

"Keep your damn tent. And your money," Jimmy said through gritted teeth. "We don't want anything from you. And Alec?" He paused to tower over the man, his face only a foot away as he looked down on him with disgust. "Stay the hell away from Sadie."

With as dramatic an exit as he could muster, Jimmy threw their stuff into his bag and stormed back to the farmhouse.

Chapter 12

An earthquake

Jimmy found no one in the barn, but the smoke coming from the chimney told him they'd gone indoors. As he approached the house with trepidation, he was hit with the strong smell of warm food. His stomach churned with hunger for a homemade meal, yet he lingered there on the verge of knocking. He leaned in to put his ear to the door exactly as it opened.

Sadie stood there, looking like she'd just had a hot shower. She wore someone else's clothes. Had she seen him coming out the window?

"We've been invited to stay the night," she said.

He shook himself off best he could and stepped into the entrance-way. She left the door open as he hung his coat. He learned why a minute later when Alec pushed his way in behind him. Jimmy had been hoping to get a minute with Sadie alone, but their company only increased when Dominic popped around the corner.

"Casserole's in the oven. Make yourselves at home. Hi, I'm Dominic." He held out a hand to Alec.

"Alec. Smells fine as heck in here. Is that paprika?" the siren asked with an ingratiating smile.

"Sure is. My late wife's recipe," Dominic said.

"My family makes a good paprika beef stew. Grow it ourselves. Have you ever tried—"

The men led the way into the dining room and Sadie followed before he could think to grab her.

Dominic turned to him. "Toilet's through there. There's towels and stuff. Either of you want to shower before supper?" Dominic asked.

Jimmy and Alec looked at each other. Jimmy was hoping Alec would say yes, just so he'd leave for a minute. When he didn't volunteer, Jimmy decided he'd love a hot shower.

By the time he'd returned, the table was set and Dominic was bringing out warm bread. Jimmy had been left the seat directly across from Sadie, from which he spent the entire meal avoiding looking at her. A task made harder by the fact that she spent the entire meal looking at him. Neither of them contributed to the conversation. In fact, Jimmy barely registered it until a particular word caught his attention.

"Seattle? The train station's about ten miles from here. If y'all are looking to go to Seattle, my neighbor's got a truck; can take you in the morning," Dominic was saying.

Jimmy sat up. "Well I don't think it's decided that we're *all* going that way," he interjected. He caught Sadie's eye. He was hoping to choose a different city, far from Alec, but persuading Sadie might take some work. She wrinkled her forehead at him.

"You don't want to go to Seattle?" she asked. "It's the nearest big city. Why wouldn't we go there?"

Jimmy couldn't think of a convincing argument for the dinner table. "Well there's a lot of places we could go. Thought we might want to consider our options," he said.

"But Seattle's the only place where we know someone. Alec's going to show us his family's casino." They all turned to stare at Jimmy, and he couldn't avoid giving a nod of agreement. They could go to Seattle. He would talk to Sadie about Alec when they got there.

The obnoxious siren waited to shower until they were all in the kitchen washing up. Jimmy was sure this was intentional, since it prevented him from getting a moment alone with Sadie. Dominic had one spare bedroom and a sofa. Jimmy, assuming Sadie would be in with Dominic anyway, volunteered to take the couch, but after a brief and awkward moment of decision, Sadie told Dominic she should probably let him rest. This was how Jimmy ended the day alone, with Sadie and Alec sharing a room upstairs. Alec, like any pest, clearly knew how to stick around. Jimmy was going to have to try a lot harder if he was going to free them of this unasked-for trouble.

But twelve hours later, the three of them were closed up together in a train car, city-bound. Jimmy had found no great ideas in the night, only restless sleep and memories of the painful day. Since the silence between Sadie and him had persisted through the morning, he sat leaning against the opposite window from her, drifting in and out of sleep. Sadie appeared equally tired. Only Alec seemed chipper, quietly reading in his own corner.

The world outside the window drifted past in a haze, matching his mood. Life had never felt so out of his control. He wanted to go back, but there was no undoing adulthood; no undoing their current circumstance.

Jimmy felt a hand on his arm and blinked up at Sadie. She had moved to sit next to him. She lifted his arm over her and cuddled into his side. His muscles relaxed; her familiar warmth and presence soothing some of his tension. His body was too consumed with sadness to be excited at her nearness, and he merely kissed the top of her head and fell right to sleep.

THEY BOTH JERKED upright at the halting motion. Sadie was thoroughly unready to move away from this moment of peace, but it seemed they had arrived. She reluctantly pushed herself up from the comfort of Jimmy and gazed out his window.

Her first impression of Seattle was rather different from her one and only previous experience of a big city. For one, there were significantly fewer people mulling about, and the roar of sound she remembered from Arlington was rather subdued here. Even the architecture gave off a simple ambience. The train station was small, though a great deal more people exited the train then boarded it.

Alec led them out the building and onto a thoroughfare. The road was built to be quite wide, and Sadie could see why. Carriages were the popular form of transport on this avenue, and the people on foot hugged the outer edges to avoid stepping in horse dung. It stank to high heaven. Entirely unlike the natural manure smell of a cow pasture or the sharp smell of automobile gasoline, this was a mix of all the crude smells Sadie had ever sampled. She tried to cover her nose and keep up with Alec's fast pace.

Jimmy pulled up the rear with an equally crinkled expression, but Alec seemed unfazed by the odor. He put up his hand and a carriage stopped to let them board. Alec sat in the middle and pointed out landmarks as their transport jostled them toward the inner city. Unlike Arlington, there were few tall buildings here. The roads were straight and seemed to run in clean grids. The businesses and houses alike were rectangular and simply constructed. Occasionally, they passed a home that was nymph-grown, but most of it looked built by human hands.

The people had a strange way of keeping their heads down. Throughout the entire ride into town, Sadie spotted not one exchange of greeting between passing strangers. She witnessed only darted glances and side-steps. She exchanged a glance with Jimmy behind Alec's back.

They were truly far from home now.

The carriage stopped in front of a four-story building, which stood out both for its height and for the ruckus of sound pouring from its doors. Alec hopped down before offering Sadie a hand. She took it gratefully as she leapt over the squelching mud under their feet.

"Welcome m'dear, to The Taste of Destiny! Where fates change." Alec gave her his widest grin. "And my home." He led them through a set of double doors into a wide expanse of a game room. Sadie had never seen so much color, from the rugs to the tables to the tapestries. She gaped at an older woman in a big black hat wearing seven pearl necklaces of different lengths.

"Ooh so close, Ms. Davy," Alec said, putting a hand on her shoulder. "But we know a woman like you don't go long without getting her due." She smiled toothily up at him.

"Irene! Suite five is taken," Alec shouted at a woman behind a counter as he led them to an elevator.

"Fourth," he ordered the operator, then added, "How's married life?"

"Same," the operator replied, while he pulled open the metal grate.

They all piled into an obscenely large elevator. Sadie hadn't seen much of herself recently, but suddenly she was in a mirror on every wall. She didn't look bad for being on the road so long, but she self-consciously tried to smooth out her hair.

"And the house?" Alec asked.

"Same," the middle-aged man replied.

They exited to an empty floor with a long hallway.

"This floor is mostly for family," Alec said as he led them down the hall. "I have a regular suite that they sometimes rent out when I'm outta town. You can stay there with me." Alec stopped at the fifth door down and pulled out a key.

He pushed open the door and welcomed them in with a flourish. The room was wide, with polished floors and glistening countertops. A minibar separated the kitchen from the living room, which sported several sofas and a sizable built-in bathtub. Sadie was confused as to why the bathing would take place in the living room, but perhaps it was just a weird city custom. Off one side was a small bedroom and bathroom, off the other was a large bedroom also with a full bathroom.

This was large for just Alec. Sadie found herself suddenly wondering if Alec had a spouse and kids she didn't know about.

"Drop your stuff anywhere," he said after the brief tour had finished. "And stay as long as you like. Just keep things looking clean. Don't wanna find moldy food under the couch when I'm entertaining."

Sadie put her bag down and Jimmy moved to follow, looking unhappy.

"Well then, ready to meet the family?" Alec clapped his hands together.

"Or," Jimmy interjected, "maybe we should stay here and rest and wash up."

"I don't feel like resting," Sadie said. "Let's go, Jimmy. We can rest when we're dead."

"Well I think I want to relax a minute," he said, wearing a strange expression.

"Okay. You can stay. Get some sleep." Sadie squeezed his hand and then turned back to Alec. "Is there a place I can change?"

He led them into the smaller bedroom and Sadie went to the bathroom to put on a nice summer dress and long white gloves. She emerged to find the two men waiting just outside. Jimmy was glaring at Alec with the strangest expression, but it turned soft when he looked back at her.

"I'll hav'er back by midnight," Alec said with a wink at Jimmy, before he grabbed Sadie's hand and dragged her outside.

She cast a worried look back at Jimmy, but found herself quickly distracted as Alec led her into the hall and spun her around. "You look nice as hell. My family's gonna love you," he said.

Sadie beamed.

"Round lunchtime we all gather up around Granddad's," he explained as he took her a few doors down and walked in without knocking. They found ten people milling about a long table. A woman who looked the spitting image of Alec came over.

"Welcome home, dear." She kissed him on one cheek. "Tuck your shirt in."

"That didn't take long. You miss us? Or did you run outta dough?" a young man asked.

"Or did you get hitched? Who's this then? She looks too good for you," said a middle-aged man.

Alec introduced Sadie as everyone pulled up a chair. The woman, Irene, from downstairs turned out to be Alec's sister. She was dressed fancier than anyone Sadie had ever seen in person and she took to Sadie immediately.

"You must sit next to me if you're gonna tell me all about yourself," Irene declared, pulling out a chair.

Sadie barely ate because the family asked her so many questions. They all seemed delighted to have her there, and Alec's mother echoed his earlier words for her to stay as long as she liked. Sadie didn't know what to do with so much positive attention. A warm feeling settled over her as she shared stories of the weeks since her Becoming. She found herself embellishing slightly, worried her life was actually quite boring, but everyone seemed perfectly interested in anything she said.

Alec must have noticed she hadn't taken a bite, because he jumped in with a distraction by asking, "Any trouble while I was out?"

"A little. But we took care of it," replied a cousin.

"Trouble?" Sadie asked.

"Human trouble. S'group in town, not a fan of our kind. They'd like to see us go out of business," the cousin explained.

That successfully turned the conversation to work matters and Sadie quickly inhaled her meal. The second she had finished, Irene leaned in and said in a lowered voice, "So... I noticed you skimmed some of the dirtier parts of your stories. No need to hold back for me. I want *all* the juicy deets."

Sadie smiled, but said nothing. She thought it a strange comment from the woman given she had little interest in sex, but then again, the images that surrounded her were filled with scenes of sexual encounters. How strange. Sadie didn't know what to make of the contradiction.

When it became clear she wasn't going to indulge her, Irene changed the topic. "You should let me show you around the casino tonight. We can get all dressed up and hit the bar together. It's Mystery Monday. You spin for a mystery drink, half-off."

Sadie thought that sounded like fun, though she wondered what it meant for Irene to get more dressed up. She nodded agreement.

Irene added, "And don't worry if you don't got clothes with you, I'm going to give you a full makeover."

After lunch, Irene took Sadie back to her room. They spent the entire afternoon trying on different outfits. Sadie had never done anything like it before and found herself immersed in the experience of putting on such different styles. In the end, she chose a dress not that unlike the one she'd arrived in, albeit a little shorter and tighter.

Irene held up some heels. Sadie laughed and shook her head in an adamant no.

Though an hour later, she found herself decked out in her first pair of high heels. They were almost boots in the way they laced most of the way up her calves. Sadie thought they were quite pretty until she tried to walk in them.

She tripped and fell at Irene's feet.

"See, what I'd tell yeah? Can't sprain an ankle if they're strapped to your whole leg," Irene said, laughing. "You just go down in one piece. Though we can't have that either. We need to give you some practice."

Irene had Sadie parade up and down the room, teaching her how to place her weight and let her hips move naturally in their new positions. After Irene had become completely satisfied by her performance, she pulled Sadie into the bathroom. This was where she learned that it was entirely possible for a person to spend two full hours doing their hair and make-up.

By the time the mission was accomplished it was turning to evening. Sadie told Irene she wanted her to meet Jimmy. "Maybe we could give him a little make-over too," Sadie suggested, replacing her elbow-high gloves.

"Definitely. I can raid my brother's closet for him," Irene said.

"I'll go see if I can persuade him to join us," Sadie said, walking with a click-clack sound toward the door.

"Oh girl, looking like that I bet you could persuade a baby outta a lolly pop."

Sadie's face broke into a wide smile.

She found Jimmy eating dinner alone at the counter in Alec's room.

"Ah there you are. I was getting worried," he said, dusting his hands free of crumbs. "Look Sadie, I've got to talk to you."

She smiled, waiting for him to say something about her makeover, but he didn't seem to notice.

"It's about Alec," he rushed on. "It was nice of him to let us stay here and all, but I really don't think we can trust the guy."

Sadie frowned. This was not what she'd been expecting.

"What does that mean? We can't *trust* him? Trust him with what?" She crossed her arms.

Jimmy cleared his throat. "Trust him with... see, I think back in the woods – uh, when we couldn't find someone for you – Alec said he'd searched all around us. He said there was no one there, but then I found that farm. It was basically right next to us."

She raised her eyebrows.

"I think he intentionally didn't tell us," Jimmy finished.

Sadie realized her mouth was open and closed it.

"Jimmy, that makes no sense. Where is this coming from? Why do you suddenly have it out for Alec?"

He opened and shut his mouth, stood up, and cleared his throat again. "No, it's not sudden. I just didn't have a chance to tell you earlier. There was so much happening and we didn't have a moment alone together. Alec didn't *want* to give us a moment alone together, not even to shower. He waited till we were all in the kitchen."

Sadie shook her head, her frown deepening in genuine concern now. She tried to step into the kitchen, but her toes caught on a tile and propelled her forward. Jimmy caught her just in time, helping her back to her feet.

"What are you wearing?" He frowned, looking her up and down.

"Alec's sister – never mind. Look Jimmy, I think sometimes you get a little jealous when I make a new friend. I remember how you were about Gabriel. But it's good for us to branch out. We're traveling the world, we should be able to meet new people; live a little."

"No, Sadie, I don't think you're hearing me. Alec intentionally tried to sabotage us."

Sadie bit her lip.

"Jimmy, why would he do that?" she asked again, a little anger coming through this time.

"He's a siren. He wanted to feed off you while you were hungry. It's how his kind do it." Sadie stood up straighter and recrossed her arms. "Yeah. It's how my kind do it too. Are succubi not trustworthy either, or is it just sirens?"

"No that's—" Jimmy's face softened. "Sadie, that's not what I mean. It's just that Alec—"

"Look, I'm going to go downstairs and have fun. You're welcome to stay up here and fret if you want, but I want to go be in the world. Let others in a little. Wasn't that the speech you gave me when you dragged me out to that party by the river? If that Jimmy shows up, you know where to find me." And before he could say Alec one more time, she turned and stormed out, her heels ringing loudly in the silence of her wake.

"HE WAS SLEEPING," Sadie told Irene. "It's been a long trip."

Irene gave a huff. "You're not sleeping."

"That's right," Sadie said, tucking a curl behind her ear and looking at her reflection in Irene's full-length mirror. Still a little shaken from the argument, she rallied herself to go have fun. Irene didn't seem to notice as she looped her elbow through Sadie's.

"Let's light it up," Irene said.

The place was surprisingly full for a Monday night in Sadie's opinion. Didn't these people have families? It was dinner time.

"Heya, who's your friend?" said a red-haired man as he pulled up next to them.

"Sadie, this is Joe," Irene said. "He's a schmuck. Don't go home with him. But he plays a mean game of cribbage if you want to try your hand. He's also a dear friend." Sadie could see it was the truth.

"Pleasure to meet you, sir," Sadie said with a slightly ironic curtsy given the introduction.

"Welcome, Sadie. Everything she says is true. Can I buy you a drink though?"

Sadie looked at Irene, who nodded.

"That'd be great," she replied to Joe.

"Over here," Irene said, taking her to join two women on the far end of the bar. Tara and Katina, sitting at the bar, were also introduced as dear friends, though in truth the friendship was only between the two of them. The relationship between them and Irene was clearly exaggerated, since there were virtually no real friendship lines connecting them, but Sadie played along.

"Oh, I just love those boots," said Tara, offering her a seat between them.

"They're, um, Irene's. She's lending them to me. I didn't really have anything like this with me while I was traveling." Sadie wished she didn't sound so nervous.

Katina jumped in, "Well you pull them off perfectly. Irene said you came from a little town up north? I'd always wanted to settle in a place like that. And I bet you're quite the hit there. You must tell us all about yourself."

Joe returned with her drink, providing a little liquid courage. For all her concern over being far too boring to entertain these women, they seemed delighted at her stories. And for the first time in her life, Sadie felt... comfortable in a crowd.

They all swapped stories of how they'd come to Seattle and Irene kept the drinks flowing. She had a knack for keeping the conversation lively too. Sadie found herself becoming increasingly giggly. When a line dance started up in the space next to the bar, Joe pulled her up. She protested only a little. The three Mystery Monday drinks helped loosen her hips though.

After a while, the women bid her farewell so they could go gamble, but expressed their hope to see her again tomorrow. Joe and Sadie were left at the bar together a while, which turned out to be perfectly comfortable as he really did know how to play a good game of cribbage, and Sadie could hang with the best of them. When it became clear she wasn't going home with him though, he too bid her goodnight and went in search of a bed warmer.

Irene was in and out as she helped cash people out for the night, but she did keep checking on Sadie. She appeared only a minute after Sadie found herself alone.

"Sorry, babe. It's been a busier night than I expected," Irene told her.

"No, I've been having so much fun! Your friends are wonderful!"

Sadie said, perhaps a bit louder than was necessary. She meant it though. She'd never felt so welcome, and now she was left with a warm feeling that she was sure was only partially due to alcohol.

"You good for a while then?" Irene asked.

Sadie nodded vigorously. She was more than good. Irene bobbed her head, satisfied Sadie was telling the truth, and disappeared.

Finding herself alone, Sadie had the opportunity to scan the room. She enjoyed these moments when she could look around at all the people and take in their complex connections and sexualities.

A couple sat gambling at one table nearby. She could tell they were a couple by the faded love lines passing between them, like thin old strands of black barely holding on. She'd come to recognize some subtle differences in color and texture of the black light that spoke of a love relationship. She felt she could tell when a couple had been together a while and if they had once loved each other, but the emotion had grown stale. The man here had a strong sexual connection with the woman dealing out the couple's cards. A full rope of red light ran from one to the other.

At the next table over was a group of people with friend lines between them. One of the men had red lines flowing from him to each of the three women, though none of them returned the interest. She could see several scenes hovering around him in which he masturbated while thinking about each of his female friends. A waitress walked by and some of his attention split to her. Sadie smiled to herself. This guy was looking for some action wherever he could find it. A potential candidate for herself that night. Sadie would certainly make his day.

Just beyond them was a woman sitting alone in a corner booth. At first Sadie didn't see much worth noticing about her and almost moved on immediately. But in the second of lingering, she became intrigued by something. The woman had almost no sexual or romantic attachments. There was a smattering of one-night stands with different women and that was it.

And notably, there was very little in the way of recent sexual interactions or interest, but in this moment the woman was yearning for companionship. Sadie could sense this despite the lack of a clear image of what she was looking for. She exuded an overall feeling of desire.

Sadie pushed back the images to focus on the physical; an easy task in this case. The woman was dressed in sturdy boots, which contrasted slightly with her elegant dark blue dress. Her fair hair was pulled up high and tight on her head. Sadie was just taking in her strong cheekbones and intense gaze when she realized that gaze was directed right back at her.

Sadie smiled, but the woman looked away.

Despite the dismissal, Sadie couldn't help but continue to watch her. There was something strange about the woman. Shortly after she'd looked away, a red line of light appeared connecting them, flowing slowly outward from the woman to Sadie.

Not so disinterested then. Or was she just desperate?

Sadie didn't think the woman would want long for company, and sure enough, several men and one woman tried to approach her. Every time, she pushed them away with a shrug or a look.

Sadie found herself doing the same, just to get rid of people and continue watching the woman. The thin red line remained steady between them, and mysteriously, the woman showed no such interest in any of the others. Sadie made sure to look away whenever the woman would glance in her direction. This game went on for what must have been an hour before Sadie decided it was time to walk over there.

Oddly, Sadie found herself nervous to approach the woman. How could this stranger affect her at all? In Arlington, she had gotten used to picking up people to feed from. She was never hurt by rejection, though she rarely received it, given she often knew ahead of time if someone was a good bet. Her biology was built for comfortably engaging in such action. And yet her legs didn't seem to want to lift her down off her stool and across the room.

Finally forcing herself into action, she popped down and turned back to face the bartender.

"Hey," she said in a slightly lowered voice, "can you tell me what the woman in the far left corner is drinking?"

"Hetia? Uh...gin. On the rocks."

"I'll take two," Sadie said.

The woman saw her coming and watched her approach without blinking. Sadie half-expected to be dismissed like everyone else, but she let her walk right up to the booth.

"Hetia?" Sadie tried. "Want to introduce me to gin? I've never tried it."

"It's Hay-sha. Hay. Sha. Not Het-ee-a."

"Oh, sorry. The bartender—" Sadie explained.

"Doesn't know my name," Hetia cut her off.

Being overly familiar had definitely been the wrong call. Sadie was seriously off her game. Trying to recover, she said, "Well then allow me to offer you a *gin*-uine apology." She set the glass in front of Hetia. She thought she saw the woman's mouth twitch, but it could've just been the light. The subsequent silence stretched so long, Sadie considered just leaving without a word, but as she shifted her weight to go, the woman said in a moderately softer tone, "You can sit."

Sadie contemplated taking the seat next to Hetia, but at the last minute sat down across from her. The woman watched her; twirling her glass with a frown.

"You've never had gin?" she asked. "Though you look like you're seventeen. How do I know this isn't your first drinking experience?"

Sadie smiled. "I'm twenty. Old enough to drink. And don't worry, I'm very experienced."

The woman laughed at her flirtation. It was a genuine laugh, and though Sadie was surprised at the sudden change, she was even more struck at her warm smile. A few moments only, though, and Hetia's face had masked over again.

Suddenly, Sadie didn't feel like putting on airs. Relaxing into the bench, she continued, "Though really I'm from a small town up north a bit. We don't get a lot of liquor. I know some kids bring it in for parties, but I was never invited to those. I'm used to a simple beer by the river, not these fancy drinks in bars in the big city."

Sadie took a swig of the gin. Ugh! She almost spit it back into the glass. Trying to play it cool, she swallowed and smiled, but the look on her face definitely gave her away.

"I guess I bought you two drinks," she said, pushing her gin to Hetia.

Hetia downed her own glass in one gulp, threw back Sadie's in a second, and asked, "So what brings you here..."

"Sadie. Sadie Hall," she said.

"Sadie. Hall," Hetia repeated back slowly, as if sampling the name on her lips.

"And what about you? Where are your people?" Sadie asked.

"Not here," she said.

Sadie responded with silence over pushing for more, but this had the same effect. Hetia conceded. Her shoulders softening an inch, she continued, "My mother left when I was young. It was just me and my dad. Then he died and his best friend raised me. We moved around a lot."

"Oh. I'm sorry about your dad. How old were you?"

"Eleven. It was a while ago." Hetia stacked the glasses in front of them and sat back, then redirected. "And what brought you here?"

Sadie looked down at her hands. "Well, actually, I decided to leave town after I became a succubus."

Hetia registered no change at this information and Sadie continued. "The news didn't exactly go over well with my neighbors. I was afraid to stay. Afraid no one would want to be with me there. And—" Sadie paused, not really wanting to talk about Jimmy.

To cover up the pause she moved on to other thoughts. "I miss it though. So much. In all these little ways."

As Sadie described everything that she loved about home, the woman's interest in her slowly grew. Hetia didn't say much herself; continuing to wear a reserved look.

Neither woman went for another drink or even acknowledged the rest of the room for several hours.

Eventually, Sadie asked, "Where are you staying tonight?"

Hetia responded simply, "Here."

For a woman clearly hoping Sadie was coming back to her room, she wasn't being very cooperative.

"Right here in the bar?" Sadie asked. "It's so public. How will you sleep? Or... do other things?"

Hetia smiled ever so slightly, but still didn't say more.

Sadie was afraid to be more direct when obvious hints were left hanging like that.

"Well, I'm staying upstairs, but I'm sharing a room with a friend," Sadie said.

Hetia merely nodded.

"It's getting late," Sadie added, feeling like she was outright rambling now.

Hetia just blinked.

"So, can I – do you want me to come up?" Sadie asked.

Outwardly, Hetia responded with still silence, but a pulse of red desire answered the question.

"My room is a mess," Hetia finally said.

Well, that was unhelpful. Sadie chewed her lip.

The woman didn't seem nervous. She did seem to enjoy talking to her. She was picturing them kissing. She did want to sleep with her. And yet outwardly it seemed like she wanted her to leave.

"Well, maybe I should get to my own bed?" Sadie asked.

Hetia looked down. "If that's what you want," she said.

Well now what?

"It's not what I want," Sadie said.

Hetia looked back up into her eyes and asked coolly, "And what do you want then?"

Sadie could think of a lot of things she wanted just then. Most of them centered on wanting to see this woman react with more than a blink to anything she said… or did.

Pulling her seat forward Sadie slid her right foot forward until her heeled shoe clicked against Hetia's boot.

"Are you wearing leggings?" Sadie asked.

Hetia shook her head once.

"Neither am I," she said, pushing her heel an inch more. Hetia's feet were together under the table.

"Do you understand how succubi feed?" Sadie asked.

Hetia nodded, moving her feet so Sadie could stretch out between them.

Taking that as some encouragement, she slipped her foot out of

Irene's heel. Hetia spread her legs just wide enough that Sadie could tuck her foot under her dress and rest it on the seat between her legs. Moving slowly in case the woman changed her mind, Sadie pressed her calf against Hetia's inner thigh.

They watched each other, unmoving, as Sadie sent the smallest wave of pleasure she could through Hetia. She had to breathe steadily, forcing the most control over herself she'd ever attempted as she kept the sensation minimal.

"I think what I want is to order some chicken wings," Sadie said, answering the earlier question. Then, when Hetia didn't weigh in, Sadie flagged down a distant waiter, a man who had long since stopped checking in on them, and placed the order. "And some more water please," she added.

As Sadie spoke, she released some of her control, letting the sensation go from arousal to a steady state of pleasure.

"Will that be all?" the waiter asked, looking between them.

Hetia's lips parted and her nipples hardened enough to be visible. When she didn't answer the man, Sadie said, "Yes, thank you," and he disappeared.

On instinct, Sadie thought it best to continue pretending like nothing was happening.

"Have you eaten here before?" she asked.

"Yes," Hetia said.

"Are the wings any good?"

"Very," Hetia said, this time sounding a little breathy. It was barely detectable, but it was the first time her tone had been anything but cool reserve all night.

"That's good. I just realized I'm starving."

Sadie could feel the heat building between Hetia's legs and made no effort to contain it as the waiter returned with the wings.

Sadie nodded once in appreciation, dismissing the man, and reached for some chicken. She moaned as she bit in. "Hmmm. This was exactly what I wanted."

Hetia watched her lips as she ate, her eyelids relaxing in a soft gaze. Sadie nudged the plate toward her, but she didn't accept. At some point she'd gripped the edge of the table and when Sadie's eyes locked on her hands, Hetia released the hold, placing her palms unnaturally flat against the tabletop in front of her.

Sadie continued to make small sounds of pleasure as she ate. Whereas Hetia, in total silence, began to breathe heavily. They didn't speak. Hetia wasn't prone to chatter and Sadie had her mouth full. So Sadie merely ate the wings, watching Hetia's chest rise and fall.

"Should I finish this?" Sadie asked, pointing to the last wing.

Hetia bit her lip at the double entendre and then nodded once.

Moving slowly, Sadie picked up the final wing and bit in as she let the plateau build to orgasm. An almost desperate little sound escaped Hetia's lips as she clenched her thighs around Sadie's foot.

Suddenly, Sadie wanted more of the woman than she could handle. Not holding back at all, she hit her full force. She knew this was trouble. The people around them were bound to notice something. But just then, something remarkable happened to cover up her moment of weakness. The whole room began to tremble. Everyone looked around as the walls shook. Hetia closed her eyes as her hips bucked several times. Sadie watched her back arching as she bit her lip in a suppressed cry.

This had been what she'd wanted; to watch this strange woman come completely undone. And she got that wish entirely as the building shook around them. Perhaps they should be ducking for cover like the others. But as everyone got under the tables, Sadie couldn't drag her gaze away from the woman's face.

The earthquake stopped only a few moments after Hetia completed the long climax. She looked genuinely shaken as she opened her eyes and caught her breath. Everyone was still crouched under furniture as Hetia looked at Sadie in open hunger and said, "Room 206."

Chapter 13

A disagreement

Oh my god, what had she been thinking? Hetia flashed to the image of herself on her back, then back to the hotel and the earthquake. How had she lost control so completely? She blushed at the memory, then flushed in anger at her own blushing. Red-faced, she jammed her stockings on so hard they tore.

And what was with the wholesome-farm-girl-sex-goddess act? First, she was all sweet and genuine and adorable, and then she turned out to be amazing in bed. Who did this woman think she was?

She probably had everyone falling all over her, too. Well not Hetia. She was taking her ass up outta here *now*. Hetia paused briefly at the door to take in the sight of auburn curls spread across two pillows, before shaking herself and stepping out into the safety of the empty hallway.

Everything about the woman had been unreal. And as her dad would've said, never trust perfection if you can't see the strings.

There was always a catch.

Hetia pushed open the door to breakfast a little too hard. She heard a smack as it made contact with the back of someone's head.

"Ouch," exclaimed a young man as he rubbed his scalp.

"Sorry," Hetia said in earnest. "You alright?"

"Good enough," he replied, as if there was some personal subtext. She got in line behind him to grab some hot scrambled eggs. If there was one thing Hetia loved, it was complimentary hotel breakfasts. She piled hash browns, eggs, biscuits and cereal onto a tray before looking around for a table at which to sit. Since accidentally bruising someone seemed like reason enough to share a table, Hetia sat across from the brown-haired man.

No one else sat with them, and neither of them seemed to be bothered by eating in silence, but when he finished much faster than she, he threw out the casual question, "You from around here?"

"Luckily no. You?" she asked, not looking up.

"Just visiting." He pushed his plate away then added. "I'm Jimmy."

"Hypatia," she said before pausing to look him over. He had a kind face. Too trustworthy for this town.

"Well, I wouldn't linger too long. This isn't a place you want to get stuck," Hetia told him.

"How do you mean?" he asked.

"Not that things were always this way," she clarified. "But this town's been extra tense lately."

He waited patiently and eventually she went on.

"It's not just the news going on about the government fracturing. It's – well, you can tell when things have gotten bad because the harpies started moving into town. I've seen it before. They come to feed off the vengeful atmosphere. *And* stir it up. But I've never seen it this bad. Things are going to blow eventually," Hetia finished.

She'd been positively chatty lately. For the second time in two days, she found herself surprised at her own demeanor. But the man had managed to neither cut her off nor annoy her for five whole minutes, and so she found herself prattling on. Or maybe her encounter with the little succubus had left her more rattled than she cared to admit. Either way, she ended up divulging enough that she felt suddenly uncomfortable. Excusing herself out of the blue, she rose to depart.

"All this to say, don't stay if you don't have to," she said and bid the man farewell before departing for work. Soon, she would get to take herself up on her own advice.

~

"Housekeeping," rang Irene's voice. Sadie stirred, but didn't want to open her eyes.

"Someone had fun without me," her new friend said.

Sadie felt Irene sit on the bed. Where was she?

"Time to move your ass though. Whoever was in this room has checked out. I gotta reset it."

She bolted upright. The woman from the bar. Hetia. She'd gone? Sadie felt a stab of anger and sadness that the woman hadn't even said goodbye after a night like that.

Rolling reluctantly out of the warm sheets, Sadie made her way back to her room in search of another bed. When she found it empty, however, she suddenly didn't feel like sleeping. Remembering her argument with Jimmy left her somber, but awake.

She wished he was there. After everything that had happened over the past few days, all she wanted was to curl up in his arms and go back to sleep while he held her.

Instead, to distract her mind from the swirl of different emotions, she plopped down on the bed with the diary. It felt like ages ago that she'd been lying in that field reading. Flipping quickly until she found her spot, she distracted herself with the troubles of some other succubus.

September 1st 1920

It is with some effort that I do not erase my last entry. Mother spoke most wisely to me regarding my actions and I must confess I cannot keep down the shame of having behaved so rashly. I understand there are many forms of power in this world, and those of the flesh can be decidedly destructive. She is

of the opinion that I wait until my feelings have calmed before accepting Thomas back into my bed. After all, he is not the father of my child, nor will he be my husband, nor can he feed me. If I had but listened to her sooner, I would not have made a mess of things. I know Thomas will not understand. It is up to me to put the distance between us. Surely if I tell him I harbor no continued interest, he will find another object of affection.

September 5th 1920

HAVING SUCCESSFULLY RID myself of Thomas, I have found a renewed desire to feed regularly and plentifully. Unfortunately, it is not always the case that lovers can be readily found who do not come with their own complications. Mother is instructing me deeply in this most grim of truths. However, she has introduced me at last to the men she keeps and says I can feed off any that interest me until I can procure my own selection. It was a concerning moment when I realized that the red-haired one preferred me drastically to my mother, but as I should have suspected immediately, my glorious mother cares not in the least that this is the case.

Unhappily, immediately after she had left me alone with the male, came another human attack, and this time they dearly wounded Father with a thick shot through the leg. None of the perpetrators have been caught, and Mother has been in quite the state that they might return during the ball tonight. I begged her not to cancel the event since I'm uncontrollably excited, and we cannot live in fear of petulant humans.

FIRST, I must say that as an, at times, insatiable young succubus, there is nothing more naturally exceptional than being the center of an event in which many of those present have come solely to throw themselves at you in the hopes you are remotely interested. I found at least four nymphs worthy of my attention. I have invited the first of them to return tomorrow, and I anticipate it will be a well-formed match.

In dreary news, Thomas came to the ball unbidden, and made such a scene my mother had to have him forcibly removed. Though I couldn't be upset for long. Mother found me in the restroom all full of self-pity and did such a job of soothing me that my make-up barely smudged. She told me the sweetest tales of her own youth, and reminded me that the life of a succubus is inherently accompanied by jealousy, rage, longing, and other strong emotions, and in time I will learn to navigate these waters smoothly.

I write these words here to reread in hard times, for my mother is a wise woman. There is no doubt she will keep our family together through any and all threats which come our way.

The door opened with a click. Jimmy's head appeared, followed by the rest of him once he spotted her lying awake with the book. He sat down on the edge of the bed.

"Good night?" he asked.

"Actually yeah. It was a very good night," Sadie said. She was annoyed at the tone of her own voice. She didn't want to fight, she wanted to hug him.

"Look Sadie—" Jimmy began.

"I don't want to hear it," she cut him off, tiredly slumping down into the bed.

He might have just been about to apologize, but she suspected from the tone of his voice that he was launching back into the same argument.

"Let me just try to explain better," he said, sounding a little frustrated for the first time.

"Explain what? Why the most generous stranger we've met on the road is secretly out to get us? Why *his kind* can't be trusted?" Her thoughts flashed to the humans shooting the father of the author of the diary in the leg. Strange she didn't even know the name of the woman whose diary she'd been reading.

"No. You're twisting my words. It's just Alec that—"

"How would you even know? You didn't want to come introduce yourself to everyone."

"Yeah, I don't want to meet his family. I want us to get out of here. We shouldn't stay here."

"Well, I disagree. I think we finally found exactly what we were looking for. Why the hell would we leave?" She looked at him sternly.

They both turned at the sound of the front door opening. A moment later, Alec appeared at the edge of their room.

"Mom's inviting you both to lunch. Says she can't wait to hear about your night here. Sis says you were quite the hit." Sadie smiled wide, then blinked in surprise at the look of murder on Jimmy's face.

"That'd be—" Sadie began to say, but was distracted by Jimmy jumping up and storming out of the room.

"What's with him?" Alec asked.

"I'm so sorry. I don't know what's gotten into him. That was really rude. I think he's feeling a little jealous."

"S'always hard when emotions are around," he said. "Heads never work right. Don't hold it against him too much. Even grown men need to pout sometimes."

"Thanks Alec. I hope he'll come out of it soon."

JIMMY DIDN'T REAPPEAR AT ALL that day and Sadie had another great night on the ground floor. This time with Alec and a few of his friends. They took to her as fast as had Irene's posse, and managed to immediately make her feel like she'd always been a part of the group. Only one of them wasn't a human feeder, and Sadie wasn't particularly interested in the slightly abrasive air nymph, so she picked up a stranger from the bar to feed from. That part of the night had been rather boring and she found herself sorry all over again that Hetia had left without warning.

Sadie decided to spend the night in her own room, despite the fact she'd have to spend it with a moody Jimmy present, but he never returned. She left space for him in the bed unnecessarily, since she woke up alone in a little patch of sunlight. The warm rays of morning reminded her that she hadn't been outside since they'd arrived.

She dressed in her blessedly comfortable traveling clothes and made her way into the fresh air. There was a bakery on the corner across the street with little outdoor tables. A little sunshine, that's what she wanted. The door to the cafe opened toward her right as she reached for the handle. Jimmy stepped out.

"Oh. Hey," she said, a little flustered.

"Hi," Jimmy said, frozen in the doorway. They stood there staring at each other until a couple pushed their way out behind Jimmy, forcing him forward.

She stepped back just enough to give him space as they continued to search each other's faces.

"Are you hungry?" He held out a bag.

"Oh no, that's yours. I'll go in and get my own," she said.

"No, it's yours. I was bringing it for you," he said.

"Oh. Thanks." She accepted the sack, feeling extra shy about their recent fight.

"Sit?" He looked at some empty chairs a few feet away. Sadie nodded and took the far one before peering into the bag in her hand. It held a fresh croissant with a mouth-watering smell.

She relaxed a little as she took a bite and looked around. It was such a pleasant morning. Eating a fresh breakfast in the sun with her best friend. Why couldn't things always be as simple as moments like this?

They looked back at each other at the same time and began speaking. After a false start, Sadie gestured for him to go first.

"I'm sorry," he said. "For pushing so hard. I understand why you want to stay here."

"Thanks Jimmy. And I'm sorry for getting so mad. I know this has all been hard on you. And you didn't have to come with me." She reached across the table and took his hand. "But I'm glad you're here."

They ate in silence for a minute.

"If we're going to stay though, we need to find work. We're almost out of money," he said, releasing her hand.

Feeling uncertain about breaking the peace with his name, she risked saying, "Alec says we can stay as long as we want. He says I'm good for business and his family likes me."

Jimmy flinched slightly.

"I'm not comfortable just living off their generosity. I need to work," he said.

Sadie remembered he hadn't stayed with them last night and wondered out loud, "Where were you last night? Not that – I guess you don't have to tell me. I've not come back before. It's fine. I'm just curious."

Suddenly the thought of him going home with someone else entered her mind and she realized she did care where he was. She cared a good deal.

"I got a room at Pine & West. It's a small inn a few blocks from here. I sold a bit of family jewelry mom gave me. Nothing special, just enough to get some extra funds."

Sadie pursed her lips. It sounded like a waste of good money to her when they already had a room. Jimmy was clearly just being obstinate.

"FEEDER LEECHES!" someone cried. Sadie's head whipped around. Two people on a bike sped past the casino. One of them threw a bottle at the door. It smashed open, releasing a green gas.

"What the?" Sadie said. A minute later, when the gas reached them, it became clear its intention. It stank to high heaven. Coughing, they retreated around the corner. They shook out their clothes, but none of it seemed to have latched on.

"Are you okay?" he asked.

"Yeah, it's just a little noxious gas with breakfast. It's not going to kill us."

"That's not what I mean," Jimmy said, looking serious.

"Yeah. They weren't out to do any real damage," Sadie said, feeling a lot more shaken than she cared to let on just then.

They finished their breakfast standing.

"Well, I'm going to go ask around about a job," Jimmy said in the end. "Do you want to come with me?"

"No, I don't think it's necessary, as I said. We're welcome guests. We can probably even help out in running the casino. Do you want me to ask about getting us jobs there?"

"No Sadie, I don't want to work for or stay in Alec's casino," he said slowly.

They were both tense again.

"Fine. If you choose to wander around like we have no friends here I can't stop you." She crossed her arms. "Just be careful out there. The humans in this town are crazy."

Jimmy made an uncharacteristic huffing sound and shook his head. He was apparently too wise to retort just then, however. He opened his mouth once, closed it, then contented himself with crinkling up the bag in his hand.

"I hope you'll be safe yourself," he said in the end, frustration and worry coming through in his tone. Without another word, he darted down the alley away from her.

∼

SADIE SUDDENLY FELT TIRED AGAIN. The consecutive late nights and emotional turmoil over fighting with Jimmy had gotten to her. Returning to her dim room, she crawled under the sheets, hugging the covers in a ball for comfort as she dozed in and out of sleep.

Eventually, she became aware of multiple voices outside her door. They slowly pulled her out of her fitful slumber. It was dark out the window. Had she seriously slept all afternoon?

She wandered as if in a trance out to the common area. There were some seven people spread out on the sofas and in the kitchen. They were all nicely dressed and engaged in quiet chatter, which ceased abruptly as they all turned to stare at her. A few nodded in greeting, but no one jumped up to explain. Alec came out of the other room.

"Sades! Perfect." He came over to her and, gesturing grandly, added, "Party's here tonight."

Sadie stepped out of the way of Alec's cousin. The man, whose name she had forgotten, placed a heavy box next to a cooler and left.

Alec smoothed down Sadie's bed hair. "Might wanna get cleaned up, it's gonna be a good one. And don't worry, sis is bringing you some fresh clothes."

Sadie disappeared to take a shower. When she emerged from the bathroom, she found a bikini and little black dress laid out on the bed. They fit her perfectly, only the dress was clearly too short. She knew it was just the style, yet she couldn't help but pull at the hem.

She didn't feel like playing around with her hair the way Irene had though. She let it air dry, and it settled into thick curls down her back. She had learned recently that was the way Jimmy liked it. When he dreamed of her, it was always with her hair down.

Ugh, why did it matter what Jimmy liked? She closed her eyes and shook her head to clear it. He wasn't even there, and if he was, she shouldn't be encouraging him to think of her that way at all. She felt like a confused mess as she exited her room. Wanting to be free of the trapped feeling in her chest, she resolved to let loose that night. No restrictions. No should or shouldn'ts.

The number of people had doubled by the time she returned to the common room. Irene and several of Alec's cousins had joined them, but all the other faces were new. Alec hopped off the couch and looked her over.

"You got the perfect little personal shopper. Sis knows'er stuff alright. What're you thirsty for?" He squatted next to the cooler.

"Surprise me," Sadie said, feeling adventurous.

He stood up with a bottle and fumbled at his key chain. A man came up next to him.

"I got that," he said, taking the bottle from Alec and popping it open. The man handed it to Sadie with a smile. His interest was written all over him. She looked him over with scrutiny and decided she wasn't uninterested. Then she glanced over the room, paying greater attention to detail. She noticed many of the people there had red threads of interest directed at her.

She raised her eyebrows at Alec. He leaned into her ear. "Mighta told a few people you were a succubus. Plus word got out on its own. Got a fan base."

She could see that. All these people were here for her? She certainly wouldn't go hungry tonight. Alec took her elbow and rubbed it affectionately.

"So if you want. You can take the gloves off. You never gotta wear 'em around here." He threw her a wink and disappeared.

Sadie felt a little nervous as she made her way into the crowd. There were three people together in the large tub and they all smiled at her. She took a swig from the mystery bottle and felt a little warmth run down her spine. Gaining courage, she made eye contact with a couple of people on one of the sofas. They scooted apart to make room for her, and she went to sit down.

Ever since her succubi instincts had kicked in, she had felt fairly comfortable picking up strangers. Or at least comfortable picking up *stranger*, singular. But not even the past few days had prepared her for this room full of attention.

"Hi, I'm Mini," said the woman on her left.

"Greg," said the man on her right.

"Peter. Maya. Kareem. Tom."

"How're you liking Seattle?" Kareem asked.

"I haven't seen much of it yet," Sadie said. They all laughed. She blinked in surprise.

"How long have you been a succubus?" Mini asked.

"Uh... a few months," Sadie said, taking another swig of alcohol.

"Do you have to feed every day?" Tom asked.

"Yeah. Supposed to," she said.

"Is it hard to find people?" Maya asked.

"Nah. Look at her. Course it's not hard," Greg said.

Sadie blushed at this. Which was strange, she realized. And yet this whole interaction had her squirming a little. To get herself back in the driver's seat, she looked over the people around her. The man Peter seemed the most genuinely attracted to her. She also found him appealing, in a rough sort of way.

"No. It's not usually hard to find people," she said, looking him hard in the face. The others smiled, heads turning back and forth between them. Sadie began to feel more in her element as she took one of her bare feet and slid it up against Peter's thigh. He went hard as his lips parted. It was exactly what the crowd had wanted. They soaked it up.

"Can you make him come like that?" Mini asked as Peter put his head back.

"Probably. But it wouldn't be as intense."

"What do you mean?"

"It matters where and how I touch someone," Sadie said this with confidence, but the truth was she was still learning so much about how it worked. She knew there was truth in her words though. Since Mini was the only other person there that Sadie found somewhat appealing, she decided to explore her idea.

Following Alec's earlier suggestion, she let the gloves come off. Mini smiled as Sadie turned to face her. She wore a bikini top and shorts, and nothing else. Sadie ran her fingertips across the woman's stomach.

"Huh. Wow!" Mini said.

"May I?" Sadie asked, even though she already knew the answer.

"The woman nodded and Sadie undid her top button. She could still feel Peter, but her attention was pulled to Mini as she slid her hand in her pants, under her underwear and cupped her already wet sex.

This had been exactly what they'd come for, she realized. The threads of red light turned into solid pulsating ropes directed at her from all directions. Her head swam for a minute with the sudden wave of ravenous attention.

"Oh my god," Mini said. "Wow."

Sadie thought her reaction was a little overblown when she hadn't even begun to take her higher. All the woman was feeling was a normal rush of excitement and the beginning stages of pleasure. Sadie began to slowly change that.

"Wow. It feels just like having sex. But better," Mini said. Sadie thought the woman must not have had much good sex if that's how she felt at this level.

Sadie tried to focus in on Peter. She wanted to see if she could take him as high with just her toe on his thigh. She slowly increased the intensity for Mini, trying to do the same for Peter with the little control she was learning to have over such things. Mini began to rock a little against her hand. Peter kept his head back on the couch. All of the other men were hard as they watched the escalation.

It was a lost cause trying to keep Mini and Peter at the same level. Clearly, she had significant more power over Mini as she was touching her directly. Sadie gave up and just focused on the woman. She sent sudden waves of pleasure through her, far outweighing what she'd been able to do with Peter. Sadie felt her own body excite as she let the waves become all-consuming and then tried to hold her steady on the edge of release.

Mini stopped babbling and describing it as she had been throughout. She also stopped her loud moaning. Her eyes clamped shut and her sounds turned into heated, genuine gasps of pleasure. Her cheeks and neck filled with blood and her head fell back. She clenched and rocked and jerked uncontrollably in the final few moments before Sadie withdrew. Sadie sent Peter over the edge at the same time, but her theory about the intensity had been confirmed.

As Mini came to, she had no more "wow's" in her. She blinked silently at Sadie. Sadie winked and did back up the woman's button. Picking her bottle up off the floor, she took another swig, but suddenly the power of alcohol paled in comparison to what else the night had in store for her. Sadie suddenly noticed the new quiet in the room. Everyone was looking their way. She stood up, locked eyes with Alec standing in the kitchen and declared for all to hear, "Let's party".

"Whew!" said one man as several people clapped.

"Water's warm," said a woman sitting on the edge of the giant tub. She took off her top as Sadie looked at her.

"Wanna join us?" The woman had a very weak line of attraction for Sadie, but how could she turn down such an invitation? The three men in the tub behind her were far more interested. Sadie walked up to one of them and turned around. Pulling her hair out of the way she asked, "Want to help a girl out?"

The man practically scrambled over himself to help her unzip. An hour later, she had fed off each of the men and was telling her Becoming story as they listened with interest. All of them were ready for more, and she could tell the night was long from over. Her head buzzed and skin tingled with so much heavy consumption of pleasure. The woman's interest had peaked after watching her work on the men, and she stood up in the middle of the tub and said, "My turn."

The tub was waist-deep in the middle, and Sadie waded out into it to join the woman.

She wondered what would happen if she just kept feeding all night long. With all these people, she could literally do just that. As Sadie scooped up the woman's breast in her hand, she caught a motion out of the corner of her eye. She turned to see Jimmy standing in the doorway. He searched the room, spotted her, took one glance at her fondling the woman as the three men watched, and turned and left.

That's fine, thought Sadie. She didn't need his moodiness anyway right now. She was having way too much fun for that. Turning back to her next conquest, she let her attention wander over the woman. Her mind and heart tried to drift back to Jimmy, but she forced her thoughts to let him go. They were both adults. They didn't always have to be in the same place. In fact, doing so had brought them both plenty of pain recently.

To distract herself, she threw her attention full-force into the woman, who had begun to tremble with the beginning of orgasm.

Something new happened. At first it all seemed business as usual, but then the images of the woman's sex life which surrounded her became sharper. Sadie saw clearly the woman's last sexual encounter. As she focused on the scene, she found herself able to see the man's face and even the room. Never had she been able to clearly make out such details.

In further strangeness, she found herself following the scene backward to the moment of their meeting. They were at a friend's house. A mutual friend. Her name was Samantha, Sadie thought, the knowledge coming seemingly from nowhere. They were having macaroni with hot dogs, but it hadn't come out yet. The smell was delicious.

The tablecloth was bright green. The man sitting to her right had a neon orange watch.

"Well, I don't think they stand a chance this year," Samantha said from the end of the table.

Why was everyone talking for so long? She just wanted to eat. She was so hungry, she just wanted to eat. Please just serve the food!

Sadie felt warm water cover her face. She gasped and sputtered for air as she re-found her footing.

"Damn Hina! You took the succubus out! I always knew you had a magic pussy."

Hina punched the guy and then held out a hand for Sadie. "You okay?" Hina asked. She looked genuinely concerned as she helped Sadie up.

Sadie was shaking from head to foot, but she didn't know what to say. "Yeah. I think maybe I've had enough for tonight." She climbed backward out of the tub and reached for one of the fluffy towels someone had left on a stand nearby.

"Alright. Party's over folks," she heard a cousin saying. "Maybe you'll get luckier next time."

She felt a hand on her back and blinked up at Alec. "You good?" he asked.

"Yeah. I uh – I think I need to call it a night." Sadie disappeared back into the little side room. She felt a sudden bliss at the safety of the closed door and leaned back against it for a minute to catch her breath. What the hell was that? Gabriel's journal hadn't said anything about mind reading. Or memory reading, as it were. At least not beyond the normal overview of someone's sexual history and desires.

She felt as if she were walking on air as she made her way to the bathroom. Her body was charged and her mind racing. She needed some release of her own. She poured herself a real bath, one without the funny smell of Alec's, and climbed into the fresh, hot water. Her thighs melted open in the heat and her own body throbbed for attention. All night she'd been engaged in sexual matters, but none of it had been focused on her.

As she felt out her own pleasure, she quickly realized that none of the people she'd met that night actually turned her on. Her thoughts found Hetia. And though this worked well, Jimmy kept popping into her head. She tried to push him away, but there were some images that wouldn't relent. His face when she'd asked him to take her back to the tent. Him standing naked in the river, so vulnerable. His hand wrapping hungrily around her ass that morning in the grass hut, the one time he'd made her orgasm.

Fuck!

She came.

It felt good for a second.

She pushed him out of her thoughts and climbed out of the tub.

Sadie knew there was no hope of her sleeping. She popped open the bedroom window and climbed onto the ledge. The air was cool and welcoming and she couldn't smell the foul street as well from the fourth floor. She looked out over the twinkle of lights. It was a pretty sight in its own way. The stars, however, looked far away, as if they were hidden behind a haze despite the fact the night was clear.

Sadie wondered what she and Jimmy would be doing just then if she hadn't turned. Would they be eating dinner with her parents? Stargazing in the orchard? Skipping rocks down by the river? Reading comics in his bedroom while his mother waged the nightly battle to get his siblings ready for bed?

What would their life be like if they stayed here in Seattle? She'd certainly have people to feed from, that was no question. And Alec's family had given them a warm welcome, so they wouldn't want for a home-cooked meal. Everything about it seemed like the right choice given her options. She was just experiencing a moment of homesickness. Such things were natural, she reminded herself. She had a sudden longing for familiarity. She wished she had someone to talk to about everything that was happening to her.

She'd gone through so much. What if she was doing it all wrong? With Jimmy. With all these strangers. Why had Gabriel's scrolls told her so little? And even with the best of books, it wasn't the same as having a mentor. That's what she really craved, she realized. Someone like Gabriel, only more like a parent. Someone who could help her figure it all out.

She envied the succubus from the diary. She had a whole family to support and love her. Her Becoming had been planned and natural. It was what was expected for her future, and everything in her world supported her fate. There was a kind of order to it all. It contrasted sharply with the chaos of Sadie's own experience. Having to flee her hometown, enter a new world which lived in sharp contrast to her old. It all felt like plunging into a cold lake without a bottom.

Was what had just happened at the party meant to be her fate? Orgies with willing and hungry strangers there to consume her the same way she consumed them? She felt a pain of deep loneliness. She had been having fun at the time. Where was all this new emotion coming from? She tried to picture the various people she'd touched that night and feel excitement again, but it had passed.

She probably just needed to get some sleep. Reset.

Looking for someone to whom she could vaguely relate, she pulled out the diary and made herself comfortable on the bed.

September 8th 1920

Oh how tiresome it is to speak of matters regarding my brother, but one day I intend to understand the fight which Father and he had in the entranceway just now. Therefore, I must record exact wording so far as I can recall it. There was a great deal of shouting on the part of Father and pleading on the part of Mother, the details of which are already slipping my mind. But Father certainly said, "The Oaths you have made to us are far stronger, how dare you put her before the family? Do not think but I won't turn you in for such illicit behavior." To which Brother responded something like, "Careful, dear father, for if it is secrets we're exposing, there are far more dangerous ones than a silly little affair between a feeder and human." I couldn't tell what the silence held, but from my watch around the corner I could see my mother's face had gone white at this. Then Brother left without another word.

. . .

SEPTEMBER 15TH 1920

WHAT A DREARY WEEK. It has done nothing but rain, and I feel quite the slave to both my education and to my feeding. It seems all I do is recite the useless Latin and bring pleasure to ungrateful humans. With the somber mood that has taken the family, I have found little impulse to set up my network of lovers, leaving me to feed most days off Mother's men. Sadly, the execution of the troublemaker who shot Father might have spoiled the men forever. Mother says I will learn in time to handle such things, and I see that she is right. Though I can't ignore the red-haired male's loathing. Fortunately, it seems to have little effect on the feeding, which his body yet craves. It is also my bad luck that the red-haired man was the one most affected by the execution. I can see in his coloring and cheek-bones that they were likely brothers. I almost wish the family had succeeded in breaking down the cellar door before they were taken. At least if the men had escaped, Mother would have more motivation to replace them.

SADIE STOPPED READING. What the hell? She couldn't be sure she understood, but was afraid to continue. She reread the last few lines several times, feeling a chasm open between her and the world of this other succubus. Suddenly a bit sick, she shut the diary and staggered backward out of bed, as if the book were a friend who had slapped her. Sliding down the wall, she put her head between her knees.

Never in all her life had she felt so alone.

Chapter 14

A crossroads

Sadie woke up with a jolt. Her head pounded as she worked to identify her surroundings. Why was someone attacking her temples with a hammer? She rolled over as the memories of the night rushed back to her. On her side, she found herself inches from Jimmy's sleeping form. He must've joined her in the night, though he rested fully clothed on top of the covers. He had even kept on his shoes.

She examined the planes of his face, and for a moment, it felt like old times. No disagreements. No hard choices between them. She had the impulse to kiss his nose and had to content herself with playing with a few strands of his hair. Sadie had removed her gloves, and so was careful to avoid direct contact.

He opened his eyes. A brief exchange of warmth passed between them before the reality of their recent interactions crashed over the moment. Both their gazes sharpened, and Sadie was suddenly aware again of her throbbing headache. She tried to sit up, but fell back against the bed frame, nausea gripping her. Jimmy pulled himself upright at the same time and glared at her.

"Looks like maybe you had a little too much fun last night," he said in a strangely accusatory tone.

"Let me guess. You don't approve," Sadie retorted, finding a price in the focus it took to speak. She plopped her head back on the wall, but kept her gaze fixed on Jimmy.

"I would if it was right for you. But really, Sadie? Are you sure about all that? Do you really want to be a theme-park attraction? And you should've heard what Alec was saying in the kitchen. I'm not wrong about him, whether you choose to believe me or not."

"Can we do this later, Jimmy? It's first thing in the morning."

He nodded to the clock. "It's noon."

"Well maybe my schedule just isn't running the same as yours these days," she said, defensive of his judgement.

"It isn't. It hasn't been. And Sadie, I don't know that I can stand by and watch you do this anymore. Alec is no good for you."

"Alec and I are getting along fine. We seem to have a mutually beneficial arrangement. And I see nothing wrong with it."

"Well I do." He ran his hand over the beard that had begun to grow in. "Sadie, I want to go home."

She blinked; pushed herself forcefully into a more dignified position and responded.

"I already said, Jimmy, I want to stay here. I can't go home now."

He nodded then looked away. He was still for so long, she considered pinching him.

Turning back to her, he said decisively, "I'm going home."

Now she did want to pinch him. Was he serious? He was so jealous of Alec he was just going to abandon her there? She'd never known him to be the stubborn one, and this new turn angered her with such volatility that she began to shake, tasting bile, sour in her mouth.

"What're you waiting for then? If after all this time such a small thing would pull you away, why waste another minute with me?" Her eyes welled with traitorous tears, but she kept them wide enough they wouldn't spill over.

He stood up suddenly. "You'll know where to find me... if you change your mind. I'll tell your parents you say hello." His voice broke slightly on this last word, then he turned and walked toward the door.

Sadie came up on her knees. How could he leave her just when she needed him the most?

"Fine! Tell them you chose to give up on me just because I finally found a place I feel welcome," she sobbed.

He stopped with his hand on the door. She watched his back as he took several deep breaths. Jimmy turned and approached the bed in a rush. He kissed the top of her head and whispered, "I love you, Sadie. Please be safe."

Then he was gone.

Sadie cried most of the afternoon. Her wracked emotions and headache-driven nausea eventually caused her to vomit, which led to an even greater feeling of self-pity. Irene popped her head in to say hello and ended up playing caretaker, though rather unwillingly. Irene made her brush her teeth and get dressed, but when it was over, Sadie just climbed back into bed with her shoes on. She'd ceased crying and now just wanted to sleep some more.

Irene huffed and went to the door. Sadie heard her say in an only mildly hushed voice, "You brought her here. Do something."

Alec approached the bed. "Hey Sades. Time to get your ass up. Meteor shower tonight. We're headed outta the city lights to watch it." He pinched her side. The sound of his brusque voice roused her out of her stupor a bit. He pinched her again, and this time turned it into full-on tickling. She couldn't help but respond.

She tossed and turned until she was laughing against her will. Pulling herself into a seated position, she hugged her knees and glared murder at him. He grinned back mischievously. This wasn't his fault, she told herself. She couldn't attack her host.

"Meteor shower?" she asked.

"It's hitting right at dusk. Can watch the sunset. Drink a couple beers with the guys. Back in time to party."

After a minute, Sadie nodded.

"Good." He slapped her leg and bounced to his feet.

AN HOUR LATER, she was jostling around in the back of a truck with Alec and his air nymph friend, Eric, who she'd met the other night. She knew Eric was an air nymph because he'd spent some amount of their first meeting blowing up the skirts of passing bartenders. There were also two new guys, named Dan, who was driving, and Sam. They both seemed alright. Sam kept apologizing for Eric, and eventually ordered him to the other side of the truck bed.

As promised, they took her just out of the city and parked against a large oak. They weren't the only ones around either – this was clearly a popular place to hang out. People were sprawled out on blankets and chairs up and down the side of the dirt road. There were a few more private vehicles like theirs, and even a few pop-up vendors.

Dan kicked open the cooler and passed around beers as Sadie watched a mom pulling along a young girl in the midst of a tantrum. They were obviously traditionalist nymphs as they had stems woven through their hair, though their species would've been obvious to anyone paying attention by the way the flowers lining the road gave a slight lean in as they passed.

Sadie hadn't met many different peoples, and she was slowly realizing how little she actually knew. Did the child feel the presence of the daisies, or did that develop in puberty?

Kicking up her feet and leaning back with the cold beer, Sadie directed at Alec, "What's it like? For you I mean. When you feed?" She hoped the question wasn't too inappropriate, but she was suddenly curious.

He nodded in thought and took a sip before answering. "S'like a hum in the air. Tingle at the base of my skull. When I'm around it, everything's right. When not, I start craving it. Only a little at first. Then more and more till my head pounds too loud to hear straight."

"When did it start?"

"I think I always felt it. Can't remember a time I didn't. But I started to need it, I don't know, round age ten I guess. Pretty typical." He laughed. "Sis was about six, and she had a little nymph playmate. I remember the sudden joy of withholding her toys. The girl would reach for them, crying her eyes out. The family stopped letting her come over. Ma said it was good for the girl though. She always got everything she wanted in her own home. Not healthy."

"I had a similar experience," Sam said. "Bout the same age. My people feed off excitement, see. It's just my dad and me and he worked down at this theme park. There was a rollercoaster and a haunted house that stayed up all year round. I always enjoyed going to visit him and I could always feel the emotion in people, but one day a kid fell out of a ride. He dropped ten feet, broke both legs. The mom saw him falling and the feeling of her struck right through me. It's a sensation in my gut, a euphoric feeling. Nothing compares to it. I felt awake after that, and started craving it all the time. Got me into some mischief over the years." He grinned.

"Yeah," Dan chimed in. "People have always feared their emotions. That's the problem with our society. Humans don't know how to embrace their own natures. Excitement, sorrow, lust, these are all a part of being alive."

Sadie nodded. The contentment at being around her own kind welled up in her. It was enough to pull her mind momentarily off her loss. If there had been a satisfaction feeder nearby, she would have made them happy, and she would have been happy to do so.

Right in that moment, the first shooting star darted across the horizon. There was a collective murmur along the road as anyone who'd been watching pointed it out to friends and family.

Sam jumped up. "'I'll be back. Anyone want anything?"

They all placed hot dog orders.

"Five hot dogs coming up," he said.

There were two stands nearby, and Sam went for the one on the right. Alec and Dan exchanged a look. "Someone's feeling feisty," Eric said, watching Sam walk away.

Sadie had missed it; what was happening?

When no one explained she prodded Alec.

"That's the human side," Dan answered. Sadie looked at the chairs and blankets and hot dog stand. Then she examined the people.

"How do you know that?" she asked.

"Oh. Everyone just knows that," Alec responded in an unhelpful clarification. Sam pushed his way in front of a young woman.

"Hey!" Sadie could hear her say. "What do you think you're doing?"

"Buying a hot dog. What's it look like?" He turned his back to her. "Five please," he told the vendor when it was his turn.

"Just in time. Got only six left," the old man told him.

"Actually," Sam said, "I'll take all six." He grinned over his shoulder at the woman. The old man cleared his throat.

"Uh, you sure? Don't want to save one for the lady?"

"Did I stutter?" Sam asked. The man didn't argue further as he handed over the dogs.

What a jerk! Why would he do that? Sadie glared at Alec.

"I know," Alec said. "Don't hold it against him too much. He's had a lotta human trouble recently. Man's gotta vent somehow."

On Sam's return, however, Sadie found she suddenly wasn't hungry. Scooting closer to Alec and further from his friend, she tried to enjoy the sunset. A few more shooting stars streamed by.

"On that subject, how's business?" Dan asked Alec.

"Another attack yesterday. They're determined to put us out," Alec said.

"They're just jealous at how well you've done. I saw it last week. Looked fine in there. Bringing in good clientele too, I noticed. Your family should talk to my dad about making some investments up town," Dan suggested.

"Like the Hare's Edge would let us move in on 'em? We'd get no business over there anyhow."

"Not yet," chimed in Eric, "but if they went out of business..."

"Doesn't seem likely at this point. They've got The United on their side after all," Sam said.

"The United?" Sadie asked.

"A pro-human group in town. Probably the ones behind the attacks."

"Well maybe if we started getting our hands dirty," Eric said. Alec shrugged, but Dan sat up straighter.

"Not a bad idea. We could teach them about messing with feeders."

"You know I'm always in," added Sam. They looked at Alec.

"The Edge?" Alec asked. Sadie's head swiveled between them as they made the decision.

"Alright," Alec agreed. "Let's do it."

Sadie asked what was going on as they began to pack back into the truck. "There's a human-run casino on the other side of town. We're going to see if we can't make them a little nervous," Dan said.

"Don't worry Sades. It'll be safe," Alec added.

"But there's still stars," Sadie protested, pointing out another one. She wasn't at all sure about messing with someone's business.

"You can watch them on the drive back," Alec said.

This turned out to be only partially true, as it took ten minutes before the view had to compete with city lights. In no time, they were parking the truck in an alleyway.

"Maybe I'll just stay here," Sadie said.

"Not the safest place to stay alone," said Dan.

"Come on Sadie, live a little," added Sam.

She wasn't particularly interested in anything the second man had to say at this point, but she was a little afraid of staying in the alleyway by herself. Fear of other people wasn't a habit she'd grown up with, but she'd heard stories about the city.

Accepting Alec's hand, she hopped down to join them. They crept along the now-dark streets and settled behind some bushes in a little park. A dimly lit sign reading *The Hare's Edge* could be easily seen from their hiding place. The neighborhood was residential apart from the casino, and tiny houses lined the rest of the street.

"The Danny?" Eric whispered to Sam. Sadie saw him nod and the two of them disappeared.

"Keep a look out," Alec told her. "Might need a distraction."

Sam and Eric crept away to fumble around next to the dumpster just inside the alleyway between the casino and little purple house. They kept pulling items out of their backpacks to assemble something Sadie couldn't see clearly, but eventually they hooked a small package to the chain on the dumpster and ran back to the bushes.

The five of them watched for twenty minutes, discussing other plans if this didn't work out. Eventually, a middle-aged man came out a side door just behind the dumpster. He unlocked the chain to open it all the way and a small fire burst to light. Sadie gasped as the man's beard nearly went up.

Eric got to his knees and reached out a hand. A strong gust of wind billowed down the alley, enraging the flames as it passed. The man jumped back in a yell as Sadie cried out in shock. A paper, pulled by the draft, soared like a fiery bird out of the dumpster and in the blink of an eye caught on the branch of the neighbor's tree.

A piercing scream erupted immediately from somewhere inside the little house. An instant later the branch went up in flames. A woman in a nightgown burst from the front door clutching her heart.

"No," was all she said, but the word was filled with such anguish that Sadie would've thought she was looking at her child burn.

"Oh shit," said Eric, jumping to his feet.

"Let's go," said Dan, pulling on Alec's shirt.

Alec looked worriedly at Sadie, but Sam let out a little laugh. Dan glared at him and he covered his face.

"Sorry, I know I shouldn't," Sam said.

Everyone except Sadie was on their feet. Alec tugged on her sleeve, but she was transfixed by the scene playing out before her.

The woman had come to her senses and run into the house. She returned a half-minute later with a wet towel. The man from The Hare's Edge ran back into the casino, but the situation was escalating rapidly. Sadie had to do something. Shaking out of Alec's grip, she rushed forward and took the towel from the woman.

"I've got this one," Sadie said.

The woman let go and ran back into her home while Sadie climbed the lower branches and tossed the towel over the highest branch that was aflame. The woman passed her a second one as several people emerged from the casino to help.

When it was finished the tree was half-blackened, though still standing. The woman knelt at its base in shocked silence while neighbors tried to comfort her.

Sadie slunk away, returning to the bushes. Everyone had gone. They'd just left her! She took one last look back at the devastated tree nymph before making her way back to the alley in which they'd left the truck. It too had disappeared.

Alec, however, stood leaning against the wall.

"What the hell was that!" Sadie raged.

"I'm so sorry. Got outta hand back there. Clearly an accident though. Eric doesn't have the best control."

"That's not even what I mean. Setting a fire! Someone could've been hurt."

"If a singed beard counts, then yeah. But he's fine. We've never really hurt anybody."

"Do you do this often?" Sadie crossed her arms.

"Often enough to remind them to leave us alone. Gotta defend ourselves or we'd go outta business. You saw what they did."

She had seen the stink bomb, but it hadn't seemed nearly as dangerous as this. She continued to glare. Alec stepped closer.

"You're right," he said. "This was uncalled for. We'll do it better next time."

That last line did nothing to placate her mood.

"I want to go home," she said, looking away from him. "How are we getting back without the truck?"

"This way." He nodded toward the road. A bit of a walk and a short carriage ride later, they were walking up the steps to The Taste of Destiny. Sadie hadn't spoken since the alley, but Alec had been making polite conversation the whole way; speaking far more than was his usual manner.

The second he opened their suite door Sadie pushed past him to her room and closed herself in. She was being rude to her only current lifeline. Would he be mad, possibly ask her to leave? She wasn't sure if she cared at the moment.

Then she remembered the feeling she'd had earlier that evening, before everything had gone south. She liked being around Alec. She could talk to him about things which they both understood. His friends were all awful, but people could get caught up in the wrong crowds. It happened all the time.

She sprawled out on the bed and glared a hole into the ceiling for what must've been an hour. Jimmy's words came back to haunt her, *He can't be trusted.* Though the feuding in this town seemed to leave no innocents. Why should she single out Alec?

She hadn't resolved her quandary when she heard several voices appear in the common space. A few minutes later came a soft knock at the door.

"Sades?" Alec asked gently. He entered and sat next to her on the bed.

"Let me make it up to you? Got a host a-pretty people out here. Even invited a fire nymph. Heard your kind like those."

She continued to glare at the ceiling, but eventually responded.

"It's not that we like all fire nymphs, it's that they can withstand a lot from us. They're particularly resilient to succubi. Doesn't mean that I'll be into them."

"Huh. Interesting. Well... wanna come find out?"

Sadie heard laughter coming from the other room and longed for the simplicity of the previous night.

"Okay," she said somberly, pushing herself to a sitting position.

"I should change," she added, feeling tired at the thought.

"Oh. About that. Sis stocked that closet. S'all just for you. Take anything you want." He threw her a smile and left.

Sadie slid open the mirrored door. Wow. She ran her hands over the various dresses, shirts, and lingerie that Irene had graciously left her. Sadie had never previously cared much for such things, but then again, she had never received such attention before either.

She played dress up for about an hour, glad Irene wasn't there to drag it out even longer, and went to join the party. There were even more people present than the previous night. In fact, everyone who had been there appeared to have returned, only now an additional twenty people helped to fill every corner of the room.

Sadie did her best to enjoy herself, but a feeling of protest had begun to bubble up in her. She fed from the three people she found most interesting, to the excitement of everyone. The bikini top chafed horribly when she got it wet, so she joined the variety of women in going topless. The fire nymph did not particularly grab her interest, but he didn't seem to realize that.

By the reactions of the women around them, she could tell he was accustomed to being the most attractive thing in the room, and he gazed at her all night like he secretly knew she was just dying to jump him. When she continued to ignore the man, he joined her in the tub.

Sadie was sitting on the edge, trying to cool off. People chattered around her, but it all felt far away, even when she heard herself respond to direct questions. Her head swiveled toward different speakers, but she barely heard them. She tapped her toe in the water to the sound of her heartbeat, fixated on the repetitive splash-splash sound.

She looked up to see the nymph sauntering toward her, grinning knowingly. His body had an impressive ripple to it as he walked. The bubbling sound of steamy water mixed with the babble and laughter around them, but it all felt muted in her mind. The nymph placed himself right in front of her and took her chin in his hand.

"Are you ready for this?" he teased.

A flash. It was an early spring day and Jimmy had tied a rope to the highest branch above the river. They'd secured a tire to the end of it and anchored it tightly to shore. The rope was long, it would be a hell of a swing when they let go. It had always been their favorite place to play since the current was slow and the water deep.

She climbed in first. Jimmy was going to jump up at the last minute. He untied the security line and was shaking with the effort of holding both her and the tire.

"Are you ready for this?" he asked.

"Let's fly," she'd said. He jumped from the ground, clinging to the rope as he jammed his legs on either side of hers.

"Ahh!" they screamed. The swing soared out over the smooth water. It tangled with a few branches on the far side of the river and swung back with almost equal gusto. She let it oscillate a few more times before saying, "Bye." His eyes grew wide as she let herself fall straight backward out of the swing.

She sank through the cool liquid, her hair engulfing her vision of the light above. A moment later, she saw him pierce the surface to her right. He spotted her and turned. Staying submerged, they swam toward each other. The water was so clear that she could see the sun glitter off his skin and the rocks just below them. They came up together, laughing with exhilaration.

They floated on their backs and Jimmy reached for her hand.

"We'll have to start every spring like that," he said.

"New tradition?" she asked.

"New tradition," he said.

"Promise?" she pressed. "Even when we get old and our bones protest the cold?"

"Promise. Spring won't start without it," he said.

Sadie staggered backward and looked around the room. What was she doing here? She scrambled out of the water. It suddenly felt much too warm; the room too stuffy. She went back to the bedroom and shut the door. Someone knocked. She turned the latch to lock it.

She couldn't breathe. How had everything gotten so lost? She ripped off the wet swimsuit bottoms and searched for clean clothes, donning her old turtleneck and gloves. She did take one of the pairs of panties out of the drawer as Irene had thrown all hers away upon seeing them, but she put on her own long traveling pants.

Sadie unlatched the door and tore through the room almost before anyone recognized her.

"Hey, where you going?" someone called as she yanked open the front door. She didn't want to take the elevator. It felt too small and she needed to move her body. She found stairs and practically flew down them.

Sadie snuck out the side door they used for garbage. The air was surprisingly chilly. When she noticed the lightening sky, she realized it was the chill of the approaching dawn that she felt.

What had Jimmy called it? She went to the street bearing the cafe at which they'd eaten. He'd nodded down that way. Cedar and west? Pine and west? She walked several blocks and realized the hotel could be anywhere.

Just as she was concocting a plan to systematically wander up and down every street, she spotted a woman out walking a dog. Thank goodness for small bladders. Sadie raced over to her.

"Just down there to the right. You're not far," the woman croaked.

Sadie broke into a run. She hoped he'd decided to stay a night.

The inn was small and all doors were locked. She paced anxiously in the street until a man opened the door to shake out a rug.

"Hey excuse me. Excuse me, sir?" Sadie ran up to him. "Can you tell me – do you have a guest by the name of Baker?"

"Baker, yes." The man squinted. "Might still be sleeping, but he said he was catching the early-morning train. Told me not to worry about breakfast."

Sadie wanted to push her way past the man and pound on his door, but she didn't think he'd tolerate that.

"Okay thank you!" she called over her shoulder as she rushed in the direction of the train station. If there were any really early trains, she would hopefully beat them. At the least she would be there when he arrived.

She ran through the deserted streets of Seattle, thinking about everything she had said to Jimmy over the past month; replaying everything he had done to take care of her and to be a part of her new life. Even though all this had been almost unbearably hard on him at times, he had stayed. He loved her. Even as he had said goodbye, he had loved her. And he'd been right about Alec. She had just been so desperate to be a part of something, to feel included, she hadn't been willing to listen.

The sun peeked over the horizon as Sadie entered the station. There were a couple of people sleeping on benches, but the room was otherwise empty. She hurried across the marble expanse and through the unlocked door on the far end.

The sun lit up the tracks in a warm glow.

There was only one person on the platform for the early-morning train out of town. He was standing, looking out over empty tracks. She knew him by the way he held himself; upright, still, strong, and thoughtful. A pillar that would hold any weight she put on it. Or was he a broken pillar? Had she gone too far?

His hands were clasped behind his back the way they had been back at the barn, the day he had made the choice to tell her there was someone else nearby she could feed from. She knew how much he had wanted to take her back to that tent. But he hadn't. He had always done what he thought was best for her.

She slowed her pace to catch her breath. The train was nowhere in sight, there was time. Her mind raced through all the things she wanted to say. Her stomach clenched and she had to blink away tears as she thought about how much she loved that man and how she had almost lost him.

When he turned at her approach, she had yet to form a plan for what would come out of her mouth. He looked surprised and she noted the redness of his eyes, as if he had recently been crying. What a fool she had been to think there was something worse than this. Worse than hurting him as she had. Whatever happened next, she knew one thing. It was time to tell Jimmy the truth.

He was looking at her with a weary expression, as if afraid of what she might say. She looked over his familiar face; the deep brown eyes she loved so much; the dimple in his chin; the strong line of his jaw. Now that she was under his gaze, however, her tongue felt like lead in her mouth. She was hoping he'd break the silence first, but that was not her luck. Letting go, she let the words come out as if they had a mind of their own.

"Jimmy, I – I'd always known you'd be the most important person in my life," she panted, still trying to catch her breath. "I figured, when I showed no interest in sex, that I'd be the closest aunt to your children. And I just prayed you'd still have time to come fishing every Saturday." She swept her hair behind her ear and took a steadying breath. "That was the future I'd been picturing for us. But everything's different now, and I don't know any more what we look like ten years down the road." She paused to breathe, but her voice still broke as she said, "But wherever I am, I know you're there with me. And that's where I need you. I always need you. And I always want you. And I'm sorry. I'm so sorry, Jimmy." A tear broke free and ran down her face.

He took her hands in his. "Sadie, I know I left in anger, but I've had the night to think. I don't know where you're headed, but I'm not sure – will there even be a place for me in your world?"

"You are my world," she said through her tears.

"I used to be, but as you said… everything's different now. I don't want to hurt you, but everything has been strained between us since the change. I don't know how to fix it. How to put it back. How to move it forward. How to—"

"I love you, James Baker. Always have. And now more than ever."

He closed his mouth and blinked, before saying in a voice barely more than a whisper, "Not like I love you."

"Actually, *exactly* like you love me," Sadie said, finding her voice steady again.

He stepped a few inches closer so that only their hands, which they still held at chest height, were separating the distance between them. When he spoke, his voice came out husky and it made her body heat. "That's a bold statement, Ms. Hall."

The familiar scent of him was intoxicating in that moment and she could hear her own arousal as she said, "When I turned, I got a new power. One I never told you about. I can see the nature of people's relationships passing as light connecting them. I see friendship, love, and… desire. I happen to know exactly how you feel about me. And I know it is exactly how I feel about you."

Jimmy's face registered so many different emotions she couldn't keep up. He blinked several times, blushed, clenched his jaw, and then teared up ever so slightly.

"You – all this time? Why—" he began.

"I don't want to feed from you." She shook her head in desperation as if trying to convince herself yet again. "Gabriel taught me about the dangers of feeding from people you love. He gave me a succubus scroll that said people can get addicted to the succubus they're in a relationship with. People go crazy, do terrible things. I was terrified of that happening to you; to us. And I thought it would be too hard to resist if you knew the truth. It was *me*, my self-control, that I was afraid of most. That's why I was trying to keep you at armslength with… a lie."

His lips parted in surprise, then he made a sound halfway between a laugh and a sob.

"Oh, Sadie," he said.

Their faces were so close now. It would be so easy to kiss him. He watched her contemplate it as her gaze flicked to his lips. Would she ever stop? If she closed that gap?

"And I still... I don't want to feed from you," she said as if in a trance, their mouths a few inches apart. He bit his lip as his gaze traveled over her face. Then he shook his head.

"Then you won't," he said firmly, but didn't withdraw. "I promise Sadie, I won't let you do anything you don't want to. If it's dangerous for us and you don't want to risk it, I'll help make sure we don't. I—" It was his turn to pause before his voice broke. "I don't want to lose what we have either. I don't ever want you to be my addiction. I didn't know... that could happen."

He brought their hands up and kissed her knuckles, then the palms of both her hands, moving slowly. Then he knelt at her feet and kissed her stomach. His hands explored her hips as he rested his forehead against her abdomen. Tears dripped from her nose as she looked down at him.

Then suddenly, he lifted her into the air with a firm grip. By the time she slid carefully down his body they were both smiling. He held her with both arms around her waist and she rested there, a gloved hand pressed firmly against his chest, her mouth only an inch from his.

"And I promise to be honest with you," she said. "From now till forever. So when I tell you that I want all of you James, you'll know it could only be the truth."

Chapter 15

A new day

Sadie and Jimmy made their way back downtown on foot. Neither of them seemed in a hurry to get anywhere other than where they were. Jimmy hadn't let go of her hand since the train station and he was continuously rubbing the back of it with his thumb. Sadie neither noticed the stench of the thoroughfares, nor the unsociable behavior of the passersby. They got lost, but he didn't seem to mind any more than she did.

They spoke little at first, but when the floodgates opened, they erupted; immersing them in a retelling of the past months from each of their perspectives. They both blushed at times as they spoke of everything that had passed between them.

"So you can tell? When I'm... thinking of you?" He used far less explicit language than she just had. She nodded and he ducked his head.

"I'm sorry. I can't turn it off," she said.

"From how far?" he asked.

"Not sure," she said, then smiled. "But we could try some experiments."

She thought he might respond to her playful tone in kind, but instead he blushed more and looked away.

She'd forgotten that despite everything, they weren't old lovers, and he hadn't spent the past year in a highly sexed world as she had. In fact, he had a very limited sexual history and had spent most of it wanting her.

They fell silent as they wandered into a large park and Jimmy let go of her hand to buy a peach off a street vendor.

"Want to sit?" she asked, looking over at him shyly.

They sat in the tall grass next to a pond and he fed them the peach bite for bite. When they reached the pit he fed her slowly, keeping his fingers just out of reach of her lips. Their tentative interaction felt suddenly like a very strange first date. They'd opened up a new world of possibility, but she wasn't sure where to start.

As he watched her lick her lips clean, he picked back up the conversation. "So, what exactly did this scroll say about succubi dating... or having relationships that are, you know, serious?"

Sadie exhaled in an audible sigh. "Uhh, it said that it's dangerous. Humans in particular tend to want more and more. It told some stories of suicide-homicides. It said that the person becomes unable to focus on anything else. It said the succubus can also suffer some of these symptoms."

"But... why?" Jimmy asked. "Why would it work like that?"

Sadie suddenly felt shy. She stared at the grass as she explained. "Because... well, I don't know, but I think that with you – things are different. The two times I touched you, once right before I turned and that time outside the bookstore – they were both really intense for me. And for you. It isn't quite like that with other people. That is, I tend to have more control, and it just doesn't feel the same. There've been exceptions. There was this woman in the casino, and that time I was really hungry with that guy in the barn, and with Ina who was an old friend, but none of that even came close to a few seconds of touching you. It's just—" She picked some grass to fiddle with. "It's just different when you love someone I guess."

He was silent, and she was afraid to look over at him. It turned out she didn't need to as she could feel the pulse of arousal as he thought back on the times she'd touched him. The image from memory turned into fantasy as he imagined kissing her; being inside her. She saw him adjust himself in her peripheral and she hugged her knees to keep herself from responding to his reaction.

The fact she could pick up such things without looking at him directly was also unique to him. Sadie recalled the morning outside the nymph hut, when she could feel him from somewhere in the field. Nothing like that had happened with anyone else. She decided not to tell him every little detail of how much she could see though. Some things were best left vague. He had an idea of what she could do and that was enough.

"It doesn't seem fair," he said. "That it should work that way."

She caught his eye. "No. It doesn't."

He looked away to say, "That means I'll never be able to... umm, kiss you. Ever."

She took his hand, imagining all the other things they'd never be able to do.

"No," she said.

They played with each other's fingers in silence for a long time, before she remembered something that would serve as the perfect change in subject.

"Oh, and the strangest thing happened to me." She turned to sit facing him. "That night in the tub with all those people. It was right after you came in. I don't know if it had anything to do with you or with the woman, but I swear, I had some kind of premonition."

"What?"

"No, not a premonition, a like, psychic reading," she clarified.

He sat up straighter, seeming comfortable again.

"I can see bits of people's sexual histories as I told you, but this was different. It was of people eating dinner and I saw very particular details, and I had thought it was a recent memory of hers, only now I'm not so sure. Have you ever heard of something like that? You were always paying better attention to such things in school."

"No, never. Did you see it from above or through her eyes?" he asked.

"I don't know. I don't even know if it was her memory, but I think I saw through her eyes. Though that's not how I see the flashes of scenes that usually surround people."

"And Gabriel's scroll had no mention of it?"

"Not unless I skipped a crucial paragraph."

"Have you tried to do it again?"

She shook her head.

"We could search the public library. I know it let us down in finding Amadi, but everyone deserves a second chance."

"Even buildings of books," she agreed.

He laughed.

It was a new day, and Sadie felt an almost childlike excitement as she imagined her life with Jimmy. They would stay in Seattle and build a life together. Somehow, they would work it out.

THEY ASKED for directions on their way out of the park and set themselves on a path toward Jimmy's hotel. Sadie knew she had to go collect her belongings, but she would deal with that later. Right now, she wanted nothing that would pull her from Jimmy's side.

On the corner of Pine and West, they found a woman in an elegant sun hat speaking to every passerby. She'd lived a full sexual life, but her encounters with someone Sadie assumed to be her husband were faded. She had only one leg and was leaning on a crutch while fanning herself with her free hand.

They watched some people scurry past her while others stopped to listen, smiling and nodding. As they approached, she turned her attention on them.

"Block party tonight in Eagle Park. Will you join us?" the woman asked.

"Oh, we're not from around here. Just staying at the inn," Jimmy said.

"All are welcome, especially newcomers." She smiled.

"Where is Eagle Park?" Sadie asked.

"Just there, love," the woman pointed.

"We'll be there," she said before steering Jimmy inside. "We should at least check it out," she added as they stepped into the elevator.

"We might have to cancel our other plans, but yeah, if you want to go..." Jimmy said.

The receptionist gave Jimmy his same room back with a warning that it hadn't yet been cleaned. The second Sadie spotted the rumpled bed in the dimly lit room, she realized exactly how exhausted she was. She collapsed on top of the covers, before rolling to smile sleepily at him. "Want to join me? I've been up all night."

He climbed in next to her and they did a dance of positioning her hair and face so that she could sleep in the crook of his arm without risk of skin contact.

"Are you sleepy at all?" she asked drowsily, hoping they could spend the whole day wrapped together like that.

"No, but rest as long as you like. I won't move," he said.

And he didn't.

She awoke several hours later in the same position, with Jimmy gently rubbing his thumb back and forth over her arm. Such tender affection contrasted sharply with all her other intimate interactions. No one else touched her like this.

She enjoyed it as long as she could, but eventually her body began to ache for more. Afraid of her rising desire, she pushed herself up out of the satisfying position.

"I should go collect my things," she said. "The diary. I feel bad for leaving it."

"Do you want me to go with you?" he asked.

"No. I think it would be better if you didn't." She kissed the side of his head. "Meet at Eagle Park in an hour?" she suggested.

"Okay. But if you're not there, I'm coming in with an army," Jimmy said.

SADIE FOUND Alec and Irene in the kitchen of his suite. He spoke in a chastising tone he'd never used with her. "Rude. Disappearing like that. Everyone was there to see *you* after all."

"If having the right to do what I will with my own body can be called rudeness, then I suppose it was," Sadie replied coolly.

"Sounds like you spent the night talking to your human," Irene said. "He's got you all turned against us. Honestly, have we given you anything but free reign? You've got some gall coming round here accusing us of anything."

"Actually, my gall's been rather lackluster recently. But I'm hoping it will make a full recovery given the right support," Sadie said.

Irene clucked her tongue, gave her a nasty look and disappeared into the bedroom. Returning a moment later with Sadie's backpack, she dropped it with a thud at her feet. Sadie bent and opened the bag. Her heart stopped.

"And the box? Where's the box?"

"Oh." Alec laughed. "That thing." He wandered around the living room looking under and behind the furniture. Eventually he peered into the tub and nodded; reaching an arm down, he retrieved the fine marble box.

"Interesting contraption you got there. Sorry. Didn't mean for it to get left in there."

She jerked it out of his hand.

"Thank you. For your fine hospitality," Sadie said, trying not to let her tone be too full of irony. She turned.

"You really going to walk outta here with my silk panties?" Irene bit out.

Sadie glared at her. Then setting down the bag and box she removed her pants, then underwear. Unabashedly nude from the waist down, she stood up and threw the underwear in Irene's face. Cinching herself back in commando, Sadie left with her head high.

THE LITTLE PARK was nestled in an alcove of old-growth oaks. Large trees cast shadows across the grass from all sides. A traditional nymph-grown home rested in the center, from which people were carrying dishes of food to cover a long wooden table.

Sadie hadn't realized there'd be a meal. She was starving, and was suddenly very aware of their lack of income. Free food seemed like a reason on its own to be there.

"There are many reasons to stay united in this increasingly dangerous time," bellowed a broad-hipped woman from the doorway, "but among those is the sharing of bread in good company. Dig in!"

Sadie spotted Jimmy sitting in the grass on the far end of the clearing and broke into a smile at the sight of him. He spotted her and a flash of emotion passed between them as they exchanged a good long stare. She hadn't liked being apart for even that single hour and regretted having ever left her resting place in the crook of his arm.

"Powerful emotion. Young love," someone said from below her. Sadie looked down to see the one-legged woman leaning back casually on a wide blanket. She sported a different colorful sun hat from earlier, and it contrasted nicely with her bronze skin.

"Are you a feeder? Can you read... that?" Sadie asked.

The woman shook her head. "Just have eyes," she said, then patted her blanket. "Join me."

Sadie ducked her head demurely before making herself comfortable on the other side of the blanket. Observing her face close up, Sadie realized she was not as young as she'd presumed. Dark eyeliner ran parallel to the wrinkles at her eyes.

"Dangerous question; asking if I'm a feeder when so much is placed on the answer."

"Is it? Sorry I didn't mean to offend," Sadie said.

"You didn't offend. Not me anyway. And where are you from, child? Clearly not here."

"No. I'm from a little place north of Arlington. My town is mostly human actually. We had zero human feeders in fact until—" Sadie hesitated, uncertain of the political water she walked, but the woman had a warm face and many loving relationships, so she finished, "Until I turned."

"None that you know of," she corrected. Sadie considered this. Of course it was possible, in fact likely, that there were other feeders. Why had she never considered that some of her neighbors might have felt compelled to hide?

Jimmy arrived, carrying food enough for two. The woman gestured him to sit and he scooted in next to Sadie.

"Luciana," the woman introduced herself. They both gave their full names.

"Your parents were not feeders then," Luciana continued. "My family is also mixed. My granddaughter is a hag."

Sadie caught Jimmy's eye and he glared the giggle back down her throat. Obviously, Luciana meant that descriptor literally.

"Ah, that's her now," the woman added.

A person rose to her feet and cleared her throat to speak. Sadie's first observation was that the woman had never had any sexual attachments or interest. So she saw a tall, rather stunning woman in a flowery dress. She clearly resembled her grandmother, though her presence was very different. Her hair was pulled into a tight knot, producing a reserved look, and she had a quality about her which made her seem in charge. The gathering quickly fell silent.

"Friends and neighbors," she said loudly. "We have all witnessed tragedy strike our beautiful city as the forces of politics, corruption, and hate spread like poison through the veins of our shared country." Sadie looked around at the crowd as the hag spoke and found many enthralled faces, including, she noted, Jimmy's.

Sadie, however, was skeptical as the woman spoke of dangerous forces in town. It seemed she'd heard this tune before. When the hag declared, "We must stand united," she began to suspect they'd found themselves in the company of the very same group responsible for attacking The Taste.

"Who exactly are The United?" Sadie asked Luciana. She merely smiled and adjusted her sun hat.

"The who?" asked Jimmy.

"What have you heard?" the elegant woman inquired.

"Just rumors." Sadie shrugged, trying to look only casually interested, and reminding herself not to put too much faith in the things she'd learn from Alec.

"There's certainly a lot of fear and confusion in this town. But I am part of The United. So is Patricia," she nodded to her granddaughter, "and neither of us have ever attacked any person or gambling establishment." This last statement was particular enough that the rumors were apparently common knowledge.

"I ask you to listen more than you speak," Patricia's words recaptured Sadie's attention, "to find common ground more than you fight over it. To not let the forces that divide us—"

"Forces like the harpies and sirens attacking our people?" a man shouted over her. "We're supposed to find common ground with them?" He got to his feet. "When they lobby to have our businesses shut down, our rights restricted, when they try and turn us against ourselves and attack us where we sleep?"

A few people nodded. Patricia stood straight-backed, looking far more patient than Sadie would've been if someone had shouted over her.

Another man stood up. "My neighbor kicked down my fence. Just got up in the middle of the night and kicked every inch of it down. With his own boot! When I asked him why, he said someone had told him it was me that destroyed his squash. Only it wasn't! I'm sure it was one of those harpies that said it. I'm sure of it. They've been running around this town causing all kind of trouble."

"Yeah," a woman chimed in. "And we're supposed to just try and be all nice to them while they abuse us?"

"Someone's gotta do something. We should be taking action!" another man said.

Patricia cleared her throat then. "I don't disagree. But there are many ways to respond to the intentional harm of the greedy. We can't control their actions, only our own. Neighbors can choose not to be so quick to listen to rumors about each other. We—"

"Well, I don't plan on being their passive playthings," interjected the same man who had interrupted earlier. "If anyone else here is tired of sitting on their hands while they laugh at us, you can follow me."

He left the gathering. Patricia watched as one by one, most of the people went after him. She looked at a loss of what to do. The exodus left about ten of them, sitting spread out around the grassy expanse.

A few more people thanked the wood nymph for the food and wandered off in different directions, leaving only Sadie, Jimmy, Luciana, Patricia, the wood nymph and a young man. Sadie knew the man was there to stay by the red light flowing from him to Patricia, though she returned only the green of friendship.

The other three came to join Luciana at her blanket.

"What a disaster!" Patricia declared to her grandmother. "The worst one yet."

"No reflections till you've eaten," said the nymph, handing her a plate. The man bounced with excitement up to Patricia's side. Though shorter and fairer than Patricia, the man's face made him look the woman's twin, though Sadie knew he was not family.

"It's not your fault people are fools. I thought you spoke like a hero," the man told her.

"Well, maybe they were right. Are we just going to talk our way out of this whole mess?" Patricia said. Instead of eating, she turned to her grandmother. "You've said yourself, sometimes we need more than words. We just lost most of the gathering! And I really thought I was getting through to people. When, exactly, will we change tactics?"

"Do you think fueling their anger will make things better?" Luciana asked her granddaughter.

"No actually. I think it will probably only draw more harpies to town," Patricia said moodily, jabbing at a potato.

"Harpies aren't the problem. Most human feeders only bring out what's there in order to feed from it. Remember Cash? He didn't try to intentionally stir up trouble. Well... maybe a little." Luciana smiled at a memory before continuing. "People are quick to blame others. You were right to remind them that they have some responsibility in how they respond to the mischief of harpies. Don't be so hard on yourself, dear. We have a difficult task here."

"Who's this?" Patricia waved at her and Jimmy. "Did they send you to join us?"

Luciana cleared her throat and gave Patricia a meaningful look that Sadie didn't understand. A brief flash of – was it embarrassment? – passed over Patricia's face, before she held out a hand in introduction.

"Patricia," she said. "I apologize for my rambling. Glad you're here."

"Welcome. I'm VJ," the man said rapidly. "And that's Nun." He pointed to the wood nymph. "We're glad you came. You lived here long?"

Sadie and Jimmy shared a little of their story of leaving home as the others joined them in sitting. When they'd finished, VJ talked quickly about everything that had been going on recently. The Taste of Destiny made an appearance in his list of recent events. Apparently, they had dropped a lot of money into buying off the city council and had come close to getting a vote to make it illegal for non-siren families to own casinos. Sadie tried not to let her shock show on her face, since she did not wish to share anything about her recent associations.

Patricia never did eat, only waved around her skewered potato as she spoke, but VJ picked up her abandoned plate and shoveled it down. The hag anxiously smoothed out her dress and plucked at the grass until the conversation turned back to how the event had ended.

"I just think things are getting worse, rapidly," Patricia said. "The sirens are capitalizing on the opportunity to get a stranglehold on the near-wish-fulfillment industry. The harpies are getting high off all the vengefulness, jealousy and other impulsive emotions. This is pretty much becoming a den for all human feeders who need big emotions. And everyone seems out for blood. The humans and nymphs included."

"It's true this city is going to hell. We might just have to let this one go," Luciana said. Patricia gasped and opened her mouth, but her grandmother put up a hand to silence her. "But there's no need to give up yet. Look, we're not alone today. These two stayed." She nodded to Sadie and Jimmy and asked, "What do you think of all this? Are you planning on settling in Seattle?"

They exchanged a look and Sadie stepped up to respond. "Hopefully," she said. "We didn't know things were so bad here though. We just want to find a place that's right for us."

"And what does that look like?" Luciana asked.

Sadie chewed her lip. "Well, Jimmy's a human and I'm a feeder. It would be nice to find a place where we're both welcome. And where we feel safe."

Luciana nodded, thoughtfully. "Safety is a hard thing to find. But I promise you're both welcome with us. The United has people from all walks of life, but the one thing we have in common is a desire to live together peacefully. If you want to get to know us, see what we're about, you should join us for dinner on Friday. You can tell me more about your home."

They accepted, and she gave them directions to a little restaurant not far from where they were staying. Sadie's face was flushed with excitement as they said goodbye and made their way back to the hotel. It felt good to be on common ground again with Jimmy as they decisively agreed that they had a good feeling about Luciana. They were still talking animatedly about the things Patricia had said as they pulled up outside their hotel room.

Then something shifted. The conversation died as Sadie picked up a pulse of desire and the image of the two of them in bed. Jimmy twisted the key wrong three times before the door unlatched.

She wasn't sure why it should feel so strange all of a sudden. They'd shared a room many times; a bed even. In fact, they'd shared a bed earlier that day. But everything was different now. Every time they'd shared a room in the past, it had been as friends. And earlier, she'd been so exhausted that all she'd wanted to do was nap.

Sadie stepped past him, giving more space than usual and highly conscious of the gap between them. They didn't make eye contact.

"I should take a shower," Sadie said. She hadn't done so since sharing that tub at the party, and she had the compelling urge to wash that all away. She beelined for the bathroom, began to shut the door behind her, and stopped. Her heart sped up.

Stepping back into the main room, she found Jimmy seated on the bed, eyes roaming over the wooden floor like he was reading a book. He looked up at her with a mixed expression she struggled to read. Sadie kicked off her traveling shoes and socks and walked to the edge of the bed.

"Help me," she said, holding out a gloved hand.

There was a long pause as he stared up at her. Then Jimmy cleared his throat and reached to tug at the fingers of her glove. He removed one and then the other. Sadie pulled her shirt over her head and let it fall slowly to the floor. Jimmy took a steadying breath as an erection appeared in the space between them. Then he reached for the top button of her pants and undid them, avoiding the flesh of her stomach. She snapped her bra open and let it fall in the space between them, then scooted a few inches away to push her pants down past her hips and shimmy them to the floor.

He'd seen her naked before, and she knew he hadn't forgotten it, but this time was wholly new. This was for him. And unlike her Becoming, when she'd been on display without caring a bit about it, this time she felt vulnerable; wide open. It was her offering. A gift that was his alone, her ability to feel shy in front of him.

She ran her hands over her own body; across her stomach, over her breasts, through her hair. They both breathed in shallow, barely audible breaths. She backed up slowly toward the bathroom, his gaze heavy on her now moving form.

"I'll be back in a minute," she whispered. It was the truth. She held her hair up with one hand to be washed another day and quickly soaped down her body. She returned before steam had even had time to form.

Dropping the towel on the bed, she looked at him hungrily and said, "Your turn." She leaned back on the bed, slightly damp and completely naked to watch him. He looked back at her intently as he stood and removed his own clothing. He looked as vulnerable as she had felt a moment earlier, but she could see in the red pulsing light coming in waves off him, that he was fiercely enjoying this new ritual.

When he pushed the last of his clothing down over his hips, she took in his firm erection like she'd never seen one before, and for a moment her self-control seemed questionable. If she hadn't just had two consecutive nights of feeding orgies, they'd probably be in trouble. But as it were, she seized the opportunity to look over his muscled body with as much deliberation as he had taken in hers.

Then, pulling back the bedding, she asked him to climb under. Sadie lay the thin layer of sheet over his legs, examining it for holes as she did so, then climbed up to straddle his thighs with her own.

"Hold yourself," she instructed, looking at exactly where she wanted his hands. Unfolding the remaining layer of sheet, she covered him to his chest. Then Sadie cupped her hands over his on the other side of the fabric. They slowly found their way toward letting her control the movement. She couldn't feel him the way she was used to with the people she fed from. She could only discern his pleasure by watching his face and reading the erotic images rolling off him. But she soaked up every line, every expression, every pant, like it was a precious resource.

When she rocked her pelvis against his hard shaft, she was shocked at the explosion of excitement in her own body. Afraid that an orgasm would overtake her restraint, she had to back off to maintain control. Holding her own body still, she resisted the urge to move with him.

The intimacy of the moment felt raw and open as she focused on all the little things; the muscles of his arms as he flexed them with each stroke, the feeling of his fingers under hers, the image in his head of her straddling him. Though they could hear the slick sound as he moved in his own hands, in his thoughts he saw himself inside her.

"Sadie," he said with a desperation so heartbreaking she thought they would both melt. She watched as a pre-orgasmic flush began to spread up his neck.

Suddenly, she couldn't take it. Almost all at once, her control snapped; her mind going blank. Releasing her grip over his hands she reached for his chest. He moved like lightning. In one instant he went from stroking himself to gripping her wrists through the layer of sheet. His eyes were wide. She'd been reaching to touch his skin. What was she doing?

"It's okay," he panted. She hovered above him, shaking; her whole body crying out, but he held her firmly.

"It's okay. I got you," he said.

It took far longer to calm her than it had taken to arouse them both. She continued to tremble in his grip for several breaths. He waited until she could open her eyes and sit back before daring to release her. The second he did, she jumped up and redressed, complete with sweater and gloves.

Coming to sit on the edge of the bed, she didn't dare look directly at his him. She couldn't handle seeing the lust in his eyes, or the need of his strained shaft. Even so, she could feel the burning pulse of his unreleased climax. She knew now, even satiated as she currently was, that she couldn't handle his orgasm without losing control completely. The truth was, she had very little experience with her own levels of self-restraint, and she would never have predicted the sheer ecstasy of finally being with Jimmy, even in this limited fashion.

"I'm sorry," she said to the wall.

He moved behind her. "Don't be. Sadie... We'll take it as slow as we need to. There's no rush." He rubbed a hand in soothing circles over her back.

"Come here." Jimmy pulled her back against him, an arm around her waist, and his erection pressed firmly along her backside. "I shouldn't have let you take things so far. It was me that got too excited. I made you a promise. And I'm going to keep it."

They lay down and she rolled into his side, hugging a leg up over his thighs. The pressure of him between her legs felt almost painfully good, and she contented herself with this small consolation as she waited for the throbbing to pass. When her body finally softened and her breathing calmed, she opened her eyes to see his arousal had in no way lessened. His erection left a mound above her thigh, and the sheet covering it was wet with precum.

She closed her eyes tight against the image and breathed deeply and slowly, praying she wouldn't get caught up again. It was hours before sleep found her; at which point the steady rhythm of their respective heartbeats had slowed to two dull thumps which beat at the same pace, only ever so slightly out of alignment.

Chapter 16

A thief

The next morning, Sadie and Jimmy broke their fast at a little place across the street. It was a cafe with mostly outdoor seating for the summer. They sat in the corner furthest from the other tables, sipping coffee as the sun gradually made its way around the corner.

Jimmy counted the remaining cash while Sadie looked on, chewing her lip.

"Three more nights. Then I'm out," he said.

"Shit, really?" That was worse than she'd thought.

She reached for her own wallet to get an accounting of their total remaining worth. The wallet was missing. No. She was sure she'd pocketed it that morning. She bent down to rummage through her bag.

"What's wrong?" Jimmy asked.

"I—" Sadie began.

"Looking for this?" asked a nasally voice above her. Sadie looked up to see a young man in a beret, flashing her a gap-toothed grin. Following the line of his arm, she saw he held out her wallet.

"Oh, thank you! Where did you find it?" Sadie asked.

"I stole it. Right off you. Ironic huh?" he said.

Sadie's mouth dropped open.

"No way. You stole it? I would've felt you!"

"Nah. You wouldn't have. I can teach you. If you're looking for money. I could use a woman. I gotta a lot of plans involving a woman. Plus, it's always easier with two. One to do the distracting, the other to do the taking," the man said.

Sadie's eyebrows were raised and her mouth open by the time his proposal was done.

"Thank you, but we're not interested," Jimmy interjected.

"If you're concerned about your moral code and all, don't worry, I only steal from the rich rats coming out of The Taste of Destiny. They don't miss it. And work's hard to come by in this town. Believe me. I've been looking for three years now." He sighed dramatically.

"What did you used to do?" Sadie asked.

"I used to work at The Taste actually. Only they fired me. And now I steal from their rich customers. Ironic huh?"

Clearly the man didn't know what that word meant.

"What did they fire you for?" she asked.

He flashed her another grin. "Stealing."

"Thank you," Jimmy said again, "but we're not interested."

The man kept looking at her. Sadie could feel her pants chafing against her bare bottom. She hadn't been able to buy new underwear to replace the ones Irene had tossed. She leaned in toward her friend. "Jimmy? Are you sure? You don't even want to hear him out?"

"Sadie, really? Stealing? You know I wouldn't."

She did know. He wouldn't. But she would.

Hoping they were about to come up with some satisfactory alternate plan, she thanked the gap-toothed man and declined.

"Ah well. Good luck to you," he said before vanishing.

Sadie opened her recovered wallet and found he hadn't taken anything from her. Then she counted out the cash and added it to Jimmy's pile. "Five more nights," she revised. "If we don't plan on eating."

~

THEY AGREED to split up to look for work. She hated separating, but this money situation was nothing to toy with. They had no safety net here. No more friends. Nothing to keep them off the streets.

Within hours, Sadie had been rejected as a seamstress, a waitress, a cook, and even as a plumber's apprentice. She wandered up and down the busy Seattle streets, convinced there would be something for her just around the next corner.

A beautiful street with gold-painted stones appeared to her right. There were tapestries of rich colors hanging out each window. Sadie strolled open-mouthed through the display. A woman dressed in green called down to her above a green banner.

Sadie understood. She'd found the sex workers. Not an inappropriate choice for herself. She knew it was a common line of work for her kind. She looked over the women and the customers wandering the streets.

It would certainly be a respectable line of work, but after her recent experience at Alec's parties, she wasn't sure she could handle being a stranger's fantasy all the time. She walked along merely to observe and then found her way back to Pine.

Sadie was finally getting hungry, and not for food. She would have to find someone soon. The thought repulsed her slightly, though she wasn't sure why. She decided it didn't hurt to wait until tomorrow. After all, she'd fed excessively earlier that week.

They both returned to the inn that evening entirely unsuccessful. Agreeing to spend as little as possible on food until they found jobs, they split a day-old baguette up in their room. Sadie bitterly missed Alec's hospitality, and was annoyed at how much it cost just to sleep in the city. When they'd left home, she'd never expected to run out of funds so quickly.

"Well obviously we can't risk going back out into the countryside," Sadie said. "Especially not now." Jimmy looked a question at her. Did she really have to explain?

"Just the two of us? Alone? Sharing a tent with possibly no one to feed from for days?"

He didn't seem to understand what a challenge it was for her to resist him when he was so near. Especially when they both clearly wanted each other and there were no other barriers in their way.

Though climbing into bed that night turned out to be a lesson for both of them in her lack of control. Resuming their cuddle position, she tried to sleep again with her head against his chest. The experience was painful. She wondered at how she had done this the previous night. After an hour of fighting off the urge coursing through every cell in her body, she shifted to move away. At her movement however, Jimmy, who she knew was also keenly awake, became aroused.

She pushed her way off his chest and there was a moment of confusion in which he seemed to think Sadie was initiating something. He lay frozen, looking hesitant even as waves of red light coursed from him.

"I'm sorry. I can't sleep like this. I should've fed today." She threw herself to the other side of the bed in frustration. Jimmy lay a hand on her back.

"Don't touch me," she said, then to her surprise, started to cry.

"I'm sorry Sadie. I don't know what to do," he said.

"Just don't touch me," was all she could manage to say.

Sadie woke up in a mood, dressed angrily and ended up with her shoes on the wrong feet. Embarrassed to even look at Jimmy, she spoke over her shoulder, "We should split up again. And I promise, even if I don't find work, to not return until I've fed."

Not wanting to give him time to reply, she rushed through the door and out into the muggy summer air.

Sadie was quite hungry at this point, and the aversion to feeding she'd carried the previous day was morphing into a carnal pull toward anyone walking by. She grabbed herself an apple off a tree and made her way in the direction of The Taste. Sadie had made up her mind in the night and tried now to keep her conviction as she ambled toward the last place in town she wanted to go.

Peering around the corner, she saw nothing of interest. She bought a bagel at the bakery on the corner and made herself comfortable at a table from which she could easily see the comings and goings of the casino. It was still early, and almost no one entered as she watched.

A man sat at a table nearby, reading the paper. When they caught each other's eye, she threw him a flirtatious smile and saw that he liked it. Her luck was looking up. Though it was morning. It was always harder to find someone who wouldn't blanch at a bold offering pre-lunchtime. A rather inconvenient fact, given she was always hungrier when she woke up.

She struck up a conversation, using the best of her charm. He came to sit with her as they spoke. When she asked if he lived around there, he pointed to a house just across the street. When she asked if he'd ever met a hungry succubus before he smiled broadly, immedi-ately understanding the situation. They rose to head to his place at exactly the same moment Sadie saw a wiry, gap-toothed man bump into someone heading into The Taste.

Damn. Would he still be there when she returned?

"Something wrong?" the man asked.

She shook her head and smiled back at him hungrily.

The man led her to his place. He took her through the living room and into the kitchen, offering her tea, but she was impatient.

"Actually, I'm in a bit of a hurry," she said, removing one glove.

"I like your attitude." He smiled as she leaned against the door-frame in front of him. She ran her fingers along the side of his face. She felt nothing. She saw from the edge of her vision that his body reacted, but she couldn't feed.

"You're a human feeder," she said in surprise and disappointment.

"True. But you were into me a minute ago. Has that changed just because you can't get everything that you want from me?"

She huffed in annoyance. He'd intentionally not told her.

"Yes, it has changed. I don't know you and I need to find someone I can feed from fast and get back to the cafe."

"You don't know me yet." He cupped her face in his hand, his expression taking on a euphoric look at the touch.

"No. Back off." She shoved him back a good six feet. He stared at her as if she were the one out of line. He looked for a moment as if he was about to move in again, but she glared him down. Without another word, she stormed out of the kitchen, keeping him in her peripheral.

Feeling mildly shaken, she practically jogged back to the cafe. Her judgement had yet to lead her into danger, and she was searching for what she'd done wrong. The man had no abuse in his history; she couldn't have known he would be comfortable trying to coerce her. Perhaps it was a surprise to him as well and even now he was regretting it.

Regardless, it wasn't her fault, she decided. Though perhaps in the future, she'd be less willing to follow a stranger into his house.

She rounded the corner. The thief was gone.

What a waste of a morning. Hungry, angry, and missing Jimmy, she stomped back in the direction of Pine & West. Turning the corner onto Pine, however, her mood improved drastically. At the same cafe at which they'd first met him sat the man with the stolen wallet; two big plates of half-eaten food lay in front of him.

He grinned toothily at her standing over him.

"I changed my mind," she said.

"Knew you would," he replied. "You've got that look in your eye."

Sadie didn't appreciate being told who or how she was but decided not to start off by insulting her new teacher.

"Drigh," he said, holding out his hand.

"Sadie," she shook it, wondering if he was going to make anything of her gloves.

"Eggs?" he asked.

"I'll eat later," she said, sitting down opposite him. "Just tell me how to get money fast."

Drigh insisted on finishing every bite of the meal before leaving, but while he ate rather slowly, he talked through some basic principles.

"You ever done a magic trick?" he asked.

She shook her head.

"Well, often the trick is over before any of the magic even begins. Ironic, no? Same's true here. Only different. The distraction usually comes during or before. But still. You've gotta make the situation about something else entirely."

Sadie thought she understood perfectly, but what it meant in practice she couldn't fathom.

It wasn't until he brought her to Eagle Park and had her practice with him the rest of the afternoon that she began to grasp some of what he meant.

"It's easier at night and when they're drunk, so we should wait till then for your first time. Meet back here?" he asked as evening settled over the park.

She agreed.

Sadie remembered Luciana's dinner invitation at the last minute and pivoted mid-stride of her idle walk back to the hotel. Everyone was seated when she arrived; Luciana, Patricia, VJ, and Jimmy. She'd been left the seat directly across from Jimmy, which meant both that there was distance between them, and that they were facing each other.

She smiled awkwardly, still embarrassed about the previous night. Whereas he looked back at her with affection and concern along with the usual wave of desire, which in this moment served to make her feel infinitely hungrier.

"And you think that excuses their behavior?" Patricia was asking of her grandmother as Sadie took her seat.

"I think condemning or not condemning behavior is an entirely useless task. I was merely saying that our actions should be made on the basis of what is effective." Luciana adjusted her hat with both hands as she spoke, appearing for all the world like they were at a garden party.

"What do you think?" Patricia directed her melodic words at Sadie. "If your neighbor uproots your turnips, do you not have the right to uproot theirs?"

Sadie gave this some thought, not wanting to appear childish in front of the woman.

"Perhaps you have the right, yeah. But I'm not sure that that is the best question. I have the right to sneeze in stranger's faces, but I don't think I should."

Patricia pursed her lips.

"A bad analogy then. If one faction of society tries to use or control another, should they not fight back?"

"Your question must be rhetorical. No one is going to answer no to that," Sadie bit back, feeling a little heated now.

"I've offered you insult with my oversimplifications. Let me be more direct. There are feeders in this city and elsewhere who would see humans reduced to second-class citizens. Should their power not in turn be reduced through whatever means necessary?"

Sadie wrinkled her forehead, glad they were getting to the meat of the matter.

"You mean by throwing stink bombs and lighting fires?"

"And more," Patricia added.

This time Sadie didn't hesitate. "Possibly, but I think I'd be a fool to rush into such things without good cause."

And a fool she had been.

"I mean, without fully comprehending the situation and having a damn good reason to attack," she added. Thinking again about her presence at the dumpster fire, which had almost destroyed that poor nymph-bonded tree, she added, "After all, everyone deserves a second chance; to be heard out. If I heard one evil fact about a person, I don't think it should be cause to condemn them. If it were, where would the world be?"

This time, Patricia gave a small smile, the first Sadie had seen on her, and glanced at her grandmother. Jimmy and VJ were both holding their breath. Jimmy looked particularly nervous as he glanced between them. What was going on?

"You have an appreciation for nuance that I rarely see in someone so young. Though to be fair, as a hag, I rarely spend much time with anyone my age."

Sadie was confused. What exactly was happening here? Why had they been invited to dinner? Just to argue? And what was it that Patricia was arguing for? Her reactions seemed so contradictory. Then a strange thought occurred to her.

"It was a test," Sadie said in wonder as she re-examined the faces watching her. Patricia nodded.

Folding her arms defensively, Sadie asked, "Well, did I pass?"

She directed this at Luciana, but the woman deferred her attention back to Patricia, who bobbed her head. "You did. You both did. Sadie, was it? You don't mince words. I like you."

Sadie's emotions had traveled down so many side streets in the past hour it took a minute to re-find her bearings. When she did, it turned out they were set on a realization. She in turn liked this woman. Though having just been played and not wanting to give Patricia too much the upper hand, she asked, "And who are you then? Why do you care what I think about anything at all?"

VJ jumped in. "Patricia is a leader in The United. We're a movement that is against the government split between humans and feeders. And we're trying to calm some of the mess that's brewing. What we need though, is more help."

"Especially from feeders," Patricia picked up. "There are very few human feeders in our group and we theorize it is more effective to speak to and reach other feeders if we do the talking."

"Then there are more than just the three of you?" Jimmy asked.

"Oh yes, but not many in this city. In fact, they sent me because of the particularly strong tensions taking root here," Patricia said.

"Because you're a feeder?" Sadie asked.

"And because I'm good at what I do. Or at least, I thought I was."

VJ put a hand on her arm.

"We haven't had much success recently. Which brings us to the purpose of tonight." Patricia turned her gaze from Sadie to Jimmy and back. "Would you be interested in joining our efforts?"

Sadie looked over their new companions slowly, taking in each of their expressions. Luciana was smiling kindly. VJ was practically vibrating with tension, his eyes wide. And Patricia. The woman gazed back with a look that was both commanding and patient, youthful and wise, warm and yet reserved. Finally, Sadie looked to Jimmy. They took a moment to assess each other's responses.

This was the first time they'd found themselves someplace they might fit in. Plus, after her involvement with Alec and his friends, Sadie had some lingering guilt for being on their side of the attack on the human casino. Maybe with these people they could finally find a little home away from home.

"We're in," Sadie said.

～

As they said their goodbyes and departed, Sadie was confronted with a moral quandary. She had promised not to lie to him, but she wasn't ready to tell Jimmy about her plans that night. She thought if she could do it safely once and come home with cash, he might be more amenable to the idea. Avoiding an outright falsehood, she said.

"Jimmy, I still haven't fed. I'll just meet you back at the room later, okay?"

"I should come with you. It's getting dark and I don't trust this city," he said.

"I'll be careful." She squeezed his hand and began to walk away. He didn't relinquish their grip, however, and she came to a sudden stop. She rotated to put her hand on his chest and they looked into each other's eyes in a way they hadn't all day.

She wanted to say, *I want to do this alone*, or, *I'd be more comfortable if you weren't with me*, but neither would've been the truth. She could only repeat, "I'll be careful."

"I know. I just wish it wasn't like this." Then as if he suddenly noticed what he was doing, he dropped her hand and stepped away. "Just be safe," he said, and then proceeded to watch her until she was out of sight.

Sadie found Drigh in the same place she'd left him. When he smiled at her, she had the momentary thought that his grin was kind of appealing, in an adorable sort of way. *Damn,* she was really getting hungry now. His sexual interest in her was mild, however, and she definitely didn't want to feed where she worked. She shook herself out of the thought and asked simply, "Time to go?"

They walked the ten blocks to The Taste and positioned themselves on a corner, talking casually as they leaned against the bricks.

"Now. As I explained earlier," Drigh said. "The good thing about a partner is how you can look real casual together and not draw attention. I can't just stand here when I'm alone, see?"

He set her facing the casino so she could practice describing what she saw.

"Now. Look for how they arrive. Do they own a personal vehicle and park in the small lot out back? This means they're rich. And what type of car is it? Can learn a lot from that. You tell me what's happening. We'll talk about what it means."

The fact that The Taste resided on one of the few streets which was paved and wide enough for cars was one of the reasons it attracted a wealthy clientele, Drigh explained. The even wealthier customers were dropped off by a personal driver, but they were rare. Sadie, who knew nothing about cars, was no help in wading these waters, however.

The second thing to watch was their clothes. Unfortunately, Sadie had not the eye for this either.

"I don't know, like, a dark-bluish uh, jacket, I guess. His shoes look... uh... shiny," Sadie said in her fourth such remarkably poor assessment.

Drigh grabbed her arms and brought her closer to him in an affectionate way. At first she was confused at this sudden change in sentiment, until she realized he'd rotated her in the process so that The Taste lay to their right.

"When you wanna turn your head to look just giggle and look like you're blushing at something flirtatious I just said. I'll be able to turn my head like I'm looking at you," he told her seriously.

She laughed at this. "Do women often giggle and blush at your flirtations?"

"No, never. Now focus. I hear a car." She turned her laugh into a giggle and did as he suggested.

The car parked in back. Out swaggered an overblown male who clearly thought a lot of himself.

"Scenario C," she mumbled to Drigh in the middle of his rapid explanation of the man's attire and what it meant.

"No not C," Drigh said. "It's family money. Look how he's

young-like. He's likely used to women showing interest and all; won't be distracted by that."

"No, actually," Sadie said, hesitant to correct, but sure of what she needed to say. "He *is* used to a lot of attention, but he also craves it. Flattery would work well."

Drigh raised his eyebrows at her.

"I can tell by his walk," she lied, not able to tell him she could see his sexual history.

They waited a while before they heard the next car. Drigh spent the time telling her about men's clothes while she spent the time imagining kissing him. She had to find someone to feed from soon. The situation was escalating rapidly if she was fantasizing about Drigh just because he was standing nearby.

She giggled and looked over her shoulder at the approaching sound.

"It's a hawk," she said, giving Drigh's code word for anyone with a personal driver. The small black car stopped directly in front of the building. A large man in a three-button jacket emerged, followed by a slender woman dressed in simple pants and shirt. They had no lines of connection between them and Sadie wondered at the relationship.

"An assistant?" Sadie asked.

"Bodyguard. Saw her in action last week. A piece of work, that man. He was my first mark, but I'd almost pay to be able to hit him again."

After an hour, Sadie asked what he was waiting for, impatient to step away from him and find someone she could actually feed from.

"Till they come back out," he told her.

"I thought you said we should hit them on the way in when their wallets are full."

"Not for your first time. We're hitting them drunk," he said.

This could take forever then. She hadn't expected to be out so late or waste so much time on this part of her two missions.

After her scouting lesson had finished, he moved them closer to the door. She was worried she might be seen by a member of Alec's family, but since Drigh had a similar problem, he found them a safe place in the shadows between the entrance and the parking lot. It was a more suspicious place for two people to stand talking and she was worried he was going to want to pretend to make-out if someone passed. Given her current hunger, such proximity could escalate quickly, but he assured her they wouldn't linger much longer. It was almost midnight and people would begin to exit.

Sure enough, a steady trickle of drunken gamblers staggered their way out and down the street in different directions. Frequently people exited alone, but occasionally an old couple would emerge or a young fresh match. None of them were the targets they'd marked on their way in.

Then there he was. He came out alone, but she saw on him a night of flirtation and an exchange of numbers with one of the bartenders. It was her scenario C gentlemen from earlier. She looked to Drigh for approval.

He nodded. They moved.

Sadie prepared herself for her role. Switching her hips in a way that was both new and yet felt entirely natural, she pretended to be looking elsewhere as she approached. She turned at the last minute to smile at the man right as Drigh bumped into him from behind, just as planned. The bump pushed him into her, creating the distraction away from Drigh.

Sadie caught the man's eye. It was the fire nymph from Alec's orgy. *Shit.* Clearly this distraction was going to be even more effective than they'd planned. The man smiled.

"I thought we'd meet again," he said.

"Yes, I—" She turned to look around for an escape route, but as she caught the man's eye, she realized she wasn't ready to scurry away. Her body heated at his look, and she changed her tense posture.

"Me too," she said and leaned in. "I was so overwhelmed the other night. I was sorry to have to leave you so soon." She said this in an uncharacteristic simper that surprised her a little. Was she still playing a role? If so, it was the one she needed right then, both to distract and to feed.

Drigh was out of sight; the task successful. It was time for her other mission of the night.

A half hour later, she climbed out of the back of the nymph's car, satiated and sleepy. Unfortunately, it was likely two in the morning.

Sadie jumped out of her skin when she rounded the corner and Drigh emerged from the shadows.

"You waited for me?" she asked.

"Course. You're a succubus I take it?" he inquired.

"Yeah. Sorry for getting distracted. I hadn't fed in two days."

"Hmm." His interest in her went up, but only a little. They walked a while in silence.

"You should've told me. Brings in a new element. If you plan on feeding from the marks, we should rework the plan."

"No, I don't! Not in general. This was an accident. It won't happen again," she said.

He shrugged.

"Right. Well, here's your cut." He handed her a large wad of cash. Her mouth hung open as she counted it.

"What is he doing with this kind of money?" she asked.

"Nothing anymore," Drigh said before breaking into a smile at her expression.

"See you again next week?" he asked. Though clearly he meant the question to be rhetorical since he turned his back and disappeared into the shadows before she could answer. She counted the cash one more time and responded to the cool, empty night, "See you next week."

Chapter 17

An experiment

Sadie cracked open the door to the hotel, hoping not to make a sound, but the bedside light flickered on immediately.

"Sadie?" Jimmy spoke with the voice of recent slumber.

"Here." She sat on the bed as he pushed himself up.

"Time is it?" he asked.

"It's late."

He was shirtless and she wondered if he wasn't entirely naked under the sheets. He saw her looking and said, "I can put on more clothes."

"No, don't. I'm covered." She ran a hand along his chest.

"I was worried," he said. "Then I thought, maybe you had just ended up staying the night... with someone." He was clearly trying to keep the sadness out of his voice, but he wasn't successful.

"No." She continued to explore his body. "I don't want to do that anymore. Not with strangers."

She ran her hand under the sheet along his thigh and felt him grow hard. He wore more clothes than she'd hoped for.

He blinked at her, lips parted.

"I thought you said it wasn't safe," he said.

"I can't go too far, but I can handle this," Sadie said.

In fact, she'd milked that obnoxious fire nymph for all he was worth just so she could come handle this. She slid under the covers and they came to rest in a close embrace. Sadie searched the mess of images surrounding him. She saw the other night; her standing naked at the foot of the bed appearing rather different than how she saw herself in the mirror. She saw him in the shower earlier that evening, thinking of her. And she saw this current moment.

An image of him running his hand down her back and over her rear emerged clearly from the surrounding scenes. A second later he did just that. He gripped the fleshy part of her lower ass, his fingers curling to rest at her entrance. She rocked gently against him and watched his excitement build at the small movement. He wanted her to stroke him, though he didn't ask for it out loud. She did her best. They were restricted by his underwear, but she was sure her glove on bare skin would not feel nice.

Sadie focused in on how he wanted to be touched. She focused in a way she'd never done with anyone before, relying on reading him to slowly bring him to a steady plateau of pleasure. When he groaned into her hair, it was almost too much for her to handle.

He was suddenly close to the edge and began to buck his hips into her grip. For a moment they were both lost in it. Then right as Sadie felt herself losing control, he stopped. He relaxed his hold on her backside and she quit rocking against him. They panted into the small gap of space between their faces. She batted her eyes open and looked up into his lustful gaze.

"You okay?" she asked when they'd caught their breath. He nodded.

"You?" he asked.

She nodded and cuddled back against him. He squeezed her tightly.

"Fuck, Sadie. Fuck," he said before they spent an hour in pregnant silence, hoping for the distraction of sleep.

～

Sadie had to leave the bed quickly in the morning. Her previous evening's feeding had worn off a bit and the memory of the night with Jimmy was hot and fresh. It was a danger to linger, but she sought solace in a warm shower.

Though her thoughts were not destined to be Jimmy-free, as a sharp, carnal pulse reached her. He had woken when she'd moved, and was now lying on his back, wanting very strongly to touch himself. He was thinking of her under the water and remembering what had happened in the night. She could feel his thoughts clearly despite the separation. She couldn't be sure, but Sadie guessed he was self-conscious of the fact she would feel it if he brought himself to orgasm and was trying to hold out.

He didn't know the full extent of how much she could perceive. She had been right to assume he would be uncomfortable knowing she could see his every little sexual thought and was suddenly glad she'd held out on sharing all the details of her powers.

His desire was intoxicating though. She put on a straight face to exit the bathroom, but had fun prancing about the room as he watched her dress. She took her time.

"You probably still want to shower," she said. "Maybe I'll go on ahead and get us a table at the cafe?"

He nodded, keeping his facial expression remarkably relaxed given his heated thoughts.

Sadie ordered two bagels and selected a table far from others. She pulled out the diary to read, but became aware of something far too distracting. She could still feel Jimmy. It was too far to make out any specific images. She wasn't sure if he was in the shower or the bed, but she knew his thoughts were heavy on her.

She took a slow bite and looked down the sunny street at the handful of people walking in the morning air. A small breeze grazed her skin and the sound of birds twittered overhead. And though half her thoughts were absorbed in her surroundings, the other half were climbing in a heat of raw pleasure. She closed the diary.

"More coffee?" a woman asked. Sadie shook her head in a quick no, an answer which contrasted sharply with the words that had just entered her mind. *God yes*, she thought, squeezing her thighs together under the table. The woman left.

Alone in the corner, Sadie stirred a bit of cream into the hot cup, watching the colors swirl as her nipples hardened into tiny marbles. She licked the dessert spoon clean, taking her time as she dragged it gently over her tongue. Then her mind went blank. Or was it Jimmy's mind?

The feeling passed and she took in a staggering breath. Becoming aware of her surroundings, she lifted the tiny cup and sipped innocently. She was just a girl having breakfast.

When Jimmy joined her twenty minutes later, she tried to keep her expression smooth, but her gaze traveled heatedly over his face. Luckily, he was avoiding looking directly at her, and didn't notice how turned on she was. Sadie tried not to think of tomorrow or the next day. She tried not to fret over how they were going to handle this long-term. Time suddenly seemed to pass very slowly, measured in heartbeats between one carnal thought and the next. She needed another shower.

Blessedly, she had an entirely different topic which would hopefully distract them both.

Shaking her head to clear it, she set down her fork and said in a business-like tone, "Now don't be mad. I couldn't tell you yesterday. You obviously didn't approve, and I didn't want to drag you into it or make you worry."

"Sadie," he admonished. "You didn't."

"I did! And it was totally safe and worked so well. And trust me, the guy didn't need it. He was uber-rich and it was gambling money. And Jimmy—" She reached across the table and put the wad of cash into his hand. He looked around nervously, but there was no one paying even remote attention to the two people in the far corner.

Jimmy brought the money under the table and counted. His eyebrows rose slowly, nearly disappearing into his hair.

"For gambling? What business does anyone have walking around with that kind of money?"

"So I can keep stealing?" she asked.

"Mmm... redistributing," Jimmy said, throwing her a mischievous smile she'd rarely seen on him.

"Can I?" he asked, splitting the wad in two. She nodded and he pocketed several large bills before handing back the stack.

It would be several hours before they'd meet up with Patricia, which gave them time to explore the city in greater depth. They found another broad park with several ponds, fields of wildflowers, and a contented flock of geese. Jimmy asked her if she'd found anything enlightening in the diary, which led Sadie to spend the morning catching him up as they walked languidly around the park.

"It's strange, though. I still can't see why a woman would've risked everything for this? Unless it was all for the button," Sadie finished.

They lounged on a spot of grass. Jimmy lay on his back and Sadie propped her head up against his stomach. It was a comfortable position from which to read the diary aloud. Having caught him up a bit, she flicked open to the book-marked page.

September 20th 1920

DR. BRONZE HAS OFFICIALLY MADE the proposal to my father. I can find no good reason to make haste now that we are certain of my future, but my mother has set the date for five weeks hence. Both her and father seem entirely out-of-sorts these days, terribly distracted by visitors. I fear they are merely hoping to remove me from the house so that they are no longer subject to my curious questions. As if I'm going to relent simply because they've sent me across town. The Maddoxes come calling nearly every day, and I know that I can get information out of Thomas if he knows anything at all. If my parents' stubborn secrecy continues much longer I will take action to discover the truth on my own. For I am convinced there is some mischief happening in this house and I am the only one as yet out of the loop.

This last fact seems evident from my brother's words to my

father, which I have now analyzed most thoroughly. We have not seen him since that day and I think his behavior proves that if anyone in this house can't be trusted with secrets it is not their dutiful daughter. I am livid that they would bestow on my brother an ounce more trust than they have shown me when we are opposites in every way and I received all the good qualities a child can possess. Hopefully their judgement will improve in time.

September 25th 1920

What a distracting week. The most frightful moment of my life occurred three days past, and I only haven't told you about it because there has been so very much to sort out since then. I awoke in the early light to the smell of smoke, as if someone had closed the chimney vent. Then came a piercing scream which ripped me immediately from my bed. The entranceway was on fire and quickly spreading to the rest of the house. There was a rapid scramble of buckets and towels to save our entire home from catching.

When the smoke had cleared, literally and figuratively, we discovered the cellar door had been removed and all of Mother's humans escaped. Not being certain of the sympathies of local law enforcement we had no recourse, but to track them ourselves.

"Wait, what is this?" Jimmy interrupted.

"Oh, I didn't tell you before. I wasn't sure of it. Her family seems to have had slaves of some kind. Humans... for feeding."

Sadie felt uncomfortable talking about this with him, and she wasn't sure why. It wasn't like this was the diary of a dear friend, though maybe she had begun to think of it as such.

"Yeah, I remember learning about that in history class. Some of the old families kept human slaves," he said. "Though I think it was pretty rare by the 1920s."

"Oh. Yeah. I didn't realize. I guess I shouldn't have been so surprised," she said.

Sadie picked back up the book to keep reading right as a new sexual image popped into Jimmy's head. It was of him tied to a bed with her straddling him. He strained against the chains. Sadie swallowed.

"That's enough for today," she said, closing the book with a firm snap.

Out of all the diaries of other young succubi, this would have been the last one in the world she wanted to read. Why had this come to her? And why in the hell did people have to be so complicated?

Patricia had given them the address of a hotel across town. They met her on the corner and she gave them a run-down of the goal. The hotel had had some trouble with an incubus guest sneaking into other people's rooms in the middle of the night. The owners, a nymph family, had kicked him out and put up a sign stating no human feeders were allowed to room there. In retaliation, someone had dumped rotten eggs all over the surrounding gardens. They were to do everything in their power to convince the family to take down the sign.

They left several hours later full of tea and biscuits, but entirely unsuccessful. They had told the family they were all humans working with The United, which seemed to be the two facts needed to get them in the door. Jimmy had come closest to winning over a member of the family, but only because he'd spent all afternoon galloping around on all fours as she rode on his back.

They met up with Luciana at a mostly empty tavern and gave her a recap of their efforts. As they were saying their goodbyes Sadie asked if they knew of any good places to go shopping for new clothes. Luciana broke into a wide smile.

"For you or young James?" she asked

"Both of us. We've been on the road a while," Sadie said.

"Well now, *that's* a way to spend an afternoon." Luciana cupped Jimmy's scruffy, unshaven face in one hand. "Such a handsome man. I could fix you up fine." She looked him up and down. "If you trust yourself in my care?"

Jimmy smiled at Luciana. Only it was a new smile; a flirtatious smile. He asked, "Will I get to wear a colorful hat?" Sadie looked in awe at his expression. Jimmy had never smiled at her that way. Where had he been hiding such things? He glanced then at her innocently and she dropped her gaze to the table, feeling suddenly shy.

Sadie was lucky, she supposed, that he'd never tried to charm her, as clearly it would've worked.

"You can wear as many colorful hats as you wish," Luciana said, grinning as she plopped her own on his head.

Patricia seemed equally delighted to take Sadie around, and thus the party split in two. The two younger women made their way into the heart of the city and entered a bustling open-air market similar to the ones Sadie had seen in Arlington. Patricia, who seemed to only wear the chicest dresses, glided along in her elegant fashion pointing out the various places she liked to frequent.

They chatted casually about their families and upbringings as Patricia held up various garments for Sadie to exhibit.

"And VJ?" Sadie asked, twirling to give Patricia a full view. "How did you meet?"

"We met a few years back when we began working together. Took to each other immediately. We're quite passionate about all the same things."

She shook her head no at the outfit and Sadie went to change.

Patricia continued, "Unfortunately he's also infatuated with me." Sadie knew this of course, but she listened attentively. "Sometimes I worry he only stays so close because he's hoping I'll return the sentiment."

Sadie came out so Patricia could do up the back of a long-sleeved yellow dress.

"And do you?" Sadie asked, knowing the answer.

"Not at all. And I don't think I'm ever likely to. Truth is, I seem to have no sexual interests whatsoever. Never have."

Sadie faced her. "That can be a hard thing when society expects something different of you."

"True." Patricia shrugged. "But then again, such is the way of the world. And a person can become uninspiring under the comfort of fitting in."

They worked a while in contemplative silence, adjusting buttons and ties. The outfit was clearly more than Sadie would ever wish to wear and had tried it on simply for the novelty. Considering herself in the mirror, she picked back up the conversation. "Neither did I. Before I turned. I didn't care at all for the idea of dating or sex even though I loved my best friend in other ways."

"Honestly?" Patricia asked.

"It's always that way for succubi. We have no interest before we turn. And yet we can't get pregnant after. Ironic huh?" she said in mimicry of Drigh.

"Interesting. So the only way succubi can reproduce is if members of the family are human born and carry the gene? With the way Congressman Siphon speaks of humans, you'd think he had no idea that his entire existence depends on them, right from birth. When clearly his mother must've been human."

"No. There is another way. His mother might've had him before she turned," Sadie said.

Patricia considered this, then wrinkled her nose. "What people will go through to keep their lineage *pure*." She said this last word like it was a curse. Sadie nodded.

"Are you pleased then, that you turned and now want him in the same way he wants you?" Patricia asked.

Sadie thought about this. "I was happy before. Our relationship was just different. And this new situation comes with its own set of challenges, trust me. I think we can only be who we are—"

"And accept it as is," Patricia finished.

By the time they were done Sadie had two new dresses and shirts, one new pair of pants and shorts, and five fresh pairs of socks and underwear. She also thought she had a new friend. They made their way back to the street in front of the bar from earlier.

"Thank you, Sadie. It's been a captivating afternoon. I feel you

will make a hag very happy one day when you reach your prime."
Sadie was pretty sure hags fed off life experience, but it didn't seem
like the right moment to ask. They pseudo-kissed on the cheek and
turned just in time to see the approach of Luciana and Jimmy.

Luciana had two canes which met up with her hands at her hips.
With these she managed to walk as if with three legs in a way which
gave her a sensual swagger.

Sadie, however, only had eyes for Jimmy as he strolled up the lane
toward her. His hair had been cut and face shaven. He wore a form-
fitting shirt, slightly finer and tighter than she'd ever seen him in, but
appropriately casual. She could see him out working the land in that
outfit, the way he would be now if they were back home, but she
could also see him dancing or selling fruit at market; handling the
produce with deft hands. This last thought reminded her that she
hadn't fed.

The way the clothes accentuated his body and movement were
not the real problem, however. After all, such things would mean
nothing to her on someone else. Rather, it was the way both of them
responded any time they saw each other. A dangerous flurry of images
surrounded him as he looked back at her and she did her best not to
pay them too close attention.

"Well, it looks like you did nearly as well as we did," Luciana said
to her granddaughter.

"I wasn't aware it was a competition," Patricia said coolly.

"You would've been had you won," Luciana said. "Come, let's let
them get home."

Patricia threw her one of her rare smiles and departed.

And they were alone.

"Sandwich?" Jimmy asked, holding up a bag.

They ate as they walked back to the hotel. Neither of them spoke
the entire time. When they reached their room, Jimmy paused at the
door. He leaned against it and looked at her.

"You were right," he said. "To take a chance on working with that
thief. I'm too hesitant sometimes, to take a risk." He cupped her neck
through her hair. "Like telling you how much I love you." His voice
dropped to a whisper. "And how much I want you."

He seemed taller as he spoke; his face a little older. Having watched him change over time she couldn't quite pinpoint the moment he had become a man, but she could see it now. He'd grown up.

"It will always be hard watching you walk out of my sight, to go do with some stranger what we won't do. It's harder now than it was before. I see why you kept the secrets you did. But I want to make this work."

"Jimmy, I want to try to explain something," she cut in. "This feeding from strangers has gotten harder for me too. I don't like it outside of the moment it's happening. And that's just the thing, something comes over me, a hunger. It feels almost out of my control. All I want is more and more. I find myself doing things that sometimes surprise me later. I don't want to be that way with you. I'm afraid of losing control."

"I know." He cupped her hands. "That's why I'm hoping you'll let me try something."

Jimmy unlocked the door then and led them in. She watched him as he kicked off his shoes and removed his shirt. He put on a new shirt with long sleeves and a pair of gloves.

Her heart sped up, excitement and uncertainty fighting for dominance in her emotions. What was he up to? She walked to the edge of the bed and sat down. Jimmy pulled her back to her feet and began undressing her, starting with the gloves. He walked behind her, swept her hair over her shoulder and unzipped her new dress; letting it fall to the floor. He undid her bra and it landed on the dress. She found her voice then.

"Jimmy. I haven't fed. I don't think—"

"Don't worry, I won't break my promise to you. Do you trust me?" he asked as he pulled her back against him and ran his hands up her stomach to cup her breasts for the first time. She could feel him hard against her back as he massaged her, and they moaned simultaneously.

She did trust him.

"Yes," she said in both encouragement and assent, leaning her head back against his.

Jimmy took her to the bed. He was still fully clothed and she moved to undo his pants, but he stopped her. Instead, he lay her down and came to rest propped up at her side. His gaze raked slowly over her, and she felt vulnerable in that way she only seemed to with him. He ran a finger along the edge of the new panties.

"So smooth," he whispered. "Do they feel good against your skin?"

She nodded.

"What if I do this?" He ran a hand over her. She arched her back, chest rising. He had barely touched her, but she wanted him so badly that the sensation ran all through her.

"Yes," she said.

And then Sadie caught the image of what he had in mind. Her heart raced. She could feel herself losing control already.

"Good," he whispered in her ear as he reached for something off to the side. Jimmy took both her hands over her head and wrapped them together in what must've been a pillowcase. He held them there firmly with one hand. Rocking his body partially up onto hers, he both spread and held her thighs with his own.

She looked at him, wide-eyed.

"I got you," he said. "Try to get out."

She struggled against his hold and found herself entirely trapped. The sensation of straining against him was surprisingly erotic, and she felt her clit throb with sudden need as he began to run his free hand all over her body, coming eventually to rest between her legs. The desire pouring off him was too much, especially as it mingled with her own. She had to kiss him, to touch him.

"Jimmy?" she half-pleaded.

"Does this feel good? What I'm doing now? Tell me," he said.

"Yes," she said, writhing against him as best she could.

"I want to take you all the way. I want to watch it happen on your face," he told her.

Her chest heaved as he spoke and Jimmy looked down at her body as she bucked against him.

"Shit, Sadie," he said in the sweetest voice. Then he bent to whisper in her ear, "Tell me how to touch you."

She whimpered, and for a second she thought she might climax just from the sound of his voice. "Your middle finger, a little higher," she panted. "In circles."

"Here?"

"Yes," she cried, bucking against his touch.

"Yes," he breathed. "I can feel it. You're all swollen. And soft."

She groaned.

"I think about licking you here," he continued. "Licking... your clit." He said the word as if testing it out. "I fantasize about it all the time. What you would taste like. How you'd feel against my tongue."

"Jimmy?" she panted.

He moved slowly as if determined to savor every second, but the pleasurable heat built in her at a rapid pace. She quickly lost all control over her own thoughts as her desire became all consuming.

She needed to touch him; needed to feed. Sadie looked into his face; his beautiful brown eyes, his mouth open in a way that made it look as if he were the one about to climax. She'd been right, now that he knew how she felt, it was infinitely harder for her to resist him. And in this moment, she couldn't remember any of the reasons she should.

"Kiss me," she begged. "God Jimmy, just kiss me."

He continued to watch her, unmoving. She was on the edge now and she closed her eyes as her mind became distracted by her own overwhelming pleasure.

"Look at me, Sadie. Look at me," Jimmy commanded, recalling her words to him during her Becoming.

Her gaze locked on his right as she cried out in a gasping moan; her whole body convulsing in rapid successions. He clenched his jaw as he watched, his face so near.

"God. So fucking hot," he said, his eyes dropping to her parted lips. "That's it. Yes. Come for me." His hips seemed to be bucking unconsciously to the rhythm of her convulsions.

When the waves had subsided, he pseudo-kissed her nose, keeping back only a fraction of an inch before retreating to a safe distance. Her chest was still heaving when he ran his hand up to rest over her pounding heart.

"Thank you," he said. Sadie could only pant, her whole body throbbing.

When the aftershocks quieted, however, her need to touch him returned ten-fold. She wanted him now more than ever and she went back to her begging.

Jimmy didn't acknowledge her pleas, just stroked her body. He took his time exploring her, running fingers over her neck and inner thighs. She felt his arousal spike as he began to fondle her breasts, squeezing them gently before finding each nipple.

The gloves he'd bought were incredibly soft against her skin and she cried out with need as he toyed with her. By the time he'd returned to the center of her wet panties, he found her swollen and ready to be touched again. Sadie balked against him.

"Jimmy. Do you have any idea what I would do to you, if you let me out?" she said, switching tactics.

He groaned. "No. Tell me."

"I would flip you to your back and climb down your body. Then I would take you between my lips. *God,* I want to feel you in my mouth."

Jimmy's hips bucked in a spastic motion as if moving of their own accord, and she felt his slick head slide along the inside of her thigh.

"I would run my tongue in a circle around the crown as I stroked you. Do you know what that would be like? The mouth of a succubus wrapped around —" her heart pounded as she struggled to say the word. "Your cock," she finished.

"God, Sadie. I might come like this," he said through gritted teeth, his hips rocking into her in tiny spastic jerks.

"No," she panted, feeling frantic now. "I can't handle it, Jimmy. Please. Let me out. Let me taste you. I *need* to taste you." She'd made it through her own climax, but his pleasure was too much. She fought against him, struggling with all she had this time.

His gaze refocused on her as he reached to undo his zipper. Jimmy extracted himself in a rush. She stopped her writhing and her eyes dropped to stare at his shaft, bigger than she'd yet seen it, as he stroked it once, twice. He cried out as if in agony, he eyes closing as a stream of hot liquid shot out of him and landed across her new panties. It seemed to go on forever, his muscles straining above her as he coated her in his release.

Sadie's whole body was trembling uncontrollably by the time he'd finished. He looked down at her in shock and she thought she might go mad if he didn't release her. The sound of his panting was unbearable, the smell of his scent on her utterly intoxicating. She needed to have him. All of him.

She began to plead with all she had. "Please. Let - I need —" But she could think of nothing that would break him. Jimmy held strong, letting her struggle as he resumed exploring her writhing body with an expression of rapture.

Eventually, he ran his hand along her slick panties and resettled over her clit.

"Ready for round two?" he asked as a wave of desire rolled off him so strong she thought her own body would explode with it.

He wasn't going to release her. There was nothing she could do to make him. Somewhere in the back of her crazed mind she realized what that meant. They really could do this safely. He would be her self-control.

Trusting herself over to him, Sadie paused her pleading just long enough to get out the word which she knew from every one of his current thoughts he craved to hear pass her lips.

"Yes," she said. "Yes."

Chapter 18

An impulse

The weeks passed in the city as the summer that had forever changed the direction of Sadie's life neared its end. Sadie and Jimmy spent most days working with The United, attending city council meetings, neighborhood association meetings, and holding their own events, trying to bring people together. Patricia usually did most of the speaking, but occasionally Sadie would take the lead. Jimmy was better with the one-on-one interactions. He had a particular knack for reaching the hearts of older women.

Sadie continued to hone her thievery and they paid up the hotel for the month. Having come to greatly like the old man who ran it, they turned down Patricia's offer to come stay with them. They also wished to keep their own room, as they seemed to make a lot of noise in the night, and the morning, and sometimes in the early afternoon.

Sadie walked around with a layer of guilt for being in such a state of happiness while the city around her seemed destined to crumble apart. Gangs of feeders had begun roaming the streets, harassing people. They'd marked themselves with a tiny bead inserted under the skin at the edge of their right eyebrow. Everyone had begun to refer to them as *the beaded*.

She and Jimmy avoided going out at night unless they absolutely had to. She found herself a handful of humans to feed from regularly and arranged with them to always meet in the mornings.

And Since it was immediately following feeding that she felt comfortable taking the biggest risks, Sadie decided to try a new game on that particular morning. As she neared their room, she could tell that Jimmy was in the shower. Slipping into the steamy room, she made herself comfortable sitting with her back against the door.

Jimmy froze. "That was fast," he said.

"I made it quick today," Sadie said, looking him up and down through the sheer shower curtain. She knew from his thoughts every morning when she came home that she was missing the best part of the day while she was out feeding. When they were together, he would usually just focus on her since he'd realized how hard it was for her to handle watching him climax. This meant that in the morning, while she was out, he would take care of himself.

"Keep going," she said. He had switched to washing his hair, but his profile would have made his aroused state obvious even if she hadn't been a succubus. He hesitated a minute, then went back to stroking himself. Today, she wanted to show him how far she had come these past weeks. Show him that she could at least handle being in the room.

Sadie hugged her knees to her chest and forced her breathing to be steady. She wouldn't completely lose herself in this. She would sit here quietly and just watch. Having had many opportunities to practice at this point, she'd found she could keep some control over her thoughts... if she really tried.

The biggest danger while Jimmy was particularly aroused came from the way she would find herself trying to seduce him. There'd been a couple of incidents already in which she thought he might just snap and give in, but he always found a way to pull them out of it. So all she had to do if she wanted to stay now was to not say or do anything. A task easier said than done.

Jimmy, in turn, remained silent as scenes from the previous night swirled around his thoughts. In one hand he held a soap bar, using it as lubricant, and bubbles appeared between his fingers. He was clearly enjoying the feel of it. His arm muscle flexed with the movement, and he put his head back, closing his eyes. The room was getting steamier, though, and Sadie didn't like the obscured view.

She considered moving just close enough to pull back the curtain, to hell with getting the floor wet, but didn't trust herself to move. Then she thought of telling him to move the curtain, but she also didn't trust herself to speak. He was getting close, she could feel it. She had to stay calm now, more than ever. Frozen in her rapt yet restrained attention, she resigned herself to not being able to see much.

But then Jimmy once again came through. Shutting off the shower he pulled back the curtain so she could see. "I'm close," he said. Not much of an exhibitionist, he was really stepping out of his comfort zone to do this for her. He put one hand on the wall below the shower head and closed his eyes as his movement became untethered.

The room was suddenly quiet except for his breathing. Sadie practically held her breath as he groaned, the sound filling the empty space between them. Her knuckles were white from gripping her own knees as Jimmy finished himself. And though there were other things she could have watched, her gaze was locked on his face.

He didn't look over at her as he caught his breath, pulled closed the curtain, and restarted the shower. When she felt like she could handle it, Sadie slowly got up and made herself leave the room. As much as she'd enjoyed that, she was left with a feeling of regret. Knowing what she could do to him, she found his quick morning orgasms in the shower unsatisfactory. Luckily, he didn't know anything else.

Jimmy emerged in a towel, still behaving shyly as he dressed. He glanced at her briefly when she handed him his socks and they exchanged small smiles. Then, as if emerging from a dream, she remembered that Luciana had given him a tip on a job opening and he'd gone to check it yesterday.

"Oh, how did it go? At the construction site?" she asked.

He smiled. "I got the job. I forgot to tell you. When we, uhh, got distracted last night it just slipped my mind."

"But that's huge. How does it pay?" she asked.

"Not well. I'm mostly just helping move things around. I think I know a lot more than they realize though. If we decide to stay here, it could be a living."

He had dressed fully, including his now standard black gloves, and so Sadie hugged him. "That's great, Jimmy," she said in his ear. They broke apart slowly, equally reluctant. He hooked his arms around her waist, keeping her close.

"Is that what you want though? To stay here?" he asked.

"Seattle? Maybe not. It's a dangerous mess, honestly. But it feels like we're always running to someplace new. And I want to stay with Patricia and the others."

Sadie moved back in to press herself against him "As for right here?" She wrapped her arms around his neck to make it clear she was now talking about her current position in his arms. "Yeah, I definitely want to stay *here*."

He pulled her tighter, looking for all the world like he was about to kiss her. "Sadie, I'm happy living anywhere if it means I can be near you." He moved his face dangerously close to hers, pseudo rubbing their noses together the way he liked to. "But if it really is dangerous everywhere, why don't we just go home?"

She put a hand against his jaw and rubbed her thumb over his lips.

"Because. Then we couldn't do this." She rubbed against him, and despite what had just happened in the shower, he hardened against her belly. "We can keep doing what we're doing so long as I have people to feed from. Lots of people. And I couldn't handle giving this up now that we have it. It feels like all I want is more and more of you and it's never enough." Sadie knew she should stop. She was doing that thing again; seducing him against her better judgement. But it was all true. It really wasn't enough. Ever.

He slid his hands over her ass and pulled her up against him. "I'm not complaining," he said.

She tugged at his lower lip before resting her thumb on his chin. "I know," she said, but she could of course see all his sexual thoughts and desires. Having become increasingly proficient at pulling them apart into coherent images, Sadie knew exactly everything that he wanted; everything they would never have. It was true, however, that he never complained out loud.

Feeling like it was her turn to get them out of this moment, she backed off slightly and continued to answer his earlier question. "And... I don't know, it feels like I'm still waiting for something. Like if we go home, I'll just always be looking for something bigger. Maybe one day... But not yet."

Then, trying to be the strong one, she wiggled out of his arms and put back on her shoes.

"Where did Luciana say we're going?" she asked over her shoulder.

"There's some trouble with a couple human feeders at a market-place across town. Apparently, there's talk of this powerful impulse feeder that's teamed up with a harpy to make some chaos."

He filled her in on some details as they made their way outside.

"So... what's the difference between an impulse feeder and a harpy exactly?" Sadie asked, putting her hand up to hail a cab.

"That's the first thing I asked. Harpies also feed on impulsive emotions, but they're into jealousy and envy and such. Also, like all of the human feeders with special names, harpies are way more common. Pure impulse feeders are rare. I also learned yesterday that rare feeders tend to be more powerful, like storm or earthquake nymphs versus wood nymphs. Your regular dryads are a dime a dozen, and they often affect the woods they're bonded to in subtle ways. But storm nymphs can sometimes *create* storms to feed from."

"I guess succubi are like that. We create the thing we feed from," Sadie said.

"Yeah, that's another thing I learned. We never got into any of this in school, but some feeders create the thing and others just follow it. Like sirens don't actually create unmet desires, they just build the situations." Jimmy looked at her out of the corner of his eye as he tested out the topic of Alec and the casino.

To reassure him, she said, "Yeah, that seems to be how they thrive. Alec's family was good at that... which happened to be bad for us."

They hopped up into the carriage and Jimmy gave the address.

"So do we know about impulse feeders and harpies?" Sadie asked. "Do they help stimulate the emotions they feed from?"

"Yeah. That's been the problem. Unlike harpies, impulse feeders can stoke the emotion they feed from. Though... they can't create something out of nothing. But this place was ripe for trouble before they got there," Jimmy said.

"And what can *we* do about that?" Sadie asked, throwing her hands up.

"For now, we're just scouting it out. We'll get a sense of things and report back," he said.

"We're going alone?" she asked.

"Yeah, for today," he said. Then putting his hand on her knee added, "Then we could get lunch. Luciana recommended a place that's both cheap and good. Our kind of thing."

She smiled and squeezed his hand in hers. "It's a date," she said. "We gotta celebrate your new job." She glanced in the mirror to check if the driver was watching before moving his hand further up her thigh.

Jimmy ducked his head and looked out the window in response. He silently caressed her inner thigh for the rest of the trip, lost in his own thoughts. Which meant that she too spent the ride immersed in a scene of the two of them in the shower, one with her back against the wall and legs around his waist, a position they had definitely never taken in real life.

The driver pulled the horses to a stop in front of a small alleyway lodged tightly between two buildings. A strangely large amount of foot traffic was pushing in and out of the alley despite its narrow size. Sadie handed over some cash and they climbed down. She adjusted her clothes to ensure she was properly covered before taking Jimmy's hand and stepping into the stream of people.

For once the scent of the city turned pleasant, as the stink of manure was quickly replaced with a clash of food smells. Cinnamon and turmeric infused the air as they exited the other end of the alley into a wide expanse. The sun shone down on what appeared at first glance to be a happily bustling market filled to the brim with vendors of every type. As they jostled their way through, however, it became clear why Luciana had sent them to check this place out.

The market was split into two parts, the smaller of which had clearly been staked out as human feeder territory. Standing on the corners of the part that appeared to belong to feeders were two of the beaded. The men were burly and standing with their arms crossed in a gesture that made them look like bodyguards.

Sadie and Jimmy positioned themselves on the edge between the two territories and openly observed the scene around them. Attuned to such things now, Sadie caught sight of several instances of thievery just within the first few minutes of standing there. The few kids in the market were all acting out in large ways, the younger ones throwing tantrums and the older ones throwing other people's wares. Sadie flinched at the parents' response to the behavior.

Someone bumped into her from behind and she distinctly felt a hand on her ass. Then the most surprising thing happened. Jimmy, looking down at where the man had grabbed her, immediately released her hand, stepped back, and punched the guy with all his force. He blinked down at what he had just done.

Sadie grabbed Jimmy's arm and pulled him to move before the man could get to his feet. He complied and let her drag him to hide between two buildings.

"Sorry. Shit. I—" Jimmy began.

"What was that?" Sadie asked.

Jimmy shook his head. "I just... I had the thought that I wanted to hit the guy and... before I knew it, I had done it."

Sadie looked around. "I guess that means our impulse feeder is present."

"Yeah. Can't you feel it?" he asked.

"No. Though maybe it doesn't affect me? Them being another human feeder and all," she said.

"Oh, right. Well, they're definitely here somewhere," he said, the last word trailing off as if he forgot he was speaking. His eyes raked over her body. Noticing her watching him, he cleared his throat and looked back out at the crowd.

"We can see if we can figure out who it is," Jimmy suggested.

"Yeah," Sadie said, feeling hot at the way he had just looked at her, as well as at the unfiltered thoughts and feelings pouring off him.

They made their way cautiously back out into the crowd and found a new observation point. Assuming that creating impulsive emotions took some focus, she scanned around for someone who looked content and otherwise unoccupied. It took a while. The action-packed horde was thick.

Eventually though, Sadie spotted a girl in her mid-teens. She had so few sexual images around her that she was nearly a child. She sat painting her nails under what appeared to be her parents' tent; they sold purses and scarves on the edge of the feeder territory. Sadie only noticed her because, despite her apparent absorption in her task, she kept looking up through her lashes at different interactions around her.

Sadie watched as a few vendors away from the girl, someone pushed a wheeled cart a couple feet further into a merchant's tent. The man was selling nachos just outside of the territory that the beaded men were guarding, and he seemed to be making a point that the cart had crossed a line into his space. The girl looked up and smirked as the owner of the cart emerged and began chewing out the man. The nacho vendor didn't hesitate; he shoved the man back, sending him toppling backward over the chair behind him.

The teen girl looked up at the woman placing cash into the register nearby. Sadie assumed this was the girl's mother. They exchanged a small smile.

"How are impulse feeders born, I wonder?" Sadie said, stepping into Jimmy to be heard. "Could they come from harpy families?"

Before Jimmy could answer, however, a commotion drew their attention back to the crowd. A fight had broken out involving multiple parties. It was escalating fast. Sadie would have never thought it possible that so many adults could behave so irrationally, but the mood seemed like wildfire, rolling over the whole market. She felt Jimmy tug on her arm right as two men crashed into each other, jostling Sadie in the process. They turned their wrath on her, and Jimmy pulled harder.

Though as he dragged her away, she caught a glimpse of something, or rather someone. Drigh was in the middle of the fray, rapidly shoveling cash from a register into his pocket. She spotted him for just a second before her view was obstructed. That didn't seem like him at all. He normally planned things out so well. Clearly, her tutor was also feeling the impulsive behavior bug.

That little feeder must really be powerful. In that moment, Sadie could see why so many people feared human feeders. Though clearly what the girl was doing was an abuse of her skills. After all, Sadie doubted she needed to cause this much chaos just to feed.

Jimmy pulled her into a tent sandwiched in one corner. It wasn't the best place if they needed to escape the market entirely, but at least it was out of the way. Trying to get through the masses blocking the two main entrances didn't seem like a good option just then, and Sadie was honestly a little afraid to leave Drigh there alone.

The owners of the tent they'd entered were temporarily away, but they could come back any time. Sadie and Jimmy made their way to the back and squeezed behind some coat racks, just as they heard voices from the entrance.

"Ha! What idiots! Abigail's getting feistier every day and the human's just dance more and more for her," a young man said.

"Yeah, feistier and prettier. Wait till she's in her prime," another man said.

"She said she was going to go all out today, invited me to watch," said the first man. "So be a good little boy and stay here to mind the booth."

They heard the second man protest as he was left alone. Sadie was glad there was just one of them now. She felt unsafe around these feeders. Jimmy must have too, because he stepped deeper into their hiding place, sandwiching her between him and the wall.

When Sadie looked up into his eyes, however, it was clear that he'd moved closer for another reason. His gaze was heavy and she felt him harden against her belly as she looked at him.

"We—" He paused to take a deep breath. "Need to get out of here."

She leaned back against the tent in surprise and was lucky that there was a hard wall of a building to catch her behind the tent barrier.

"Jimmy?" she said as an image of them kissing and locked together hit her like a storm. The roar of the fight outside picked up, and Sadie watched as the wave from the impulse feeder reached Jimmy. His thoughts were so tightly fixated on what he wanted in that moment that all the myriad of scenes that made up his whole sexual self disappeared behind one desire. He bucked forward, catching himself with his hands against the wall at her back. He held himself a few inches from her as he closed his eyes.

"Shit. Goddammit," he whispered, balling the curtain into tight fists on either side of her head. The lust rolling off him was overwhelming. Her head swam as she tried to escape it. He emitted a deep rumbling groan as he breathed out. Then, taking in quick, shallow breaths, he continued making a sound that was half-growl and half-moan as he pressed in tight to her.

"Push me away," he said in a tone that was half begging and half command.

Sadie pressed hard against the wall behind her, but she made no move to meet his plea. She'd closed her eyes too, trying to block out his presence, but she could feel him breathing against her mouth, continuing to groan on every exhale.

She was going to kiss him or he was going to kiss her. There was no way she could bring herself to push him away, and his impulse control was at a loss without her input. And she knew that once their skin touched that would be it. They wouldn't hold back. He was going to end up fucking her against this wall in this very public market, and she was going to do nothing to stop it.

Knowing the end result though, didn't seem to help her do as he'd asked. She wouldn't push him away, not now, not ever. He was begging her for help and she had nothing to give. Instead of complying, she threaded her hands up between their bodies and wrapped them around his fists. Her hands gripped his beside her head as she arched her back to press against him. She managed only the slightest bit of friction before he slammed his body into her, pressing her tight against the wall and making the tent shake. Their eyes opened as he cupped her face in his hand, his gloved thumb stroking over her lower lip.

A bang as loud as a gunshot went off. It only barely disturbed the moment, but it was just enough that he managed to pull his hips back to a safe distance. Gasping with the emotional effort of it, she pushed him just enough to step to the side. Sadie moved several feet away as Jimmy sat on the floor and put his head between his knees.

She was shaking with the impulse to pull him back to his feet and do what they both wanted, and she wasn't even the one being hit with what must be a very powerful wave from the misbehaving teen. From the sounds going on around them, there was some serious trouble happening.

"Stay here," Sadie said unnecessarily to Jimmy's compact form as she turned to peer out the curtains. A large group of beaded had strolled into the center of the action. It was difficult to see exactly what was happening, but the noise had died down considerably. What was going on? She needed to get closer. Slipping through the fold, Sadie crept along the outer edges of the tents while trying not to look as though she was sneaking about.

"Thousands of dollars. All gone," someone was saying as Sadie pushed her way between two tents and peered out at the now still crowd.

The market was half as full, even with the arrival of the beaded, and Sadie could see why. The feeders were armed, all of them. Sadie slunk back a few inches. She'd never seen guns like those. They weren't at all like what her neighbor used for hunting. Where could they have gotten such things? And so many of them?

Adding to the threatening environment was the fact that they'd surrounded a group of what she assumed to be humans and nymphs. The people from the human feeder part of the market were standing around watching smugly, while everyone else was trapped in the circle of beaded.

"Who was it?" a man said somewhere to the right and out of sight from where Sadie was standing. The question was met with silence. Then another bang went off. Sadie jumped back with shock at the volume of the sound. A woman directly across from her had fired, shooting directly upward. It was the most terrifying thing Sadie had ever seen. She decided they needed to get the hell out of there.

As she began to turn her back on the scene, however, someone said, "It was him. I saw it." Sadie paused to look, then groaned as she spotted Drigh with a finger directed accusingly at him. Shit.

Then she looked again. Drigh had a tiny bead next to his right eyebrow. Had that been there earlier?

He put his hands up. "No, actually, what you likely saw was me working," he said. "Unlike you lot, *we* work hard for our money." He moved to the outer edge of the trapped crowd. "Excuse me," he said as he nestled in next to the woman that had just fired the shot in the air.

For a minute, it looked like he might get away with this. The beaded looked back into the crowd unsure for a minute what to do, then the woman narrowed her eyes at Drigh.

"You're a feeder? In this market? Why haven't we met?" she asked him.

This really wasn't good. Sadie's mind raced frantically through different ways she could help. Some large distraction might do it. If only she happened to have some fireworks or something.

"Just moved here," Drigh said, putting his hands in his pockets and looking casual as he rocked back on his heels.

"What kind of feeder are you?" a man asked from his other side.

"An incubus," Drigh said without hesitation. Sadie really hoped he was telling the truth, but she had the strong suspicion he wasn't.

"Incubus? Really?" the woman said. "Prove it."

"Uhh, how'm I gonna do that? Can show you tonight though, when folk are sleeping," he bounced casually, looking only slightly as if he was nervous.

"Yeah?" a guy said from somewhere to the left, coming into view a few seconds later. "What specifically would you do?" he asked Drigh.

"Oh, you know," Drigh shrugged. "Give people exciting dreams, then feed off 'em."

"Yeah?" the man repeated in the same tone as earlier. "And will you need to touch their skin to give them these dreams or not?"

Sadie held her breath. He had a fifty-fifty shot of answering correctly, though he couldn't pause to think about it. Before she could worry, he said in the same casual way he'd been doing, "No, of course not."

The man smiled, then shook his head. With a small flick of his hand, he gestured to the woman. She reached out and held Drigh as the man approached. He grabbed Drigh's scrawny face in his hand and flicked the supposed bead with his right. It came off easily. The man snorted and stepped back. The woman holding Drigh tossed him to the ground.

"Let this be a lesson," the man that had interrogated her tutor said, turning full circle to address the group still trapped in the center. "This city – this world – it's ours."

Then as if in some bad, unbelievable dream, Sadie watched as the man raised the weapon and fired at Drigh's head. The shot went out as loudly as the others, but the sound felt far away as Sadie watched the body of her friend drop immediately into a limp puddle on the ground.

She couldn't believe her eyes. She wouldn't believe it. Her feet stayed locked in place as she watched blood pour slowly from her mentor's head and onto the surrounding concrete. When it really seemed like Drigh wasn't even going to twitch, she finally shook herself awake. The crying of a woman trapped in the circle jolted her back into herself and Sadie decided it was really time to collect Jimmy and get the hell out of this place. She saw the woman that had fired the earlier shot reach into Drigh's pocket, pull out the cash and throw it on his limp form before the circle began to disband, releasing its captives.

Sadie scrambled backward, tears obscuring her vision. She jumped as someone touched her from behind. Heart pounding, she turned to see Jimmy. He had a hold on her waist and a finger pressed to his lips. He released her before silently retreating backward. She followed him as he turned and ran in a silent crouch.

Jimmy looked back regularly as he led them to a different corner tent and squeezed out to a lesser-traveled alley. It was as wide as his shoulders and he had to turn sideways to make it the last few feet to freedom. Emerging on the calm and mostly empty street in front of them, Sadie looked around and let out a sob.

"Drigh..." was all she managed.

"I know. I saw," Jimmy said, pulling her into a hug. He held her for some time while she cried. Eventually she relaxed to the feel of his hand rubbing her back and lips kissing her head.

"I can't believe that just happened," she said when she'd regained her voice. He responded with one final squeeze before standing them both upright.

"Let's keep moving," he said.

They called Patricia from a pay phone, and a large group of The United gathered at Luciana's home to hear about what had happened. Jimmy brought Sadie some tissues and sat next to her as she told the assembled group what she'd seen. Patricia, as always, took studious notes, nodding along with every detail. Sadie did her best to describe the man and woman who had actually fired their weapons. Jimmy filled in some details about the woman, but had been too far back to see the man.

Shortly after nightfall, Luciana called them a ride and insisted they get to bed. The grief and shock of the moment had faded slightly in the retelling. It was a strange kind of therapy, having everyone gasp in horror at what had occurred.

Drigh would be remembered, she'd make sure of it. She only wished she'd had a chance to say thank you for helping her. She couldn't remember actually having expressed her gratitude. His mousy little face was burned into her mind as they returned to their room. *Ironic, huh?* she thought, intentionally misusing the word.

Once alone with Jimmy, however, a new memory surfaced: one of him slamming her against a wall and cupping her face in his hands. She'd almost forgotten about the impulse feeder and her mischief.

When it was clear that her mood had finally shifted away from grief and shock, Jimmy's interaction with her shifted in kind. He kept his distance as she sat on their bed. Picking up a water bottle, he chugged it before sitting as far from her as possible on the comforter. They were both silent as they reflected on everything that had just happened.

She knew what he was thinking about in particular though when he looked away shyly as her eyes sought his.

"I'm sorry," he said.

"No, don't – don't put that all on you. And besides.... it's okay. Nothing happened," she said through stuttering gasps.

"But it would have," he said. "If that gun hadn't gone off. I would have kissed you."

The words hung in the air as they finally looked at each other.

"Or I would have," she said. "The way you were feeling back there, that's how I feel every time something happens between us. I couldn't have held back any better than you. It feels like every day we're playing with fire, and we just take it moment by moment."

He moved to sit against the wall. It put him further from her and she wondered if it was his intent to move away.

"Then maybe we shouldn't be doing this," he said. "We're just tempting fate. I admit, when you first told me how you really feel, I was a little mad at you for keeping it all from me. But now—" He shook his head. "I can see how it was the only safe choice."

"What are you saying?" she asked, her heart racing a mile-a-minute.

"I'm saying I don't want to break my promise. And I also don't want to lose our relationship in some lust-fueled dependency."

Her stomach clenched. "Then we won't. We'll keep doing what we're doing and—" Her voice broke and she stopped.

"Sadie, you know it's only a matter of time before we're back in a situation like today. Hell, if you feel like that all time then we're always in that much danger of losing control and I've just been stupid and selfish not to realize it."

She felt tears breaking loose now and tried to stifle them. If nothing else, she wouldn't lose control of this conversation. "Jimmy, think about this. What's the alternative?"

He looked down. "We—" He huffed. "Ahh fuck, we could put some distance back between us." His voice broke this time, but he finished the sentence firmly.

"No," she said. "No, we can't. That's worse than losing you the other way. I'd rather our relationship change than say goodbye to it all together. I need you with me. I can't lose you now. These past weeks have been so—" She gulped. "We have to keep trying."

"But we'll fail," he said. "If we keep doing this, I won't be able to keep my word. I can't make sure we don't do something we'll regret."

"Then that's just how it is," she said.

"You don't mean that," he replied.

"Yes, I do," she said, the tears finally stopping.

"You want us to end up like those stories in that scroll?" he asked.

"Yes," she said. "Or no, but I want to take that chance. It's worth it to me. And if something happens... it won't be your fault. Okay? I reject your promise. You didn't know what it meant when you made it. I want to stay close to you even if it means we eventually end up in the one place I said I wanted to avoid. I want you more... more than I want to avoid that fate. I accept the consequences Jimmy, whatever they are."

He was silent for so long she thought she would explode waiting for his reply. Eventually, Jimmy stood to look out the window and she wiped her face clean, hugging her knees as she watched him.

"But we'll continue to try and hold out?" he asked.

"Yes. We'll try," she said.

Jimmy was still for what felt like forever, picking at a spot on the window. But in the end, he cleared his throat. "Okay," he said to the glass.

Chapter 19

A decision

Sadie woke up with a pounding headache. The tragedy of the day before had become a physical presence in her body. Her limbs felt like lead. The image of Drigh dropping to the ground played on repeat in her mind. The situation in this town had really escalated if the beaded felt comfortable with public murder.

She jumped at the sound of the hotel door closing, and blinked away tears as Jimmy joined her on the bed. Her stomach churned at the smell of food wafting from the paper bag he placed between them. In his other hand was a rolled-up newspaper. He dropped that between them too and stroked her hair.

Scooting up next to her so she could rest her head against his thigh, Jimmy massaged her temples. She relaxed into his lap as he soothed her, and for once, neither of them was thinking about sex. The black light that indicated loving relationships swelled slightly between them as a strong need for affection overwhelmed her. She felt like her heart had undergone some grueling exercise and was now tender and sore.

"It's not mentioned," Jimmy said. "There were other people killed yesterday that made the news, but the stuff that happened at the market wasn't worth a footnote. The violence in the city was all over the place this past week. They gave some numbers and then included details only for the deaths they thought were *important.*"

Jimmy pushed away the paper and food and sprawled his legs out next to her. She rolled her weight up on him, swinging her thigh over his, and relaxed on his chest. Sadie soaked up the feel of him as she inhaled his musky scent. If things were different, she might have wanted to make slow, sweet love just then. The kind that she saw in other people's minds, but had never experienced. But as it were, she contented herself with the feeling of him pressed tightly against her.

"Where should we go next? Keep heading south you think?" he asked.

She lifted her head. "What? No. I—" Sadie rested her chin on her hands while he propped up his head to look down at her. "I think I finally know what I want," she said. "I want to stay and fight against what's happening. I never knew the world was such a mess and I'm tired of running from it. After... what happened yesterday, I'm sure of it. I want to stay. I want to help. For Drigh."

Jimmy nodded, looking thoughtful. "Okay. I'm in," he said, and a little fire of determination lit up his expression. "So long as we're safe, we can get more involved. I just don't want you to get hurt. We need to be careful. It's getting dangerous around here."

"I know, but it won't be risk-free." She propped herself up then. "And on the subject of taking risks, I think we should give them the box."

Jimmy pushed himself up too. "Are you sure? Maybe we should just ask them if they know of an Andre Amadi. If Ocean said this would help stop the war, and that's the goal of The United, it seems like they might know of him."

"Yeah, maybe. I think it's time I finish reading the diary. I've been putting it off since it didn't seem like a rush and I hate reading that thing, but we should at least check that there's not more info in it before we say anything."

Sadie had in fact read more of it and it was filled with some rather gruesome scenes of the succubus feeding off a new haul of human slaves. She hadn't picked it up since. It seemed mostly useless anyway. That is, unless it really was some kind of codebook.

"So we have a plan then?" he said. "You'll finish the diary, then we'll ask about Amadi and possibly tell them about the box."

She relaxed her weight back on him as he lay back. "A plan," she said with a decisive nod.

He reached for her thigh and pulled her tight again. The mood changed instantly. All at once, her libido kicked back to life as she felt him hardening under her. His thoughts were again fully on her as he ran a finger under the curve of her ass.

"I should go feed," she said, rubbing herself once against him before propping herself back up. She traced a finger from his collarbone to lower abdomen, sighing regretfully. With one last glance at the bulge in his pants, she climbed moodily out of bed. It seemed nothing was fair in this world.

She indulged in the feeling of self-pity for the rest of the morning. The fifteen minutes she spent feeding from one of her regulars provided a temporary distraction, but the second she stepped back out into the cool air of early fall, she was back to her frustration. For some reason, she didn't have the patience to deal with restraining her desires just then. The feeling of having made a choice for their future had lit a fire of action and it left her with a wave of rebellious angst.

Sadie was wandering the streets in the direction of their hotel when she made a decision. She had just the way to satisfy her mood for action. Pivoting, she redirected her path toward The Taste. It had been two weeks since her last real, hefty take, and Jimmy's job wouldn't provide for them for a while. It'll be in Drigh's honor, she told herself. One. Last. Time.

Sadie scouted out the casino from a shady corner. It was now mid-afternoon, and she'd never actually done this in the daylight. She sat under a maple tree whose leaves had begun to change into beautiful burnt oranges and vibrant yellows which seemed to match her mood. Holding up a newspaper which had been showing strong support for the feeder vigilantes, she pretended to read.

It took hours, however. She could've read the paper five times had she actually been reading. It was probably beginning to look suspicious if anyone was paying attention. Yet she waited. She didn't want to risk herself for just another couple bucks. She wanted a big fish.

Eventually, her patience paid off. A tiny black car pulled up in front and discharged a large man in a suit. Sadie moved. She examined his jacket and pant pockets from her peripheral as she walked casually, pretending to still be engrossed in the paper. She marked the wallet, right pant pocket, as she approached.

Just before he turned at the sound of her, Sadie bumped into him, retrieved the wallet and dropped it into a pouch sewn into the underside of her skirt in one fell motion.

"Oh dear! I'm so sorry. My head was far away." She flashed him the paper.

He narrowed his eyes. She kept walking, though worry crept through her as she realized he suspected her and was probably even now checking his pockets.

Abruptly, the ground felt unsteady under her feet as if she had suddenly become overly intoxicated. She fell flat on her face as the earth trembled, but rolled quickly to her back to look around. Before Sadie could suss out what on earth had just happened, the man's bodyguard stepped out of his expansive shadow.

It happened in a second. The person was slight, but moved quickly. Sadie tried to stand, but was tripped and pinned so effortlessly that she felt she must be a clumsy toddler flailing about under the steady, confident hold of an adult.

In her panic, it took Sadie a moment to take in the features and images of the person holding her, but when she did, she gasped. It was the woman Hetia. The one-night stand she had been idly fantasizing over ever since their fortunate meeting. Sadie relaxed, smiling up at her. However, when Hetia pinned both her hands in a forceful grip and began patting her down with her free hand, Sadie remembered they were not on the same side here.

Struggling against the hold, Sadie tried to buck her hips and twist her wrists out of the grasp, but to no avail. Sadie marveled at the strength of the woman. Though Hetia stood several inches taller than Sadie, she was much leaner. Clearly, she was a paid bodyguard for a reason. With an unimposing physique, her skill and strength were probably frequently underestimated.

Hetia's hand ran down the length of Sadie's side, from armpit to hip. Then she felt along under and between her breasts. She was searching so meticulously there was no way she was not going to feel the pouch. She ran over every inch of her stomach and Sadie began to worry in full for what was going to happen to her when she was caught stealing, but the fear was confusingly mixed with the excitement at the way Hetia was so intentionally searching her.

Wisely keeping away from skin contact, Hetia reached for Sadie's knee, which was just barely covered by the hem of her skirt. She moved firmly up Sadie's thigh, her thumb running along the inseam and bound directly for the pouch.

Was it Sadie's imagination or was Hetia moving rather more slowly than the task called for? Her hand reached the pouch, nestled against the top of Sadie's inner thigh. Hetia's eyes locked on Sadie's as she made contact and a triumphant, albeit short-lived, grin flashed over her face. Oh god, what had she done? Sadie lamented, even as she looked longingly at Hetia's thin, slightly parted lips.

But Hetia's hand kept moving, traveling up over her hip and stomach as if she hadn't already found the bounty. She scooped up under her breast once more and traced along her bra line before returning to rest on the side of her ribs. Hetia's gaze flicked for a moment from Sadie's eyes to lips and back, looking for all the world like she was about to lean in and kiss her. Then she rose abruptly to her feet in one swift motion, leaving Sadie on her back, breathless and confused.

"She's clean," Hetia told her employer.

"Are you certain?" the man asked haughtily.

"Have I ever failed you? The woman must've bumped into you after the wallet had already gone missing."

The man considered this a moment, but in the end nodded; immediately losing interest in the woman who'd just been tackled for suspected robbery on his behalf.

"Sorry for the confusion. You're free to go," Hetia said with a perfectly straight face that betrayed none of the underlying truth of the situation. She turned to follow her employer.

"Wait! Het—" Sadie had started to say, before realizing she couldn't possibly call after her, especially not by name, without arousing suspicion. She watched dejectedly as Hetia disappeared into a place she certainly couldn't follow.

Her bad luck continuing, Sadie turned grumpily away from the entrance only to find herself face-to-face with Irene. Irene... sporting an eyebrow bead.

"Sadie? What are you doing here?" Her tone was cold, but the question genuine.

"Uh..." She panicked, searching her thoughts frantically for a safe explanation. "I've left my human and... I've been feeling a bit lost. But um... wanting to get more involved so... I'm here looking for you." She was praying that Irene never played on her family's poker tables.

Irene narrowed her eyes. "What changed your mind?"

Sadie got hold of herself and relaxed into the role. "I overheard some humans talking about raiding The Taste and, you know – I know we didn't part on the best terms, but I didn't think you deserved that." The story seemed believable enough, and in fact, Irene's expression softened.

"Where did you hear this?"

Sadie was not confident she could continue fabricating details on the spot.

"There's more than just that, I've heard other rumors too, extending way beyond just The Taste. I was hoping you could help connect me with the right people so I can share my full story." She said, proud of her fast thinking.

Irene looked at the casino behind her then down at her nails, her expression tense in thought.

"Tonight. You're not welcome here, but there's a gathering tonight and I'll bring you as my guest. I won't tell you where. You can meet me back here at eight."

Irene looked her up and down with a curious frown as Sadie nodded. Then before she could say another word, Irene turned her back on her, nose in the air, and vanished through the entrance.

An hour later, Sadie was sitting in an emergency meeting to discuss the idea of her actually showing up to the appointment with Irene.

"I don't like it," Jimmy said from his place standing in the doorway. A small crowd had gathered in Luciana and Patricia's tiny living room.

"Of course he doesn't," VJ, the man infatuated with Patricia, chimed in. "It's dangerous. If something went wrong, you'd have little back-up support."

"And to what end?" Patricia questioned. "Our goal is to calm the troubles here, not stir them up. Feeding evil rumors to the most dangerous elements of the city seems far astray from our intentions."

"Not if they were the right rumors," Sadie argued. She had convinced herself on the way over here that she'd accidentally fallen into a great opportunity by running into Irene. "If we were able to somehow distract and divert their efforts, it might protect real people from harm for a while." She was filled with fierce determination as she said this. After Drigh's death, Sadie had never been so desperate to act.

"Or it might make things worse for everybody," Jimmy said.

He rarely spoke this much in meetings. He was clearly going to fight all he could to kill this idea.

"That's why if we can't come up with a well-thought-out plan before eight, we won't do it," Sadie said. "But I have to add, it's more than just having a chance to feed false information, it's also about possibly getting information. If I can get them to trust me a little, maybe I can learn something useful."

Jimmy opened his mouth to argue again, but Luciana put up a hand to silence the room. She rarely offered her opinion, doing so only in moments of sharp contention.

"My dear granddaughter asked me once when we know it is time to take greater action. The beaded have been intent on doing harm, without needing provocation, from the beginning. We're not going to change their minds, one way or the other. They've decided what they're about. But information as to their plans could be useful. I think if Sadie is willing, we should take this risk."

The room contemplated this in silence, looking anxiously around at each other. Slowly, people began to nod.

"Vote?" Patricia said. All hands went up except Jimmy's, but at a glare of betrayal VJ returned his to his lap.

Sadie felt a fire in her belly as she said in triumph. "Now. Let's see if we can't come up with a good story."

It was only a few hours later before Sadie was staring back into the face of her once-playmate. Irene blindfolded her before Sadie felt a hand on her head push her down into a car.

"Hi Sades." Alec's voice came from her left.

She did her best to make small talk. A little nervousness was only to be expected under the circumstances, but she couldn't give herself away through panicked babbling.

The blindfold came off once they'd reached some indoor location. Luckily, the ride had been short. Sadie looked around at a vast church. It had been emptied somehow, except for the beaded, who now stood on all sides of her. The lighting was natural, a rich glow coming through the stain-glass windows above.

They'd placed her in the center, probably to intimidate. Everyone was on their feet except for two women that Sadie recognized as the pseudo-friends of Irene, Tara and Katina. They were dressed in heels and fine clothes as if they were back sipping cocktails at the bar, and perched on the edge of the balcony.

Irene came to stand in front of her, arms crossed. "The floor is yours."

Sadie cleared her throat.

"I don't know most of you, but I was shown a lot of kindness when I first came to this city. Out of pride, I behaved rudely to my hosts. I want to first apologize to Alec and Irene, who I was once happy to have as friends. I hope you can forgive me. It's been a confusing year, coming into my own identity, and I've made a lot of mistakes along the way."

Stick close to true emotions, Luciana had told her, *you never know who might be reading them.*

"But while I was wandering out there in the world, I learned several good lessons. The biggest one is how dangerous some people can be; to our world, to our very existence." Stony faces stared back at her. Was her tone too preachy?

"There are feeders who've arrived from out of town. At least ten of them that I know of, but I suspect the network is much bigger than that. They intend to infiltrate your group slowly and turn on you in one fell swoop."

There was a collective murmuring at this.

When it had died down, a man stepped forward.

"And how are we supposed to believe you aren't one of them? It's what I'd do, send in someone with a previous tie."

"I am one of them," she said boldly. "That's how I know all this. Up until a week ago, I was actively planning on participating." That lie would account for the feeling of guilt she was experiencing. "The thing is..." she continued, thinking of the day Jimmy had told her he was leaving Seattle; of the desolate sorrow and confusion she felt. She let the emotion wash over her until her eyes welled with tears. Then she thought of Drigh.

"The thing is, they killed someone, a feeder, right in front of me, all because he had said a kind word about Congressman Siphon. I don't think all of them are dangerous. I think there are others like me who want out, but the leadership—"

Sadie looked around. "I think the leadership wants you all dead."

Irene's expression showed fear and interest, but still suspicion. "And the raid on The Taste?" she asked.

"That's part of their plan. They were going to send feeders in to gamble who would pretend to fight against the human attack. This was how they intended to gain your trust." Sadie looked at the ground, trying to feel ashamed before continuing. "I know I don't have such a good plan, sweeping in here with no reason for you to believe me. But I didn't have much time. I panicked, and my feet brought me to Irene as if in a trance." Hopefully that would explain her strange behavior from earlier.

The feeders looked around at each other, turning slowly to defer to an older man in the back. The man spoke in a cracked voice, "What do the harpies say?"

Tara spoke from the balcony. "We taste no vengefulness or envy. She certainly isn't here for revenge."

"Sam?" the man spoke again.

Alec's friend Sam chimed in from her right. She hadn't noticed him.

"I'm getting something. A great wave of excitement. Could be fear. Or just a thrill at being here. Even if it's both, it doesn't necessarily mean she's lying, but she's keeping her face much calmer than her emotions."

As they discussed her possible guilt or innocence, she studied the lines of connection between them. Trying not to look too intentionally, Sadie made note as best she could of who was present and how they were related.

"Well, it does us no harm to assume she's telling the truth, but I don't think we can put much trust in her," Irene said. "She grew up with humans; her parents, her lovestruck pet. She'll have to earn her way in slowly."

Sadie bobbed her head. "I understand."

The man in the back spoke again in his commanding tone. "Take her back, Irene. We have other business here."

"Wait. There's one more thing," Sadie cut in, pretending she'd only just remembered. Looking around anxiously she said in a voice barely above a whisper, "I also learned today, that two of their members have already infiltrated your group." She paused for dramatic effect. "They could be here now."

This had been Patricia's masterpiece, and Sadie thought it an idea worthy of her wise friend.

The air fell so silent, you could have heard a feather fall to earth.

"Right uh, Irene, get her out of here," the man said in a tone that one would use if they'd just learned their ship had a fractured hull, but they wanted to keep the crew calm enough to not jump overboard.

Irene directed her with an arm on her back. She didn't speak to Sadie on the car ride back, apparently not ready to resume their friendship. "Come back tomorrow," Irene said, as they exited the car at the corner of The Taste. "My family and I will talk about hosting you again." She gave Sadie a not unkind look as she added, "Thank you. I hope we're right to take a chance on you."

She did her best to not look guilty, returning a small smile she hoped was somewhat warm. Then, having successfully completed the most delicately challenging task of her life, Sadie departed.

Yes, this was definitely where she was meant to be. A wave of excitement and pride filled her as she thought about what she'd just done. Because as terrifying as it had been, she knew now that she was born for this.

THE NEXT DAY, flush with their success, The United organized an outdoor party in a human and nymph neighborhood. It had been a while since they'd tried to merely bring people together for pleasure alone. With live music, dancing, and good food, they hoped it would be a welcome distraction from the fear and tension gripping everyday life.

Luckily, Irene told Sadie that they were not ready to have her come stay with them, but that she should instead come visit daily. The visits would be dangerous, Sadie knew, but they would allow her to practice her role as spy. It was also good that Alec and Irene wanted distance, since it would have meant separating from Jimmy, something that wasn't an option.

As exciting as her life had become, the high stress of it all made Sadie immensely grateful for the coming party. Patricia was organizing the set-up crew, and Sadie and Jimmy arrived late in joining, that is according to Patricia's thoroughly organized schedule. They were gathered under an oak tree in the field that would host them.

"Sorry, we uh, overslept," Sadie announced to no one in particular, but blushed under Patricia's narrowed eyes.

"As I was saying," the hag continued, "we still need people to bring in the tables. How about you three." She pointed to three people who had recently joined the group. "Sadie and Jimmy, I am putting you on the baking crew. Everyone else, you know what to do. We will meet back here to start having fun at 5 p.m."

Sadie smiled affectionately at Patricia's particular way of viewing the world. As for Sadie, the fun began immediately. Jimmy and she were placed alone in Luciana's kitchen with an abundance of ingredients, music blaring from the living room, and baking instructions written in Patricia's precise hand.

"No, it says here to knead firmly." Jimmy pointed at the instructions with a floury finger. "You've really got to put your back into it," he said before coming up behind her and sliding his gloved hands over hers.

She arched her backside against him. "Like this?"

He grew hard as he pressed down the dough with her hands, both of them bending forward with the effort.

"Yeah, just like that," he whispered in her ear.

Jimmy had learned a lot about how much she could take before entering the danger zone. He showed off this earned skill by toying with her all afternoon. The moment she bent towards over excitement, he would back off and wait for her to reset. Unfortunately, this game had an escalating effect over time, leaving her with a hunger to feed despite having done so that morning.

Dusting off the handprints of flour which were at this point all over her body, she ran a few houses down to one of her regulars while Jimmy went on ahead with the fruits of their labor. Or rather, the breads, muffins, and scones of their labor.

By the time Sadie reached the party, situated in a large, shared lawn at the center of a ring of houses, the festivities were well underway. A couple dozen families, plus the ever growing membership of The United made for several hundred people.

Sadie had changed into a beautiful baby-blue dress with long sleeves, appropriate for the cooling air of September. As she strolled into the field, dodging running children and inhaling the smell of barbecue, she felt more at peace than she had in a long while. A small knot of homesickness tightened in the pit of her stomach, and she resolved to call her parents the next time she was at Luciana's. After all, she'd been slightly inconsistent in her promise of weekly calls.

"Ah, there you are love." Luciana gestured her over. The grandmother was standing with half her weight on one arm. The cane which was looped about her other wrist flailed as she gestured, speaking animatedly. Next to her was another woman of about the same age.

"Tam, this is the one I was telling you about. Marched right into the lion's den and delivered the poison."

Sadie blushed.

The woman surveyed her carefully. "Hmm. It sounds like you've got yourself into a dangerous game. It's a hard life, spying. What made you want to do it?" The woman had a bland face in a way that made it almost hard to notice her, even when Sadie was addressing her directly.

"Well, I think because I could be good at it. I didn't know I would be. Though," she thought back over her time with Jimmy after she became a succubus, "I have had some practice at controlling my emotions. And – I think I like dangerous games." Sadie concluded, smiling at her inner thoughts.

"Still, can't imagine it would hurt if she had some training," the strange woman said, looking her over as if evaluating every detail.

Sadie didn't hear the rest of the conversation as she had just spotted something which struck her like a punch to the stomach.

Her heart stopped.

She muttered an excuse to break away and let her feet carry her across the field. She tried to walk normally, but was having a hard time remembering exactly how her hips usually moved. Sashaying in a way she was sure was not her regular manner, she smoothed her dress over her waist and cleared her throat.

"This is the third chance meeting for us," Sadie said with a smile to the woman standing alone. "Feels like fate."

Hetia had been facing away and hadn't seen her approach. At the sound of Sadie's voice, a wave of hot red light rushed from her. Outwardly, however, the woman did not react in the slightest. Without turning her head to face Sadie, she retorted, "You don't actually believe in such things?"

Sadie pulled up next to her to survey the gathering and to remove herself from staring awkwardly at a person who was not staring back.

"I don't know," she said. "There's so much of life we don't understand. Who am I to say why we end up where we do?"

"I don't buy it. We all have choices to make and are responsible for where they land us," Hetia said.

"Like the choice to work as a bodyguard for a rich feeder who likes to frequent The Taste?" Sadie peered at her.

"Everyone has to make a living," Hetia said.

"Or the choice to ask a girl to dance or to leave her standing alone in the corner?" Sadie asked. She regretted the flirtation almost immediately. She didn't know what came over her, but her head didn't seem to be working quite right.

Hetia looked askance at her.

"Woman," Sadie corrected. "Full-grown, strong... woman."

Hetia's mouth twitched for a moment and Sadie thought she might get to see that warm smile she'd glanced once during their first encounter, but a second later Hetia redonned her mask.

"No, uh... I don't dance," Hetia said, before adding firmly, "but I'm sure there are plenty of other people here who would love to dance with you."

Hetia was a study in contrast. Sadie had never seen someone make a summer dress look like a battle uniform. She held her head high, shoulders back and feet steady at hips width apart. Her cold, apparently indifferent manner, also sat sharply against the emotions and images Sadie read on her. What was she to make of the situation?

Instead of replying to Hetia's comment she asked, "What are you doing here then? I thought you were attached to The Taste?"

Hetia glared at her. "I could ask you that."

Sadie suddenly felt uncertain about her connection with Hetia. What *was* she doing here? She couldn't tell her she was connected to The United. That could get her in trouble if her instincts were wrong about the woman.

"I don't need to though," Hetia continued. "Since I already asked Luciana about you."

"What? You know Luciana?" Sadie said.

"Yes," Hetia said, offering no further information.

Sadie stared at her patiently, waiting for her to elaborate.

The technique worked once again. Maybe she was learning some things about this woman.

"I've been undercover until recently. That's all I'll say," Hetia told her.

They stood in silence for what felt like forever while Sadie desperately tried to think of any safe topic. Hetia had dismissed her offer to dance. In fact, despite the images of their night together which covered the woman, Hetia was outwardly rejecting her in both word and posture. In the end, Sadie did the only thing she could.

"Well anyhow, it was nice to see you again. Take care. Hetia," she said, before backing away slowly.

Hetia turned to look at her then, her striking eyes flitting up and down Sadie's form as she moved, before she jerked her gaze back to the gathering. As Sadie turned, she heard a barely audible "Goodbye" at her back.

As she walked, Sadie was distracted by boring a hole through the grass with her gaze and didn't see Jimmy approach. She ran into his chest before she stopped and looked up.

"Oh. Hi," she said breathlessly. He looked her over, steadying in on her eyes.

"Is that one of the humans you've been feeding from?" he asked, gesturing with his head back in the direction of Hetia.

"Uh, no. Well, once. But no," she said.

"Who is she? She looks familiar," he said, rubbing a hand absent-mindedly over her back.

Sadie was about to say that she was nobody, but her tongue caught. She'd made a promise, and the truth was, regardless of how Hetia had reacted to her just then, she was not nobody.

"That's Hetia. I met her at the bar of The Taste and we spent the night together," she said.

His face registered something and he nodded.

"I seem to like her. I like her a lot actually, but she is... uninterested in being friends I guess." She looked over his expression carefully, suddenly wishing she were a harpy.

"What are you thinking?" she whispered.

"I'd just never considered – I know it is my fate dating a succubus to share you, but I had never considered the idea that someone else might come along who..." He glanced back at Hetia and Sadie followed his gaze. By the way her head snapped, she had apparently been watching them up until they'd looked her way.

Jimmy continued to frown in contemplation, losing interest in expressing himself in words. Sadie took his hand. "But she's not interested. It's a moot point." By his ongoing furrowed brow and searching expression, Jimmy didn't think the point was closed at all. She pressed her body into his, finally redrawing his attention.

"It's such a lovely evening. Can we talk about this later? Honestly, what's a girl gotta do to get a dance around here?" She smiled.

He matched her expression before sweeping her up. They danced for hours, until their feet were sore and their faces flushed and sweaty. When the air began to cool into evening, they found a little bench off to the side where Jimmy fed her barbecue wings. Having removed his gloves so as not to stain them, he teased her with how close he could get his fingers to her lips, licking them clean in front of her.

This was the game they were engaged in when a whisper overtook the gathering. They looked around to see adults hurrying children in doors and The United rapidly gathering up plates and chairs. What was going on?

They stood, exchanged worried glances, and wordlessly decided to beeline for Luciana.

"What is it?" Sadie hissed to the grandmother who had been like her kin these past months.

"Trouble. In the city," she said. "Some people were killed. There's a large gang of beaded moving this way."

"What can we do?" Jimmy asked.

"Run. Get indoors. Back to your hotel if possible, though take the northern route as you leave." She secured her hat, kissed him on the cheek and hurried away. Sadie took Jimmy's hand and without another word they bolted. As they ran, however, Sadie couldn't help but look back over her shoulder.

The field was in disarray. Everyone was scrambling to gather their belongings and get out of there. Only one person remained unmoving. A tall, slender figure stood steady against the backdrop of the low hanging sun. Hands clasped behind her back, Hetia stared at Sadie as if there were nothing more important in the world she should be doing than watching her retreating form.

Chapter 20

An ending

They ran down side streets and through alleys, avoiding any sounds of life. A challenging task as it seemed half the city was out of bed that night. Jimmy pulled Sadie behind a dumpster as a cluster of people passed. Peering through the crack between dumpster and bricked wall, she reported back to Jimmy in a whisper, "They're not beaded, though they are carrying baseball bats and rifles." She looked again and added anxiously, "They look seriously angry."

They changed course five times as they maneuvered around similar packs, ending up further from the hotel than they had started. After they were forced back yet another street, Jimmy suggested, "Maybe we should lay low away from the hotel."

"No. The diary, I have to get it! What if something happens to the hotel? I'm an idiot for getting out of the habit of always having it with me. And now... if it's taken... We can't disappoint the last wish of a dying woman." She was panicking. Jimmy held her steady in a firm grip.

"We'll get it." He took her hand. "This way."

They had to do a wide loop to reach Pine from the east side of the city, but it was much quieter in that part of town. The few people who saw them pass turned out their porch lights and scurried inside.

They found the main entrance to Pine & West locked up. Jimmy banged furiously until someone responded and opened the door just wide enough for them to slip inside. No one presided over the elevator, forcing them to make their way up through the stairwell. After only one flight, Sadie cried, "Wait. I have to catch my breath." She leaned against one wall, heaving.

When she could talk she exclaimed, "What the hell was all that?"

"I don't know, but it didn't look good. Perhaps we should get out of the city?"

"But Patricia and Luciana? Oh god, their house! It's right in the thick of it."

Jimmy chewed his lip. "I think there's a phone downstairs. Maybe we could call them to check they're alright?"

They agreed in a silent exchange and traced their steps back down to the landing.

"Hello?" Sadie called over the front desk. No one answered.

"On it." Jimmy flung his legs over the counter, grabbed the phone and dialed. Sadie was grateful he could think under the circumstances as she found she'd entirely forgotten the phone number in this desperate moment. It rang. And rang. And rang.

"Maybe they fled?" Sadie suggested hopefully. Then added in a panic, "But then how will we ever find each other? We don't have any other way to contact them!"

Jimmy hopped back to her side of the counter and extracted something from his pocket. "That's not entirely true. Luciana gave me this. It's directions to a place just out of the city. I agreed we'd meet her there if things went south. At the time, I couldn't imagine what that would mean, but now..."

Sadie looked over his shoulder at the slip of paper.

"It'll be dangerous going back out there. Might be best to stay put for tonight," Sadie said.

Jimmy considered a moment, then nodded.

They made their way upstairs and began to pack. The hotel had become a second home to them and they had sprawled out into every corner. Sadie gathered underwear flung over bed posts and lamps. Jimmy rolled up the various sketches they'd made of everything she was able to recount of the beaded in the church and their connections. Sadie watered the little flowerpots she'd bought and placed in the windowsill.

"Sorry, my friends. I hope you find a new caretaker soon," she told them.

The final thing she packed was the diary, securing it safely back in the succubus box and shoving it to the bottom of her backpack. And then they waited. The light grew dimmer as sunset loomed. Jimmy stood watching at the window, unmoving, as Sadie paced.

They both turned their heads at a sound in the hall. That was strange. The hotel itself had been so quiet. Maybe it was another guest returning to safety for the night? Then came a loud knocking at the door. They froze, exchanging wide-eyed expressions. Sadie gestured for Jimmy to stay where he was as she crept to the peephole. Her heart skipped. It was Alec.

"Sades?" he asked. "Are you in there?" Jimmy shook his head. She was in agreement. They certainly weren't home. She heard Alec ask in a different tone, "Are you sure?"

In a horrifying turn of events, a familiar voice responded. "I'm sure. I saw them together. The man exactly matched the description you gave of her pet human. I followed them right back here." Who was speaking? Sadie knew it from somewhere.

"Well maybe they're out," Alec suggested.

"One sure way to find out," the voice replied.

"How? By—"

"I can break it down. You know I can."

Then Sadie realized. It was that awful wind nymph who had stoked that dumpster fire. Abruptly, her senses caught up to her and she realized what was about to happen. Finding her legs she commanded, *run!* as she hissed the word to Jimmy.

Sadie bolted for the window and pried it open; searching frantically for the fire escape. Jimmy took one look at the panic on her face and asked no questions. No sooner had they thrown on their backpacks and hauled themselves onto the tiny ladder attached just outside the window than the door burst open. An explosion of wind soared over their heads.

Sadie was grateful she hadn't closed the window as they would have had shards of glass to contend with on top of everything else. She tried to move quietly, hoping that Alec and Eric would believe the window had just been blown away, and not that it had been recently opened.

As Jimmy's feet touched ground, they both looked up just in time to see two heads peering down at them.

"Run!" Sadie cried. They sprinted down the alleyway as a gale assailed them head-on. Sadie ducked her head and dug in her heels, reaching blindly for Jimmy's hand. The progress was slow. They'd likely have been moving faster if they'd been walking at a leisurely stroll with no headwind. Sadie couldn't hear behind her and didn't want to risk falling over by attempting to look.

Fear began to grip her as she waited for a hand to grab at her, but the only hand which pulled her was Jimmy's tugging her sideways. They cleared the building and the pressure on them died immediately. Apparently the nymph couldn't send it around corners. They dashed forward to Pine.

Whipping around the corner, Sadie caught a glimpse of the two men emerging from the other side of the alley, but she wasted no time turning to look. They moved as quickly as her skirt and their packs would allow.

"We have to lose them. They'll catch us," Jimmy panted.

They could hear a ruckus of voices somewhere to their left.

"This way." Sadie pulled him toward the clamor, hoping she wasn't about to get them both killed. They traveled one block, turned a corner, and emerged into what Sadie could only think to call a mob.

Adapting quickly, Sadie slowed her pace and tensed her stance into an angry stomp.

"Death to feeders!" she shouted in chorus. Jimmy stared at her wide-eyed. He fell in line beside her, however, and also took up the chant, albeit in a more hesitant tone.

The assembly was moving much slower than she wanted, but the streets were darkening. Sadie hoped they'd be able to hide if she could move them to the middle. Cursing her light blue dress, she squeezed her way deeper into the crowd, pulling Jimmy behind her.

They appeared to be heading toward the heart of the city which was not the direction they wished to go. Casting furtive glances down every street they passed, Sadie could see no sign of Alec. When an uproar of voices sounded ahead, followed by a gunshot, they knew it was time to disconnect.

They slipped through an alley the width of their shoulders and emerged onto an empty avenue. It was wide and smelled of horse dung, but was also blessedly deserted. As they traveled away from the setting sun, their bodies cast long shadows out in front of them. Within what was probably a few minutes, but felt like hours, they found themselves alone with only the sound of their pounding steps.

Occasionally, Sadie thought she heard another set of footfalls, though when she'd try to listen closer, she could catch only the distant rumble of fighting.

They slowed to a walk. Her legs and lungs were on fire. They couldn't keep up the pace and they did seem out of immediate danger.

"I think we should arm ourselves," Jimmy said, glancing sideways at her. She didn't like the idea, which must've shown on her face because he added, "Just in case."

"What if it just makes us more of a target? Makes us stand out?" she said.

"I think everyone out tonight is armed. I think it would make us fit in," he said.

As they dropped down a deserted residential street, Jimmy scanned the surroundings. Sadie watched him anxiously while he veered left onto a porch.

Sadie pulled up next to him as he ran his hands over a smooth wooden rocking chair.

"Do you think anyone is home?" she whispered.

"Don't know. Stand back," he said in a commanding tone she rarely heard from him.

Lifting the chair above his head, he brought it down hard against the steps; once, twice. It broke off into two parts. Picking up the smaller half, he worked at it with a heavy foot until it came apart into two smooth wooden legs.

Sadie looked it over, impressed and yet surprised at his behavior. She gave it a test swing and nodded approvingly. Could she swing it at a human head though? If she had to? Sadie had never contemplated such a notion, and she prayed to make it through the night without having the opportunity to find out.

They continued to travel east and the din of fighting reached their ears from both the north and south. It seemed they were charting a course through the middle which was fortunate enough to be left out of the action; for the time being at least.

They walked in tense silence for a while.

Jimmy was the first to break it.

"Sadie, I don't know how we ended up in this mess, but I just want you to know... that if I could go back and do it again, I would." He clasped her fingers. "I wouldn't give up a moment that I had with you this summer, or all the years before that."

Sadie didn't like to hear him speak as if they weren't going to make it out the other side of this. She tried to reply, but the words caught in her throat as a tear fell from her eye. Giving the only response she could, she squeezed his hand in hers.

Abruptly, the houses fell away into an empty expanse. Sadie gaped at the sudden open scenery. There were no buildings or trees here, only a lone road connecting one side of the city to the other. As they crossed, Sadie pointed out a sign reading "Danger, Fault Line."

"Are there earthquakes here?" she asked.

"Not that I've heard," he said.

The racket closed in as they moved, and before long, they could hear the distinct sound of voices. Their heads whipped side to side as they resumed jogging.

The fighting sprawled out into the path ahead, forcing them to an abrupt halt. They looked to both sides and could see trouble. They were boxed in.

"What do we do?" Sadie asked.

"In here." Jimmy dragged them toward a clothing store. He broke a window and hoisted her inside. The terrifying sounds of fighting were muffled within the thick walls of the expansive building. Sadie floated through the round clothing racks, getting the lay of the land.

"Jimmy, back here," she called over a shoulder.

Next to the restrooms, there was the entrance to a second, much larger room filled with sewing machines and long, wooden tables. There were no windows here.

"I wonder if we could barricade ourselves in," she suggested.

A crash came behind them and they leapt forward through the door. It did not lock from the inside.

"The table." Jimmy gestured, running to hoist the far side.

"Sades? You in here?" Alec's voice echoed in the outer room. They froze. They had kept following them! "S'okay. We just want to talk," he said.

Sadie covered her lips with a finger. The table was heavy. She couldn't lift it off the floor. It would probably make a ruckus if they tried to move it. Jimmy gestured that they should just move away from the door.

Searching in near darkness for a place to hide, they felt their way under a workstation in the back just in time as lights flickered on in all directions.

They heard the men split up, each one coming up on either side of the room. It was inevitable they would spot them crouched there; nowhere else to run.

"We're armed," Sadie said weakly.

"We're not," Alec said, walking casually now as if he no longer felt any need to disguise himself.

"Lied to the family, Sadie. No one's gonna to be happy to learn that. Everybody was rooting for you. Even Sis."

Jimmy gestured her to stay put as he bear-crawled his way around the station and out of her sight. Unable to communicate, she could only trust he wasn't about to do anything stupid. Then before she could form another thought, Alec appeared to her right and she found herself staring at him over the barrel of a gun. He stood over her with a grin as he said, "Make you a deal. I won't tell 'em, so long as you promise to take the secret to your grave." He cocked the trigger.

Sadie flinched at the cracking sound of Jimmy's chair leg colliding with the side of Alec's head. The gun fired a hole in the ceiling as Alec smacked hard against the cement floor. Eric appeared at the end of a row to her left and she stood to face him. She had to keep him from assisting his friend. Sadie stepped forward with a fire in her eyes and pulled back her makeshift bat, preparing herself to swing.

A wind pushed her back as Eric pulled out a long knife. Her bat was longer, she told herself, hoping to imbue confidence as she pushed forward. She didn't find nearly the resistance she had in the alleyway outside the hotel. Apparently the nymph couldn't create as much of a gust in this enclosed space.

Abruptly she fell on her face. He'd switched the direction of the wind nearly instantaneously. Jimmy swung over her head and Eric was forced to hop back. Sadie kicked her feet around and tripped him. Jimmy put his foot on the wrist holding the knife as Sadie was grabbed from behind and dragged backward. She lost hold of the bat as Alec threw her against the wall.

Enough, she told herself. Shaking it off like she'd merely tripped in the woods, she rose to her feet in a huff. He laughed as she moved toward him in determination. Making as if she were about to throw a punch, she instead kneed him in the groin with all her strength. He buckled over.

Sadie felt a rush of victory, though she knew that was a trick she would only get to use once. It seemed unlikely she would win this fight. Alec clearly had experience in these ways and she had never even intentionally killed a spider. Then a thought occurred to her. Hadn't she done it once before? Sucked the life out of a person? Alec picked up the bat, looking angry, but taking his time. He strolled toward her. She was backed into the wall.

"What a waste," he muttered sadly.

She doubted. What if it didn't work on other feeders? Then before she could talk herself out of it, she moved. As he pulled the bat back to swing Sadie crashed forward, locked her lips to his, and pulled. She felt it immediately. Sadie forcibly withdrew something from deep inside him and he fell in a heap at her feet.

She staggered back against the wall, retching. A sickness clutched at her stomach.

She slid down and put her head between her knees. Jimmy's hand appeared on her shoulder.

"Eric's down?" she asked through her heaving, unable to lift her head.

"Yes," he quickly assured her.

"Dead?" she asked.

"Unconscious."

"And Alec?" she asked.

She heard Jimmy shift.

"He's alive."

Relief flooded her.

"We should move before they wake up, unless we want to do this again," Jimmy said. "Can you stand?"

"In a minute."

He squatted next to her and they sat back against the wall. She leaned into his embrace, looking at Alec's crumpled form in front of them.

When she could speak, she asked, "Did it feel good? Getting to knock him to the ground?"

He rubbed her arm a minute in silence, before responding, "No. Do you think it should have?"

She looked around at the damage in front of them.

"No," she said sorrowfully.

Sadie waited for the pounding in her head to subside to a manageable ache before letting Jimmy help her to her feet.

They exited through the door, having had enough crawling through windows. Armed again with their tiny bats, they stepped out into the chaos and stared in the direction they had previously been heading.

"The only way out is forward," Sadie said. "No more trying to go around."

Sticking as close to each other as they could, they made their way into the thicket. Sadie wondered how the two sides would even have been able to fight each other if the beaded hadn't marked themselves artificially. What a horror, she lamented.

They dodged two men slicing at each other with kitchen knives.

Another man scrambled to reach a woman holding a hose. She was clearly a nymph, as the water was firing unnaturally into three different people's faces.

Then, dreadfully, Sadie spotted a woman standing next to a tree that happened to stand in the center of the fray.

"Please don't! Not here," the woman begged, hugging the tree with her back, arms splayed. "Go anywhere but here!" she shouted.

A man hopped up into its branches to load a gun as an unnatural gust of wind tried to snap the branch free.

Gaze flitting frantically over the rest of the scene, Sadie spotted two figures in heels perched on a roof. The harpies beheld the spectacle as if they'd come to see a play and weren't disappointed. Disgust flooded her.

Sadie hopped up into a wagon to dodge an oncoming duel of fiery torches and Jimmy came in behind her.

"Is there anything we can do?" she cried, looking again at the solitary tree nymph caught in the center.

"We can stand with her. Try to beat people back," Jimmy said. It seemed unlikely they would succeed, but Sadie couldn't bring herself to leave the woman to fight alone.

"Through here!" She hopped off the front of the wagon and squeezed through a narrow opening in the throng.

Though right as Sadie pulled up to the tree, the dryad reached for a fallen baseball bat, one much bigger than Sadie's. The woman turned to swing it at her with a determined expression.

"It's okay." Jimmy gripped the bat from behind. "We're here to help."

Some of the madness softened in her eyes, only to return tenfold as she faced the surrounding mob.

Sadie felt her own mind cave under a delirious rage as she swung with all her might at a woman brandishing a knife and a murderous expression. Over her head, Sadie glimpsed a teenage girl peering out of a window. It seemed their impulse nymph was again fueling the flames.

Somehow, despite their best efforts, they'd found themselves in the center of the clash. *No.* She thought back to Hetia's words: *We all have choices to make.* Theirs had led them here.

She spotted a head in the distance. Was that—? No, it was only that she'd just been thinking of her words.

But then the figure neared, and there could be no mistake. A woman walked through the crowd, upright and assured. She dodged the brawlers as if such blows were beneath her and she were merely stepping out of the way because she'd seen a better path. One man attempted to throw a punch right at her and ended up flipped to his back.

Sadie heard a rumble to her right and noticed the building supporting Tara and Katina had begun to sway. Then, as if all at once, the whole world moved. All the buildings danced on their foundations; the ground rattled under their feet. The fighting slowed as people tried to find their footing. Several car alarms went off in the distance.

Sadie looked for Jimmy. He was staggering toward her, barely keeping his feet under him. The nymph slid down against her tree and began to pray. Jimmy grabbed her hand as they both relinquished their weapons. Sadie looked back out at the turmoil for Hetia.

She stood not ten feet from them, unmoving. It was a strange kind of unmoving. Her back was straight; shoulders upright. And though the ground moved below her as for everyone else, she seemed to move with it, like a veteran captain on a ship.

As Sadie stared in awe at her, she saw a person in the corner of her vision was also taking note of Hetia's strange behavior. A shirtless man carrying a rifle, gaped at Hetia before taking aim.

"Look out!" Sadie cried. Hetia gazed languidly in the direction of the man trying to point the gun at her and dropped into a crouch. At first Sadie thought it was her strangely ineffective way of dodging the shot, until she placed a hand to the earth and the shaking increased precipitously.

Sadie heard one of the harpies scream as she fell from the roof. The ground cracked under the nearby carriage and one wheel sunk into the earth. Most people were on their hands and knees now, including herself. Jimmy tried to haul her back upright. "We have to move!" he shouted. Hetia joined them in front of the tree, the rumbling quieting as she came back to her feet.

A man shouted, pointing a finger in their direction, "Get them!"

Hetia looked away from the man to lock her gaze on Sadie's.

"Run, succubus," she said.

Sadie didn't want to leave her, but was yanked so forcefully by Jimmy that she thought he might toss her over his shoulder if she resisted. Not wanting to endanger him further, she complied with being pulled away.

They staggered up the hill as quickly as was possible. The sound of resumed fighting mingled with that of the earthquake behind them.

When they were again alone, and the shaking under their feet only a muted rumble, Sadie cried, "Wait!" Looking back down at the scene they'd fled, Sadie watched as the mob focused their attention entirely on Hetia, finding a sudden shared purpose. The woman bent again and placed one hand to the earth.

Everyone who wasn't already on their knees, landed there then. One building came down. Then another. They watched in shock as the store housing the unconscious bodies of Alec and Eric was reduced to dust. Tears streaked down Sadie's face. She wouldn't let herself be moved further as she watched the chaos play out. The quake didn't reach outside of the one neighborhood, but in a perfect circle around the fighting, every building was leveled.

The sun set behind the rubble as Sadie stood there gaping, Jimmy's arm over her shoulder. The smoke cleared in what appeared to be a natural wind, and she caught sight of a tree. It now stood taller than its surroundings, its leaves blowing in the evening breeze as the sun's rays illuminated its golden leaves like fire. Sadie thought she could make out the tiny figure of the tree nymph at its base, and a small wave of relief washed over her.

Finally, she let Jimmy drag her away. They traveled with heavy hearts to the edge of the city. The location Luciana had given them turned out to be a tiny hut of a house on the side of a grassy hill. The grandmother sat there on that hill, watching what was turning out to be a spectacular sunset.

Sadie and Jimmy joined her wordlessly. The dust from fires and rubble all over the city fought to cover the view, but the sun rays peeking out from over the horizon won out, as the entire sky filled with dark pinks and warm oranges.

"Earthquake nymphs warned against building a city here," Luciana said. "That quake was inevitable."

Sadie wondered if she should tell her that that particular earthquake was not the workings of natural order.

Instead she asked, "Where are Patricia and VJ?"

"I sent them to safety. A difficult task, but they obeyed in the end," Luciana said.

"Where will you go now?" Sadie asked, stuttering through her desire to replace the word *you* with the word *we*.

"Well, Sadie Hall, James Baker." Luciana nodded to each of them. "I think you've earned a right to know. "Our work here was actually our above ground operation. It was set up to try and calm tensions." She looked over the city burning at their feet and adjusted her hat. "Clearly, we uh, failed here."

They gazed again in silence at the landscape before she continued, "But we could really use you behind the scenes. You see, our underground operation has a larger purpose."

Sadie looked wide-eyed at Jimmy before asking, "And what's that?"

Luciana looked from Sadie, to Jimmy, to the setting sun before replying, "To prevent the war at its source. To bring down the feeder government."

Chapter 21

A beginning

Sadie and Jimmy stayed the night in the little hut on the hill. She slept restlessly on a tiny bed shared with Luciana, her arm dangling over the side to clasp Jimmy's hand on the floor. They rose at dawn into a world which, to Sadie, felt entirely new.

Luciana packed them food and a map. "You'll find huts like these along the way, with extra supplies and a warm bed. After my granddaughter returns and we have a chance to clear out the house, we'll follow."

She pushed a coin into Sadie's hand. At least she pushed something Sadie mistook for a coin. On closer inspection she saw it was a rather large golden disk, engraved with three intersecting rings.

"Flash this to anyone who questions you along with the words *is that a dove's cry I hear?* They should respond *only if you've got an ear to the ground.* And when you arrive at camp, tell them I sent you with my highest recommendations." Luciana spoke with uncharacteristic haste.

"Now, I must attend to my belongings before they are ransacked by anyone using last night as an excuse to steal twenty cherished hats." She kissed them both, taking care as always with Sadie, and scampered down the hill.

Three days. That was how long Luciana said it would likely take for them to reach The United encampment nestled high in the Cascades. Worried about making such a long journey with likely no one to feed from, Sadie set a brisk pace as they traveled down the other side of the hill and out of Seattle. She looked back only once, but the ash from the previous night's event had settled low, obscuring the city from sight.

They spoke little as they wound their way up and down hills and through forest. Lost in their own thoughts, they walked in a meditative state. The houses dropped off slowly, until they found themselves in a woodland far denser than they'd ever seen. The trail shrunk down to a size accommodating for two, but clearly not meant for carts or cars.

Great firs and cedars loomed over head, their roots often running right through the path. Ferns filled the undergrowth in a thick blanket of light green, which glowed emerald when struck by the patches of sunlight. Sadie looked up, suddenly noticing her surroundings, and inhaled as if it were her first breath of life.

They found the first hut exactly where it was marked on the map. It was even smaller than the one they'd slept in the night before, and a dangerously leaning spruce tree framed the door with one of its roots. Bending to walk under the thick root, Jimmy called, "Hello?"

Sadie watched him disappear inside. "It's cute," he said. "And there's a bed and, ooh beef jerky."

The sun was setting earlier now that autumn had officially arrived. Since they had no additional light with them, they had no choice but to eat and prepare for bed early.

"We should finish the diary before we get to the camp," Sadie said. "Was it really just three days ago that we made the plan to hand it over?"

Jimmy thought a minute. "I guess it was."

"Again, we got distracted," she said. "But enough of that. It's time to find out how this thing ends, and if it's anything but garbage shoved in with an important button." She pulled out the leather-bound book and, snuggling up in the base of the spruce, read aloud by the soft glow of dusk.

. . .

September 28th 1920

Brother is dead. He came pounding on the door late last night, only to engage in another row with Father. With some final threatening words which I did not comprehend, he turned to depart, but Father had pulled down the sword from its fireplace mantel and with a swift strike, pierced him through the back. Michael turned as he fell to his knees. He saw me standing on the landing. Looked at me and fell forward. And now he's dead and no one else knows I saw what happened.

My parents told me this morning that a human killed him on the doorstep as he was attempting to get to the safety of his home. Mother said that because of the recent altercations between him and her and Father, that there might be suspicion laid on them, particularly on Father. Perhaps cook, or driver will say something against Father. Mother said that I can help protect his innocence if I can say I witnessed the attack.

She said she's arranged for the red-haired male to be a part of the line-up tomorrow. He was gathered up in the search for all red-haired young men, which is the description Mother said I gave her of the attacker. All I have to do is go down to the station and vilify—

"Or is it identify? Damn, it's too dark already." They felt their way into the hut in the near total darkness. Sadie thought that Jimmy and Luciana referring to the thing on which she now rested as a *bed* was a generous assessment. The hard cot kept them from having to lie directly on the ground, but she could say no more of it than that.

Sadie had not only become accustomed to a soft bed in a warm room, but also to the near-nightly shenanigans of her and Jimmy. Having not fed that day, such a thing would be far too dangerous now. Between her own restless body and that of Jimmy's beside her, she once again slept very little.

They rose with the sun to make the best of daylight. The birds chirped all around them as they consumed the salty jerky with Luciana's sweet plums. Casting furtive glances, they didn't speak of the fact that they were alone and Sadie hadn't fed since before the party. Nor did they speak of the fact that it was unknown whether they'd meet anyone else in the next two days.

They traveled mostly uphill from then onward, while the trees thinned and the air cooled. They met no one, and by the late afternoon Sadie was beginning to feel quite weak.

"Rest," she panted, flopping down on a rock. Jimmy made to sit next to her before changing his mind and stepping back awkwardly to sit on the ground. To distract herself from staring at him, she pulled back out the diary. Searching for the line she couldn't read in the dim lighting, Sadie cleared her throat and continued.

ALL I HAVE to do is go down to the station and identify the killer as Mother's previous man. I pray that I can do it. I haven't looked Father in the face since the incident. I fear he will see it in my eyes and know I was there. Would he strike me too? Would he ever treat me as he has Brother, or did the fool just have this coming all along? I'm not sure what choices are available to me, except to give my mother's story as she has told it. I hope they do not ask me too many questions, I've never had cause to practice delivering such momentous lies.

SEPTEMBER 29TH 1920

IT IS DONE. And before you judge me, know that I'm only exchanging the life of a human. How can you ask me to choose such a creature over my own Father? Is the world not a better place now that Father is safe, Brother is gone, and that human has suffered some consequence for his earlier offences?

At least now we can all get back to the business of planning the wedding and move past this dreadful time.

Many details are still to be sorted, but Father has made two things perfectly clear to that uppity doctor. The first is that I will naturally bear my father's name, as will my son, and the second is that I shall act as head of household in all important affairs. Both requests seem reasonable enough given my family, but it seems I shall be the one to enforce that second point. How I rejoice now that I will not have to sign Vivienne Bronze when I see how unvisionary the man can be. I refuse to fret over his faults however. In fact, I wonder if it isn't a blessing that I will play the head of the household as I am already much more equipped to do so.

One thing I have surely learned from all this is how capable I am of withstanding any difficult task. Having made the decision and taken action I must be grateful to my parents for all the qualities of character they have given me.

Now that Brother is gone, it will be left to me to carry this household forward.

And I do swear here, as my father's daughter, Vivienne Siphon, to do so properly.

"Siphon, like the congressman?" Jimmy asked.

"Probably."

"Well that's some family drama," he said.

"You don't think that's what this is all about? Trying to slur a politician with family history?" Sadie posed.

"Maybe," Jimmy said.

She shrugged in annoyance and shut the diary.

They moved more slowly in the second half of the day. Sadie's head hung low as she fixated on putting one foot in front of the other. Sunset was approaching by the time they'd reached their destination. She awoke from her concentration when Jimmy gasped next to her. A great mountain hemlock had fallen on its side. Under it, just barely visible, could be seen the remains of what was once a tiny hut.

They put on all the clothing they had to protect against the cool air, which threatened to turn downright cold, and trampled wild-flowers in their attempt to find the softest patch of ground before laying out backpacks as pillows and raincoats as bedding. Jimmy had to force her to eat. She chewed grumpily. Food was not what she wanted.

High in the mountains as they were, they could now see the sky full of stars. They lay on their backs staring up at it with a foot of space between them and tried to sleep. Sadie was grateful for her extreme tiredness, which pulled her under after only an hour of wanting desperately to cuddle up to Jimmy.

Though, unfortunately, she woke in the night. It was cold. The air nipped at her face and her body shivered subconsciously. Jimmy was awake beside her. She could tell by the nature of his arousal. Over the past month, she'd learned to distinguish dreams from waking feelings, and in this moment, he was awake and thinking hard of a night they'd spent together a week past.

The memory seemed worlds away, but as he pored over it, the feelings rushed back fresh into her own body. She had to fall back asleep. Sadie rolled onto her side away from him and covered her ears as if that would somehow block him out. Hours passed. She began to shake with more than just cold. Eventually, Jimmy drifted back to sleep, releasing her.

Sadie's brain crept slowly back to consciousness. Why were the birds so loud? And why did her body ache? Jimmy was wrapped around her from behind. By the way he slept with a hand cupped around her breast and an erection pressed hard into her back, she had a feeling it was going to be a good morning. Abruptly, she felt all too impatient. She wanted him awake now. Rubbing her backside against him, she began to massage her breast with his hand. She felt him stir as he took over the massaging.

Then the strangest thing happened. He gasped as if burned and jumped out of bed. She sat up and faced him. Oh. He hadn't jumped out of bed. They weren't in a bed. They were on a mountainside. She looked him up and down hungrily; the reality of their situation returning to her. She bit her lip, on the edge of begging him to lie back down.

"Stay here," he commanded. Then, watching her to see if she would obey, he disappeared back into the trees. Sadie wished he had traveled further before stopping. She watched the path of an ant intently, trying to ask herself questions about where it was headed and what it would do that day. Then she made up elaborate stories of ant adventures, doing everything possible to distract her mind from Jimmy.

He emerged from the trees after what felt like an eternity. She sat up, hugging her knees as she watched him approaching. Her calm focus snapped at the sight of him.

"I could do you better," she said in a breathy tone, the words surprising even her. His gaze locked to hers; surprise coating his features before he looked away in a blush.

"We should get moving," he said, making a wide berth to grab his bag. It took him a while to get her walking, but once on the road, she was able to drop back into a meditative concentration.

She barely noticed the hours pass. Jimmy made them eat on the move, wisely not wanting to break her focus. Their shadows were running long when he broke the silence with a "Damnit!"

She jumped at the sound. He was standing up ahead looking from the map to the surrounding countryside.

"We should have reached it by now," he said, not looking at her.

"Maybe the map's a little off," she said quietly. Her words sounded far away.

"Maybe," he mumbled. "It could be on the other side of this peak, but that's what I thought an hour ago." Sadie had rarely seen him look so worried. A bit of an over-reaction, she thought, given their circumstances. Nevertheless, she tried to calm him.

"I'm sure it is. The map-maker probably just lost count."

They kept walking over one false summit and then the next. After the third one, a tiny hut appeared. Jimmy's shoulders relaxed and he smiled back at her. Then, catching himself under her hot gaze, he blinked and looked away.

He insisted on sleeping on the floor, and he placed both backpacks between the cot and himself. The night was long, but at least the room was warmer than the open air. For Sadie it no longer mattered if she were awake or dreaming. It all felt the same; one long sequence of lascivious thoughts.

She awoke in a cold sweat to the sound of Jimmy digging in a bag.

"Time to get moving," he whispered, not looking at her.

She watched his hands as they deftly handled their belongings. Sadie found herself desperately wanting his attention. She needed to see his warm brown eyes locked on her with desire; to feel him against her.

Sadie removed her gloves and slid her hands up under her shirt. He looked up at her movement and then quickly away once he saw what she was doing.

"You need to get dressed," he said breathily. She took off her shirt, bra and pants before rolling to face him. She slid a hand between her legs.

"No, Sadie! That'll just make it worse." He grabbed at her hands. He had taken to wearing gloves consistently so they could touch affectionately whenever they wanted.

He was now leaning over the bed, holding her down. It was reminiscent of other times they'd shared, and his body responded, despite his stern face.

"You have to get dressed," he said again, only this time the words came out as a plea.

She didn't trust herself to speak. At least he was looking at her now. Sadie soaked up his gaze as she bit down on her tongue. She would have to be content with this much, she told herself.

Listen to him, said a voice in her head, *he will get you through this*.

He dressed her in new clothes while she did her best to cooperate. Then he dragged her outside for breakfast.

"Here, eat this." He put a loaf of bread on the log between them.

"I can't eat." She put her head down on her knees.

"Water?" He held out a bottle. She gave it a dirty look before taking it and chugging the whole thing.

"Jimmy. I don't feel good. I don't know if I can walk another day."

He looked as if he were about to lean forward to comfort her, but switched to sitting back on his hands.

"It's just a few more hours. We should be there by mid-afternoon." He pushed the bread closer. "But you have to eat something. It'll give you strength." She looked at the bread as if it were ash and then up at him.

"That's not what I need," she said in a low voice. He swallowed.

"Eat it, Sadie. It is what you need to get through this day. Here, do you want me to read the end of the diary to you while you eat? Do you want to know how it ends? Eat and I'll read."

October 11 1920

Dearest diary. I cannot bear it a moment longer! I have been sworn to silence. And though my mind cries with every instinct to break it, I shall keep my word, as is expected of the loyal daughter I am, and the particularly clever daughter I am, though recognition from my family of this latter fact has come only recently. But silence I must keep.

After all, the wedding is in less than a month, and soon I shall find myself at the helm of my own household, and it would be unwise for me to carry on playing the child. But prudence aside, I must speak readily, one last time, even if it be only to that of your dry and taciturn pages.

My parents have bestowed their greatest trust on me. They've revealed their plans for the future of our family and for that of our country. They intend to unite feeders and nymphs, (who they'd like me to now call nature feeders; we will henceforth call ourselves human feeders), with the goal of putting all humans in their subservient place. As we are vastly outnum-

bered by the humans, Mother has come up with the most brilliant strategy for bringing nature feeders along.

She's formed a coalition with two other high feeder families, the Maddoxes and the Griffiths. Together we're going to slowly turn the nymphs (that is, nature feeders) against the humans. With them on our side, it will be possible to take control. It will be feeders versus human and we will win. We're going to convince the nymphs that humans are a dangerous threat to them. The three families developed a plan together, but to protect against another incident like what happened with my brother, they agreed to only pass on a third of the plan to each new generation. That is, until we reach our prime and take over. Thomas and I, it seems, will have ample opportunity to work together one day, as this plan will take generations. I am grateful to still have affection for him, as I feel we will make a powerful team. I should get to know the eldest Griffiths son as well, for we must stay united in this. Though I swear I will keep my family's part of the plan from them so long as I am ordered to do so.

Though I do not know the whole story, I am proud of Mother for her vision and regret my earlier weakness and hesitations. We shall put together several attacks against nymphs for which we shall then frame humans. Mother wants me to come up with one myself to show my initiative and I have just the idea. It's all terribly exciting!

And there. I said it! I now go to cast you into the furnace! You. The only refuge for my private thoughts. Forgive me, as fate has forced my hand.

"My god," Jimmy breathed. "Do you know what this means?" He glanced up at her wide-eyed.

But she wasn't listening. Her gaze was locked on something over his shoulder.

"Jimmy... look." She pointed to the little sign at the crossroads nearby. He frowned, then pulled out the map. The color drained from his face.

"That's why it took so long to get here!" He said. "This isn't the right hut. We were supposed to make a left."

He looked up at her, making prolonged eye contact in a way he had been avoiding all morning.

"Sadie, we're now a good two days away."

His eyes glazed over with a faraway expression as his mouth fell open.

Sadie stood up on shaky legs and went to stand on the rock edge overlooking the landscape. The sun was spreading its fingers along the majestic mountains and valleys below.

"It's beautiful up here," she said, just loud enough to be heard. She stood there for several long minutes, taking in the trees and little shining blue ponds sprawled out before them. Then she answered his earlier question.

"Yes. I know what it means. It means we're probably taking that diary to exactly where it needs to be." She paused for one slow breath. "And we have two more long days of walking to get there."

An eagle soared by, scanning the land.

Sadie turned around. Jimmy had come to stand nearby. Perhaps he was concerned she might fall over. He was always looking out for her; always doing the right thing, even when it was impossibly hard.

Her love. Her friend.

She took a step toward him. Jimmy stood still as stone. Another step. He held firm, watching her. She pressed a hand against his chest. He didn't look away or retreat. He stared back into her eyes as if they were the core of the world.

"James," she whispered. His heart pounded against her palm in reply because he knew, as she did, what was about to happen. If they were two days away, things would only get worse for her, possibly even dangerous if they took action once she was already in such a state. Even now, she feared she would drop into acting on pure instinct the moment they touched. Sadie ran her hand up the solid planes of his chest and cupped the back of his neck. Stepping forward one last time she pressed her body flesh with his.

He gave her the smallest of smiles, both joyful and sad.

"No regrets," he said.

Then, very slowly, she kissed him.

Nothing in the experiences Sadie had had over the past year could have prepared her for what it was like to finally kiss Jimmy. It felt as big as the world, filled with every shared moment of their lives, and as real as the feeling of skin on skin, tongue on tongue. He made the sweetest sound of raw pleasure as their lips and breath mingled and Sadie lamented every moment she had denied them this. Every wasted second of their time together. Her reasons seemed inconsequential.

He exhaled into her mouth as she deepened the kiss and Sadie wanted to crawl inside him, to soak up every sensation. The pumping of his heart pounded out a rhythm in her mind which entranced her. But just as she was about to lose herself in the feel of him, Jimmy cupped her face between warm palms and pulled her back.

She gasped, surprised to find them in the bright light of morning, looking into each other's eyes. She remembered this was him, that this would be their first time doing this, that she loved him, and then she realized she'd been wrong. She wasn't going to act on instinct. Sadie wanted to be present, to see him, to enjoy this. And against all expectation, she found she had the strength to. This time, she would be strong for him.

She removed her gloves and undid the top button of his shirt. He blinked slowly as she looked up at him through heavy lids. He didn't move as she removed his top layer. She'd missed touching him. *God,* she'd missed it. Though never in their previous life had they touched each other like this. She ran her hands up his chest and rested her arms there as she cupped the back of his neck.

Sadie held steady as the sensation of their contact spread pleasure for the first time throughout his body. She kissed his jaw on one side and then the other, pausing to look at him in between. The moment was so still as she showed him what they'd been missing. But it wasn't until he made a sound she'd never heard on him, a deep-throated growl, full of the pain of raw pleasure, that the dam broke.

She reached for his belt buckle in the same moment that he pulled her lips back to his, and she knew there would be no taking it slow.

Not a force on earth could have stopped them now that they'd had a taste of each other. As she undid the top button of his jeans, Jimmy, her pillar of self-control, ripped her shirt in his effort to remove it. And in the space between one feverish thought and the next, they were naked, frantically kicking their feet free of their pants.

The air was probably cold, but she didn't notice as they made an awkward attempt to spread out their clothes while not breaking contact. She lay back on the poorly arranged pile and he rested his hips between her thighs. It felt so strange, as if they'd never been this close before. Sadie followed his gaze as he looked down at his erection resting on her abdomen.

She'd never been so aware of all the little things. This was Jimmy, her Jimmy, between her thighs.

"Are you sure?" she asked him, knowing there was only one answer.

He responded by pulling back his hips to align himself between her legs. When he pushed against her, however, he didn't slide inside, but rather up over her. He tried again, this time using his hand, but couldn't seem to figure out how to enter her. That's when she recalled he'd only done this a few times before.

"Here." Sadie wrapped her fingers around him. He groaned as she spread out the precum along his shaft. Then she awkwardly guided him just inside. "Now. Push now," she whispered.

He slid into her slowly until his hips were flush with hers. They watched each other's faces as he filled her and he seemed as surprised as she at what was happening. As much as she'd longed for this, it still came as a shock that it was possible. He was inside her and up against her. His weight was heavy; the feeling of his skin on hers surprisingly intimate.

They explored each other as if for the first time. She caressed his muscled arm and back as he ran his hand over her breast. They both looked down at his thumb tracing her nipple as if surprised to find it there.

The shock of the moment didn't wear off, but their desire for more became a cascading effect which drove them onward. He caressed her lips with quick kisses in between whispering her name;

his hand slowly traveling to grip her hip as they increased the pace of his thrusts together. She was panting as hard as he as she met his movements halfway.

"Sadie. Fuck. I didn't know. I didn't know it could be – like this," he said in a husky voice as he pulsed inside her.

His gaze flitted over her face as if he'd never seen her before, and for a moment she was scared. Scared of the loving heat in his eyes, of how much she wanted it. But mostly, scared of the fact that Jimmy had never worn lust so boldly. She was lost in him, and he was equally as lost in her.

None of her sexual experiences that summer could hold a candle to this. And as his desire filled her, Sadie's mind began to clear, her uncontrolled hunger somewhat abated.

Her thoughts gradually refocused after her long hunger and the terrifying realization that they had finally gone and crossed this line punctuated the immediacy of the moment. Now that they'd had a taste of each other, it seemed nothing could stop them. And this only led down one of two paths. Either they separated forever, or they lost themselves to it. Either way, this was the end of what they had known.

That would have to be a choice for tomorrow though. Since if this was the beginning of the end for them, she was determined to get all she could out of it. And it seemed so was he. Jimmy cradled her face in his hands with a gentleness that contrasted with the demanding feel of his hips. They couldn't break away long enough to speak, but everything they would say was clear in their movements. His body became an extension of hers until she couldn't distinguish his pleasure from her own. Every sound he made reverberated through her, clear and perfect, as he claimed her mouth like a lifeline.

And for the rest of the morning, it didn't matter what they did, how many times he convulsed with completion, trembling and panting before starting over. Throughout it all, he never stopped kissing her.

Epilogue

Troy's legs burned as he crested another false summit high in the Cascades. He paused to sip cool water from his almost-empty flask. He could have taken the longer, flatter route, but where was the fun in that? He pulled up the base of his shirt and wiped at his forehead. When his face re-emerged, it was to the sight of company, the first he'd had in days.

A figure stood atop a boulder ahead. Her long, fair hair whipped in the wind as she gazed down at him.

"Is that a dove's cry I hear?" he called.

"Only if you've got an ear to the ground," she said, sliding off the boulder and landing on her feet. She approached him slowly until they were close enough to inspect each other properly.

She pulled back her hair into a tight bind as piercing gray eyes examined him with scrutiny. He pulled out the coin and flashed it at her.

"This way," she said, turning her back to him and walking up the steep path.

He felt reassured that she would show him her back. Clearly, he had some immediate measure of trust.

"I'm Hetia. Hypatia Pierce, that is," the woman said over her shoulder.

He introduced himself in turn.

"I know. We got word you were joining us," she told him.

She steered him off the path and down through some thicket. For a minute she completely disappeared in front of him, but after he pushed through the branches and underbrush, he nearly ran her over as they emerged abruptly into a very different scene.

Twenty or so thatched houses were spread across a valley, complete with footpaths, livestock, and gardens.

She glanced back at him before continuing her journey downward. Two women carrying buckets on their heads paused to nod at them as they passed.

"Fresh haul?" one of them asked with a smile. His guide gave a single bob of her head. Troy ducked his head in greeting as the women looked him over with approval.

A few houses later, they passed a man milking a goat. He didn't stop as he looked up at them, only called out, "He's over at the planning tent. A working lunch again. That man wouldn't sit down if he lost both his legs."

"Thanks," Hetia said before backtracking to make a left down a smaller path. A larger, more permanent building emerged from around the corner. Made of stone with a wide archway in place of a door, it held five people pouring over papers on an expansive table. They looked up as the newcomers entered.

A tall, Black man dusted off his hands and approached them. He gave Troy an assessing look and then a smile.

"Good afternoon, sir. I'm Troy Hyun." Troy held out his hand, wishing he'd had a chance at a shower before meeting him.

Though the man didn't seem to mind his sweaty palm as he accepted the handshake with both hands. "Troy Hyun. Welcome. I'm Andre. Andre Amadi."

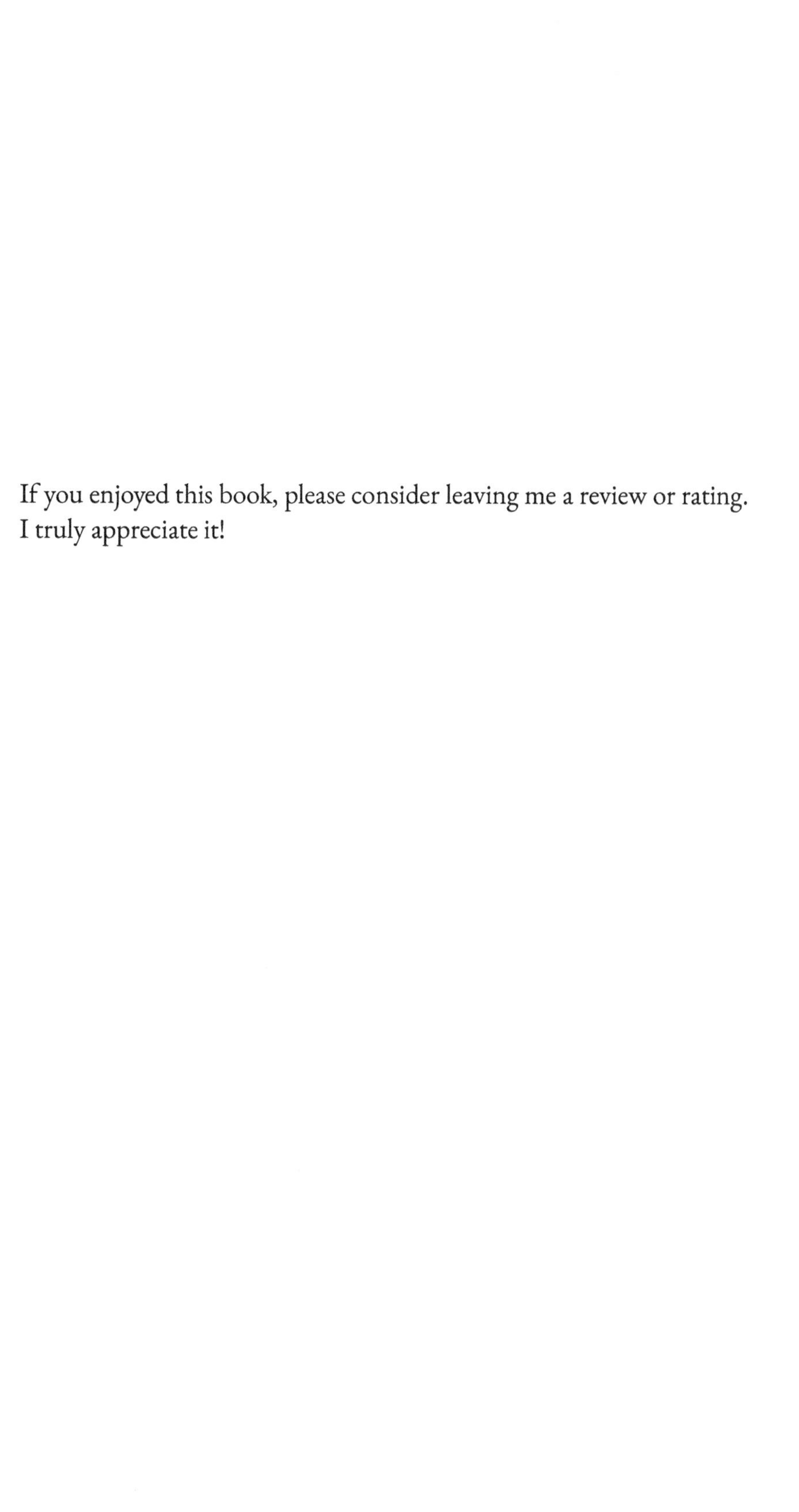

If you enjoyed this book, please consider leaving me a review or rating. I truly appreciate it!

Acknowledgements

Thank you to all my beta readers for their feedback and for talking about my characters as if they're real. You helped bring them to life. Thank you to my editor, Julie Mianecki, my interior designer Joe Donley, and my cover designer Ebook Launch for putting up with all my requests.

About the Author

Riley Kade is a romance erotica writer from the pacific northwest. She loves writing high-tension story arcs with big payoffs.

To stay up-to-date on new releases, you can sign-up for my newsletter on my website at rileykade.com.

You have finished book 1 in The Carnal Fever Trilogy.

Book 2 is coming your way February 13th, 2023!

DEATH *of a* DOUBLE DIPPER

A STORMY DAY NOVEL

BOOK #5

ANGELA PEPPER

CHAPTER 1

The dispatcher on the phone tried to talk me out of opening the bathroom door.

"Well, I'm here already," I said bravely.

I pulled a fresh handkerchief from my purse and used it to delicately turn the door handle. My overactive imagination helpfully played horror movie music in my mind—the kind with screaming violins.

I nudged the door open with my toe and quickly took a few steps back. If someone had been trapped in the room and wanted to escape, they could do it right past me rather than through me.

Nobody ran out.

The only sound was water dripping.

I steadied myself and looked inside.

There was a man lying in the tub, staring lifelessly back at me.

Michael Sweet.

Someone had stabbed him.

Someone had stabbed him a *whole bunch* of times.

Who could have done this?

Off the top of my head, I could think of a few people.

Oh, Michael, I thought with sadness. *You had to keep pushing, didn't you? Now look what you made someone do, you bully jerk.*

His lifeless body didn't offer any thoughts. For someone who always had to get in the last word in a fight, it was strange to be near Michael and not hear him.

But here we were. Just me and another dead body.

Time was ticking.

There were a few things I wanted to do before the authorities showed up, including getting an estimated time of death. I turned away from the horror in the tub and opened the vanity over the sink in search of a thermometer.

CHAPTER 2

SATURDAY

(2 DAYS BEFORE MURDER)

"Stormy, you've slept in long enough. I've already eaten breakfast, so you'll have to eat yours on the way. Would you *please* tear yourself away from the arms of your lover and get your butt out here?"

I opened my eyes and stared at the closed door of my bedroom.

Groggily, I called out, "Jessica, why don't you come in and join us?"

The door opened. My best friend and roommate, the blue-eyed and red-haired Jessica Kelly, smiled as she shook her head at me. "Look at you two, tangled up in each other's arms. It's almost revolting."

I blinked innocently. "How can you say that about a love as pure as ours?" I snuggled up closer to my sleeping companion, a sleek gray cat named Jeffrey Blue. "Ours is a true love that transcends space and time. I think we were cuddle buddies in a previous lifetime."

Jessica fixed one of her looping red braids, tucking it up into her elaborate hairstyle. "No wonder Logan gets jealous of you two."

I rolled my head to the side to give Jeffrey a kiss on his shiny gray nose. The air in the room was dry, though. I accidentally gave him a static electricity shock on the nose. He jumped up on all four paws and gave me an indignant look before stomping over me on his way off the bed.

He padded over to Jessica with his tail held high, then wove a figure eight around her pale ankles. She was already dressed for our Saturday plans, wearing a pretty flowered sundress that made her look even more like the sweet-as-a-peach small town girl she was. She'd been living with me for nearly eight months—since February—and my big-city cynicism hadn't rubbed off on her yet.

My cat continued his dance around her bare ankles. He was fully grown now, a year old, and while he retained his kitten-like vigor, his lovely green eyes were different now—more focused. Maybe my cynicism was rubbing off on him? The poor cat heard all the worst stories from my private investigation business. Last night, my furry friend had consoled me with his calm, detached listening style. I'd come home late with my faith in humanity being tested yet again. Sometimes I didn't know who was more pathetic—the guy who lied about a disability claim to scam his employer for more money, or me, the thirty-three-year-old woman who recorded video of the man from her banged-up car and then scurried out with a bathroom scale to weigh his bags of garbage.

Ah, the glamorous life of the private investigator.

On the plus side, handling bags of other people's garbage did transfer plenty of interesting scents onto my clothing for Jeffrey to inspect when I returned home in the wee hours of the morning.

Jeffrey let out a sweet meow, still rubbing Jessica's legs.

"Now I'm your favorite person," Jessica teased as she looked down into his eyes. "Cat, if we knew each other in a previous lifetime, I bet I was a sucker in that one, too."

She was feeling sorry for herself again. "Jessica, you're not a sucker. You have a good heart." I pushed my covers aside and rolled out of bed.

"That's exactly what makes me a sucker," she said, her lower lip trembling. "I'm so busy trying to see the good in people that I don't notice them taking everything."

I raised my eyebrows. "Anything you want to talk about?"

"Not really." She wrinkled her nose. "Why does it smell like garbage in your room?"

I feigned ignorance. "Garbage?"

She narrowed her eyes at me. "And the bathroom scale is missing. You were out weighing garbage again weren't you? Was it to catch insurance scammers?"

"It wasn't for recreation."

She chuckled and waved the air under her nose. "You shouldn't bring your work home with you."

I grabbed the jeans and sweater from the floor next to my bed and tossed them into the hamper. "Most of the stink is contained now." I sniffed my hands and arms. "Give me ten minutes to have a quick shower, and we can be on our way to that open house."

"Five minutes," she countered. "You're always bragging about how low maintenance your short pixie haircut is, so let's put it to the test." She crossed her arms and in a more serious tone added, "I want to get there before the start of the open house. Poor Samantha is losing her marbles over this one. Don't tell anyone, but she hasn't had so much as a low-ball offer."

"Since when do you care? Weren't you the one who threw a hissy fit over how Samantha staged that little house with undersized furniture to trick people?"

"I still don't approve of her tactics, but the poor girl is doing the best she can, raising two kids while running a real estate business. It turns out Michael Sweet isn't exactly the world's best husband. Surprise, surprise."

"Who knew," I said dryly. We'd gone to high school in Misty Falls with Samantha's husband, and I'd never been a fan.

A blood-curdling howl came from the vicinity of the kitchen.

Jessica shook her head. "Sounds like His Royal Fluffiness is either being murdered or has noticed his kibble bowl is less than 90% full."

I made a horrified expression. "How *could* you," I said breathlessly.

Jessica rolled her eyes and left to fill Jeffrey's bowl. She called back over her shoulder, "Five minutes or I leave without you! And don't forget to use soap, Stinky McStinkerpants."

* * *

It was the last weekend of September, and the weather that Saturday was almost too good to be true. We'd had a cold snap and frost two weeks earlier, but the seasons had changed their minds. Now we were enjoying a hazy, smoky sort of heat in our little slice of Oregon—a true Indian summer. The monotone grayness of a Pacific Northwest winter would be upon us soon, but not yet. I'd worn my strappy summer sandals to give them one last fling before the snow returned.

Jessica and I stood on the sidewalk admiring the work our real estate agent friend, Samantha Sweet, had put into that Saturday's open house.

Since we'd last seen the hundred-year-old home, the porch, gingerbread trim, and even the front door had been painted. The home now had a lime-green door that made the raspberry hue on the wood siding look fresh and vibrant.

"Good colors," Jessica said. "It's a good thing I don't have any money, or I'd be in danger of buying this place."

Keeping my voice low, I said, "These heritage houses are a money pit for maintenance. Notice how Samantha has added those boxwood bushes along the front. It's probably to disguise a crumbling foundation."

"I'd never buy without a full inspection," Jessica said.

"Even if it is stable, even the cutest paint job can't make the house any bigger on the inside."

Jessica laughed and punched me on the arm. Hard. As usual. "You don't have to talk me out of buying it. I'm broke, remember?" She looked up and down the sidewalk. "Where's Samantha?"

I looked around. Thanks to Jessica rushing me, we'd arrived a full thirty minutes before the open house was to begin. Samantha's car was parked on the street in front of the house, but there was no sign of the realtor.

"Looks like the house is unlocked." I pointed to the freshly painted lime-green house door, which was open a crack.

"She must be inside."

We walked up the steps of the house and across the porch. The paint was not fully cured, and I could feel it threatening to stick to the bottoms of my shoes. If I knew Samantha, she'd been on her hands and knees the night before, finishing the painting herself. For a real estate agent, she really went above and beyond for her clients.

Jessica knocked on the doorframe as she entered. "Samantha? I'm here with Stormy. We're here to talk up the place for you!"

I chimed in, "And eat cupcakes!"

There was no response.

Jessica entered the house hesitantly. "She's probably putting out signs and balloons on the main cross streets."

I made a straight line for the home's kitchen, following the scent of cupcakes. "Samantha would want us to make ourselves at home."

Jessica followed me into the kitchen and watched me attack a pink cupcake.

"Easy, killer," she said.

"This one was asking for it," I said around a mouthful.

She swished her lips from side to side. "You really have changed, Stormy."

I swallowed down half a cupcake and gave her a questioning look. "What's that supposed to mean?"

"When you moved back to Misty Falls a year ago, I'd have to twist your arm to get you to eat a cupcake. And you'd freak out if anyone tried to eat in your car."

I shrugged. "So?"

"I was just in your car, and I found wrappers." She paused, as though preparing to accuse me of a horrific crime. "Wrappers from gas station hot dogs."

"Are you saying I've let myself go?" I crammed the rest of the cupcake in my mouth. "Just because I regularly wake up smelling like garbage doesn't mean I'm not a classy"—crumbs of cake and icing sprayed out of my mouth—"sophisticated woman."

She stared at me. "Gas station hot dogs," she repeated.

I used a napkin to wipe my mouth daintily. "It's the weird hours. Surveillance can be boring, and when I get bored, I eat."

She looked at my midsection pointedly. "You're lucky you've always had a good metabolism, but it's going to catch up with you one of these days."

"Everything in moderation." I waved my hand past the cupcakes and over to the platter of vegetables. I chose a handful of baby carrots and swirled one through the dip, followed by another. "I think this is hummus," I said around my mouthful.

Jessica's bright blue eyes widened. "Double Dipper," she gasped. "I saw what you did. You double dipped your carrot. Now your spit's all mixed into the hummus."

"I'm not a double dipper. I took *three* baby carrots and dipped them separately. You can't even double dip a baby carrot. It's too small."

She made a tsk-tsk sound. "Dirty Double Dipper."

We stared at each other in silence. I couldn't tell if she was teasing me or if she genuinely believed I was a filthy Double Dipper who'd completely let herself go.

In the silence, the old house squeaked. I knew instantly the sound was coming from upstairs.

We weren't alone.

My heart pounded, and the skin on the back of my neck prickled.

With another creak of the home's old wood, I was transported back in time, to the first day of January that year. I'd entered the too-quiet house of a fortune-teller, expecting nothing more than an afternoon's harmless entertainment. Instead, I'd found the poor woman upstairs in a pool of blood. And the killer who'd shot her might have still been there in the house, hiding in a gap between rooms, watching me make the grisly discovery.

My mind made a horrible leap. I pictured Samantha Sweet lying upstairs in a pool of blood, her pretty blond hair turning red and her bright green eyes staring vacantly at the ceiling.

Jessica furrowed her brow and asked, "Did you hear that? Like someone's upstairs?" She turned to go up the stairs. "Samantha?"

I ran after her and passed Jessica halfway up the creaking stairs.

I had to lead the way. If something had happened to Samantha, I would protect Jessica. Thanks to me, my best friend had already been exposed to too many horrible things that year. She'd seen Logan get stabbed in the stomach, and then she'd climbed a tree while hallucinating after an accidental poisoning. Plus there was our adventure getting snowed in at the Flying Squirrel Lodge, trapped with a zombie-like victim and his killer, whom she'd inadvertently flirted with. Poor Jessica.

Recent events hadn't been good for her nerves. She was sensitive. She hadn't grown up the way I had, hearing stories from my father the cop.

Upstairs, I held up my arm to block her from passing me. She stayed behind, albeit with an impatient sigh.

One of the bedroom doors was closed. As I lifted my knuckles to knock on the door, I heard voices inside.

A man was saying, "Mikey doesn't deserve a fine woman like you."

A female responded with a flirtatious laugh.

I yanked my hand back and used it to cover my mouth. I turned to Jessica, who was doing the exact same thing, her blue eyes wide with surprise.

Samantha's husband was named Michael Sweet. Back when Jessica and I went to high school with him, he'd been known as Mikey. Whoever was in this room, he wasn't wrong. Mikey was a bully, and he didn't deserve a woman as fine as Samantha. But he was the man she'd married, and the two had kids together. From the outside, their marriage was picture perfect—the sort of attractive family you see in the sample picture for photo frames. At the gift shop I owned, Glorious Gifts, I had a whole assortment of families who resembled the Sweets.

Behind the closed door, Samantha said something softly. I couldn't make out her words through the door. Unfortunately, getting my private investigator's license didn't magically give me superhuman hearing.

The man in the room said, "How about next Monday? I've got the whole day off. No responsibilities. Let me take you out for lunch. I've got a few things to discuss with you."

"Not about Michael, I hope. Honestly, I don't want to know what he's been up to."

"So, you've heard the rumors?"

She paused before replying, "I'm not a fool. Plus I have an excellent sense of smell."

"You've smelled other women on him?"

"I... I don't know what it is. Maybe it's just paranoia."

"How could a man do that to you?" His voice got low and husky. "Those green eyes. Those beautiful lips. Kissing you must feel like falling into heaven."

She didn't say anything.

There was the sound of furniture creaking.

I turned to Jessica, who was silently mouthing what looked like *holy crap*.

We had to do something. We certainly couldn't stand outside the door and listen to some guy kissing our married friend.

Before I could interrupt, someone at the front of the house stomped noisily across the porch and rang the doorbell.

DING DONG!

At the sound of the loud chimes, Jessica made a startled noise beside me. By the look on her face, you would have thought she'd been busted kissing a married person.

Downstairs, a woman called out in a singsong voice, "Hello? Are we too early? We're here for the open house!" There was the sound of shoes on the hardwood floors. "Larry, take off your shoes," she instructed someone. Larry grumbled in response, and she hissed, "She's going to know we're lookie-loos if you don't take off your shoes."

Jessica and I had barely taken a few steps back from the bedroom door when it swung open.

Samantha Sweet met our eyes and made a strangled noise even squeakier than the one Jessica had made.

"You two," she wheezed. "I didn't hear you come in." Her hands fluttered up around the fringe of her blond hair and then down the front of her crisp white blazer.

Behind her stood a man who was very clearly not her husband.

"Stormy Day," the man said, grinning right at me. "I was just talking about you. What's that saying? Speak of the devil, and she appears?"

CHAPTER 3

"If it isn't the industrious Mr. Colt Canuso," I replied to the handsome, broad-shouldered, black-haired man.

Colt grinned and adjusted the strings of his bolo tie. He was sporting his usual look, a dark gray suit with a bolo tie, and western-style boots with pointed toes. As I looked down at his footwear, he shifted his feet so the toes pointed directly at me.

"That's my name," he said. "Don't wear it out." His deep voice squeaked up at the end, reminding me of the younger, skinnier version of Colt Canuso I'd known in high school. He'd been shy and reserved as a junior, but by the time we graduated, he was the class clown who'd do anything to make girls laugh. He and I hadn't stayed in touch after graduation, but I'd been seeing him around town in the last year since I'd come back to Misty Falls. He'd even helped me with a case during the summer, supplying me with eye-in-the-sky surveillance video from the casino his family owned, out on Canuso Lake. Who needs a warrant when you've got old friends?

I was glad to see his friendly face that day despite my concerns about how close his face had been to my married friend's face.

The room we'd caught him in was a child's bedroom with a narrow bed. The bed had been neatly made, but the duvet was rumpled with two butt imprints, right next to each other.

I lifted my chin and fixed Colt Canuso with a businesslike stare. "And what brings you here today, to *Mrs.* Sweet's open house?" I put a strong emphasis on the word *Mrs.*, for all the good it would do. By the two butt imprints on the bed plus the guilty look on

Samantha's face, the horses had left the stables already.

"Same as you, I imagine." He flashed me a luminous grin. He'd always had big, naturally straight teeth. They'd been too big for his face when he was a skinny kid, but he'd grown into them perfectly.

I blinked at him and licked some icing from the corner of my mouth. "Oh? Same as me? You came to taste Samantha's sweet little cupcakes?"

Beside me, Jessica made a horrified squeak.

Colt's lips twitched as his smile broadened. A dimple appeared in one bronze cheek. "Stormy, I never realized you were so funny."

"I'm no class clown, but some people find my directness amusing."

His dimple deepened. "I am, indeed, amused by your directness."

Samantha Sweet hadn't said anything. She was looking down at her white blazer, flicking away imaginary spots of lint.

Jessica cleared her throat.

The four of us surveyed each other in uncomfortable silence. The doorbell sounded again. Jessica broke away to go downstairs and greet the visitors who were muttering to each other in the entryway. Larry was still grumbling about having to take off his shoes.

Samantha Sweet finally looked up at me, her lower lip trembling and her sparkling emerald-green eyes filling with water.

Not again, I thought. *Please don't cry on me, Sam.*

I gave the real estate agent what I hoped was a friendly, supportive look.

Samantha took in a sharp gasp of air. She darted out of the bedroom in a bright flash of blond hair and white blazer, heading for the stairs.

The first couple who'd come in were still bickering over the removal of shoes. And even more people were arriving and ringing the doorbell.

Over the din, I heard a shriek behind me. I twisted around in time to see Samantha's arms flail into the air as she stumbled down the stairs. Jessica, who was partway down the stairs, calling out a greeting to the open house visitors, wheeled around in the nick of time and caught Samantha in her arms.

Colt and I dashed to the top of the stairs to make sure everyone was okay.

Jessica's elaborate hairstyle had come partly undone, and her cheeks were pink, but she'd caught Samantha. Jessica was the hero of the day.

"I'm okay," Samantha huffed and puffed. "This stupid cheap shoe tried to kill me." She leaned over and pulled off her shoe to show everyone the snapped heel that had caused her fall.

Jessica quickly took off her own shoes and handed them to Samantha. The blond real estate agent thanked her, donned the borrowed shoes, and continued on her way to greet the visitors with a cheerful ring to her voice. That was Samantha Sweet. She wasn't the most confident person or even the brightest penny in the jar, but she was a hard worker, and she did everything wholeheartedly. I'd never gotten a text message from Samantha that didn't contain enough exclamation points to warm up my mood a few degrees.

As Samantha got to work greeting the visitors, Jessica followed behind, barefoot, stuffing Samantha's broken shoes into her purse.

Colt and I still stood at the top of the stairs. As I turned to him, he followed Samantha with his gaze and quipped, "Samantha keeps saying this house will be the death of her, but I didn't believe her until today."

"Was it really the house, or the shoe?"

He turned his dark brown eyes toward me and quirked an eyebrow. "You should launch a private investigation into that suspicious accident," he said. "Someone looking to sabotage this open house must have loosened the heel on *Mrs.* Sweet's shoe." He also put a strong emphasis on the word *Mrs.*

I snorted. Ever since word had gotten around Misty Falls about me being a licensed private investigator, people had been making lame jokes about me looking into not-so-suspicious events.

"She's lucky Jessica was there," I said. "Back when we were in the cheerleader squad, Jessica was the one person you could count on to never, ever drop a girl."

Colt leaned toward me and tipped his head forward. A section of raven-black hair crossed his raised eyebrow. "I try to live my life with no regrets, but I do regret never trying out for the cheerleader team."

I tilted my chin up. "Colt Canuso, you would have been a great cheerleader, except for one thing. You were so scrawny back then. No hips at all. Even the smallest skirt would have fallen right off you."

He chuckled. "I'm not so scrawny anymore, but you're as mean as ever."

"Mean?" My jaw dropped. "I was *never* mean to you in school."

"You were downright cruel. You wouldn't let me buy you a root beer."

I rolled my eyes. "Colt, you never offered. You'd buy yourself a root beer and try to get girls to share your drink, with all your spitty backwash."

"Backwash?" He pretended to be horrified. "I'm a careful sipper. I never backwash."

He hadn't made a move down the stairs yet. We were alone on the upper floor, listening to Samantha giving the early bird open house visitors a tour of the downstairs. She expertly listed off the home's unique features: original stained-glass windows, pocket doors, wood wainscoting. Her pitch was almost good enough to take my mind off what I'd witnessed in the small bedroom. Almost.

I cleared my throat. "Speaking of other people's spit, how long have you been conducting business with Samantha? You two seemed to be having a very friendly meeting in here."

Colt didn't blink. "Stormy, you know I'm a big flirt. That's just how I am. I'm generous with my compliments and attention." His brown eyes remained fixed on mine, unwavering. A little too fixed. Liars always overcompensated with too much eye contact.

"You weren't trying to taste Samantha's sweet little cupcakes?"

He looked me steadily in the eye and swore, "There's nothing inappropriate going on."

I grabbed his hand and held it tenderly.

He blinked three times in a row. He hadn't been expecting physical contact.

I brought his hand up to my mouth and whispered, "It's good to know you're still available."

He kept on blinking rapidly. "Aren't you dating the lawyer with the beard? The one who dresses like a hipster urban lumberjack?"

I batted my eyelashes. "He hasn't put a ring on my finger," I said breathily. "And I see you've taken off your wedding band, which must mean you're up for grabs again."

Now *his* jaw dropped. While Colt was distracted, I looked down at his hand. Colt was left-handed, so I'd grabbed his left hand, which was where the lipstick he'd rubbed off his mouth had transferred. With my free hand, I grabbed a cloth handkerchief from my pocket. I used the crisp white cotton to quickly scrub the top of his hand.

Then I dropped his hand, took a step back, and held up the white handkerchief as though performing a magic trick. A telltale pink mark stained the center of the square.

"Ta-da," I said. "Samantha's lipstick, from her mouth to yours, and then onto your hand, and now on my hankie. Which confirms you lied to me."

Colt frowned. He straightened up, and a dark look flashed across his face. A monstrous look. That of a person caught up in their own lies. And then, just as quickly, he hung his head in shame, gazing down on the floor.

Without looking up, Colt said. "I take it back." He shuffled his feet so the toes of his western-style boots pointed away from me. "You're not as mean as you were in high school. You're meaner."

I put my hands on my hips. "She's got little kids," I hissed. "I know Mikey was a jerk to you back in the day, but we're all adults now. Let it go."

He glanced up, his dark brown eyes darker than ever. "Michael Sweet wasn't just a jerk," he spat out tersely. "He was a bully. He made my life a living hell."

"I remember," I said softly. "He called you Tonto, and he used to make all those insensitive jokes." I shook my head. "We grew up in different times. That racial bullying wouldn't cut it today."

"You'd be surprised," he said, moving his head stiffly. "Things are not as progressive as some folks would like to believe. Not even here in Oregon." He tilted his head to the side. "It's a small town, and no matter what I do with my life, some people will always dislike me for the family I was born into."

I broke eye contact, looking down at the handkerchief. I tucked it in my pocket and deliberately softened my posture. "Colt, I'm sorry," I said. "I shouldn't have invaded your privacy like this." I remembered a phrase I'd read a number of times in my investigation training manuals. "A person has a reasonable right to privacy." I gave him a sheepish grin. "I don't know what got into me."

"You're a force of nature, Stormy." He took a step back and rolled his shoulders forward, slouching the way he had as a scrawny teen. "And I'm sorry I called you mean. That wasn't fair. You're not mean. You're..." He gave me a blank look. "Well, you're just Stormy."

"Thanks," I said dryly. It wasn't the first time someone had used my name to describe me. It always stung, no matter how many times I made the same self-deprecating cracks about myself.

Colt glanced over at the stairs. Samantha's voice was getting louder as she herded the lookie-loo couple and more visitors toward the access for the upper floor.

He said without looking at me, "For the record, I'm glad you're here. You always did know how to talk sense into me. I still remember that day in the cafeteria, and I owe you one."

That day in the cafeteria? A memory started to surface, albeit slowly. I felt the emotions first. The fire inside me. The desire for justice. The details of who did what to whom and who started it were jumbled.

"And another thing," he said, his luminous grin gradually coming back. "That kiss I stole from Samantha was the first one ever. I swear."

I met his gaze. "First and last?"

He nodded once. "First and last. I've got a new crush now." He looked me up and down. "Technically, it's an old crush, but it's back with a vengeance."

I said nothing. He knew very well that I was dating "the lawyer with the beard," also known as Logan Sanderson. My boyfriend really did dress like a hipster urban lumberjack, with his smart suits and his neatly trimmed beard. Despite a few minor quibbles, I was quite happy to be dating Logan. It didn't hurt that he lived under my roof, renting the other side of my duplex. A girl couldn't ask for more convenience than that. Our situation was comfortable. Convenient and comfortable.

Colt Canuso turned toward the stairs and started down. "See you around, Stormy Day. Let's share a root beer real soon."

CHAPTER 4

Colt Canuso left immediately, without saying goodbye to Samantha.

Jessica and I both stuck around for the open house. We did the duties we'd promised to perform for Samantha—pretending to be interested in the house, saying positive things whenever prospective buyers were within earshot.

I played up the positive investment angles of the house, since anyone who knew of me and my history in venture capital would know I was good with money. And I wasn't lying. The surrounding neighborhood had been increasing in value lately, as more and more young families turned away from new homes on the outskirts of town in favor of fixing up older homes in walkable neighborhoods near amenities. In fact, the more I listed off the home's potential, the more I wondered if it might make a good addition to my own portfolio. If only I could get past the strange upstairs bathroom with its awkward sidesaddle toilet.

Jessica wasn't nearly as positive. She struggled to talk up the house while staying true to her beliefs. She wanted to help our friend, who'd been struggling for months to make a sale, but Jessica was a terrible shill due to her unflinching honesty. I heard her tell one couple the house was "perfect for embracing minimalism," due to its lack of closets. The couple, in their early twenties and expecting a baby any minute, hadn't noticed the lack of storage space until Jessica mentioned it. The young woman's eyes bugged out as she glanced around, noting the size of the bedroom. It held a single bed because there wasn't room for anything bigger.

The husband said, "But it's in our budget."

She replied, "I'd rather live with your mother than live without closets."

His eyes bugged out to match hers. "That bad, huh?"

She grabbed the features sheet from his hand and discarded it on a dresser.

As they exited, I overheard the man telling his wife, "We really dodged a bullet, thanks to the chatty redhead."

Samantha must have overheard this as well, as she called us over for a private meeting in the walled-off kitchen and politely dismissed us from our shill duties.

Jessica stuck out her lower lip. "But we're barely twenty minutes into the open house."

"You've done more than enough," Samantha said through a tight smile.

Jessica turned her pout in my direction. "But what else are we supposed to do for Roomies' Day Out? We can't go home without doing something fun."

"Movie matinee? Shopping?"

She scrunched her lightly freckled face. "Until my next payday, I can afford a non-fancy coffee and a leisurely stroll in the dog park. But only if you buy my coffee."

"I'll buy you a coffee, silly. In fact, I think I've got a—"

Jessica cut me off with a raised hand. "No, Stormy. Don't you dare tell me you have a two-for-one coupon for coffee. I won't be your charity case. I'm on to your little tricks."

"Tricks? Me?" I shrugged and tried to look innocent.

Samantha interjected, "If you're looking for something free to do, I have the perfect thing." She opened her brown leather briefcase, pulled out a newspaper, and handed it to Jessica. "They're doing an open casting call at the casino."

Jessica asked, "Is that what you and Colt were talking about?"

Samantha's cheeks flushed pink. "Sure, along with other things. He's really excited about it. They're casting actors for the new *House of Hallows* series on HBO."

"That's still happening?" I shook my head in amazement. I had fallen behind on my entertainment news. The last I'd heard, the epic fantasy series had seemed as good as canceled following the death of its creator. Samantha and Jessica, who were both fans of the books, quickly caught me up. According to them, a young woman named Piper Chen had taken over the writing of the series. Rumor was, she was being aided by the ghost of author George Morrison. Either that or she was a prodigy. Regardless of the implausible paranormal details, all the *House of Hallows* franchise plans were moving ahead.

Samantha excitedly told us how the Sweets' eldest child, Sophie, was trying out for the role of Kinley, the precocious young dragon master in training.

"Sophie's been practicing all of Kinley's lines for weeks," Samantha said. She glanced over her shoulder at the new group who'd entered the open house and gave them a friendly wave.

Jessica frowned and gave Samantha a sidelong look. "You don't let Sophie read the books, do you? They're not exactly family friendly."

I chuckled at her understatement. "But the royal family in the series sure is friendly. Maybe the *wrong kind* of friendly."

Jessica pretended to gag.

Samantha pushed us toward the door. "Michael tore out the chapters with Kinley and made the girls a mini booklet. Sophie and her best friend Q have been rehearsing like professionals. Q is so confident. She says she'll get the role of Kinley for sure, but has graciously offered Sophie the role of stunt double."

"Aww," Jessica said. "Kids are so cute. With all their naive hopes and dreams." She looked down at the newspaper. "Why are they doing a casting call all the way up here in Misty Falls?"

"Publicity, I guess," Samantha said with a shrug. "They're doing a whole national talent search. Plus, you know, there's the whole neutral accent thing for child actors."

I did know what she meant. A number of child actors had come from our area, because their natural accent was close to what some call General American, the neutral style favored by news anchors.

"Sounds like it might be crowded," Jessica said.

"The casino's huge," Samantha said. "You'll have fun. You might even bump into Michael."

I asked, "How is Michael?"

Her face reddened. "You know Michael," she said vaguely, herding us toward the front door. "Busy, busy."

As I stared at her, fascinated by the depth of her blushing, I noticed something was wrong with one of her eyes. Her left eye was swollen, puffier than the right, and she seemed to have the telltale purple of a bruise peeking through underneath yellow-tinted concealer.

"Is that a black eye?" I leaned in to look closely.

She turned away. "It's nothing. I wasn't paying attention, and he bumped me with his head."

"Who bumped you?"

"Michael." One of the visitors asked another person where the agent on duty was. Samantha jerked her chin up and called out, "I'll be there in a minute!"

I wanted to ask more questions about her black eye, but the woman was practically shoving us out the freshly painted door. I could take a hint. She didn't want me staring at her, trying to figure out if her husband had hit her on purpose or what she and Colt Canuso had been up to in the bedroom. And she sure didn't want Jessica talking about the lack of closet space and scaring away buyers.

We both wished her luck with the house, complimented her on the work she'd done sprucing up the porch, and walked over to my car.

Jessica was still barefoot due to loaning her shoes to Samantha. I popped the trunk of my car and sorted through my EDC—Everyday Carry Kit. Before becoming a private investigator, I hadn't given much thought to the assortment of items I kept in my purse and car. Now that I was a professional, though, I'd stepped up my game. The newest addition to my EDC was a can of Crisco. Shortening is useful for so much more than creamy frosting. It's a great source of emergency calories, a lotion for chapped skin, and with the addition of a simple twist of paper, can be burned like a candle for several hours, serving as a source of light and heat.

I unzipped my clothing bag and offered Jessica her choice of two types of footwear.

"Gee, I don't know," she said flatly. "Tough choice."

"Let me guess. You want the sandals?" I snorted and tossed the army surplus combat boots back into the bag. "You're such a girly girl, Jess."

"You are getting to be so weird," she said with a laugh as she pulled on the sandals.

She opened her purse, took out Samantha's broken shoes, and looked back at the open house. "Do you think Sam wants these back?"

I glanced at the shoes. "You could put them in the mailbox, but she's right about them being cheap. The soles may be red, but those are not Christian Louboutins. They're probably not worth fixing."

"Are you a shoe expert now?"

I smiled. "At Fairchild Capital we did a few rounds of funding for a company that was designing a new kind of stiletto heel. The heels are slim and exposed metal, like actual stiletto knives."

Jessica grinned. "If I ever see your ex Christopher again, I'm going to hit him up for free samples. Or volunteer as a shoe tester." She tossed the broken shoes into my trunk. "I'll keep them at the house in case Samantha wants them back for sentimental reasons."

I closed the trunk and dusted off my hands. My car was dirty, which shouldn't have been surprising, since I couldn't remember the last time I washed it.

"Jessica, are you sure you want to go to a crowded casting call at a casino?"

"If we go home, I'll bake things and eat them."

"Doesn't sound so bad to me."

"Let's go to the casino," she said with a swing of her arm. "Come on, it'll be fun."

"Nothing fun has ever started with the phrase *come on, it'll be fun.*"

Jessica made a puzzled face and then an ah-ha face. "That explains why my mother said it all the time before family road trips with my brothers."

CHAPTER 5

While we drove away from town and toward the casino, I told Jessica about the lipstick-stained handkerchief and my exchange with Colt Canuso.

Jessica's first question was, "Are you going to tell Logan?"

"Tell him what? This has got nothing to do with Logan."

"Colt was kissing Samantha, but told you it was over, because he's got his eyes on you now. I may be unlucky in the love department, but that doesn't sound like nothing to me."

"Nothing happened," I said with an exasperated sigh. "You know how Colt is."

"Exactly. He comes on pretty strong, and when he looks at you, those eyes are like tractor beams. It can make your knees weak."

"No kidding." I cleared my throat. "I mean, I can imagine. But those big brown eyes have no effect on me." I swallowed. "None whatsoever."

She snorted. "The flirting was mutual. I saw you looking up at him while you twirled your hair. And you really don't have much hair to twirl, so it took some serious effort on your part."

"I've never twirled my hair in my life!"

"Hah!" She held her hand out toward me, directly over the center console of the car. "We'll discuss your hair twirling another time. Show me the smoking gun, please. By which I mean the stained handkerchief."

"I was thinking we could dig into your love life. What happened on your date with Mitch, the fireman?"

"His name is Mitch. It's not Mitch the Fireman. You make him sound like a character in a children's book."

He actually looked like a character in a children's book. He was tall and enormous, like an oak tree, or Vin Diesel, or a cross between an oak tree and Vin Diesel.

I bit my tongue on describing him back to her and asked, "How did it go?"

"Not great. I don't want to talk about it." She wriggled her fingers. "The handkerchief, please?"

"Is he still calling you chipmunk? Or was it squirrel?"

"I don't want to talk about it," she said tersely.

Jessica was easygoing as a roommate, but she did have rigid boundaries about a few things. Talking about her dating life was one of those things.

She had a deep fear about guys calling her "weird" or making sweeping generalizations about redheads. She got along with Logan easily and had plenty of male friends, but they were all firmly in the friend camp. As soon as someone crossed over into being a potential boyfriend, her behavior changed. She became the thing she feared the most—weird. I'd seen it myself, and I couldn't explain it, except as a self-protective behavior. By never letting a man in close, she'd never have to worry about being rejected. It would be simple to blame her father, a con man who'd abandoned her family, for her condition, but I sensed there was more to it.

Or maybe not.

Occam's razor states that the simpler explanation is often the true one. Her father was unreliable, so she perhaps feared all other men would abandon her as well.

"Don't make me dig into your pocket myself," she threatened.

I gripped the steering wheel with one hand while I pulled the white square of cotton from my pocket and handed it to Jessica. The handkerchief was part of my personal everyday carry. I always kept one freshly laundered cotton square in my pocket as well as another two in my purse, along with paper towels, zipper-seal bags, self-defense spray, and a whole array of goodies, including items for stabbing or crushing.

Jessica examined the lipstick evidence on the white cotton. "Good job swabbing Colt's luscious lips. That was a really clever trick. I don't know why I'm surprised. You were always the smart one."

"Growing up with a cop for a dad means you pick things up by osmosis."

"Sure, but you've been learning so much more lately. If you don't watch out, you're going to be famous some day." She waved one hand at my windshield as though gesturing to a brightly lit marquee containing my name. "Stormy Day," she intoned. "The world's sneakiest private eye."

I chortled. "I'm sure you meant that as a compliment, but forgive me if I'm not flattered by praise for being sneaky, or devious, or crafty." I gave her an exaggerated stern look. "Word choice, Jessica. Word choice matters."

"Okay, I won't call you sneaky. But I truly do admire the way you get the truth out of people. I tried to talk to Samantha a couple times during the open house, but she wouldn't admit to anything going on with Colt. If it wasn't for this hard evidence," she waved the pink-stained handkerchief, "I'd probably convince myself that my eyes were lying, and I hadn't seen anything inappropriate in that tiny bedroom."

"You mentioned something this morning about Samantha going through a rough time. Is it just the house that won't sell, or is she having problems with Mikey?"

She hesitated before answering. "They've got some money problems, but who doesn't?"

I didn't have money problems, but I kept that to myself. I'd been thinking about the bruise on her eye.

"Mikey always was a bully," I said. "Do they fight over money? Or how to raise the kids?"

"Not too much. Sophie's going to need braces, but they're in agreement. The kid's teeth are super crooked. I didn't want to say anything in front of Samantha, but there's no way her daughter has a chance of getting cast in a TV show. She's a cute kid, but with those teeth, she won't get an acting role in anything, except maybe a before-and-after commercial for braces."

"Poor thing. It's too bad she didn't inherit her father's teeth. Mikey always had a great smile. That's probably why the teachers let him get away with murder." The more I thought about Michael Sweet in high school, the more my old memories came back. At that moment, a song that had been popular fifteen years ago started playing on my car's radio. As the chorus played, more old emotions returned in a flood.

In my mind's eye, I could see Mikey Sweet's perfect angelic smile as he stuck his foot out and tripped the unpopular kids in the cafeteria. I could also see his outraged expression when I "accidentally" dumped a tray of fries and gravy all over him. And then again the next week. And the next, due to Mikey Sweet being a slow learner. By the time he finally smartened up, I had started to wonder if Mikey actually *enjoyed* me dumping food on him.

It had been fifteen years since those cafeteria lessons. Had he learned how to be a better person, or had he simply switched to abusing people someplace I couldn't see him?

"This song reminds me of that spring dance," Jessica said. She leaned over and turned up the volume on the radio. "Remember how Quinn got all the cheerleaders to wear the same outfit?" She laughed. "I thought I looked exactly like Britney Spears."

"I thought you were going for Christina Aguilera?"

She giggled. "My hair was so straight, it looked like a red sheet of plastic."

"At least your hair would go straight," I replied with a groan. "My curls just sizzled and fried in the flat-iron. I spent a fortune on lotions and oils that didn't do anything. Hey, do you remember putting a raw egg and olive oil in my hair as a conditioner? Did that really happen, or am I mixing up home beauty treatments and Caesar salad recipes?"

"Was there anchovy paste?"

"I sure hope not. The fishy smell would have clashed with that sweet body spray we all used to bathe in."

"I remember an incident involving your hair, and mayonnaise. I bet I have the photos to prove it."

"You'd better not. As soon as we get home, I'm going to find all those photos, and the negatives, and make a bonfire."

She flipped down the passenger-side sun visor and looked at herself in the small mirror. "Thankfully my eyebrows eventually grew back from those little comma shapes that were all the rage."

"You had *perfect* eyebrows. You looked like a redheaded Gwen Stefani, especially with the rhinestones glued onto your forehead."

"Thanks." She flipped the visor up with a snap. "And you were a true friend, the way you stood by me through my tanning salon phase. I was such a sucker, the way I believed the girl at the counter. She swore my freckles would disappear once I built up enough of a base tan. She probably worked on commission. I hope she's as wrinkled as a raisin now." She shook her head. "Thank goodness I switched to bronzer."

"Sorry, but your self-tanning lotion phase wasn't much of an improvement. You were so orange, people kept asking me if you were sick. You looked like a Cheeto."

She snorted. "Oh, yeah? Remember your chunky blond highlights? You looked like a zebra."

"My zebra hair went perfectly with the eye shadow with sparkles so sharp they made my eyelids bleed." I stared at the road ahead. "Guys are so lucky. The worst high school fashion crime they can commit is growing a wispy mustache."

"Remember when Mikey Sweet came back from spring break in senior year with a goatee? He was so proud."

"Yup." I shifted uneasily in the driver's seat. "And when our history teacher teased him about it, Mikey got up and punched the guy in the face. I can't believe he didn't get expelled."

"He was such a psycho," Jessica said.

The song on the radio finished, and the DJ started talking about the *House of Hallows* casting call at the casino. The local rock station would be broadcasting live from the event that day. It was also the Casino's grand re-opening following extensive renovations. We listened for a few minutes, until the annoying jingle for the furniture store came on and I switched it off.

After a few minutes, Jessica asked, "Do you think people ever change their nature?"

"We're all capable of change. Is there some way you want to change?"

"I dunno."

"Something's bothering you," I said. "Are you sure you're up to this casino thing? It's going to be crowded and noisy. You always get wiped out by too much stimulation."

"I want to go," she said. "I just keep thinking about Samantha. She's so much like me. I wonder if she lets Mikey boss her around."

"You think he's still the same bully he was in high school?"

"Yeah."

I stole a glance over at my best friend. "Has he ever hit her?"

She answered quickly, "Of course not."

"I saw the bruise on her eye. And she said it was from Michael."

After a pause, she said, "I've never heard about him being abusive, physically. But then again, Samantha knows I tell you everything. If I ever did find out Michael hit her, I'd tell you, and then you'd tell your father, and then Mr. Day would jump into action. Michael would find himself dangling upside down from a suspension bridge over a creek, like what happened to that other guy."

"Allegedly," I said, clearing my throat. "You're referring to the rumored incident when my father *allegedly* dangled an abusive man over a canyon by his boots."

Jessica snorted. "Sure. Allegedly. They must have gone up there for the after-hours bungee jumping."

"No comment." I turned my head away from the road to give Jessica a quick eyebrow waggle. Could I help it if I was proud of my dad? He drove me nuts, and his texting skills hadn't improved at all over the last year, but I loved him fiercely and admired him for the good he'd done in our community.

* * *

We arrived at the Canuso Casino, where I let out a low whistle of surprise at the quantity of vehicles on the premises. It was amazing Samantha had gotten any visitors to her open house, since it appeared the whole town of Misty Falls had driven out to the lakefront casino.

Since the main parking lot was completely full, we followed the hand-lettered signs to overflow parking. We eventually squeezed into a spot in the parking lot for the lake's campsites.

As we got out of my car and stretched from the drive, Jessica squinted at me in the autumn sunshine.

"Stormy, is it true you made Samantha cry?"

"I didn't *make* her cry. I said some things, and she cried, but I didn't *make* her cry."

"Hmm."

"It's been ages since we had one of those incidents," I said. "Last winter, I simply pointed out some fundamental problems with the business investment opportunities she presented me with.

Sometimes the truth hurts. But I never tried to tear her down. If anything, I've done my best to build her up. I've given her a number of pep talks."

"That explains it." Jessica made a face, wrinkling her nose. "No offense, but your pep talks could use more *pep*."

"What's that supposed to mean?"

"Just that it's hard for other people to keep up with you and your high level of standards." She reached into the car and grabbed her floppy, wide-brimmed hat.

"My standards aren't that high," I retorted. "And I think the fragrant aroma of garbage currently coming off my clothes hamper will attest to that."

"True. You're not exactly a perfectionist, or a neat freak. And your diet lately leaves a lot to be desired. When I say high standards, I mean something else. It's hard to put into words, but I can see why men like Colt always chase after you. You're like a wild horse."

"Thanks, I think."

She donned her floppy hat, glanced up at the clear blue sky, and then sneezed three times from the bright light. She muttered, "Why do I always do that to myself?"

Her question was rhetorical, but I answered anyway. "People are paradoxical," I said. "We want what we can't have, and we do things we know are bad for us. And then we lie about it."

She reached into the car again, grabbed the wrapper from my recent gas station hot dog, and playfully flung it over the roof of the vehicle at me. "Tell me about it, Miss I Never Eat Gas Station Hot Dogs."

I picked up the wrapper, folded it roughly into a paper airplane shape and sailed it back at her. "That's not mine," I lied. "My dad borrowed my car last week while the Torino was at the garage. It must be his."

She caught the wrapper, unfolded it, and examined the interior while she rubbed her chin thoughtfully. "There's a smudge of mustard in here, but the real evidence is the *lack of evidence*. No ketchup or green relish. Being a close friend of the Day family, I happen to know that Mr. Finnegan Day would never eat a hot dog without every kind of condiment."

She had me. "No comment," I said.

She pursed her lips in my direction before walking over to the parking lot's bear-resistant garbage bins to dispose of the hot dog wrapper.

I opened the trunk of the car, grabbed two bottles of water, and cracked the lid off one as I looked down the long access road at the distant casino. I'd never seen the place so busy. People must have come from miles around to audition for a few roles.

The DJ on the radio had been talking about the odds of a local kid landing the role of Kinley. Paradoxically, the more he talked about it, the more I actually wanted to win the role for myself. And I was twenty-some years too old for the part.

Funny how we always want what we can't have.

CHAPTER 6

The casino had finished their costly expansion since my last visit in the summer. It was no longer just a simple casino with an attached boutique hotel. It had been officially renamed the Canuso Lake Casino and Resort, with a sign boasting about its new conference and spa facilities.

Between the upgraded Canuso facilities and the Flying Squirrel Lodge up in the nearby mountains, our little corner of Oregon was becoming quite the tourist attraction.

As we entered the crowd of people milling around in the entry atrium, Jessica took my elbow and murmured, "The whole town must be here."

"Plus a whole lot of the surrounding area." I scanned the crowd. "Times like these, I wish I was taller," I commented.

Jessica saw me scanning and asked, "Are you looking for someone in particular? Maybe Colt Canuso? He probably came right back here after he left Samantha's open house. This is a huge event for the casino, and I'm sure he'll be around to keep an eye on everything."

"I've seen enough of Colt Canuso for today," I said with a snort. "The man I'd like to have a few words with is Michael Sweet."

"No!" She made a face like she'd just eaten a lemon. "You and Mikey don't mix."

"We're both adults now. We can have a simple chat about current events."

"You'd better not breathe a word about Colt kissing Samantha. Give me that handkerchief."

She moved with surprising speed, grabbed the handkerchief from my pocket, and stuffed it into her bra.

"You've lost your mind," I said. "I just wanted to talk to Mikey and see if I get a guilty vibe from him. I could drop some hints that if I ever see a bruise on his wife, he might find himself dangling over a canyon."

"Let it go," she said, still making the lemon-pucker face. "This isn't one of your detective cases. I get that you're bored of weighing people's garbage, but you can't go stirring up trouble for no good reason."

"Stirring up trouble?" I was genuinely surprised at my best friend's vehemence. She was usually more supportive of my wacky schemes.

"Don't you have some sort of ethics code? We don't even know if Samantha willingly kissed Colt back. He might have *stolen* that kiss."

I gave her a dirty look. "I'm not a monster, Jess. I'm not going to tell Michael Sweet his wife has been smooching other guys all over town. I just want to chat with him for a few minutes and get a feel for whether or not he's changed since high school. I've barely seen the guy since I moved back to town. Maybe he's become a totally decent person."

"And if he hasn't? Then what?" She looked down and adjusted the handkerchief she'd stuffed in her bra. "This isn't one of your cases. It's none of your business." Softly, she added, "Plus you might make everything worse for Samantha if you start asking questions."

I stared into her serene blue eyes. In addition to being an excellent baker and cheerful roommate, Jessica did have some sensibilities where I was lacking. Sure, she was the first one to jump into freezing cold water at the annual Polar Bear Dip, but when it came to personal boundaries, she knew when to be cautious.

Jessica made a good point. If Samantha was having problems with Michael, the best thing we could do was be patient and listen to her. Unfortunately, one side effect of becoming a private investigator was that I'd forgotten how to be patient and let things unfold in their own time. Or maybe it wasn't the PI thing. Maybe I'd always been pushing people into motion, poking at problems to move conflicts toward their conclusion. Was this the indescribable character trait people were alluding to when they said I suited the name of Stormy?

"You're right," I said begrudgingly. "The Sweets' marriage is not my business now. But I swear, if anything happens, I'm going to *make it* my business."

She gave me a patient smile. "Your heart's in the right place."

"It's not my heart that Mikey needs to worry about." I glanced around the crowded atrium.

The local news crew was interviewing people on an elevated platform. Daphne, the clueless weather girl, was handing a microphone to a dark-haired young woman in a sparkling dress. It was Della Koenig, the town's wealthiest widow and an aspiring pop singer. I quickly turned my back to the platform before Della could catch my eye. She'd hired me for a few small investigative jobs over the last two months, and I was in danger of becoming someone she considered a friend. People's tongues already wagged about me now, just being a private investigator, but if I started hanging out with Della the Diva Widow, all those tongues would be moving at light speed. We'd need to get a tongue specialist set up in Misty Falls to reattach all the tongues that went flying off people's faces.

The scent of baked goods hit my nostrils. Bagels? Panini sandwiches? I sniffed the air.

Jessica must have smelled the delicious aroma at the same time. "Soft pretzels," she said. "I see a sign over there. Eee! Free samples!"

"Sold," I said, moving in the direction of the heavenly scent. "Let's go line up for a soft pretzel. If we just *happen to* bump into either Colt or Michael, I'll try to be normal. I'll even make"—I pretended to gag—"small talk. About the weather and stuff."

"Good," she said. "Do you want your hankie back?"

I eyed her chest. "It's yours now. Do you want another hankie for the other side, to even them out?"

She rolled her eyes as she grabbed my elbow to steer me through the crowd and into the line for the free soft pretzels.

We found a gap in the crowd and took our places.

Behind me, an indignant male voice called out, "Hey, lady! No budding in the line."

Hey lady? I knew that voice. A chill ran up my spine.

He called out again. "Hey, lady, the line starts behind me."

I knew that voice. Hearing it brought me back to a day of tragedy. It was last November, not long after I'd returned to Misty Falls to help my retired cop father following his hip replacement surgery. On that crisp winter day, I'd met my sweet little cat, Jeffrey Blue, as well as my future tenant and boyfriend, Logan Sanderson. But I'd also discovered the frozen body of my father's neighbor. And I'd had my first encounter with Chip the Mailman.

I turned around slowly. "Hello, Chip," I said through gritted teeth.

It was Chip, all right—the mail carrier whose regular route included Warbler Street, where I'd grown up and where my father still lived. Chip the Mailman was in his early thirties, like me, but bigger and taller—average height for a man. Despite his job that had him walking around most of the day, he sported a build that could be kindly described as "big-boned." He had a round face, pale with splotches of red on his cheeks, and fair hair that was straight and fine, like a baby's. In many ways, he resembled an extra-large toddler, albeit one who was constantly sweating.

The air conditioning inside the casino was working well, and the space was almost uncomfortably cool, even with the large crowd. Chip wore shorts and sandals, yet he was sweating, drips of moisture beading on his wide forehead. I'd seen him sweating outside in the middle of winter, which was one reason I'd initially suspected him of killing my father's neighbor and hiding the body in a snowman. Chip and I had encountered each other a few times since last November, but we'd never gotten over our first, suspicious impressions of each other.

"It's you," he sputtered, his pale blue eyes widening. He looked so much like a surprised baby, I expected him to squeal and clap.

"In the flesh," I said, still through gritted teeth.

"Miss Day," he said. "Sunny's sister. Finnegan's daughter. The private eye."

I raised my eyebrows. Did he still not know my name? If so, he'd be the only one in town.

"Chip, if you're looking for another thing to call me, I'm also your second-cousin's boss and the owner of Glorious Gifts."

He shook his gaze off me and looked down at a pint-sized blond girl who was tugging his hand. "Daddy, is that her? Is that Stormy Day?"

Daddy? Chip the Mailman had a daughter?

She let go of her father's wrist and clapped her hands together. "It's really you," she said excitedly.

Since it was the most enthusiastic greeting I'd gotten from anyone who wasn't my cat, I knelt down to be eye level with the kid.

"That's me," I said, offering my hand.

The girl had a round, friendly face and perfect teeth. She looked like a miniature professional newscaster as she shook my hand.

"You're famous," she gushed. "Your name is on the wall at the coffee place."

"You must mean the House of Bean," I said. "I don't know if I'd call myself famous, but it's true they named a drink after me. It's a latte with vanilla, cinnamon, and a dash of the same chili pepper powder they put in the Mexican hot cocoa."

She gave me a dazzling, angelic smile. "I know." She seemed to be about eight years old, or possibly a precocious seven-year-old.

Chip leaned over and asked the girl, "Q, Mom doesn't let you order coffee, does she?"

"I can get a small one," she said defiantly.

Chip shook his head. "Sweetie, coffee's bad for kids. It'll stunt your growth."

She used both her pointer fingers to jab him in the round stomach. "Dad! You drink coffee all the time, and you have this big belly!"

He rubbed his stomach and frowned. "It's true. I'm addicted to their Teenie Weenie Beanie Steamer."

Still kneeling, I tilted my head up and looked from Chip to his daughter and back again. This was a side of the mail carrier I hadn't seen before, and it did a lot to soften my impression of him. How could I have been so shortsighted? But *of course* Chip the Mailman had a life away from his delivery route. The big-boned man didn't just appear by magic to deliver mail to my father's neighborhood and then puff away to another dimension once the mail bag was empty.

Jessica joined me in kneeling before the precocious child. She said, "Q, it's not nice to comment about people's tummies. Not even if they're family."

I asked the girl, "Your name is Q?" I made the connection to the conversation we'd had with Samantha Sweet at the open house. Her daughter, Sophie, was best friends with a girl named Q. I hadn't known it was Chip the Mailman's daughter.

The blond girl nodded. "Q is short for Quinby. Q-U-I-N-B-Y. Some people call me Queen Bee, but it gets confusing, because that's my mom, too. You can call me Q."

"Quinby," I said, nodding. "And you know Jessica?"

Jessica answered, "I used to babysit Q when I lived in the apartment, which was near her house."

The little angel-faced girl said, in a very mature voice, "Jessica used to babysit me, but now we're just friends."

She reminded me of someone. I smiled and told her, "Jessica and I went to school with a girl named Quinn. She was a real queen bee."

"I know," the girl said. "That's my mom. She was the head cheerleader when she was in high school. We have the trophies on our fireplace. One day, I'm going to be a cheerleader, too. But first I'm going to be an actress."

I looked up at Chip in yet another whole new light. "You're married to Quinn Baudelaire?"

He gave me a big grin. He had gaps between all of his undersized teeth, which didn't take away his giant-baby appearance.

"Actually, I'm married to Quinn *McCabe*," he said proudly. "She changed her last name when we got married."

Quinby said, "That's spelled M-little-C-big-C-A-B-E. There are two Cs."

Jessica and I both stood up again. I looked from my friend to the mail carrier and back again.

My inner voice was screaming *Quinn the Perfect Queen Bee married a chubby mailman! Oh my God!*

Stupidly, I said to Jessica, "So, Quinn still lives here in Misty Falls?"

"I told you that," Jessica said. "You were invited to her birthday party, in the summer, but you were too busy to come with me. Remember?"

"Right," I said hesitantly. How was it I could clearly remember the sting on my butt from Quinn slapping me when I wavered in the pyramid fifteen years ago, yet I couldn't recall what month her birthday party had been? It had to be shock over seeing who she married. "That was back in..." The date didn't come to mind.

Jessica caught on and covered for me. "Stormy, you couldn't make it because you had a business appointment with Countess Octavia of Krengerborg."

"Ah, yes. The Countess," I said with the snooty tone we used for talking about the woman.

Quinn and Chip's daughter, Q, couldn't have looked more interested if she'd tried. She whispered, "You know the Countess, too?"

"We famous types stick together," I joked.

Chip said, "You should invite us along some time. I'd love to meet Countess Octavia when she's in town."

"Sure," I said. "And I do hope to catch up with Quinn very soon." I smiled at the round-cheeked mail carrier and his precocious daughter, who'd very luckily gotten her mother's good looks. "And her adorable family, of course."

"Of course." Chip wrinkled his nose and lifted his upper lip in a baby chipmunk expression.

He gave me a long stare before saying, "I know what you're thinking, Miss Day. How could someone as hot as Quinn end up marrying a chunky guy like me? Trust me, I've heard all the jokes. Our friends say we're like those sitcom couples, where they pair the comedian guy with a hot wife. Like Kevin James and a supermodel."

"For the record, I happen to like Kevin James," I said.

"Sure, but you wouldn't marry him."

I tried to look nonchalant. "Who knows? He hasn't asked."

Beside me, Jessica chuckled softly.

Chip didn't laugh. He stared at me with a look no less accusatory than the one he'd given me back when we'd first met.

I quickly reviewed everything I'd just said to Chip. I hadn't made any comment about his physical attractiveness. But I *had* been thinking about it.

Quinn was a nine or a ten in high school—long legs, blond hair, button nose, flawless skin, big blue eyes, and the kind of perfect hourglass figure that all the guys ogled and all the girls longed to have. Even if she'd let herself go these last fifteen years, surely she was still a seven.

Chip the Mailman, however, exuded all the sex appeal of an organic turnip. How much better shape could he have been in when he'd snagged Quinn as his wife?

As he stared me down, I tried to picture them as a couple, but I couldn't. In high school, Quinn had dated athletic guys, some good ones but mostly jerks. She'd taken Michael Sweet to the senior prom, despite my protests.

"Quinn used to date jerks," I said to Chip. "If you're good to her, that's all that matters."

"I am," he said. "I'm her devoted subject, and she's my queen."

"I'm happy for you both," I said, and I meant it. I looked down at the girl they called Q. "Just the one kid or are there more cuties?"

Chip pulled a handkerchief from his pocket and mopped his sweaty forehead. His cotton square was the red-and-white kind, not like the plain white ones I carried.

"We've only been blessed with one little firecracker so far," Chip said. He lifted his upper lip in the chipmunk expression again. "I run hot. That's why I always wear shorts on my delivery route, even in the snow. The doctors say there's nothing wrong with me. That's just how some people are. But body heat's bad for the little swimmers."

"I've heard that," I said, nodding sagely. "Not about you specifically, but about"—I looked down at the kid to make sure she wasn't listening too closely to our discussion of her parents' baby-making issues —"the little swimmers."

The crowd around us shifted. The scent of hot bread wafted through. A space opened up, and we found ourselves at the counter being asked what heat level of mustard we wanted with our soft pretzels.

I was thankful to have the conversation changing away from talk of Chip's body heat and its side effects.

We placed our orders, and Chip graciously bought us a round of refreshments.

We thanked Chip, and before we parted ways, I made a vague promise that I'd be seeing him again soon.

"Not if I see you first," he quipped, and then he held his stomach with both hands and laughed silently. "See? I'm funny, just like Kevin James."

Jessica and I exchanged a look.

I started to step away and excuse myself, but young Quinby grabbed my hand and looked up at me with her big blue eyes.

"Stormy Day, I'm going to be famous, just like you," she said. "I'm going to get my own drink named after me."

"How are you going to do that? You need to get *super* famous to get your own beverage."

"I know."

"Do you want me to put in a good word for you with Chad? He's the manager at House of Bean. We're pretty tight."

Jessica snickered as she took a big bite of her soft pretzel. Chad and I weren't tight, but he had stopped rolling his eyes at the other baristas whenever I came in and refused to order their version of a vanilla latte by its full name: Teenie Weenie Beanie Steamer.

Quinby covered her mouth with both hands and smothered a laugh. Then she flung her arms in the air and dramatically whisper-yelled, "I know a secret!"

Jessica and I made the appropriate *ooh* faces.

Chip made a fatherly growl. "That's enough, Junior Queen Bee."

Jessica asked the girl sweetly, "What will they put in this drink they name after you? Lots of honey? Honey from the queen bee's hive?"

"No." She gave us an adorable you-grownups-are-always-so-stupid look. "Warm mead with cinnamon. Like what Kinley drinks after sword fighting, in the books."

Chip clamped his hand over his daughter's mouth and gave us a nervous laugh. "That's enough making new friends for today." He began herding her away. "See you around. Miss Day, I hope you can make it to the next party. It's our annual hootenanny."

"I wouldn't miss it for the world," I said. "It's high time I caught up with Quinn Baudelaire. I mean, Quinn McCabe." I smiled at the little girl. "And the future most-famous-person of Misty Falls."

"It really is a hootenanny," she said brightly. "With a live band and everything!"

"Will there be straw bales for sitting on?"

"Duh!" She shook her head at me adorably before taking another bite of her pretzel and walking away with her father.

I turned to Jessica and said, "Duh! Of course there are straw bales. It wouldn't be a hootenanny otherwise."

Jessica took a bite of her pretzel. "Quinn wants us to wear our old cheerleader uniforms to the hootenanny."

"You'll have to kill me first," I said.

"The party's in three weeks. We can do lots of jogging before then."

"But we always jog a route that leads us to the bakery. It sort of defeats the purpose."

She murmured that I had a good point about the fatal flaw in our exercise plan.

I turned and looked in the direction I'd seen the McCabes walk away. "That is not the man I expected Quinn Baudelaire to marry."

"Who'd you picture her with?" She giggled. "Quick. Say the first name that pops into your head."

"Voldemort," I said.

She doubled over with laughter. "The wizard villain from Harry Potter? But we hadn't even heard of him when we were in high school."

I shrugged. "You told me to say the first name that popped into my head."

Her expression sobered. "It's actually a good match," she said.

CHAPTER 7

Three hours later, after Jessica and I had partaken in many free food samples, played some games, toured the renovated areas of the resort, and even gotten two-for-one manicures at the beauty spa, we headed for the exit, exhausted and smiling.

Roomies' Day Out had been a marvelous success, we both agreed as we admired our new nails. Jessica had gotten her fingernails painted pink, to match the flowers in her sundress, whereas I'd opted for the no-polish men's manicure with just a cuticle trim and nail-buffing.

My decision to not get any polish was met with cheeky comments by Jessica, who thought I might be embracing the role of "macho film noir old-timey detective" a little too hard. Her jokes stung enough for me to allow the bubbly girl at the makeup counter to give me a quick makeover. I just had to prove I could still be a girly girl if I wanted.

Now I had *smoky eyes*. Or as my father would have called it, *raccoon eyes*.

Each time I caught sight of myself in a reflective surface, I looked over my shoulder to see who was following me.

We were on our way out of the casino when we bumped into Samantha Sweet.

"Wow," she exclaimed as she took in my raccoon eyes. "Stormy, are you..." She struggled to find the right words. "Oh, it's makeup!"

I squinted at the dark mark next to her eye. How ironic that the woman with an actual bruised eye had been upset by my fake ones.

I turned to Jessica and said, "I told you my coloring doesn't suit dark eye shadow."

"You need more color on your lips to balance it out," Jessica said.

"It looks nice," Samantha lied, wincing. She looked around at the crowd with tired, half-lidded eyes. "No wonder my open house was slower than molasses in January. The whole town is here."

Jessica asked, "How did the rest of the open house go? Did you get an offer?"

"No," Samantha said tiredly. "Have you seen Michael and Sophie around?"

"We didn't see your family, but we did bump into Sophie's friend Q. She's really something."

Samantha raised her eyebrows. "Q is full of... confidence."

We were being jostled by the crowd, so we moved away from the door and toward what seemed to be an open area in the atrium. It turned out to be a gurgling water feature, a pint-sized replica of the waterfall Misty Falls was named for. The sound of the water crashing over the rocks created a powerful white noise that canceled out the din of the people around us.

"Ooh, misty," Jessica said, waving her hands through the air over the base of the water feature, which was surrounded by a rock wall with not-so-subtle signs reading DO NOT SIT, STAND, OR PLAY ON ROCK WALL.

The three of us breathed in deeply, commenting on how pleasant the misty air was around the fountain.

"It's like a misty oasis," Jessica said.

Samantha stuck her tongue out like a thirsty lizard.

I handed Samantha an unopened bottle of water from my purse. She thanked me and drank it while giving me an appreciative look.

A few minutes later, she had rejuvenated thanks to the hydration. Her emerald-green eyes were glowing again.

"The power of water," she said, smiling.

"Sorry your open house didn't go well," I said. "The home does show nicely. Maybe an offer is just around the corner."

Samantha pulled a tube of lipstick from her purse and applied it using a compact mirror. Jessica and I exchanged a look. The pink lipstick was, without a doubt, the same shade I'd wiped off Colt Canuso's mouth earlier that day. Was she here at the casino to meet her husband, or was she hoping to see Colt again?

Samantha put her lipstick and compact away. "Actually, girls, I did get a proposition today, but it wasn't the sort of offer I was looking for."

"Oh?" I tried to keep my face neutral. If she was going to tell us what happened with Colt, I didn't want to overreact.

"And what an offer it was," she said, laughing. "A ninety-five-year-old gentleman offered to give me a ride on his electric scooter."

I said, "Sounds like you had quite the eventful day."

Samantha's emerald-green eyes darted around nervously, and she reached up to fix her hair but succeeded only in making the blond fringe at the front stick straight up.

"The guy on the scooter wasn't even the weirdest part of the day," Samantha said.

"Oh?" *Here comes the confession about kissing Colt.* I leaned in expectantly.

She fluffed her hair again, sending more blond fringe straight up. "At the end, when I was closing up, I walked into the kitchen and found a guy in there. By himself. Just standing there."

"Creepy," Jessica said.

Samantha nodded. "And he was clutching an enormous knife."

Jessica gasped and covered her mouth. "What did you do?"

"I screamed," Samantha said matter-of-factly. "As one does when they encounter a man in the kitchen with a big knife. But then he screamed, too. And he immediately dropped the knife. Then I started apologizing to him for scaring him! Can you believe it?"

Jessica slowly lowered her hand from her mouth. "Was this the ninety-year-old with the scooter?"

"No, just a regular guy, about our age. I didn't know him. He said he just moved to Misty Falls."

I asked, "What was he doing with the knife?"

"Cutting a cupcake in half," she said. "It turned out he only wanted to have half a cupcake. Isn't that bizarre?"

I shook my head. "Those mini cupcakes are already pretty small. That is suspicious. You should put in a report with the police. I can ask around for you. Dimples is always at my father's house."

"No need," Samantha said. "The guy seemed harmless enough. We chatted for a few minutes. He said he was on a low-carb diet and it was making him crazy for sugar. But on the plus side, he said he might come back to take a second look at the house."

"Make sure you bring Michael with you," I said. "You shouldn't be alone with this guy. It could be dangerous."

Jessica said, "Next open house, we're staying for the whole thing. I'll be quiet, I swear."

"I'm not an idiot," Samantha said with some irritation. "We do have security. We always get people to sign in and out of the visitor's book."

I shook my head. "A book? Someone could kill you and then rip the page out of the visitor's book."

Her emerald-green eyes widened. "Really?" She swallowed. "I guess you're the expert on these things."

"Better safe than sorry," I said. "A logbook is not security."

Jessica cried out in alarm.

Someone in the crowd had bumped into her, nearly sending Jessica tripping over the rock wall into the fountain. I caught her by the arm and hauled her back to safety.

"Speaking of safety," Jessica said with a laugh. "Maybe we should move this party out of here to the relative safety of home."

"We were just heading out," I said to Samantha. "Can we help you here with anything? Are you looking for someone?" *Like, say, Colt Canuso?*

"Michael wasn't at home, or answering his phone," she said. "I thought he might still be here with Sophie and the McCabes. They all came down here as a group to have the girls audition for that acting role."

I said, "Speaking of the McCabes, did you know that Chip is my father's mailman?"

"Mail carrier," she corrected. "That's the preferred term. Not that Chip cares. Chip marches to the beat of his own drum."

"His daughter seemed confident about getting a starring role in *House of Hallows*. She reminds me a lot of her mother, Quinn, as a teenager. A chip off the ol' block." The word *chip* rang a bell. I couldn't help myself. "You could say she's a chip off the ol' Chip."

Jessica gave my bad pun a pity chuckle.

Samantha gave me a blank stare. "I wouldn't know," she said. "I didn't grow up here like all of you did. I've only known Quinn the last five years, since our girls met in school and became inseparable. Those two are like sisters."

"Like us," Jessica said, looping her arm around my back.

"You're better than a sister," I joked. "I actually get along with you."

The three of us chatted for a few minutes about little girls and sisterhood before the sound of an angry altercation distracted us.

"Oh, no," Samantha said. "Does that sound like my husband to you?"

Jessica leaned from side to side, trying to peer through the crowd in the atrium. "You mean the guy yelling? I can't tell. Just sounds like an angry man to me."

The three of us cocked our heads and listened.

Over the noise of the crowd, I heard a male voice yell, "You dummies spent a fortune to class this place up, but it's just lipstick on a pig! You can't polish a turd!" And then he followed up with a few racial slurs for good measure. The casino and lake were on reservation land, and he had a few opinions about that.

Samantha's eyes widened and her skin paled, like it was covered in a fresh snowfall.

"Oh, dear," she said, and then she used a few stronger words.

Jessica gave me a grim look. "That does sound an awful lot like good ol' Mikey Sweet."

"He must be drinking," Samantha said. "He gets belligerent after a few drinks." She made a high-pitched, keening noise. "I told him not to drink today!"

I jumped up onto the rock ledge surrounding the water feature to get a better view over the crowd. "I see him," I said. "He's by the pretzel stand."

And there was Michael Sweet, red-faced and belligerent, being held by two of the casino's security guards. I couldn't hear what he was saying at the moment, but based on what I'd already heard, it was probably for the best that his speech wasn't being broadcast clearly.

Samantha was frozen in horror. Their real estate business was based on their reputation and trustworthiness in the town. Michael yelling and making a scene in front of the whole town was bad news on many levels.

I reached down for Samantha's hand to pull her up onto the stone ledge with me, but she wouldn't budge. She put her hands around her mouth and called out, "Michael! Where's Sophie?"

I'd forgotten about their daughter. I scanned the crowd near Michael and the guards, looking for a small blond girl. I spotted a dozen kids who could have been Sophie. The place was packed with children who'd come for the open auditions. The kids couldn't go into the gambling areas of the casino, but there were plenty of little girls here in the atrium, where the free food samples were.

Samantha screamed again for her husband and daughter.

Michael swiveled his head and glanced in my direction. There was about fifty feet between us. He looked at me and then through me. As Samantha screamed his name again, he yanked away from the two security guards. The crowd reflexively pulled away, giving them room. I watched helplessly from my elevated position on the rock wall as Michael wound up his fist and punched one of the guards in the face.

A shockwave of gasps went through the crowd. The few people who'd been minding their own business were now paying attention.

A hand tugged on mine. It was Jessica, wanting to join me up on the rock wall. I took her hand and pulled her up to stand beside me.

Samantha had left our side. I saw the back of her head as she wove through the crowd toward her husband, who was still yelling while fighting with the uniformed men.

The crowd moved as though choreographed, stepping back to give Michael and the two security guards space to fight.

Here we go again, I thought. This was a familiar scene, indeed, right down to me observing the fight with a raised view. Jessica and I had climbed up on cafeteria chairs back in high school. History was repeating itself. Once again, Mikey Sweet was goading other guys into fights and taking on anyone who stood up to him. *Once a bully, always a bully*, I thought grimly.

Michael and the two security guards circled each other within the makeshift boxing ring.

Suddenly, a new person entered the fight zone.

Colt Canuso.

He shrugged off his suit jacket and tossed it at a woman wearing a casino uniform. He entered the ring, fists raised. Now it was three against one. Michael was a big guy, but even he couldn't take on three grown men. And Colt had muscled up since high school. He was no longer a slouching, scrawny teen who could be pushed over by a strong breeze.

The crowd got quiet—so quiet, I could hear a small child, unaware of what was happening, demanding more ice cream, and the parent shushing them.

In the center of the ring, Colt pointed an angry finger at Michael.

"Mikey, this is not your domain," Colt said coolly. "This is Canuso territory. Our land, our rules."

Michael straightened up and ran one hand over his fair hair defiantly. "Isn't it enough that you and your family don't pay your fair share of taxes?" Michael rolled up his sleeves and raised his fists. "You need to stay out of my business."

Colt cracked his knuckles. "You stay out of my business, and I'll stay out of yours. I'll make it easy for you. Michael Sweet, you are hereby banned from entering these premises. For life."

Michael puffed his chest out. "I go where I want. I'm a free man."

Colt shook his head and backed away slowly. "We're done here." He pointed his finger at Mikey again. "If you ever show up here again, on my turf, it'll be the *last thing* you ever do."

A shocked murmur rumbled through the crowd. That was a threat, for sure.

As Colt backed away, he nodded to the incoming wave of reinforcements dressed in black security uniforms.

Michael hurled another racial slur at him, but Colt didn't take the bait.

Colt said to the new wave of security, "Show Mr. Sweet to the exit, please. Make sure he gets all the way to his vehicle safely. We wouldn't want him to trip and mess up that pretty face."

Colt started to put on his jacket and then seemed to think better of it. He lay the jacket neatly over his left forearm then whipped around and sucker punched Michael Sweet in the stomach.

The whole crowd collectively gasped.

Jessica made a strangled sound next to me on the rock wall.

Back in school, Colt had never hit Michael back. Not once, despite all the times he'd been picked on. But today, after years of simmering rage, he had. And what a punch it had been.

Outwardly, I was calm as can be, but on the inside, I had to cheer. It may have taken fifteen years for the karma to come around, but Mikey Sweet truly did deserve at least one punch in the guts. There was a poetic beauty in that it had come courtesy of Colt Canuso, who'd grown into such a powerful, self-assured man.

People started talking, murmuring to each other. Kids started pestering their parents for more ice cream and mini donuts.

Over the fray, I heard Samantha again. She was yelling for her daughter. "Sophie! Michael, where's Sophie?"

Michael was still reeling from the gut punch. His head swiveled around, looking for his wife or his daughter or both. Two security guards had him by the arms. He tore away from them and rushed forward, into the crowd of people. He wasn't being careful about where he was going. Elbows flailed as people bumped into each other and got knocked over.

The crowd's noise got louder. People were getting out of the way now, trying to get their little kids to safety, but they didn't know what was happening or where to go. The atrium was even more packed than it had been minutes earlier. A brawl always draws spectators. As panic levels rose, more people went sprawling. I watched helplessly as the crowd turned into a stampede.

Panic turned to terror. People screamed. The stampede changed direction, and before I could formulate an escape plan for myself and Jessica, a group of people started tipping over toward me, like a chain of dominoes.

Arms, heads, and bodies struck me from the waist down. I couldn't keep my feet under me, and I had nowhere to go except... straight into the splashing fountain.

I reached out to steady myself, but all I caught with my hands were the red braids of Jessica's hair. I tried to let go, but my fingers curled in reflex.

I tried to warn her, but another body from the crowd hit me hard enough to knock the words from my lips.

Over we both went, straight into the misty, rushing water beneath the replica waterfall.

CHAPTER 8

After the security guards fished us out of the water feature, they took us to a staff area for a towel-off and a talking-to.

The casino's head of security, a jowly man with dyed black hair, gave us a stern lecture about not standing on ledges that were clearly marked with signs reading DO NOT SIT, STAND, OR PLAY ON ROCK WALL.

We asked about the Sweet family and were assured that everything was under control.

I asked, "Did Samantha find Sophie in the crowd?"

"She's just a little girl," Jessica said. "I hope she didn't see her father getting beat up."

The jowly man snorted. "Nobody got beat up."

"I know what I saw," I said evenly. "Michael Sweet better have made it to his vehicle without further incident."

The man lifted his jowly chin defiantly. "He strikes me as the clumsy type."

I shook my head. "This may be private property, but the laws regarding assault are still applicable here."

The man raised his gray-specked eyebrows. "Oh, really?"

I explained, "Fourth degree assault is a Class A misdemeanor, carrying up to one year in jail and a fine up to six grand. But if one were to commit this offense in front of a child, it could be elevated to a Class C felony. And Class C felonies can carry up to five years in prison and much higher fines." I gave him my steeliest look, which took serious effort with fountain water dripping down my face. "And the atrium was filled with families and seven-year-old girls."

"Then it's a good thing nobody assaulted anyone," the man said. "I'll make sure everyone with the last name of Sweet makes it safely off the property."

"Good," I said. I could feel my cheeks flushing. I'd just rattled off some facts about misdemeanors, but if the casino was on Native American land, the laws and fines might be quite different. I was certainly no expert on Tribal Council law. But I had learned, from spending time with my lawyer boyfriend, that if you talk fast and spout off a bunch of numbers, people take you more seriously. Even if you're wrong. And even if you're sopping wet and dripping fountain water on the carpet.

The head of security checked his phone screen. "Everyone's been accounted for," he said. "Safe and sound."

"I'd like to see Colt now, please."

"Sure. Let me arrange a meeting." He grinned. "Do you two young ladies promise to stay out of the fountain?"

Jessica said, "It was an accident, honestly."

I added, "There should be a guardrail around the base of the fountain."

He stared at us.

"We promise to stay out of the fountain," I said.

"We do," Jessica agreed.

That seemed to satisfy him. He called over two security guards and gave them instructions, presumably to take us to see Colt Canuso.

We followed the guards down a hallway.

"Your meeting is right through here," the smaller security guard said.

He opened the door and shoved us through.

It wasn't a corridor leading to Colt's office. We'd been kicked out through a side door, into the bright autumn sunshine. The crisp breeze made me shiver in my wet clothes.

Jessica and I exchanged a look.

She muttered, "So much for saying goodbye to Colt."

"We can still make a dignified exit," I said, and started walking along the side of the building.

Our wet shoes made squip-squip sounds with every step. So much for a dignified exit.

Over the squip-squip sounds, I heard the security guards chuckling over how much fun it was going to be reviewing the video footage of us "frolicking like water nymphs." They went on to say some things that were less delicate, concerning the sheerness of our outfits when wet.

I stopped my squip-squip walking and wheeled around to face them.

"You two chuckleheads had better watch your mouths," I said fiercely. "My associate and I are old friends of your boss's, and I don't think he'd appreciate that sort of talk."

Jessica grabbed my elbow and whispered, "Stormy, your smoky eye shadow is dripping down your cheeks."

"So?"

"You look exactly like a scary clown who's just escaped a carnival of nightmares."

"That's perfect," I hissed back.

At the doorway, standing in the bright sunshine and casting perfect cinematic shadows against the stucco wall of the new building, the two guards continued laughing at us.

I lifted my chin defiantly. "Gentlemen, I believe the words you're looking for are *I'm sorry*."

The bigger and more mountain-shaped of the two uniformed men made a scoffing sound. "You two ladies don't know the boss," he said. "You're nobody."

"We're old friends of Colt Canuso's. The three of us go way back."

The bigger guy waved one wide mitt dismissively. "You and every other lady in this town. Especially the broke ones." He chuckled, his big voice a deep rumble. "Especially the *crazy*, broke ones."

Now he had my interest, but for a different reason.

I changed tack, the apology forgotten. "Exactly how many crazy, broke girls? Is Colt dating anyone in particular? Maybe a blonde?"

The two men exchanged a confused look.

Mountain-Shaped Guy lifted his chin at me and demanded, "What's it to you, lady?"

This wasn't my first day on the job. I already had the cash in my hand. I stepped forward and casually presented him with my offering like a professional.

The big guy handed half the cash to the other guard, and they both tucked the bills away. Their postures softened.

"No blondes," the large man said. "Colt's not dating anyone, even though he could have his pick."

"But you said he's friends with all the crazy, broke girls."

"Just friends," he replied. "Colt's all talk, like a dog who barks a lot but doesn't do nothin'. If you ask me, he's still not over Susan." He added in a softer tone, "That's his wife who died a few years back."

I nodded. I knew about Susan. Jessica and I had gone to school with her as well, though she was two years younger than us. The Mountain-Shaped Guy's words rung true. The last time I'd seen Colt before today, he'd been wearing his wedding band. The ring had not, however, been there today.

The other security guard piped in, "I always try to get him to open up and talk to someone about his pain. Grieving doesn't have to be something you go through alone. But Colt's one of those tough guys who doesn't know how to talk about his feelings. I don't know what to do. If he doesn't get it off his shoulders, I'm worried he might crack some day."

I sniffed. "Some day? You mean like just now, when he punched an unarmed man in the stomach?"

The big guy puffed out his chest and fixed me with a serious glare. "You didn't see anything like that. You couldn't have seen nothin' while you were swimming in the water feature."

The other guy said, "Today wasn't the first time Colt lost his temp—"

The big guy elbowed his buddy to shut up. And then he gave me a stone-faced look I recognized. The interview, such as it was, had ended.

I thanked them and started walking away. I'd gotten what I wanted to know.

Under her breath, Jessica asked me, "Now you're bribing people?"

"Would you prefer it if I'd challenged them to a two-on-two kung fu battle?"

"Oh, Stormy."

It was a long, soggy walk back to the car with our shoes going squip-squip the whole way.

My heart felt heavy for Colt. I wondered if he had many friends to talk to about his feelings. I did worry, like the smaller security guard, that his pain might cause him to lash out or find trouble.

CHAPTER 9

My boyfriend, Logan Sanderson, hummed to himself as he scraped the carbon off the barbecue racks. We were in the backyard, enjoying what might be the last Sunday barbecue of the year.

I sipped a beer from a can and checked my phone for messages from my roommate.

"No veggie burger," I told Logan. "Jessica's having dinner with her mom."

"What?" He hadn't heard me over the sound of his scraping. I started to repeat what I'd just told him, but he impatiently started scraping the racks again before I could answer.

I yelled, "No veggie burger!"

He paused long enough to say, "Does she want it well done? I never know how long to cook these stupid mushroom-oat-bran-quinoa things." And then he tossed one of Jessica's veggie burgers onto the grill with a sizzle.

I got up from my patio chair and went to hug him from behind. He pushed me away. "Hot grill!"

I took a step back and bit my tongue. Logan had been working long hours, and today had felt like the first time I'd seen him in years. But with that treatment, I was feeling like a stranger in his life. I wanted to yank the spatula out of his hand and paddle his butt with it for not listening to me, but you know what they say. Violence is not the answer to relationship problems.

"Jessica's not coming home for dinner," I said.

He gave me an indignant look. "Why didn't you tell me? Now this lemongrass-tofu burger is going to waste."

"I'll eat it," I said. "And it's a lentil-cashew burger."

"It smells like wet cardboard," he said. "If you eat this, who'll eat your steak? Will your father eat two of them?"

"Dad's not coming tonight," I said. "Which you would know if you actually listened to me."

"Oh?" He returned his attention to the grill, turning his back to me, but there was no mistaking the fight in his voice. I could imagine the facial expression that went with it.

The urge to hit him with the spatula returned. I retreated back to the picnic table and my beer.

Logan glanced back over his shoulder at me, eyebrow raised. "That's it? You're not going to talk to me?"

"I'm letting you grill in peace."

After a few minutes, he asked, "Is it just the two of us tonight? What are the neighbors up to?"

"Dean and Eve? Beats me."

Dean and Eve Lubbesmeyer had just moved into the house next door in August. They'd arrived on the day of the town's annual Forest Folk Run, a charity event that people walked or ran while wearing costumes ranging from furry Forest Folk monster suits to zombies. The zombie look had been increasing in popularity lately. Dean and Eve had been driving their moving truck, which was packed full of all their earthly possessions, when a volunteer stopped their vehicle to let a group of zombies cross the street. Dean and Eve had looked at each other in horror, doubting their decision to move to Misty Falls. Did people in the town normally dress in tattered clothes and walk at a shuffling pace? Wave after wave of zombies surrounded the moving truck, all moaning and groaning. A few muscular troublemakers came up with the fun idea to shake the moving truck, so they did. And the squeaking of the truck only spurred the zombies on. Now, the Lubbesmeyers didn't have a Forest Folk Run where they came from, and they'd never seen zombies outside of Halloween, so what were they to think? Confusion turned to panic. After a few terrifying minutes of having their truck rocked by zombies, Dean leaned on the horn. The zombies all jumped back. That was when Eve noticed the blood and falling-off body parts were just makeup and monster effects. The whole spectacle was all in good fun. They rolled down their windows and congratulated the zombies for giving them a good scare. After the zombie horde cleared away and let them continue on their way, Dean and Eve laughed the rest of the way to their new home.

Other than their colorful entry to the town, I didn't know much about Dean and Eve Lubbesmeyer, except that they were empty nesters whose kids had all left for college, and they'd been flirting with the idea of early retirement when they discovered that the factory that made their favorite potato chips was for sale. They visited Misty Falls in the spring of that year on a zombie-free day, toured the factory, and soon became the new owners of Aunt Jo's Crispy Spuds. The first time I met Dean and Eve, we bonded over our shared love of the chip company's logo featuring Aunt Jo, with her curls freshly set from the hairdresser, and her good pearls worn proudly around her neck.

"We should see if Dean and Eve want these other steaks," Logan said. "We can't let them go to waste."

Suddenly, a face appeared over the fence separating my backyard from the Lubbesmeyers'. It was Eve, with her spiky, pale purple hair. She must have climbed a ladder to peer over at us with comically good timing.

Logan laughed. "Speak of the devil!"

She asked, "Did I hear somebody talking about steaks going to waste? That's a crime where we come from. Punishable by public shaming in the local newspaper."

Logan replied, "Were you doing some gardening just now?"

"No," she said with a straight face. "I always kneel on this side of the fence and listen in when you two lovebirds are back here. Between your law practice and the private investigation business, it's my best way to get all the local gossip. Then I go down to Ruby's Treasure Trove and sell the intel to Ruby piece by piece."

Logan laughed again. I couldn't help but notice he found Eve's antics far more amusing than my own. I sipped my beer and watched him chat with Eve. She called for her husband to come outside, they negotiated with Logan on side dishes, then they disappeared into their house to rustle up a salad. Logan finished grilling the three steaks and lone veggie burger without saying a word to me.

I got the sense I'd done something to upset him, but I couldn't think of what.

I recalled what one of the security guards had said about Colt, about how he was the kind of guy who bottled up his feelings. Was Logan bottling something? I watched his careful movements as he set the platter of grilled food on the picnic table. He barely even glanced up at me. He could have been